I0405797

NAKED CAME THE

Florida Man

ALSO BY TIM DORSEY

Florida Roadkill

Hammerhead Ranch Motel

Orange Crush

Triggerfish Twist

The Stingray Shuffle

Cadillac Beach

Torpedo Juice

The Big Bamboo

Hurricane Punch

Atomic Lobster

Nuclear Jellyfish

Gator A-Go-Go

Electric Barracuda

When Elves Attack

Pineapple Grenade

The Riptide Ultra-Glide

Tiger Shrimp Tango

Shark Skin Suite

Coconut Cowboy

Clownfish Blues

The Pope of Palm Beach

No Sunscreen for the Dead

NAKED CAME THE
Florida Man

Tim Dorsey

WM
WILLIAM MORROW
An Imprint of HarperCollinsPublishers

This is a work of fiction. Names, characters, places, and incidents are products of the author's imagination or are used fictitiously and are not to be construed as real. Any resemblance to actual events, locales, organizations, or persons, living or dead, is entirely coincidental.

NAKED CAME THE FLORIDA MAN. Copyright © 2020 by Tim Dorsey. All rights reserved. Printed in the United States of America. No part of this book may be used or reproduced in any manner whatsoever without written permission except in the case of brief quotations embodied in critical articles and reviews. For information, address HarperCollins Publishers, 195 Broadway, New York, NY 10007.

HarperCollins books may be purchased for educational, business, or sales promotional use. For information, please email the Special Markets Department at SPsales@harpercollins.com.

FIRST EDITION

Library of Congress Cataloging-in-Publication Data has been applied for.

ISBN 978-0-06-279600-4

20 21 22 23 24   LSC   10 9 8 7 6 5 4 3 2 1

For Larry "Montana" Fletcher

NAKED CAME THE

Florida Man

Prologue

Don't shoot guns into the hurricane."
        Elsewhere this would go without saying, but Floridians need to be told.

This was an actual warning issued by the Pasco County Sheriff's Office just north of Tampa Bay as a major storm approached. After all, a local man had just been arrested for DUI when he tried to order a taco in a Bank of America drive-through.

The alert was a reaction to people posting plans on the Internet for a party to shoot at the hurricane and make it turn away. The sheriff's notice even included a scientific diagram showing how the vortex of the core could curve bullet paths to come back and hit the shooter.

"Shooting at a hurricane!" said Serge. "That's the most brainless thing I've ever heard!"

Coleman looked out the rear window of their muscle car racing over a bridge. "Why is everyone else driving the other way?"

"Because they're evacuating. It's the smart move."

"Then shouldn't we be evacuating?"

"Absolutely not," said Serge, turning on tactical silicone windshield wipers. "They have to flee because they don't know what they're doing. We're professionals."

"How's that?"

"Everyone else gets ready for storms according to the official instructions." Serge reached under his seat. "Which is fine if you want to survive. But if you're taking it to the next level, all that jazz will just slow you down. Hurricanes are the marrow of Florida history, and my history always goes bone-deep. That's why I prepare for storms with an encyclopedic set of state guidebooks, every conceivable new gadget, and bags of provisions exclusively from the candy and snack aisles. Think about it: Little kids are programmed to thrive and that's the first place they go. That's how a pro has to think."

"I'm still not sure." Coleman flicked a Bic. "We're like the only car heading this direction."

"I've taken every conceivable precaution," said Serge, absentmindedly waving a pistol out the window as Coleman did a bong hit. "What can possibly go wrong?"

1928

The bloated, decaying body rolled into the ditch.

It fell onto its back, cloudy eyes still wide open, creating a frozen expression that bookmarked the last thoughts from a long, brutal life of hardship, hunger, harrow and few complaints. The final thought in those eyes: *What kind of shit* now?

"It creeps me out the way he's staring like that," said a voice at the top of the ditch.

"He's staring at God," said someone else, grabbing a pair of lifeless ankles.

Another body tumbled down the dirt embankment, and another, and so forth. The dead were all African American, just like the dozens of perspiring, shirtless men laboring with shovels.

The shovel gang most likely would have pitched in anyway, out of a sense of community, but this time they didn't have a choice. They occasionally glanced back at the white lawmen with shotguns propped against their shoulders and pools of tobacco spit at their feet.

"What are you looking at—!" The next word was impolite.

It actually should have been quite a nice day in late September. The sky was clear as a dream, and a cooling breeze swept over the fields covered with thousands of tulip-shaped orange wildflowers. The wind made the acres of bright petals sway as one, back and forth, like an immense school of tropical fish. Then the sun rose higher, and the breeze left. The air became stubbornly still, baking in that Central Florida humidity so thick it seemed to have weight. But worst of all:

It stank.

Blame history. It doesn't bother to knock. It doesn't even come in the front door. It's like those newspaper articles about a car that crashes through the wall of a bedroom in the middle of the night. This was before storms had alphabetical names, and it was called the Great Hurricane of 1928. Later it would become the forgotten storm. The victims didn't have money.

It began the afternoon of September 15. All the fancy weather instruments that now give residents a head start on hurricanes had yet to be invented. You'd be chopping carrots for a stew, and then a hurricane was just *there*. But if you were really paying attention over the years, there was one early-warning system. The Seminoles.

Something about pollen and a rapid blooming of the sawgrass. The Indians watched the plants down in the swamp, and when a low haze in front of the setting sun got that weird color, they seemed to know the exact moment to make for high ground. Many scientists have looked into the phenomenon and scoffed at the notion. But the Seminoles were always dependably on the move before each Big Wind, so they'd figured something out.

This time, the tribe had come up out of the Everglades on trails leading to the ramshackle towns of South Bay and Belle Glade, then made a right turn toward West Palm Beach. There was no panic in their march. Simply a parade of native families out for a very long stroll. Some of the townsfolk remembered a similar migration two years earlier, before a lesser hurricane, and decided to follow the Indians out. But most stayed put.

On the morning of September 17, the storm that had peaked at category five made landfall at the Jupiter Inlet lighthouse in northern Palm Beach County. More than a thousand homes were destroyed along the coast before it continued churning inland, unimpressed . . .

Now, a few days later, the digging of massive, macabre pits continued with a sense of urgency. Fear of disease swept the survivors, and in the immediate aftermath the locals were on their own. Many of them were about halfway up the east side of the big lake, which would be Okeechobee, in an empty place that would soon become known for its mass grave, which would be Port Mayaca.

The same frantic scene was replaying itself miles away, in opposite directions, at two other South Florida locations. Even as mass graves go, there wasn't remotely enough room. At least two and a half thousand dead by most accounts. Some said more than three. The nation's worst toll ever, save for the Galveston storm in 1900.

Here was the problem with the hurricane of '28: the storm surge. That's often the case, and almost without exception, the deadly waves come from the ocean. But this time around, death didn't come from the sea; one of the strongest hurricanes in recorded history made a direct hit on the nation's largest freshwater lake sitting within a state. Who saw that coming? There was no dike, and the storm's rotation easily shoved much of the lake's contents south, in an inescapable ten-to-twenty-foot wall of water that blanketed hundreds of square miles.

In the following hours and days, the water began to recede, and then came the snakes, but that's another story.

As the overwhelming scale of death became clear, they started digging a second grave pit on the other side of the lake in some unknown place called Ortona, and then a third in West Palm Beach, just off Tamarind Avenue. It was back-numbing work for all those residents pressed into service. But here's what really pissed them off: The bodies of black victims filled the pits as fast as they could be thrown in on top of one another. Each white person got their own private pine box.

Then those boxes were loaded onto wagons and taken to the nearby Woodlawn Cemetery for proper burial.

A shotgun man stuck two fingers in his mouth for a shrill whistle that got everyone's attention. Shovels stopped.

"You three! Over there!" The shotgun waved east. "They need more help!"

A trio of drained men trudged toward a separate pile of work, and stared down at a pale corpse.

"Great. The pine boxes," said one of the larger men, named Goat. "I don't mind burying our own, but this is bullshit."

"Just grab him," said a stubby but deceptively strong neighbor. He went by "Stub."

The first worker began lifting the body by the armpits, then suddenly dropped him and jumped back.

"What the hell's gotten into you?" said Stub.

Goat just pointed with a quivering arm. "He's got a bullet hole!"

"Where?"

"In the forehead."

"Jesus, you're right!"

They composed themselves and lifted him into a box, providing a better view. "Wait a minute, I know this guy. It's Mr. Fakakta."

"Who's that?"

"Sugar man," said Goat. "Lived in that big colonial house out past the bend by the ice plant."

"That big place in Pahokee was his?"

"Ain't doing him no good now."

They grabbed the next body, a woman, and just as promptly dropped it.

"She's got a bullet hole, too," said Stub.

"That's his wife," said Goat.

"What on earth is going on?"

The pair quickly scanned nearby bodies. "There's his son. Head almost blown off . . ."

Stub was Catholic, made the sign of the cross. *"Ave Maria."*

Goat glanced back twenty yards and watched a stream of brown juice shoot from between gapped teeth. "Think we should tell the deputy?"

"Definitely," said Goat. "Some monster murdered this whole poor family—"

A shotgun blast went skyward.

Everyone froze.

"Shut up over there and get back to work!" barked the lawman.

The pair nodded respectfully, then began hammering penny nails into the lid of a pine box. "Screw 'em."

Part One

Chapter 1

"Help me!" yelled Coleman. "I'm trapped again!"

"Hold on. I've got my own problems." Serge pushed away a piece of plywood and crawled out from under a debris pile of dresser drawers, chunks of ceiling and a toilet lid. He stood to examine all his scratches and bruises, but saw nothing major. He looked around. "Okay, Coleman, where are you?"

"I don't have a clue."

"No, I mean just keep talking and I'll follow your voice."

"Okay," said Coleman. "Hey, Serge, I just realized that 'slow up' and 'slow down' mean the same thing. That's fucked. I'm still stoned."

Serge cleared a path, pushing aside fractured furniture. "Keep talking."

"Have you seen my weed anywhere out there?"

Serge cast aside a torn-down kitchen cabinet and lifted a soaked mattress. "There you are."

Coleman sat up, and his face suddenly reddened as a cord from mangled window blinds tightened around his neck.

Serge flicked open a pocketknife and sliced the thin rope. "Don't you know that's a choking hazard?"

"I didn't have a choice." Coleman rubbed his neck. "It just got me."

Serge stood again and stared thoughtfully at the bright, panoramic view out the front of the building where the wall used to be. "It got everyone."

Coleman checked his own bruises. "Is it over?"

"All over but the shouting," said Serge.

Coleman joined him, looking out across the calm waters of Bogie Channel. "So that was the big Hurricane Irma everyone was talking about?"

Serge would have opened the door, but there wasn't one. He hopped down from the building and walked toward the street. The only sound was the crunch of gravel and broken glass under his sneakers. The air had turned mild and comfortable, nothing to betray what had come before.

Serge placed hands on his hips as he surveyed what had recently been a historic row of quaint old fishing cottages in the backcountry of the Florida Keys. All had been knocked off their foundations, lying helter-skelter practically on top of each other.

Unless you've seen the aftermath of a major hurricane, you wouldn't realize how much of the damage appears to be the result of high explosives. Little pieces of shrapnel everywhere. Slivers and confetti. Most of the other cottages were missing their front walls as well, allowing the wind to go to work inside like sticks of dynamite. Cabin number 7 had no walls at all, just a roof lying on the ground, which had been pushed against the base of a palm tree that neatly cut it open like a jigsaw. The cabin with the least damage, still barely clinging together and listing like a floundering ship off the edge of its concrete slab, was number 5.

Serge looked the other way, toward the landmark two-story clapboard office and bait store at the Old Wooden Bridge Fishing Camp. It had stood apart from the cabins, alone, unprotected, with no trees to shield it on the edge of the channel. Now there was little evidence there had ever been an office, except for the matchbook-size pieces that littered the ground and floated in the water like another bomb had gone off.

Serge wiped his eyes.

"Are you starting to cry?" asked Coleman.

"Why couldn't it have taken out a Starbucks or some shit? We keep losing all our best places." He blew his nose. "I'd bet the bat tower on Sugarloaf is gone, too."

It was.

One of the island's endangered miniature Key deer sprang from the brush and bounded through the debris like an antelope.

"I've never seen one run that fast," said Coleman.

"I'm sure it has a lot on its mind."

Coleman turned back around toward their cottage. "Jesus, we could have been killed! Why did you want to stay here and ride out that hurricane? Didn't you realize it would be this hairy?"

Another doe darted by.

"I knew it would be strong," said Serge. "But these little deer always figure out how to make it through storms, so I figured how hard can it be? Second, I love cabin number five."

"It's your favorite," said Coleman. "You always kiss the number by the door when you first arrive."

"I knew that if God would allow just a single cottage to survive relatively intact, it would be Five. I figured this island would get pretty much torn up, so I wanted to spend a final night in that special place. And last but not least, I seriously miscalculated."

"Wait. Stop," said Coleman. "You mean we really could have been killed? But you promised me I'd be safe."

Serge pulled car keys from his pocket. "What was I thinking?"

"Hey, where are you going?"

They don't call it Big Pine Key for nothing. The day before, Serge had found a spot where he was able to back his car about twenty yards into the woods, surrounded by thick pine trees. The kind of place where the little deer hide.

"It barely has a mark on her," said Coleman. "So we're heading out of here now?"

Serge shook his head and opened the trunk. "It will take a few days for workers to clear the roads, so we'll be camping until then. Help me with this gear."

They pitched a tent with sleeping bags behind the row of battered cabins. A small campfire began to glow in a little pit surrounded by rocks. Bottled water and beer cans bobbed in the melted ice of a cooler. Serge returned to the car for a last item and brought it back to the fire.

"What's that thing?" asked Coleman.

"The beginning of my latest science project." Serge sat down with a clear plastic storage bin in his lap. He opened his pocketknife again and poked a six-inch grid of tiny holes on the end. Then he taped a small, battery-powered fan over it. Then another grid on the opposite end. "This project has an extremely long gestation, and I don't know when it'll come into play, so we might as well use this downtime to get a head start."

Serge grabbed a soggy package from the cooler. He took the lid off the bin and began evenly arranging the bag's contents across the bottom.

"Bacon?" asked Coleman.

"Your universal food group."

"It's the only thing that goes great with everything," said Coleman. "Eggs, pickles, ice cream, Twinkies, other bacon. It's just impossible to go wrong."

"You can with this pack. It seriously spoiled overnight." Serge held out a slimy, uncooked strip. "Unless you dig trichinosis."

"I'll stick to beer," said Coleman. "But why are you putting it in that bin?"

"Read it in a medical journal," Serge said. "In our advanced world of modern medicine, sometimes the best treatment is still low-tech."

"Treatment for what?"

"I'm not treating anything, just using the principle for my experiment," said Serge. "All will be revealed in due time."

Serge finished his task and picked up the bin. He walked over to the edge of the woods, setting it down behind his car . . .

TWO DAYS LATER

Serge listened to the morning news on his emergency radio. He reached inside their small dome tent and began shaking Coleman to no avail. "Come on, wake up! The road's clear. It's time to go."

Serge shook harder and harder until he heard primitive groans. Then Coleman woke up all at once. He had somehow managed to turn himself around in his sleeping bag during the night.

"Help! Help! Something's got me again."

"It's just your sleeping bag. Hold still."

But Coleman had the reasoning ability of someone drowning. "Help! Help!" He thrashed around like a giant caterpillar trying to molt. Then he jumped up and dislodged the tent's poles, and soon he was wrapped up in that, too, rolling left and right.

Serge watched without expression until his pal wore himself out. A piled entanglement of nylon heaved as he panted.

"You finished?" asked Serge. "Because the tent isn't completely wrecked yet."

"Just get me out of this."

Serge extricated his friend and they began breaking camp.

When everything was stowed in the car, Serge walked over to his science project. "Well, I'll be. It worked." He sealed the lid on the storage bin, started the battery-powered fan and stuck the whole business in the back seat.

A gold 1969 Plymouth Satellite emerged from the trees and drove away from the Old Wooden Bridge Fishing Camp. Soon, they were almost out of the Lower Keys, approaching the bridge to Bahia Honda. The debris piles that had been pushed aside by heavy equipment appeared like small mountain ranges down each side of the highway.

"Discussion time. Where were we?"

"When?" asked Coleman.

"I don't know. The hurricane destroyed our train of thought," said Serge. "Which is a plus because a train of thought is just another one of society's cages."

"Why don't we talk about society?" asked Coleman. "Your thoughts?"

"These are dark times." Serge tapped fingers on the steering wheel. "The decline of society can be boiled down to the culture of airline flights."

"I've seen the videos on the Internet."

"You take a couple hundred people from our savagely polarized nation, cram them cheek by jowl in a metal tube and send them up to altitudes where there's no oxygen. Then people read the headlines: 'Wow, I didn't see *that* coming,'" said Serge. "Plane travel used to be glamorous, people getting dressed up, wearing hats. But now it's devolved into a subway in the sky, cursing, shoving, public urination, removing socks from smelly feet."

Coleman popped a can of Schlitz. "Preach."

"It starts before you're even off the ground," said Serge. "Especially if you're in one of those planes where the coach passengers have to walk through first class to get to their seats. It trends Darwin in a serious hurry. First-class passengers watch the coach people walking past them in the aisle and they're like, 'Yeah, you lazy losers, this is what you get for being assholes: inadequate legroom.' . . . Simultaneously, all the coach passengers are checking out the elite in their giant, comfy seats: 'That one clearly doesn't deserve to be up here.' 'What has this guy ever brought to the table?' 'There's another cosmic mistake of seating assignment.' 'Don't even get me started on this prick.' . . . Then on the next flight, for whatever reason, some of the first-class people have to fly coach and vice versa, and they all immediately switch teams: 'God, I hate those fuckers.'"

"Then the plane takes off and the fun really begins," said Coleman.

"Something about flying makes people lose their freaking minds," said Serge. "And I'm not talking about getting grumpy over the food or a kid kicking the back of your seat. I recently spoke with some flight attendants, and the true stories of psychotic breaks at thirty thousand feet would send you screaming for Amtrak. They said the public would be amazed at the number of people who freak out and try to open the doors."

"It's a senseless crime," said Coleman.

"That's why flight crews have to carry so many handcuffs nowadays," said Serge. "One woman was refused alcohol, so she drank liquid soap and bit a stewardess. Two groups of football fans had a brawl from rows seventeen to twenty-eight. During night flights, passengers ask for blankets and then leave spent condoms in seat pockets. Guys take off their shirts, try to light cigarettes, sleep on the floor."

"Sounds like every traffic intersection in Florida."

"And I swear this one's true: Another dude jumped up on the serving cart, dropped his pants and took a dump in the peanut basket. I think you lose frequent flier points for that one."

"It's just not right," said Coleman, pointing out the window at a jet overhead. "There's one now."

"Take a pass on the peanuts."

They were four miles into the Seven Mile Bridge. "Oh man!" said Serge. "Irma whacked Pigeon Key!"

"What's that?"

"Coleman, you've asked the same question the last fifty times we've driven over this bridge!"

"Was I here?"

"Under the old Seven Mile, it's all deep water, except partway across there's a single peculiar little island under the piers, with a steep ramp rolling down to it. Very popular with postcard photographers," said Serge. "Tourists driving down to Key West on the new bridge can't miss it. They all look over and go: 'Aw, how cute.'"

"Like a puppy?"

"Roughly the same level of low-grade gratification. But then puzzlement sets in, especially when they see the ramp. 'What the hell is its deal?'"

"Serge, please tell us."

"I cannot deny the public!" He leaned toward the window for a closer look. "A bunch of Henry Flagler's people lived there when they were working on the oil baron's Overseas Railroad, which opened in 1912 and at one point had four thousand employees toiling under the sun to erect it."

"You said 'erect.'" Coleman giggled. "I see a bunch of wooden buildings that got clobbered."

"Some of the most beautiful examples of old Keys wooden construction. You'll find verandas and gables and tin roofs. Tin is key to my roofing pleasure . . . Damn, it even hit the Honeymoon Cottage."

"They look kind of familiar."

"That's because back in Key West I've dragged you through every art gallery on Duval Street."

"I hate that!"

"I've noticed," said Serge. "Might have something to do with the galleries being sandwiched between the bars."

"So close and yet so far," said Coleman. "I also hate it because whenever we go in galleries it means you're going to get me in a headlock."

"You won't look at the paintings otherwise. You just keep pointing out the door with a trembling arm: '*Beer,*'" said Serge. "Culturing you up requires wrestling moves."

"But then they always throw us out."

"It's so unfair," said Serge. "Doesn't opening a gallery mean they want people to admire art? And that's what we're doing, minding our own business looking at paintings with you in a full nelson. But no, they want us to do it *their* way. I try to explain that the whole concept of art is about individual expression, and I haven't seen any signs that say 'No Wrestling.' They just fixate and respond that all your thrashing to get free is driving away the others."

A burp. "And breaking vases."

"That's on them. They distracted me and your arms got loose."

A fresh can of Schlitz popped. "What were we talking about?"

"The buildings that look familiar to you on Pigeon Key," said Serge. "Before we got eighty-sixed from those galleries of shame, you'd seen dozens of killer paintings depicting quaint pastel cottages with fiery azaleas under vibrant coconut palms. A disproportionate number are from that little island under the bridge, because artists are always setting up easels down there to feel the muse. My favorites are the watercolors. Nothing captures the palette of the Keys like that medium, and I always get pumped visiting Pigeon Key and watching them work. They seem so happy. So I point out that the best art is spawned from a tortured soul, and offer to help. But here's the thing I've learned about these art types: They're highly sensitive, and as a general rule they don't like their easels knocked over when you wrestle."

The Plymouth came off the Seven Mile Bridge into Marathon.

Coleman hung out the window. "Man, there's a whole lot less trash on the sides of the road."

"It's amazing what a difference twenty miles one way or the other makes when the eye comes ashore."

Coleman pulled himself back inside the window and shotgunned the Schlitz. "Where to now?"

"Where we were going before the hurricane interrupted us," said Serge. "Continuing our cemetery tour of Florida."

"Is that what we were doing?"

"Cemeteries rock! They're portals to our roots with all the obvious history, not to mention upbeat landscaping and bitchin' statuary," said Serge. "The perfect places for a picnic, except I always seem to be the only one with a basket and checkered blanket."

"And playing a kazoo," said Coleman. "Remember the one time they were lowering that guy into the ground?"

"I thought the music would cheer them up."

"Instead they stomped your picnic basket."

"That's the downside of cemeteries," said Serge. "The only occasions most people go is when there's a lot of hysterical crying and they drag a dead body along. I don't have room for that kind of negativity."

The Plymouth crossed a couple of small bridges onto Grassy Key. Serge made a left turn near mile marker 58.

Coleman's head was back out the window, staring at a round, blue-and-yellow sign.

Dolphin Research Center.

"This doesn't look like a cemetery."

"It's not *technically* one," said Serge. "But I'm including famous individual grave sites. My tour, my rules."

"So who's buried here?"

Serge parked. "Follow and find out."

Moments later, the pair stood solemnly in a secluded corner of the property near the water, crowded by mangroves and other lush vegetation. In the middle of the plants was a statue. There was a marker below it. Serge knelt with a large sheet of paper and a block of colored wax, making a grave rubbing.

Coleman scratched his head and squinted at the statue of a tail-walking dolphin. "I thought you were taking me to where some scientist or soldier was buried."

Serge continued lightly rubbing. "Back in the day, this majestic creature was arguably the most famous Floridian in the whole country."

Coleman read over Serge's shoulder. "Flipper?"

"The iconic dolphin was introduced to the world in 1963, but few viewers realized the star was actually a female dolphin named Mitzi. And even fewer know that this is her final resting place."

"But why here?"

"Before becoming the research center in 1984, this place opened in 1958 as a roadside attraction named Santini's Porpoise School, and Hollywood came calling. Mitzi trained and resided here until passing away in 1972." Serge stood with his wax rubbing in hand and sniffled.

Coleman put a hand on his shoulder. "You okay, buddy?"

"We're in the presence of gentle greatness," said Serge. "Mitzi was a genius in the industry, able to pop out of the water and make clicking sounds that caused humans to respond: 'What is it, Flipper? You say that an evil research scientist trying to poach rare tropical fish is trapped in his personal submarine near the coral reef surrounded by unexploded mines from World War Two training exercises?'"

"Wow," said Coleman. "Next to that, 'Timmy fell in the well' makes Lassie look like an idiot."

Chapter 2

EIGHT YEARS EARLIER

J ust before dawn. The horizon was on fire.

Literally.

Across hundreds of distant acres, bright orange flames whipped violently in the wind.

The sky began to lighten, revealing dozens of columns of black smoke rising hundreds of feet along the rim of the Everglades.

A rusty 1968 Ford pickup truck raced down a lonely dirt road, kicking up a dust plume. The truck was dark red, and the Florida outdoors had made the metal rough like sandpaper. The dirt road stretched through uninhabited miles of open fields. The road was elevated like a causeway, and on each side were canals. Water flowed broadly from Lake Okeechobee down into the Everglades, giving it the nickname River of Grass. The canals had been dug to divert the water and create hundreds of square miles of arable farmland. The canals were deep, and vehicles regularly sank in them. Drownings weren't rare. The pickup truck stayed in the center of the bumpy road, bouncing on old springs. Its bumper was held on by twisted coat hangers and rope. It was doing fifty. The bed of the truck was full of children.

Most of the children held empty canvas sacks and pillowcases. Their clothing was hand-me-down-and-down-again. Striped pullover shirts and ripped denim shorts and even a pair of swim trunks. The ones who had shoes didn't have shoelaces. There was a lot of chatter and laughing in the back of the truck. Bragging. Who had been champions in the past, and who would do even better today. Then the merriment trailed off. They were getting close.

The pickup sped straight toward the nearest fire. It approached upwind, but smoke still wafted over the truck. Some of the kids pulled the necks of their shirts up over their noses and mouths . . .

Palm Beach is the largest of the state's sixty-seven counties, and this was the *other* Palm Beach, the unknown one. Along the Atlantic shore: Worth Avenue, the Breakers Hotel, Rolls-Royce and Mar-a-Lago. On the opposite side, along Lake Okeechobee: boarded-up buildings, empty streets, burglar bars and poverty so corrosive that even the local prison moved out.

The area is now oddly known for only two things: sugar and football players.

These burning fields are where they meet.

From October to April, the harvest is on, and some of the nation's largest sugar growers set fire to their fields in controlled burns that remove leaves and weeds, making way for the mechanical harvesters. The procedure is done with straight lines and right angles. There will be a giant, perfectly square patch of flat, jet-black land where the last burn took place, right next to a thriving green square of waving cane stalks. From the air it looks like a checkerboard. When the fire and smoke start, the children head out, from Pahokee to Belle Glade to South Bay and Harlem.

The '68 pickup skidded to a stop on the dirt road, and the kids in the back hopped out over both sides like troops jumping down from a combat helicopter. They took off running full speed across a black square, their sacks flapping by their sides. Ahead, a wall of cane. The far half of the field was already on fire. They charged into rows of stalks that would soon also be ablaze.

It was a decades-old tradition.

They were hunting rabbits. By hand.

But this wasn't some thrill sport like running with the bulls in Pamplona. It was economic. Each pelt brought a few dollars, and what was left was dinner. Only if you lived around here could you realize how much of a difference that made. From years of experience passed down by word of mouth, even the youngest kids knew how to approach a burning field and head off the rabbits being flushed out.

The kids continued sprinting with all they had, smoke getting thicker. Then they saw them. The first child planted his foot and cut sharply left, diving through a row of stalks and pouncing. A cottontail went into his pillowcase. Then another child cut right, diving on another rabbit. Then another child, and so on as sacks filled.

The cottontails weren't exactly easy to grab, but the jackrabbits were another matter entirely. Almost nobody could lay a hand on them. Almost. Some of those who had accomplished the feat . . . well, everyone knew where they were now.

Amazingly, this short strip of tiny towns along the bottom of Lake Okeechobee has produced more than sixty players in the National Football League. A number so insane that there must be a catch. Word got around, and soon, each fall at high school games, there were almost as many college football scouts in the stands as parents. At first the scouts couldn't believe what they saw. But seeing was believing. These kids were *fast*. Except how was it possible, so many players from such a small area?

The legend began.

Chasing rabbits.

It didn't lead down to Alice's Wonderland, but turned them into professional football players. It even reached a point where ESPN sent journalists down to cover the hunts in the cane fields, reporting how the kids could nimbly cut, change direction and speed up again as the rabbits required. It was a heartwarming myth, but the real reason was more sobering: The kids had been dealt such a cruel hand of hardship at birth that it cultivated a fierce drive to succeed.

And on this particular day, instinct kicked in again. The children knew in their blood exactly when they had pushed it to the last second toward the advancing fire. Then they retreated as fast as they had charged in, regrouping joyously in the safety of the adjacent blackened field, peeking down into their sacks and comparing their hauls. One had four cottontails and proclaimed himself champion of the day, until a heated dispute and a recount. Another sack actually contained a fifth bunny. Hooray!

Then on to the next burning field. Young, lanky boys who had just experienced a growth spurt raced into the cane stalks, dashing and darting with stunning speed. Behind them came the younger kids from grade school, who idolized the older boys and tried to be just like them. They weren't nearly as fast but getting there. They caught the occasional cottontail, but most of the quarry eluded their grasp as they fell facedown in the dirt, and the older boys laughed. Then there was one final youth, the scrawniest of all. Named Chris. But lack of weight didn't affect this child's velocity; in fact it seemed to help. Chris ran on tiptoes. And was surprisingly consistent, nabbing at least one rabbit per field. Then, just as consistently, an older boy would snatch the animal away. "Give me that!" And shove Chris to the ground. "Now go play with your Barbie dolls."

Poverty prevented a lot of things, but not bullying.

They reached the next field and the mad hunt was on again. This time Chris actually came up with *two* rabbits, one in each hand, grinning ear to ear, until getting slammed to the ground again. The critters went in older boys' sacks. Chris just jumped up and took off after another cottontail.

The pickup truck arrived at the last field of the day. This time the haul was so bountiful that the kids pushed the time envelope beyond good judgment. Most were coughing on smoke, feeling the heat of nearby burning stalks, eyes watering as they dove for one more bunny.

Moments later, they burst out of the cane field, initially stunned silent by their own success, then celebrating. As the joy died down and the stinging in their eyes cleared, an odd sensation arrived. Something seemed off. Just a vague gut feeling.

"Is someone not here?"

"Where's Chris?"

"Shit!"

Three of the older boys dashed back into different rows on the edge of the cane field that was rapidly reaching full burn. After only ten yards in, one of the boys found a much younger, skinny kid with a big grin and a bigger jackrabbit.

"Gimme that thing!"

The grin left town. "No! It's mine! I caught him!"

The older boy seized the rabbit by the scruff of the neck, and used his other hand to shove the smaller child down into the dirt and smoke. The child clawed in the soil and fought for breath.

"Now get the fuck up and follow me," said the larger youth. "And don't tell anyone about the jackrabbit or I'll kick your fucking ass! I know where you live!"

The rest of the gang was waiting in the harmless black square, watching nervously as flames grew higher and nearer.

Finally someone pointed. "They're coming out!"

The older boy raised his trophy in triumph.

"Look!"

"James caught a *jack*rabbit!"

"He's going to play college ball for sure!"

On the ride back to Pahokee, the bed of the pickup was much louder than usual. Laughter and tall tales. Everyone had rabbits in their sack. Except one.

Chris just sulked with chin down, the way most of these trips ended.

The others wondered why Chris even bothered to come along. After all, she was a girl.

Chapter 3

THE FLORIDA KEYS

Piles of hurricane debris continued to appear down the sides of the road as if snowplows had been at work. Branches, dresser drawers, broken mirrors, toilets, tires, ceiling fans, cans of food, ripped shirts, rolls of carpet, a deflated basketball and a cuckoo clock.

A Plymouth Satellite raced east.

"Stop the car!" yelled Coleman. "Stop the car!"

Serge screeched the brakes and skidded off the side of the highway.

"Jesus! What is it?"

"Wait here." Coleman jumped out and waddled fifty yards before reaching into the trash. He returned and climbed back in the passenger seat.

Serge pulled back onto the highway. "What have you got there?"

"Check it out!" Coleman thrust his arm an inch from Serge's eyes.

Serge swatted it away. "I'm driving over here."

Coleman cradled his find and brushed off dirt. "It's a squeeze bottle for Florida honey. I remember these from when I was a kid. See? It's a cute smiling alligator from one of those roadside places."

"The old citrus stands," said Serge. "The kind that sold tourists boxes of navel oranges that got crushed by baggage handlers and leaked on the luggage belts, leaving sticky slicks that contaminated other people's suitcases in our state's way of saying, 'Please visit!'"

Coleman twisted off the top and stuck an eyeball in the hole. "I'd been watching the road for something like this."

"You're kidding." Serge looked quickly toward the passenger side. "You were seriously looking for a cool vintage souvenir?"

"Oh, sure. It's just what I wanted."

Serge turned back toward the road and shook his head with a smile. "Well, I'll be. There's hope for you yet . . ."

A half hour later, the gold Satellite sat on the side of the road near mile marker 82 in Islamorada.

Serge glared across the front seat.

"What?" said Coleman.

Serge shook his head again, but with different import. "Hope with you is a fool's errand."

Coleman shrugged and stuck the alligator's head in his mouth, taking a hit from his new honey-bottle bong. He exhaled and pointed. "What's that on the edge of the street? The thing with orange lightbulbs?"

"Temporary highway sign to alert motorists," said Serge. "Don't bother me right now."

"I know it's a road sign," said Coleman. "But they usually say something like 'Detour Ahead.' Why does that one say 'Screw Worm Inspection Station Mile 106'?"

Serge was trying to concentrate on a file folder in his lap. "Because they inspect for screw worms. Probably not now because of the storm. But they'll be back up and running soon."

"I don't even know what a screw worm is," said Coleman. "And why would they need to inspect?"

"It doesn't concern you. Leave me alone." Serge intently flipped through the file.

"I just wanted to know. You're not the only curious one." Then Coleman lapsed into his stoner pastime of playing with the sound of words. "Screw *worm* . . . *screw* worm . . . *screwwwwwwwwww* worm . . . screw *wormmmmmmmmmm* . . . screw wormy-worm . . ."

Serge slowly raised his reddening face and stared out the windshield.

". . . Screwy-screw worm . . . Worm screwy worm . . ."

"Fuck it!" Serge emitted a deep sigh and closed the file. He grabbed a thermos of coffee and chugged. "Okay, most flies—like houseflies—lay eggs in dead stuff. But there's this nasty other fly from Central American called *Cochliomyia hominivorax*. It needs living flesh and deposits eggs in open animal wounds. To up the gross-out factor, the larvae burrow into the meat as they feed, using a screw-like anchor that is so strong it can penetrate bone. It gets pretty ugly and is often fatal. You don't want to see the photos."

"Maybe," said Coleman. "But what's that got to do with the Keys? Why do we need that sign here if it's in Central America?"

"The United States eradicated screw worm flies in the early 1980s, but somehow they got back in and caused the current outbreak that is confined for now to the Florida Keys. That's why they need the signs. Any tourists who bring pets with them on vacation must have them inspected before returning to the mainland."

"They're eating poodles and stuff?"

"Not yet, but the outbreak has already caused much sadness down here." Serge pointed back over his shoulder. "You know those cute little miniature Key deer back on Big Pine that are found nowhere else in the world?"

A pot exhale. "Know 'em and love 'em."

"They seem all sweet and everything, but they're still wild creatures, and during mating season all bets are off. The males have these tiny antlers and they start butting heads for primacy. To watch these little suckers go at it, it's actually kind of funny."

"Kind of like babies fighting."

Serge paused. "When do babies ever fight?"

Coleman puffed and shrugged. "They can't all be nice."

"Whatever. So all this head crashing leaves the tops of the deer's scalps with bunches of antler gashes. That's when the screw worm flies move in, and they work fast! In as little as eight hours, the fleshly laid eggs can hatch and bore down almost an inch. Necrosis follows with equal alacrity, and if immediate care isn't sought, it's game over."

"Cool."

"But here's the freakiest part: Although the host animal is already hopelessly doomed, they're still alive and semi-functioning. That's what happened recently on Big Pine Key. Nobody knew there was an outbreak until they started seeing these zombie-like deer staggering around with parts of their heads gone. They had to euthanize around fifty of the poor fellas. It was the big news down here all season."

"Now I'm sad."

"Maybe this will cheer you up." Serge pulled a photo of a headstone from a manila folder.

Coleman blew another cloud out the window and leaned over. "Whatcha got there?"

"I've begun collecting tombstone rubbings." Fingers flipped through pages. "And the Keys are the best place to start! Whenever launching a new hobby, always pick a starting point that provides immediate success and encourages an obsessive-compulsive lifestyle of more and more hobbies until you retreat from all human contact, subsist on delivered pizza, and remain behind the closed curtains of a house crammed to the eyeballs with comic books, Civil War figures, postage stamp albums, ships in bottles, Coca-Cola signs, prison contraband, display cases of dead moths from across North America, jars of dirt from all fifty states, the world's largest ball of Scotch Tape, and a life-size model made entirely from matchsticks of the Lee Harvey Oswald shooting in the Dallas police basement."

"Never thought of it that way." Puff, puff, puff.

Serge nodded hard as he held up pages. "Take a gander. These are from the Key West Cemetery. The first one is obvious, from the verdigris bronze statue of a sailor overlooking twenty-seven graves of those killed in the 1898 explosion of the USS *Maine* in Havana Harbor . . ." He raised another page. "From there, a severe mood swing to the tombstone of B. P. Robert: 'I told you I was sick,' and Alan Dale Willcox: 'If you're reading this, you desperately need a hobby.'" Serge turned and chuckled. "I fooled him . . . You getting this?"

Coleman exhaled smoke and nodded. "Ball of Scotch Tape."

"The Key West Cemetery is my visual favorite, with above-ground crypts like New Orleans, fantastic statues of angels in various moods and severe tropical landscaping."

"All I know is you woke me up extra early."

"For my Maximum Key West Cemetery Morning Routine: Arise just before dawn and shuffle over to the tiny Five Brothers Cuban grocery on the corner of Southard Street, order pressed cheese toast and café con leche, stick coins in a metal box for a copy of the *Key West Citizen,* then stroll into the cemetery and stretch out on a slab with a great sunrise breakfast while reading an article about a homeless man with no pants arrested for knocking tourists off mopeds with coconuts."

"It doesn't get any better," said Coleman.

"But here's a fun fact to put the perfect coda on that first tour stop. About twenty-five thousand people live in Key West, but there are roughly seventy-five thousand in that cemetery." Serge raised a knowing eyebrow. "Makes you think."

Coleman pointed at the rubbings in Serge's lap. "What's that one?"

"From a cat grave on the grounds of the Hemingway House." He held up another. "And this is from where one of Hemingway's roosters is buried behind Blue Heaven restaurant in the island's Bahama Village section. And finally Mitzi the Dolphin, bringing us up-to-date."

"Was I there?"

"Yes, but pot gives you the short-term memory of a fungus." Serge stowed the file and pulled out fresh pages and wax.

Coleman followed his pal as they left the car behind. "Ever think about what you'd like on your own tombstone?"

Serge tapped his chin. "Maybe something like: 'This is bullshit.'"

"I can dig it." Coleman took another hit. "You know what I'd like?"

"You've stumped me."

"'Dave's not here.'" Giggles.

Serge slowly began nodding. "I like it. On a couple of levels. First, for its simple philosophical truth. Second, as an Easter egg for Cheech and Chong fans who lose their way going into a cemetery."

Serge entered a small, open park and snapped a few photos, then approached a monument and went to work with his wax.

"Wow," said Coleman. "That's the biggest tombstone I've ever seen!"

"Roughly the same shape, but not a tombstone." Rub, rub, rub. "It's the monument to those who lost their lives in the Labor Day hurricane of 1935. The cremated remains of nearly two hundred people are interred just under your feet."

"It looks kind of cool."

"Because it is." Rub, rub, rub. "A giant slab of coral with a bas-relief sculpture of blowing palms. Due to the era, the design is art deco. But it's so subtly placed and presented that most visitors just drive right by without noticing the massive history treasure . . . I don't think I'm going to have enough paper."

Coleman stared down and idly scraped the ground with the toe of a sneaker. "Whew, two hundred."

"Get ready," said Serge. "I have a feeling our next stop is going to be insane."

EIGHT YEARS EARLIER

Boys yelled from all directions.

"I got one!"

"I got one over here, too!"

Chris raced between rows, crashing through cane stalks. She had a bead on another jackrabbit. She began coughing in the thickening smoke, but there was never a thought of giving up. Her technique was to chase rabbits *toward* the fire and confuse them.

More slamming through the cane, scraping her arms up but good. Then she left her feet and stretched out in the air for her pounce.

"Got you!"

She was happily carrying the rabbit out of the field when something collided with her hard from the side, knocking her to the ground. A boy much older and bigger reached down. "Give me that fucking rabbit."

Chris was immediately back on her feet. "He's mine! Give him back!"

But she was just shoved again in the dirt.

This time Chris didn't get right back up. She felt she was about to cry, and she couldn't let that happen. She strained for composure, and dug her fists, clawing, into the rich soil. Then:

"What's this?"

Her left hand felt something strange. She pulled it from the soil and opened her palm. It was a coin. She rubbed the dirt off on her shirt and looked again. A *gold* coin. She read the date.

1907.

From collecting Lincoln pennies, Chris knew about other coins, too. And she still couldn't believe her eyes. It was a Saint-Gaudens twenty-dollar piece, one of the crown jewels of the numismatic world. She knew its value from her guidebooks and always figured she could only dream of having one. This was way better than a rabbit. She found a foot-long marking stake with an orange ribbon and drove it into the ground.

Chris was still studying her find as she came out of the stalks, so distracted she bumped into another of the big boys.

"What do you have in your hand?"

She clenched her fist shut and stuck it behind her back. "Nothing."

"Give it here!"

"No!"

He twisted her arm and pried her fingers open. "Thanks!" Then the final shove to the ground of the day.

Chris went home in a fuming funk and sat outside on a milk crate.

Bells jingled as a door opened in Pahokee.

The pawnshop owner set a jeweler's glass down and looked up. Pawnshops are universally the eyes of the community, and their eclectic brand of commerce tracks the town's secrets: who's gambling, on drugs, getting divorced, quitting the trombone.

Right now, these eyes gazed toward the person entering his shop and told him: *This isn't positive.* It was one of the junior high kids, nothing to buy, nothing to sell. But they were damn fast, and forget trying to catch them once they stole something and made it out the door.

"Stop right there, young man." The owner looked and sounded like James Earl Jones. But his name was Webber. "What's your business here?"

The boy reached in his pocket and held up a yellow circle between his thumb and index finger. "I found a coin."

This was different. A thousand-candlepower smile lit up the shop. "Come on over here, son! Let's see what you've got there."

But the pawnshop owner already knew. Such coins had been dribbling in over the years about one every six months. Always from kids he initially sized up as trouble. They claimed they found them in the cane fields while hunting rabbits, but who knew? Maybe someone's collection was getting poached. The fewer questions the better.

"I found it in a cane field," said an unusually tall fourteen-year-old named Ricky.

"You look like a football player." Webber examined the coin and poked the boy in the shoulder, buttering him up. "I'll bet you're going to win the Muck Bowl for us!"

Ricky bloomed with pride. "I still have a year to go, but Coach says I'm a natural tailback."

"I'm sure you are." Webber set the coin down on a cloth. "Did you take a look at this? Did you read what it says on the back?"

Eager nodding. "Twenty dollars! But it's old, and it's gold!"

"Except you realize that they don't use these coins anymore. They took them out of circulation."

"What does that mean?" asked the youth.

"It means I don't want to give you any bad news. What do you think is a fair price for this coin?"

Ricky pointed. "The back says twenty dollars."

Webber opened his register and pulled out bills to mollify negotiations. "How about fifteen? That's more than I should."

It had the desired effect as the boy stared at the cash and thought: *Shit, yeah. I just snatched it off that sissy girl anyway.*

"Deal."

Thus continued a daisy chain of underhandedness.

They shook hands.

The boy pocketed bills as he headed for the door.

"And bring me any others you find," Webber called out. "I'm good for fifteen dollars each, even though I'm probably losing money. But I can't help it; I'm just a nice guy."

Bells jingled again as the door closed.

Webber had just made his whole month. If melted for just the weight in gold, the coin was worth more than a grand. And a 1907 in this condition could fetch double.

An ebullient moment took a slight, sullen hit. Darn, he would have to notify the police as required under the law for anything of this value.

A beat cop arrived three hours later. Webber had sent the declaration fax of his purchase to police headquarters, and normally it would have stopped at that. But he knew the drill. Word of the coins was slowly getting out.

Bells jingled. The officer entered and twirled his nightstick. "So how many does that make now?"

"How many what?"

"Rare gold coins these kids are finding just laying on the ground."

"I don't know." The pawn owner wiped the lenses of his reading glasses. "A few."

"Seventeen by our count."

"That many?"

"Imagine the odds," said the officer. "Seventeen different kids just walking along and looking down."

"I understand some were under the dirt."

"Whatever you say." The officer walked along the glass display cases and resumed twirling his stick. He stopped and leaned over. "Is that the coin? May I see it?"

The owner sighed and handed him the small plastic protective holder.

"Real pretty," said the officer, turning it over in his hand. "It's just so unbelievable. If I didn't know you better, I'd say you might be fencing coins stolen from some collections."

"Really, they're just kids," said the owner. "You remember the million juke joints we had around here when the town was big? All those workers getting paid and drunk on a Friday night. I'm surprised they didn't drop more of these things stumbling around."

"Okay, I'll go along. And I'm sure you always pay these kids fairly." The officer held up the coin. "How much did this baby set you back?"

Webber stood mute.

"Did I stutter?" asked the officer.

"I-I don't remember."

"Now *you're* stuttering. Come on, it was only a few hours ago."

Webber was a very bad actor as he searched the top of a cluttered desk. "The paperwork's around here somewhere . . ."

"I'm sure it is," said the officer. "By the way, you know my boss's daughter?"

Webber welcomed the change of topic. "Great girl!"

"She's starting high school next fall and wow, is she fantastic in the band. Especially the trombone, except she—"

Webber sighed with renewed resignation as he turned to the shelf. "Just had one come in, real cheap. You probably heard the rumors . . ."

The officer nodded sadly. "Slide McCall. Who would have thought?"

"I just feel for his family," said Webber, handing the instrument across the counter as the daisy chain completed another link.

The officer whistled a merry tune as he headed toward the door with a long piece of brass over his shoulder. "Remember that fencing is a serious offense."

"They're kids. Really."

"Whatever."

Bells jingled.

Chapter 4

THE FLORIDA KEYS

Serge slapped his pal on the shoulder. "Look alive. Next stop."

"Okay." Coleman headed back to the car.

"Where are you going?" asked Serge.

Coleman grabbed a door handle. "Next stop, like you said."

"No, this way."

He led Coleman in the opposite direction, down local roads a couple hundred yards toward the ocean. They arrived in front of an ultra-luxury resort where the first President Bush often stayed during fly-fishing vacations.

"I get it," said Coleman. "We're going to crash another rich place and find a business conference reception with free food and booze. I'm down with that. Let me straighten myself up so we can get through security because this shit is worth it."

"Not necessary," said Serge. "Act however you want."

Coleman wiped his nose on his shirt. "What do you mean?"

"Just be yourself," said Serge. "It is indeed a world-class resort, but we're allowed to cut through the side of the property because the public has the right to access my next stop."

"Be myself? Okay." He pulled a pint of Southern Comfort from his pocket and lifted it to the sun as he guzzled.

"Once again, my words were not chosen with adequate care," said Serge. "Be like *other* people."

"That's different." Coleman stowed the bottle and stumbled after his friend.

They ended up on a sandy beach behind the hotel as waves from the Florida Straits lapped the shore.

"What the hell?" said Coleman.

"Told you it would be cool."

Before them stood a white picket fence surrounding a small cluster of graves and tombstones.

Coleman took a furtive swig from his flask and grabbed the fence for balance. "I never expected a cemetery in the middle of a beach."

"It's not just a cemetery but a *pioneer* cemetery." Serge snapped photos. "You've got three main family plots in there. The Pinders, Russells and Parkers, who settled here back in the 1800s and kicked off what this island is today."

"But how is it allowed on a beach?"

"Because of history lovers!" said Serge. "The die-hard locals knew this stuff here meant a lot, so despite the prevailing wisdom that tombstones are not your first choice for a tourist draw on the beach, they stood firm and dutifully tended the flame of heritage."

"*Whooooaaaaaa.*" Coleman hung on to the top of a picket with one hand, swinging off-balance and bouncing against the fence a few times like a screen door in the wind. "Getting a little funky here."

Serge was lost in the focus of the moment. "But I view the whole tourist-cemetery interface from an optimistic viewpoint that history is the future. A lovely family from Elk Rapids comes down here, and they're like: 'This is paradise. We've got a beautiful sun and sky, our blankets spread out, sodas and baloney sandwiches in the cooler, our kids laughing and splashing in the surf. How can it possibly get any better? . . . Wait, are people buried here?'"

"Where else can they get that?" asked Coleman.

"This is what I keep trying to tell people, but it's always the same closed-mindedness: 'Don't hurt me.'"

"I kind of dig that angel statue in the center."

"Remember the big hurricane monument by the highway? True story: When that storm blew through, it picked up that angel—I'm guessing by the wings—and sent it flying all the way back to the road. I mean, that's a pretty heavy chunk of rock. And it barely got scratched. The local history heroes returned it to its rightful place."

"Must have been a big storm to blow it that far."

"One of the biggest." Serge placed paper to headstone. "And Islamorada was particularly hard hit, with scores of victims. But of course all the people in this cemetery were already dead."

"So they survived?"

Serge stared at Coleman a moment and returned to his rubbing.

Soon they were strolling along the beach, Serge in a straight line, Coleman on a much looser course. His veering became more and more generous until he was offshore.

Serge sternly folded his arms and yelled at the ocean. "Can you please not do that?"

"Sorry." Coleman splashed back toward land. "Having a little trouble coloring inside the lines."

They continued on. Then they stopped and stared down.

"A dead seagull?" said Coleman.

Serge raised his eyes up the shore. "There's another one, and another . . ."

After walking twenty more yards, Serge paused again. "That's weird. Six dead birds, but no clues. No fishing lines or oil or trauma."

"Maybe it was the hurricane," said Coleman.

Serge shook his head. "The bodies are too fresh. Oh, well . . ."

They resumed strolling again and heard a chorus of rambunctious yelling. Three young boys charging down the beach to the water's edge.

"Now that's what I like to see," said Serge. "A footloose childhood like mine spent in the Florida outdoors instead of moving pieces of candy around on cell phones."

"What are they doing?"

"Looks like a bread sack. They're throwing pieces."

"Here come the seagulls." Coleman ducked as they swooped in. "How do they do that? Not a bird around, and then a million."

"Seagulls are the FBI surveillance teams of the animal world. You never know the FBI is there until the shit goes down, and then they're *everywhere*," said Serge. "Likewise, seagulls often don't make their presence known until someone tosses aside the last bite of a hot dog, turning the beach into a Hitchcock movie."

"What are those kids throwing now?" asked Coleman. "It doesn't look like bread anymore."

"What *are* they throwing?" asked Serge, heading off in a trot.

The trio of young boys giggled as they tossed stuff to the frenzy of birds.

"Excuse me," said Serge. "May I see what you're feeding them?"

One of the boys quickly hid something behind his back, and they all stopped laughing.

"Come *onnnnnn*," said Serge. "I just want in on the fun."

"Then okay," said one of kids. He produced a box of generic Alka-Seltzer.

Serge gasped and grabbed his heart.

From behind: "What the hell are you doing? Get away from those kids!"

It was a voice from someone Serge hadn't noticed on the beach before. He turned and saw a man running down from the palm trees around a resort swimming pool.

He arrived and got between Serge and the boys. "What are you, some kind of pervert?"

"No, but why do you have a video camera in your hand?"

"None of your business! And you're wrecking my shot!"

"I know what you were doing," said Serge. "You told these kids to feed Alka-Seltzer to the birds. And because birds can't burp, they would explode."

"No, I didn't."

"You're lying," said Serge. "And then you were going to film the whole shameful episode with your camera. That level of cruelty is a sickness."

"So what if I was?" He shoved Serge hard in the chest. "What are you going to do about it?" Another shove.

Serge stumbled backward a couple of steps. "Don't you know the whole tale about birds exploding is an urban myth?"

"What are you talking about?"

"They don't explode," said Serge. "They *can* burp, or whatever the avian equivalent is of dealing with the social awkwardness of unpleasant gas that gets looks from the rest of the flock."

"Then what's your problem?"

Serge pointed back up the beach at the half-dozen fallen seagulls that they'd just passed. "While the birds may not explode, you've given them an overdose of aspirin and anhydrous citric acid, the active ingredient in those tablets. A gull that weighs a pound or two can't handle what's meant for an adult human."

"I don't believe you."

"Believe this: The overdose symptoms include high fever, double vision, respiratory distress, cardiac distress, abdominal agony, brain-swelling, seizures. It's such a horrible way to go that those birds probably wished they *had* exploded."

"You—!" The man with the video camera noticed something out in the water and paused. "What's he doing?"

Coleman was up to his belly button in the surf with a strained look on his face.

Serge cupped hands around his mouth. "Coleman! No taking dumps in the ocean! We've talked about this." He turned back around to the man. "Sorry, where were we?"

"You were just about to leave!" Another shove.

"Jesus, there are kids here," said Serge. "What kind of example are you setting as a parent?"

"Ha! I'm not their father. I'm their uncle."

"Well then, by all means, ruin them, Uncle Jack Wagon."

"I've had enough of you!" A final shove, sending Serge down to the sand. "Fuck off!"

"Okay, now you're really being a bad example," said Serge. "Using profanity *and* ending a sentence with a preposition."

Coleman trudged his way back to shore. "What did I miss?" He received his own shove to the chest and toppled over. "Hey, what was that for?"

Serge got up and dusted himself off. "I've really tried to be nice, but now you're being mean to Coleman, which is a broad form of animal cruelty."

The man gritted his teeth in rage and lunged for another shove. This time, Serge quickly slipped aside, grabbed him by the wrist and locked up the man's arm under his armpit.

Now, in fights it's often the bigger combatant who prevails. But sometimes it's the little things. Like the little finger. Bend it back to the breaking point, and people bend to your will.

"Ow! My finger!"

"Tell the kids to go home."

"You mean to the motel room."

Serge rolled his eyes. "Whatever." He bent the finger harder. "Now."

"Boys! Go back to the room!"

"What about the birds?" asked a child.

"Get going!"

The young trio skedaddled.

"Alone at last," said Serge.

"Now will you let go of my finger?"

"Yes." Serge pulled a pistol from under his shirt and stuck it in the man's ribs. "I never got your name."

"Clyde."

"Clyde, start walking."

"Where are we going?"

"Oh, this is going to be a real blast, a regular humdinger," said Serge. "Have you seen the Pioneer Cemetery? . . ."

A little while later, Serge stared down into a car trunk. "Comfy?"

"W-w-what are you going to do—"

The lid slammed shut.

EIGHT YEARS EARLIER

Chris was a weird little kid.

In a good way. Other children take to education like they're being force-fed. But Chris was so naturally curious that she practically became another piece of furniture in the library, spending hours on the computer to look up more data than her course material had to offer.

Then the next day in science class, where they were discussing the basics of our sun, its age, distance. A hand shot up. "I found out that our sun bends time and space. The planets, too. It makes wormholes possible."

"What are you talking about?"

"Einstein. Others proved his theory with a telescope during an eclipse when a star appeared from behind the corona when it shouldn't have."

Then math class and a triangle with equal sides. A hand flew up again.

"The Romans killed Archimedes while he was working on a problem. 'Don't disturb my circles,' he said."

"What?"

Soon, other teachers were showing up out in the hall, pointing through the window of the classroom's door at the odd little kid in the front row with a hand enthusiastically in the air. Still more educators began joining Chris in the library to look up her tidbits, their own curiosity piqued. They glanced over at the young girl sitting a few desks away, leaning farther and farther forward, as if knowledge would pull her right through the computer screen.

Saturday meant no school, but Chris had her own curriculum. She grabbed a notebook, pens, an old compass, some tape and a lunch bag. Chris had grown up alone with her grandmother due to the broken-home epidemic that was going around. The old woman looked up as Chris wheeled her bicycle through the living room of their apartment.

"Where are you going, honey?"

"Treasure hunting."

"Have fun."

The ride was at least a mile, possibly closer to two, but when Chris put her mind to something, get out of the way or prepare to be run over.

Other kids probably didn't remember, but Chris could recall every word of the old schoolyard folklore stories about the evil sugar baron named Fakakta who was found shot to death after the 1928 hurricane. And of course the lost treasure. Kids are allowed to dream.

She was a cute little sight, tiny legs churning as she pedaled her pink bicycle up the side of Hooker Highway. She finally arrived at a cane field from one of her recent rabbit hunts, and turned down a dirt road. Chris had a good memory as she walked her bike through the rows of sugar stalks. She came to a marking stake with an orange ribbon. Then she got out her compass and triangulated her position with a pair of distant power lines. Numbers were jotted in her notebook. Then she commenced digging. It was a scientific sampling grid that only she would have thought of, moving out from the stake. The afternoon wore on under the unfiltered sun, her face filthy from wiping away sweat with dirty hands. She was quickly reaching the logical conclusion: probably just a one-time find. And she didn't have any proof that the bogeyman of the sugar field ever existed. That's when her fingers hit it.

The second coin.

Now Chris had two geometric points to work with. She stood up and aimed her compass, dutifully recording new figures in the notebook. She turned the page and drew a second diagram. The search field had become an elongated oval. Digging continued till she could barely see in the growing darkness, but no more finds. She stuck the coin, compass and notebook in the lunch bag she had brought along, and taped it flat to her stomach under her shirt. No way anyone was going to steal this stuff.

Two boys stopped her a block from the apartment building. "Hey, Milk Crate! What have you got there?"

She hated that nickname. "None of your business!"

"Empty your pockets."

"No!"

"I said empty!"

She turned them inside out. Empty.

"Okay, you can go."

As she put her feet back on the pedals, one of them punched her in the shoulder with an extended knuckle.

"Ow!"

She left laughter behind as she pedaled away . . .

Good thing the next day was a Sunday. Her power of will was locked in, and there was little chance she would have been able to focus in school. She rode her bike back to the cane field again. This time it only took her three hours to find the next coin. The compass and notebook came back out. Coordinates plotted, a new shape diagramed. She stopped and aimed her compass in the direction of Lake Okeechobee, squinting with one eye closed, the tip of her tongue sticking out the corner of her mouth in concentration. Math and science were just intuitive to Chris. Her mind's eye instinctively drew a line from the lake to where she stood, envisioning the shape of the debris field if some treasure chest burst open around here in a storm surge. She decided to load her search southeast of the last coin.

It was only an hour before grimy fingers pulled up the next gold piece. Excitement bubbled. There was a lot of time left before sunset. But that would be it for the day.

Chris pedaled home and ran inside.

"Where have you been?" asked her grandmother.

"Out." She dashed into her bedroom and closed the door. Chris ripped the tape off her stomach and lay on the floor next to her dresser. She stared up as she pulled out the bottom drawer. The two newest coins were taped underneath next to the previous one. She closed the drawer and jumped up just as her grandmother came in.

"Good gracious, child, you're filthy."

Chris dropped into the chair at her small desk and opened the notebook. "I'm fine." A pen clicked open.

"You go wash up right now before you make a mess of the whole place."

"Don't disturb my circles."

"Are you sassing me?"

"No, it's a math joke." She stood from the chair. "I'll go wash up. I love you!"

The next day in school, the teachers had a nagging feeling that something was different in class, but they couldn't quite put their fingers on it. By fourth period, the science teacher figured it out. Chris was unnaturally quiet. She hadn't asked a single question or added something arcane to the discussion, like, "Thomas Edison never slept more than four hours a night." And Chris kept glancing at the clock on the wall. Before this day, she always seemed as though she wanted class to go on forever. Maybe she had the flu.

The bell rang, and the teacher caught her at the door. "Chris, is everything okay?"

"Great! I just got a cool compass that I've been thinking about!" She ran off down the hall.

Weird little kid, the teacher thought. *But in a good way.*

Chris burst through the door of her grandmother's upstairs apartment, rolling in her bike. She ran right for her room. She rifled through papers and magazines and library books on her little desk. It became frantic. She ran out into the living room.

"Grandma, have you seen my green notebook? . . . *Grandma?*"

"In here."

Chris ran to the kitchen. "Grandma, what are you doing reading my notebook?"

"I wouldn't read it if it was your diary because that would be private." The old woman turned the page with sausage fingers. "But you left it open on your desk. All these numbers and complex diagrams, for a child your age no less. So this is how you always get straight A's?" She handed the book back. "I'm very proud of you. Just remember not to care what anyone thinks; you're going to do great things someday."

"Thanks, Grandma." A kiss on the cheek, and then she was off again with her bike.

Today would be a watershed, but it didn't look that way at first, taking two hours to find the next coin. But shortly after, her hands hit something else in the soil. She pulled out a piece of wood. A short thin plank with rusty rails on each end like it had been part of a packing crate. She tossed it aside and began excavating with vigor. The hole was wider than her others, exposing the surface of two more broken planks. She lifted them up and froze. Six more coins in a cluster. There was now no doubt that this wasn't just stray dropped money. The folklore was true. Chris wanted to tell the world, but "I can't tell anybody."

She made all the required documentation in her notebook, then taped everything to her stomach again, and pedaled her bike home like a maniac.

Now she had a problem. An embarrassment of riches, so to speak. If her hunch was correct, she would quickly run out of room under her dresser drawers. And the bag she taped beneath her shirt wasn't going to cut it much longer. She started taping coins inside her shoes, but that just made pedaling too hard. She had a stroke of brilliance.

The next day she raced home from the fields again. Boys stopped her bike at the corner of the apartments. There was a basket on her handlebars with daisies.

"Hey, Milk Crate! What have you got there?"

"None of your business."

The tallest boy looked in the basket. "Textbooks? *Ewww!*" A punch on the shoulder and they let her go.

Chris ran up to her room and removed the rubber strap holding the books together. She opened an old algebra text that she had found discarded behind the school. In the middle of the carved-out pages were her coins for the day.

Next order of business: Improve storage. This would be more difficult. She stared out the window. Then she got down on the floor and began removing tape from under dresser drawers . . .

And so it went. Days, weeks, then months, slowly building her haul. She had depleted all that apparently could be found from that first crate, and there had been a dispiriting lull. But it was followed by the wooden remnants of a second box. Then a hundred yards south, the discovery of the next planks.

A year passed. Then two years. At first it had been pure excitement. Nothing goes together better than kids and buried treasure. But now that she was getting older: "Am I doing something wrong?"

Chris sat at her usual computer in the library the next afternoon. She looked up site after site on salvage laws. She read about how if something sinks in a body of water, under certain circumstances, it's up for grabs. Then she went back to meteorology pages showing detailed computer models and maps of the tidal surge from the 1928 storm. The highest water levels rose twenty feet over the field she'd been working. She sat back and bit her lower lip in thought. "Technically, the treasure *did* sink. And I'm the finder."

Back to work.

More time passed, more trips to the cane fields. But all good things must come to an end. Chris's efforts dwindled in results as she depleted her find, until there was nothing. And she was sure about it, too, because she had dug her scientific sampling holes far and wide in the logical drift directions.

She was happy and sad at the same time. What an adventure it had been. On the other hand, Chris always felt unanchored when she didn't have an obsessive goal to focus her mental energy. She would just have to come up with something else.

It only took a few days. She rode her bike as fast as she could, hyper as hell, down to the high school. She knocked on a door . . .

Chapter 5

SOUTH FLORIDA

The Plymouth Satellite wound its way east on U.S. Highway 1 and crested the bridge out of Key Largo at mile 107. Then it entered what locals call "the Eighteen-Mile Stretch," a no-man's-land of mangroves and wild scrub from the bottom tip of the mainland to the first dribbles of civilization at Florida City. Do not break down, do not run out of gas.

Coleman sucked on his gator bottle and blew smoke out the window. "I never heard about trying to explode birds."

"A sad state of affairs," said Serge. "And not just Alka-Seltzer. Do any kind of Internet search on animal abuse, and it brings up a trail of tears. Pelicans get it especially bad for some reason, and now these ass-heads are filming the brutality and proudly posting it on the web. Rice is another one."

"Rice, like the San Francisco treat?"

Serge nodded. "People feed uncooked rice to birds, waiting for them to burst. It's another myth, and luckily, in that case, the birds aren't poisoned and can fly away. But the intent is still there. I can't get my head around that brand of cowardice."

"But, Serge, there must be another way."

"There is." Serge checked the clip in his pistol and stowed it under the seat. "That's one reason why a lot of people have stopped throwing rice at weddings. Instead they hand out bags of birdseed. Of course they don't realize that the rice is safe, but I'm heartened to see they care enough to err on the side of caution."

"You said it was one reason they stopped throwing rice?"

"The other reason is all the documented slips and falls on the tiny kernels," said Serge. "It dampens the mood when the lovebirds are driving away with tin cans bouncing behind the car and then Grandma Petunia takes a spectacular header in the driveway."

"You know, I admire the way you respect animals," said Coleman. "Really?"

"Yeah, I like my little nature friends," said Coleman. "Squirrels dig my potato chips."

"You are noble in that way," said Serge. "Although the salt contributes to hypertension. Those tiny fellows are wound way too tight as it is. Especially the flying ones. What is their fucking hurry? I mean, damn, just slow your roll, man."

"What about jelly beans?"

"Diabetes," said Serge.

The Plymouth entered southern Miami on the Dixie Highway. Soon, they passed a church, and Serge craned his neck around as people entered. "Well, I'll be."

Coleman turned. "Someone's getting married?"

"We were just talking about weddings, and one's about to get started," said Serge. "This gives me a chance."

"For what?"

"To restore tradition," said Serge. "Whole generations know not of the rice joy."

"What about Grandma Petunia?"

"My solution is elegantly designed not to break any hips."

Serge drove on until he found what he was looking for. The Plymouth skidded into a parking lot.

An hour later, the pair waited alone in front of the church.

"So we're going to be wedding crashers?" asked Coleman.

"No, that would involve dishonesty," said Serge. "But there's nothing unethical about standing outside a church and rooting for strangers not to get divorced."

"The doors are opening," said Coleman.

"Here they come," said Serge. "Get ready."

Guests poured down the steps and formed crowds on each side of the walkway leading from the church. Finally, the happy newlyweds emerged. They headed down the walkway, showered with cheers and birdseed. They were halfway to their car at the curb when suddenly:

Plop . . . plop, plop, plop . . .

"What on earth?" said the bride.

Plop, plop, plop . . .

The groom looked up in rage. "Who's throwing rice? *Cooked* rice?"

"Me!" Serge raised his hand. "Because I care! There's no way those old geezers over there will crack their noggins."

The groom looked down at his chest. "It's brown! And greasy!"

Serge grinned sheepishly. "It's pork fried rice. Sorry, I got a little hungry and that's my favorite." *Plop, plop . . .*

"My dress!" screamed the bride. "It's ruined!"

"You bastards!"

Serge held out an innocent hand. "What? I'm so happy for you! This is your special day! Don't get divorced!"

"Special day?"

"Yeah," said Serge, "but keep up this kind of gloomy fixation on laundry and tonight you'll be wanking off into a honeymoon suite bathrobe."

"Fuckers!"

"Get 'em!"

"Coleman, time to run again."

Serge easily slipped out of grasp as usual, and just as usual, Coleman was captured. They had him squirming by the arms, and Serge was about to disperse them with a display of the Colt .45 pistol in his waistband. But Coleman was even more effective at the task by jackknifing over and rainbow-vomiting a bouillabaisse of Southern Comfort and Cool Ranch Doritos across the hems of black tuxedo pants.

"Son of a bitch!"

The Plymouth patched out and raced north on Dixie Highway. They heard a banging sound from the trunk.

"Jesus, can't I get any peace?" Serge slapped the steering wheel while fishing bullets from his pocket. "*I'm* being mellow, but everyone else is rowing against my harmony stream."

O n an overcast afternoon, a gold Satellite sat in the parking lot of a sub-budget motel on Highway A1A. Across the street, a nearly deserted beach in Fort Lauderdale. Purple clouds rolled in over the unstaffed vintage lifeguard stands. The sign above the motel office featured a smiling mermaid, in an attempt to make up for everything else.

Serge and Coleman crashed through the door of room 6.

"This is going to be the best party ever!" said Coleman, dumping a shopping bag on one of the beds and chugging from a bottle of Jack.

"Damn straight," said Serge, emptying his own bag. "We're going old school. And if you're going old school, then go all the way!"

"You don't mean—?"

"That's right!" said Serge. "Kindergarten!"

"Man," said Coleman. "That's off the hook."

"Those were the last of the truly great days," said Serge, pawing through his new stuff on the mattress. "All fun all the time, running around screaming on the playground, crayons and construction paper, those little milk cartons and nap time. No grade-point average yet, no pressure whatsoever except tying your shoes and trying not to spit up."

"But then the janitor could always come with the sawdust," said Coleman.

"It was like watching a miracle," said Serge. "The first time I saw it, I didn't give the sawdust a snowball's chance, but then *damn*! For a while, life was perfect. If there's ever a problem, just throw sawdust on it and everything will be lollipops and unicorns again. And one evening my mom was sitting at the kitchen table, crying over a pile of unpaid bills. She suddenly sits up straight and starts brushing all this stuff out of her hair: 'Serge, what the hell?' I say, 'Sawdust, Mom. Everything's okay now.' But instead I got a time-out in the corner. That was the death of innocence."

"Look at all this cool stuff on the bed!" said Coleman.

"And not a speck of digital." Serge stood. "That's how we lost our way."

"Where are you going?"

"To get the rest of our haul out of the car. I'll need your help."

It had been a whirlwind shopping spree, with stops at quite varied retail outlets until brimming bags filled the car. After several unloading trips, Serge and Coleman were safely ensconced back in the room, enthusiastically sorting their recent purchases on the bed. Paste, safety scissors, pipe cleaners, finger paints, glitter, tinfoil, clothespins, buttons, Play-Doh.

Coleman picked up a couple of the buttons. They were clear, with something round inside that rolled around. "What are these?"

"Eyes you glue on a drawing of a bear or something to make him look wacky."

Coleman held the buttons over his own eyes. "Serge, what do you think?"

"Overkill."

Coleman cast them aside and picked up the scissors. "Remember in kindergarten when you could make a costume out of just a pillowcase?"

"That was the best!" Serge grabbed a sixty-four-count box of Crayolas. "You cut holes for your head and arms and could color whatever your imagination dreamed up. You could be anyone you wanted."

"I was an Indian for Thanksgiving," said Coleman. "What about you?"

"Chief Justice Warren."

"Hey, let's make costumes!"

"Great idea!"

They dashed toward the head of a bed and stripped cases off pillows.

Coleman plopped down at a table and grabbed crayons. "Do you think the motel will mind?"

"We'll just slip them back on the pillows when we're done. They've seen worse."

Coleman leaned over the table, ready to go. "What do you think our costumes should be?"

Serge grabbed a blue crayon. "Superheroes. The pillowcases will imbue us with special powers."

"What hero are you going to be?"

"It's a secret." Serge began coloring furiously. "And don't tell me yours either until you're done."

"I love surprises." Coleman joined in the vigorous scribbling. "So where'd you get this idea for a kindergarten party, anyway?"

Serge intently colored on his own case. "You know how sometimes I like to leave my cell phone in the car and take off on foot?"

"I've been wondering why you do that."

"You take away someone's phone today, and it's like you've cut off their oxygen. They can't survive," said Serge. "But kids used to spend entire childhoods without phones and do just fine. That's why it's essential to leave my phone in the car every so often. My wallet, too. Because I have no money or credit cards, it recalibrates my senses back to grade school, forcing me to appreciate all the free stuff in life, like skipping or rolling around in the grass for no reason. It's about rekindling the lost art of being silly."

"I remember that one time you left your phone and wallet behind, and you were hanging upside down on the monkey bars, making farting sounds with your hands on your mouth."

"And the park officials made us leave just for that? I even explained it was part of my phone-and-wallet-free therapy, like EST, insulin shock or primal scream."

"I think you were freaking everyone out."

"They said it was inappropriate behavior for an adult, which I explained was the exact kind of thinking that now has everyone at each other's throats." Serge grabbed a different color crayon and scribbled. "Anyway, I realized I was severely limiting myself with those brief childlike excursions. I needed to invoke the Total Kindergarten Protocol. But of course society isn't ready, like the monkey-bar fiasco or how they laughed when the Beatles joined that ashram in India. So we need the privacy of a motel room."

"What do you do for this proto— . . . proto— . . ."

"Protocol," said Serge. "In order to cleanse ourselves of the toxicity from the growing-up process, we must revert and do nothing beyond the level of a five-year-old."

"Cool." Coleman grabbed a crayon in one hand and a bottle with the other. Chug, chug, chug.

"Ahem!"

Coleman looked up. "What?"

"I don't think Jack Daniel's is on the lunch menu next to the beanie weenies."

"Oh, judge me for a little snort?" Coleman pointed with a yellow crayon. "I don't remember *that* from childhood."

Serge looked over at a man tied to a motel room chair and gagged with duct tape. He slapped himself in the forehead. "I'd completely forgotten about Clyde."

Coleman scoffed sarcastically. "Did you tie people up in kindergarten?"

Serge walked over to the hostage. "Actually, there was this one incident. It's pretty funny now, but at the time: 'Where the hell did Little Serge get all that rope?'"

The hostage wiggled violently. "*Mmmmm! Mmmmm!*"

Coleman grabbed the bottle of whiskey and resumed coloring. "Sounds like he wants to tell you something." Chug, chug, chug.

Serge rapped knuckles on Clyde's forehead like it was a door. "Is that true?"

Vigorous nodding.

"Promise not to yell?"

More nodding.

Serge quickly ripped off the tape.

"Owwwwwwwww!"

"I thought you promised?"

"Please don't hurt me!"

"Hurt you?" said Serge, innocently pointing to his own chest. "Oh, *I'm* not going to hurt you."

"Then what are you going to do?"

Serge gestured toward the arts-and-crafts table. "First I need to continue my kindergarten reversion therapy, and then we'll have an after-school party. How about it? . . ." His gleeful expression became a frown. "What? You don't like parties? You're not in a festive mood? . . . Then you leave me no choice . . ."

Serge turned his back to Clyde and bent over a bed.

"No! Please! Whatever you're thinking . . ."

Serge spun back around. Two buttons were over his eyes. He shook his head back and forth, and the little objects in the buttons rattled around in circles. He removed the buttons. "Pretty wacky, eh?"

Clyde just whimpered.

"Jesus," said Serge. "I give and I give." He tore off another long strip of tape and forcefully wrapped it over Clyde's mouth again. Terrified eyes looked up at him.

"Hold that thought," said Serge. "I'll be back after I'm a superhero . . . But you can't tell anyone my true identity."

There were a number of stray crayon marks on the table, but Coleman was able to get most on the pillowcase.

Serge sat back down. "Wow, you're really going at it!"

"Yep, I dig kindergarten." Scribble, scribble, chug, chug. "And I'm just about done . . . There!" Coleman beamed proudly as he held his case up to Serge.

"It's wonderful! It's . . . It's . . ." Serge didn't want to discourage his buddy. "Absolutely fantastic! . . . Uh, what is it?"

"Can't you tell by the shield on the chest?"

"All I can make out are the letters *B* and *M*," said Serge. "I hope that's not supposed to be bowel—"

"Of course not." Still smiling wide. "Don't you get it? I'm Bong Man!"

"I think it's safe to say that this particular superhero name isn't taken yet." Serge scratched his head. "But you don't have a superpower."

"Oh, I've got a superpower all right." Coleman grabbed the safety scissors. "It's a doozy!"

"What is it?"

"Just go back to your own pillowcase, and by the time you're done, I'll show you."

"If you say so." Serge resumed scribbling, skeptically watching Coleman out of the corner of his eye. *What's that idiot doing?*

Coleman had become a rare blur of industriousness. Construction paper, glue, tape and most of their other supplies came into play.

It was a race to the finish, and it was a tie.

Serge slapped down a crayon. "I'm done."

Coleman tossed an extra clothespin on the table. "Me too." Like poker players: "Show me what you got."

Serge held up a pillowcase with flamingos, rockets, sailfish, race cars, Cinderella's castle, Bok Tower and the lighthouse on Key Biscayne. In the middle, Serge had his own chest shield.

"What does the *CF* stand for?" asked Coleman.

"Captain Florida."

"What's your superpower?"

"I can name the state's sixty-seven counties in under a minute, sometimes." Serge pulled off his T-shirt and tried on the pillowcase. "Your turn. What are you hiding under the table?"

"Close your eyes and promise not to peek."

Serge did. He heard the unmistakable telltale sound of a Bic lighter coming to life. Then a familiar smell of smoke.

"Hey," said Coleman. "I didn't say you could open your eyes yet."

Serge's jaw came unhinged. "Your superpower is that you can make a bong out of ordinary kindergarten craft supplies?"

"Pretty super if you ask me." Puff, puff, puff.

Serge sat back and studied the contraption, held together solely with glue and tape, plus pipe cleaners and clothespins for extremities. Colorful construction paper was bent and rolled and folded like the work of an origami expert. "Coleman, your bong, is that a robot?"

"Robots rule! What do you think?"

"Danger, Will Robinson."

"And I used Play-Doh for the seals." Puff, puff, puff. "Your turn to put up."

Serge took a deep breath before spitting out words rapid-fire like an auctioneer. "Alachua, Baker, Bay, Bradford, Brevard, Broward . . ."

"Mmmmmm! Mmmmmm!"

Serge grabbed a tape dispenser and flung, ricocheting it off Clyde's soon-to-be-bloody nose. "We're trying to be five-year-olds, motherfucker!"

A pot cloud exhaled toward the captive. "Serge, could you hand me those two eye buttons? I want to glue them on my robot to make him wacky."

"Here you go."

"Thanks." Coleman squirted Elmer's Glue. "By the way, what are you planning to do with him?"

Serge reached into a shopping bag. "I've given this one a lot of careful thought." He pulled out a small blue box.

"Alka-Seltzer?" asked Coleman.

"No, a generic brand called Fizzing Circles because I wouldn't want to cast a pall on the good people at Alka-Seltzer."

"That's a weird name."

"Apparently, someone's tightening up trademark infringement laws, because generic names are getting pretty strange in order to keep their legal distance. You need look no further than the cereal aisle. I swear these are all real: Fruit Rings, Square Shaped Corn, Circus Balls, Crispy Hexagons, Pranks instead of Trix, and a knockoff of Life cereal called Live It Up. Children see right through those bowls of bullshit."

"So what's the plan with the tablets?"

"Stalled for now," said Serge. "The first hurdle was how do I get enough tablets in him without them activating before the Big Fizz? I finally found a solution, but the technique was so tediously long that I grew weary of the wit involved. So I went hard the other way . . ."

Serge grabbed a bottle of glue off the table and reached in his grocery sack again. Then he went over to the hostage with the safety scissors and began snipping off his clothes. "Sorry, I know this must be one of your favorite T-shirts because of the slogan on the front: 'I'm Not a Gynecologist, but I'll Take a Look.' Damn, that's funny."

Serge stopped snipping and began smearing glue across Clyde's bare chest. He opened a product from the supermarket and placed the pieces in a careful arrangement. "Now we just wait for the drying process."

Chapter 6

Tequesta, Florida.

The northeastern tip of Palm Beach County on the ocean. Named after the Native American tribe who lived, loved and built shell mounds here for two thousand years until ancestors of the current residents put a stop to that, clearing the way for golf.

It is a quiet, affluent bedroom community with many dockside homes and waterways, making it popular among sportsmen. Most prefer sailing out into the Atlantic under the bright sun for their recreation, but some are nocturnal. Night scuba diving is an exciting change of pace, with all the local reefs. So is night fishing.

On a Tuesday evening, just after eleven o'clock, a twenty-seven-foot Boston Whaler with twin Mercury engines cleared the jetties at Jupiter Inlet and began bouncing across the waves out to sea. The continental shelf off this coast is among the narrowest on the whole U.S. seaboard, sometimes barely a mile wide before precipitously dropping off hundreds of feet, where they call it deep-sea fishing.

The Whaler continued cresting small swells. Four heavy-duty spin-casting rods swayed in their holders like radio antennae. The boat's only occupant, a loner named Remy Skillet, also had two rifles and a shotgun. He was going *shark* fishing. He felt a slight pain in his mouth and thought of missed dental appointments.

A mile out, on the edge of the continental shelf, Remy cut the engine and drifted with the current. All lines went in the water, along with a dumped bucket of bloody chum that spread a grease apron off the stern. Seasoned anglers understand that the sport requires mental stamina, and Remy had the kind of patience of someone who brings guns with him to fish. He began blasting the water with an assault rifle before he realized he was shooting at his own chum slick, now glistening under the moon. He opened another beer. He was so far offshore that the lights of the oceanfront homes formed a single, horizontal thread of light, which was his only indication of where black sky left off and black water began. The ocean wind was more loud than stout, and carried a salty mist from the bow slapping the waves. The salt made Remy reach for another beer. That's when the shark hit the bait.

It was a seven-foot mako, gauging from dorsal to tail, and it began swimming back and forth under the boat, bending one of Remy's thickest rods to the breaking point. This required the shotgun. The water exploded off the port side, then the starboard, then port again. The next blast was decidedly louder than the others, and Remy took a step back and stilled his weapon. "That couldn't have been my gun. What was it?" Then he turned around and recoiled even more. "Holy shit!"

Remy's face glowed in the orange light as a fireball mushroomed into the sky a few hundred yards away. What remained after that was some kind of vessel, at least forty feet long, but it was difficult to determine much else because it had burned practically to the waterline. Remy started up his engine and headed in the direction of the explosion.

Minutes later, Remy idled his boat as it circled the smoldering wreckage. He felt his vessel bump something, and it wasn't the other boat. He looked over the side and couldn't see anything at first, because it was black. Not the water, but the scuba suit that the floating dead guy was wearing. Then he saw a second body in a wet suit, and a third, all bobbing in the waves. The toll ended at four, the last guy wearing jeans and a T-shirt with scorch marks.

Remy scratched his head. "What on God's green earth happened here?"

Then more confusion as one of the previously motionless bodies began to thrash. Remy fell into his captain's chair. "Jumpin' Jesus!"

In all the excitement and beer, Remy had completely forgotten about the shark on his fishing line that he'd dragged over to the scene and that was now devouring the bodies.

"Stop that! Stop that right now!" He racked his twelve-gauge. *Blam! . . . Blam! Blam! Blam! . . . Blam! Blam! . . .*

A steadier hand could have accomplished the objective with less ammunition, but Remy was still able to get the situation under control. The last shot sent the shark away from the bodies and diving under the boat . . .

In the days to follow, Remy would be arrested as the prime suspect, mainly because all the victims were presumed to have died from multiple shotgun blasts.

"No, really," Remy told them. "I was trying to preserve the evidence."

"How's that?"

"A shark was eating them."

"You do realize it's now impossible to determine how they died? And we wouldn't even have been able to identify two of them if it weren't for tattoos."

"Am I in trouble? . . ."

But right now, as the bodies were still bobbing around Remy's vessel, he had another question. "Where's that last Schlitz?"

A half mile away, night-vision binoculars watched a sinewy man crouching near the bait wells of a Boston Whaler, then standing up and appearing to drink from a can.

A whisper: "What's going on?"

"I think we just caught a big break."

"But what the hell was all that shooting?"

"That was the big break." The binoculars followed Remy as he headed toward the front of the boat, tripped over something and disappeared from view, then popped back up. "This clown just shot up the evidence."

"Why?"

"He was night-fishing. They use beer."

The three men continued hashing out their predicament in muted tones as they lay on their stomachs across the bow of a six-hundred-horsepower go-fast boat. The boat was as black as their jumpsuits, and all the running lights were off.

They waited silently. The reason was obvious. They were about to slip away from the crime scene, as they say, scot-free. All they had to do was remain dark and quiet until Remy departed without detecting their presence, and pray he didn't lose his navigational bearings and head toward them.

He headed toward them.

"Don't panic," said one of the jumpsuits. "He's still too far off to be on dead reckoning."

They waited.

"He's not veering."

"He'll veer."

Remy's bow light grew brighter.

"He's not veering."

"He'll— . . . Shit!"

The trio vaulted back behind the controls and gave it full

throttle. At the last second, the black void of a large powerboat with its lights off shot out from in front of Remy.

"Whoa!" Remy cut the steering wheel in a classic overcorrection, careening for a slalom to port. And because all fishing boats are required to have way more engine than they'll ever need, the centrifugal force flung Remy over the side into the water.

Fortunately, the boat had a "kill switch" in the event the captain went overboard, and the fishing vessel quieted to a stop and settled into the water just a short swim away.

Remy sighed with relief as he floated. "What a night..."

Oh, and when the authorities would eventually question Remy, it would be in a hospital room. Because as Remy dog-paddled back to his boat, the shark still on his fishing line came over and bit him.

Chapter 7

FORT LAUDERDALE

Chug, chug, chug. "What are we waiting for?" asked Coleman. "It looks like that stuff on your prisoner is dry now."

Serge glanced out the window. "The weather's still really crappy."

"Is it going to rain?"

"You'd think it would cut loose any second," said Serge. "But it's holding up. Just a full canopy of black clouds. To this day, whenever the weather is crappy like this, I get a joyous sense of childhood déjà vu. Instead of becoming glum, we'd use our imaginations and play endless games indoors."

"You don't mean—"

"To the shopping bags! . . ."

A few minutes later, Serge chased Coleman around the room, running over the tops of beds. "I got you! I got you!"

"You did not!"

"Yes, I did!" Serge blasted his friend in the face.

"Hold on," said Coleman. "I need to refill my squirt gun . . ."

"Mmmmmm! Mmmmmm! . . ."

Minutes later. "Coleman, look! I'm walking the dog! Now I'm doing the cat's cradle. You try."

"Okay." *Zing, clack*. "Ow! My forehead!"

"It's bleeding," said Serge. "Apply pressure."

"I just remembered I hate yo-yos."

"Mmmmmm! Mmmmmm! . . ."

Moments after that: "Coleman, here comes the paper airplane."

"I've never played with paper airplanes like this before."

"It's no fun unless they're on fire . . . Oooh, shit, get it away from the curtains."

"Mmmmmm! Mmmmm! . . ."

More stuff came out of shopping bags. More games ensued. Until finally Serge had his eyes closed tightly as he walked around the room with outstretched arms. "Marco!"

"Polo!"

"Marco!"

"Polo!"

Serge grabbed a face and squeezed a nose. "Is that you, Coleman?"

"No," Coleman yelled from the bathroom doorway. "It's Clyde."

"Sorry."

"Mmmmmm! Mmmmm!"

Serge opened his eyes. "Fun's over."

Coleman took a slow sip of whiskey as he surveyed their room: Hopscotch chalk on the carpet, jump rope wrapped around a broken lamp, a burned smell from a cap-gun battle, a horseshoe sticking out of a wall, pencils stuck in ceiling tiles, scattered marbles, baseball cards, jacks, a pogo stick, a robot bong and a hostage. "This was the best party ever!"

Serge checked the window again. "Looks like the weather's

not going to clear. We'll just have to take our chances and pray there's no cloudburst."

"Cool," said Coleman. "I finally get to see what you have planned for him."

Serge ripped the tape off Clyde's mouth and grinned. "Bet you just can't wait to find out what's in store."

"Y-y-you, you're completely insane!"

"Me?" said Serge, tapping himself in the middle of his pillow-case costume. He reapplied mouth tape. "Coleman, look alive. It's time to get ready and head out."

"Are we going in our pillowcases?"

Serge shook his head and grabbed another shopping bag off the floor. "I've got a better idea." He dumped the sack on a bed. "Let's put these on."

"Where'd you get that stuff?"

"The Party Store has everything!"

Soon they were dressed again.

"Won't this attract extra attention?" asked Coleman.

"Just the opposite," said Serge. "This is like the concept of orange vests, clipboards and safety cones. If you're wearing these, the general public simply assumes that you're authorized."

Coleman looked in the mirror as he adjusted his red Afro wig and rubber-ball nose. "Are you sure about this?"

"When have you ever seen anyone question someone dressed like this?" Serge jauntily snapped his polka-dot suspenders. "People see clowns and they automatically think you know what you're doing."

Serge freed Clyde from the chair and walked him to the door. He peeked outside to make sure the coast was clear, then hustled Clyde into their car's trunk again and slammed the lid.

They began driving south, pulling up to a red light. Some teenagers in the next car began laughing and pointing. "Look! Clowns!"

Serge flashed a clown badge. "We're authorized."

The light turned green and they sped off.

Coleman sucked on a robot. "Where are we going?"

"To the far end of the beach, just before the port. It's a longer walk from the hotels and usually empty, especially with this kind of overcast weather."

They parked on a secluded corner of a public-access lot. "Coleman, grab that duffel bag at your feet."

A couple came off a walkway over the sea oats from the beach. Serge nodded seriously and respectfully.

"Who are those guys?" the wife asked her husband.

"Couple of clowns."

They drove away, leaving Serge and company alone with unfinished business. He popped the trunk. "Time to rock and roll!"

Serge led Clyde across the sand in the grim weather, poking a pistol in his ribs.

Coleman struggled to keep up alongside, continuously re-hitching the duffel's strap over his shoulder. "Serge, I still think the guy looks too weird with all the stuff glued on him. We're bound to get caught."

"And that's where you're wrong." Serge poked the barrel harder for motivation. "We're out in the open with a clear view of any approaching cops. If we do see any, I'll just slice off his wrist bindings and remove the mouth tape. What's he going to say? 'Help! Help! I've been held hostage by two guys who played kindergarten games all day while wearing pillowcases!' He'll come off like designer-drug fiend. Then if the cops question us we say that we just met him in the parking lot, and he must have relapsed after getting off the bus from rehab."

"But what about our clown suits?" asked Coleman. "Won't that make the police suspicious?"

"Again, just the opposite," said Serge. "I'll tell them: 'Look at us. We're professionals. Do we seem like pillowcase guys to you?' Of course the answer's obvious."

"Mmmmmm! Mmmmmm!"

"Where are we taking him?" asked Coleman, trudging through the sand in big, floppy shoes.

"Over there, behind that clutch of palm trees for a little privacy." Serge's own large shoes slapped the beach.

Moments later: "That's far enough." Serge poked a gun in a stomach. "Now sit down and don't give me any trouble or . . . or . . . well, there's really nothing left to hold over your head. Just do it out of politeness."

Clyde sat in the sand, and Serge began going through the bag Coleman had carried. First the rope, tent stakes and hammer. *Wham! Wham! Wham! Wham!* The captive's ankles were secured to the ground. Serge pulled out a bottle of drinking water, the tape and a baggie of pills.

Coleman puffed a robot. "What are those?"

Serge held the baggie to his face. "This was a real bitch to prepare, so I hope it works. Remember the Fizzing Circles I showed you before? And I mentioned a tedious process that caused a mood swing and change of heart? I've since come around on that kind of constipated thinking. I've decided to go for a two-pronged project."

"Dear God," said Coleman.

"That's right," said Serge. "All the most critical pieces of scientific apparatus have redundancy circuits, so why not me?" He tossed the baggie in the sand next to the captive and held up a video camera. "Those babies in that bag might not do the entire trick, but the added visuals will put it over the top. When you commit to a project, you can't just phone it in."

Chug, chug, chug. "I still don't know what those are."

Serge knelt next to Clyde. "It took three whole boxes of Contac. Except not Contac, but the generic called Colored Capsules, because the folks at Contac are good people, too. And since they come in capsules, I twisted them all apart and dumped out the original contents. Then I wiped a bowl down and hit it with a hair dryer to ensure a moisture-free receptacle. I mashed up a whole bunch of the Fizzing Circles until there was just powder in the bowl. Next I carefully spooned it into the empty halves of the previously disassembled capsules and twisted them back together. It took *forever,* but one of the strongest motivational forces in the universe is irony."

Serge reached into Coleman's bag again and pulled out thick plastic goggles. "Clyde, you're going to need these. Safety comes first." He fitted them over the hostage's head with a thick rubber strap.

"Mmmmmm! Mmmmmm!"

"Man, hold your horses," said Serge. "The tape is just about to come off."

Rip.

"Ahhhhh!"

"Keep it down or . . . or . . . just keep it down." Serge uncapped the bottled water and wedged it in the sand. Then he opened the baggie and scooped out a handful. The other hand stuck the pistol in Clyde's cheek. "Are you going to play nice with others? A nod will do."

He nodded.

"Good. Now, as you heard me explain to Coleman, this isn't poison or any addictive prescription, because I just say no to drugs. The ingredients in these capsules are just for upset tummies, and yours must be doing backflips right about now. And in your self-crafted rationale that I observed on that other beach, it's totally moral for me to force you to take them. So open wide and don't chew; the water will be coming right up to wash it down."

The capsules were crammed in his mouth, then the water bottle. It was a struggle at first, but soon Clyde managed to get them swallowed.

"Good student," said Serge, reaching back in the bag. "Just a few more times and I won't bother you in this way again." He repeated the process as needed until the baggie was empty.

"Excellent!" Serge reached in the duffel for more tent stakes and rope. *Wham! Wham! Wham!* The hostage's arms were now stretched out over his head with wrists held fast to the ground.

Serge ripped off yet another strip of duct tape. As he pressed it in place: "You know, I did some Internet research on the subject of cruelty, and the stuff I read brought tears to my eyes. Someone actually crucified a pelican on a wooden light pole. I'll spare you the rest of the ghastly details, but the horrible deaths animals experience in the name of idle entertainment are nothing short of heartbreaking. Not to mention that the tormentors proudly post the videos. What's wrong with people like that?" Serge gestured skyward with the hand holding his own video camera. "I guess I just can't understand the concept of torture."

"Mmmmmm! Mmmmmm!"

Serge grabbed a pocketknife. The blade flipped open and stuck between the captive's lips. "Hold still," said Serge. "I'm going to cut a small slit to give you a little extra air, but I don't know why. I must be going soft or something." Slice. He inserted a drinking straw. "There! You still can't scream, but feel free to go 'toot, toot, toot' like a toy train . . . And now that I've thought about it, I require it. Go ahead."

The captive just stared up with horrified eyes.

"Come on!" said Serge. "Don't make me regret giving you that slit. 'Toot, toot, toot.'"

Clyde was tentative, and it came out more like a question. "Toot, toot, toot?"

The clowns doubled over with laughter. "I don't know why that's so funny," said Serge. "Maybe it's the goggles."

"Or maybe all the corn chips you glued on his chest and legs," said Coleman.

"You might have something there," said Serge. "I'll call him the Bandito."

Puff, puff, chug, chug. "What now?"

"We have to time this perfectly." Serge reached into the

shopping bag a final time. "The capsules in his stomach are just about dissolved."

"He's getting that look on his face like when I have gas," said Coleman.

"Here we go!" Serge reached into a bag of corn chips, and tossed a handful high into the air.

Coleman ducked. "Where'd they come from?"

"FBI surveillance team." Serge tossed another handful toward the sky. Seagulls swarmed and cawed and fought each other for crumbs.

Coleman held out his left arm. "Poop."

"We better back up." Serge looked skyward. "Today's forecast calls for a shitstorm."

"Damn!" Coleman felt the top of his head. "Another one got me. They're following us."

"Because they think we have all the chips." Serge stepped forward and dumped the rest of the bag liberally on the ground. And across Clyde.

"Look at 'em go!" said Coleman. "They're all over him. I think they're accidentally pecking him going for the chips, and he doesn't like it."

"What gives you that idea?"

"Just listen."

"Toot! Toot! Toot! Toot! Toot! . . ."

Serge doubled over again. "I don't know why that's so funny because it shouldn't be."

"I can barely see him anymore because of all the feathers," said Coleman.

Serge raised a video camera. "And for the record, I used non-toxic kindergarten glue. No animals were harmed during the production of this film."

"The tooting stopped," said Coleman.

"There's a good reason for that," said Serge. "Watch."

It began slowly at first, then a growing fountain of white fizz shot up from the tube in the mouth tape.

"You sure gave him a lot to think about," said Coleman.

"It's kind of pretty, like those dancing-water fountains."

"But, Serge, there's one thing I don't get." Coleman tightened the red ball on his nose. "How are birds eating chips off him supposed to teach any lessons?"

"Seagulls are widely misunderstood creatures." He zoomed in with the camera. "We think they're cute little guys nibbling popcorn and tacos. But that's just because they're creatures of opportunity. Did you know that gulls often grab clams, mussels, crabs and even small turtles, then fly to great heights and drop them in parking lots to crack them open for food? Amazingly, that's something they have to learn from scratch each generation because back thousands of years ago when genetic memory was forming their survival instincts, I don't think they had much pavement."

"That's trippy," said Coleman.

"But there's more. We really don't comprehend a seagull's primal nature because all we observe is their behavior around us: 'Let's see. I can bust my ass flying around with this tortoise or, fuck it, I'll just eat these onion rings.' But in the absence of human handouts, they're highly aggressive carnivores, often feasting on rodents, reptiles, amphibians, carrion. Even working in teams on severely injured larger prey that can't escape."

"By the way, what were the safety goggles for?"

"Gulls find the eyes tasty," said Serge. "I have a weak stomach. Another favor I did him, but do I get any thanks?"

"So which do you think will get him first?" asked Coleman. "The circles or the birds?"

"It's neck and neck," said Serge.

"The fizz is shooting higher."

"The circles have the edge."

"Hey, why is that one bird all pink?" asked Coleman.

"I think it nicked his femoral artery," said Serge. "The gulls have retaken the lead."

They stopped talking and watched the spectacle unfold a few more minutes.

Coleman stowed his flask and raised his smoking device. "I have to admit, this is one of your cooler projects."

"Society has become too fast-paced and jaded." Serge looked down at his clown suit, then the robot bong, then a corn-chip-covered hostage spewing fizz and blood through a blizzard of feathers. "But see all the fun you can have if you just leave your cell phone back in the room?"

Chapter 8

FOUR YEARS EARLIER

The office walls were concrete blocks painted with high-gloss institutional enamel. Framed photos, some decades old, hung sparsely. A couple of felt sports-team pennants. A bookshelf with trophies. The people in the photos wore football helmets.

The desk was standard fare for high school coaches. In other words, junk. Anything nicer, and they'd lose credibility. Behind it, almost overwhelming the desk, sat someone whom the whole town had known and talked about for years. This was the result of both the man's accomplishments and how small the town was.

Back in the day, Lamar Calhoun had been a star running back for the Pahokee Blue Devils, helping claim their first state championship in 1989. He had that rare combination at his age of college-level speed and size. Lamar could cut back in the open field at such mystifying angles that he made the fastest safeties and cornerbacks look foolish. But his specialty was leaping over the defensive line in short-yardage situations. And if one of the linebackers did meet Lamar at the peak of his jump, well, he was just along for the ride, falling backward with Calhoun into the end zone.

College scouts were all over him; cars practically lined up at the curb outside his house as a parade of famous coaches sat in the living room making offers, some quite generous, others NCAA violations. He left for an education in the Midwest. Everyone was certain they'd one day see him on television in an NFL uniform.

Then nothing. It was like he had just vanished. People talked for a while, and there were the typical rumors. But then more high school seasons came and went, more state titles, and even more stars, many of them reaching the pros.

Almost three decades later, when Lamar was all but forgotten, he was suddenly just *back*.

It was minutes before the final bell of the day when he simply strolled in the front entrance of Pahokee High School. Word swept the hallways. People peeked in the widows of the principal's office as faculty and the coaching staff surrounded the towering Lamar, showering praise and recounting glory on the nearby field.

"Appreciate you stopping by."

"Glad you haven't forgotten about us."

"So what brings you through town?"

They all just figured he was a big deal somewhere else and had taken a detour on a business trip to see the school where it all began.

"Actually, I'm not passing through," said Lamar. "I'd like a job."

It got quiet in a hurry. Then stammering from the principal. "Well, uh, sure, I, I mean yeah; it's just so out of the blue."

But it was Lamar after all. The principal said there was an assistant coach opening, running backs, no less, but . . . uh, they were a small-budget school. Would he mind also driving a school bus?

"That's great," said Lamar. "Thanks."

The former gridiron legend smiled and shook hands all around and walked out of the office.

Everyone stretched their necks to watch him leave, thinking: *Who comes back to Pahokee?*

L amar Calhoun sat in his coach's office going over report cards. Player eligibility. Tutoring.

There were some towel-snapping hijinks up the hall in the locker room. Calhoun shouted out the door to knock it off. It was quiet again. He looked back down at grades.

A timid knock at the door and an equally timid voice: "Coach C? Do you have a minute?"

"You again?" He was annoyed but also amused. He made himself smile.

A student walked in. "Have you thought any more about what we discussed?"

"I'm sorry, but it's just impossible," said Lamar.

"Why?" Chris took a seat on the other side of the desk. For the tenth time. Like a bad penny.

"Don't take this wrong, but you're a girl," said the coach. "Why don't you try soccer?"

"Because I want to play football," said Chris. "I've seen stuff in the news. A few girls have actually made boys' teams."

"And all of those were kickers," said the coach. "You want to be a running back."

Chris nodded. "I'm pretty fast."

"Why are you pestering me instead of the head coach?"

"Duh, because you're the running-back coach."

Lamar sighed. "What grade are you in anyway?"

"Junior high. Eighth."

"There you have it," said Lamar, relieved at the conversational escape route. "You've got another year before you should be bothering me again. End of conversation."

He resumed going through report cards.

Chris cleared her throat.

The coach looked up and raised his hands in frustration. "What do you want from me?"

"Make me a manager."

"What?"

"I'll carry water bottles, equipment, help with paperwork, anything. I just want to be around the team."

Lamar was actually smiling inside, but he'd learned that sometimes not being firm wasn't doing anyone favors. "Check back in a year. Now, if you'll excuse me, I have work to do . . ."

V iolent grunting and shouts. Shoulder pads crashed. A running back slammed into the defensive line and purely willed himself for a two-yard gain before the punishment of a gang tackle.

A coach blew a whistle.

Water break.

The teenagers pulled off helmets and gathered round the coolers. Panting, dizzy, sweating, jerseys caked with dirt. They guzzled from paper cups, spitting most out and swallowing the rest. High school football practice was tough enough in the rest of the country, but rarely like out here in what they called The Muck, under the Florida sun in a withering soup of humidity from Lake Okeechobee and surrounding Everglades crop fields.

Another assistant coach sidled up to Lamar Calhoun. "What's going on over there?"

"Where?"

The other coach pointed. With all the players on the sidelines now, the view was clear to the far side of the field. Two rows of truck tires were lined up for high-stepping agility drills. A tiny person was running through them. Or trying to. There was a trip and fall every few tires. The person got right back up for the next several tires and promptly went down again.

"Oh geez," said Calhoun.

"You know who that is?"

Lamar nodded. "Can you take over for me a few minutes?" He headed across the field.

A whistle blew behind him, and the boys lined up again to scrimmage.

Lamar reached the tires. "What are you doing?"

Chris pushed herself up from the vulcanized obstacle course and managed a couple more steps. *Plop.* "I'm practicing, Coach."

Calhoun's voice was more perplexed than angry. "Okay, first, I'm not your coach, and second, you can't be out here."

"Why not?" Huffing and turning around at the end of the tires, then heading back.

Lamar watched as she ran by and fell again. "Because only players are allowed on the field."

"I'm going to be a player."

"Please don't make me throw you out," said Lamar. "It's . . . insurance. Yeah, insurance."

Chris stopped. A resigned "*Allllll* right."

Calhoun watched with conflicted emotions as the young girl slunk off the field. He scratched his head and had no idea what to make of it . . .

•

Chapter 9

A 1969 Plymouth Satellite sat quietly and alone in the shade of an oak tree. It was lunchtime.

Coleman finished chewing a bite and swallowed. "What are we doing here?"

Serge stuck a fork in his mouth. "Eating pie."

"No, I mean *here*," said Coleman. "This place."

"It's our next stop." Serge chased the bite with more coffee. "The Antioch Cemetery, a few miles east of Micanopy and Cross Creek."

"I'm surprised you picked this one," said Coleman. "It's small and kind of dumpy. Just dirt with some brown grass and weeds."

"That part's a disappointment, but one Floridian buried here makes it more than worthwhile."

"So who is it?"

"Hold on," said Serge, digging in again with his fork. "I'm letting the moment build with pie. This is a celebration of astounding dimensions."

"If it's a celebration, I would have guessed you'd buy a cake."

"I'm done with cake!" said Serge. "Cakes are flashy and get way too much attention compared to pie. All that garish frosting. It's just gratuitous."

Munch, munch. "Why do you say that?"

"Because cakes are the pole dancers of the bakery world, but a pie is the girl you take home to Mom. If cakes had names, they'd be Jazmine, Sunshine, Cinnamon, Duplicity; pie would answer to 'Sarah' and 'Beth.'"

"Never thought of it that way."

"There are defining times in your life when you just have to speak up."

"I can dig it." Coleman took another bite. "And I have to say it's pretty damn good pie. But I've never tasted anything like it."

"It's sour orange pie." A fork scooped.

"Never heard of it." Munch.

"Almost nobody has." Serge chewed and slurped from his coffee mug. "But it's one of our state's most fantastic native dishes ever, made from centuries-old family recipes that are now virtually forgotten. Key lime pie gets all the headlines today. And Key lime's great, don't get me wrong. But sour orange is nirvana. And because it's so unknown, you have to work like the devil to get it. The main ingredient was brought here by the Spanish in the sixteenth century, and now grows wild across the peninsula, characterized by its extra-bumpy and thick skin, like a giant citrus golf ball. Just finding the fruit is a bitch, involving hiking boots and trespassing, or long drives to specialty grocery stores like Cuban bodegas in Miami, where they're sold to make mojo sauce—I like saying 'mojo.' Then boil to a syrup, add eggs and sugar, graham-cracker or saltine-crumb crust, whip more syrup into the meringue, and the crowd goes wild. I found several recipes online, including one in an article for *Gardens and Guns*."

"Is that a real magazine?" asked Coleman.

"I thought it was a joke, too, but it's quite real," said Serge. "I can just see the early organization board meeting to come up with a name: 'We need a concept that appeals to the broadest possible audience covering the entire spectrum, something no other magazine has ever dared! Let's shoot it around the table . . .' Second place was probably *Kittens and Whiskey*."

"I'd buy a subscription to that."

"This pie delivers more than a taste-bud party." Serge yanked the napkin from the neck of his shirt. "Symbolically harkening back to the glorious time and place of the legend laid to rest here. It was out in these sweltering pioneer badlands of Central Florida near Lochloosa Lake, where she had the fruit trees growing off her veranda, and it's a safe bet she baked sour orange pie. Today, a couple of local rustic restaurants in her area are among the few places left where you can still order the real deal."

"So that's why we made that long detour on the way here."

Serge opened the door. "We have rubbing a-callin'."

They strolled across the field until they came upon a slab with no tombstone, just statues of a family of deer, mom, dad, and baby.

"Marjorie Kinnan Rawlings." Serge got down on his knees with an oversize sheet of paper. "Most known for her classic novel *The Yearling*, hence the animals on her grave."

"They look cute."

Rub, rub, rub. "This tour stop is special, and not just for Rawlings. It marks a turning point in our odyssey, where we've picked up the beginning of a long strand of Florida connective tissue that will bring our trip to a fever pitch of heritage, lore and motel antics."

"So where to now?"

"It's amazing how you can jump across the shoulders of Florida giants." Serge stood with his finished page. "By no coincidence, our next stop involves one of Rawlings's writing students . . ."

FOUR YEARS EARLIER

They call it the Treasure Coast.

Why not?

Florida already had the Gold Coast and the Space Coast, and above that, the First Coast with St. Augustine and all its oldest-everything-in-the-United-States signs.

That left three counties in the middle—Indian River, St. Lucie and Martin—orphaned with no coast of their own. It was hurting business.

Then, in 1961, a group of treasure salvagers made international headlines by discovering wrecks from a silver-and-gold-laden Spanish fleet that disappeared in a hurricane in 1715. A total of eleven ships were lost after departing Havana and ultimately sinking off the Sebastian Inlet near Vero Beach. The local *Press-Journal* newspaper swung into action and coined the term *Treasure Coast.*

Today, there is an annual pirate festival commemorating the 1715 wreck, and souvenir maps are sold everywhere with the locations of the ill-fated ships. Divers still search the well-known and charted sites, occasionally finding an artifact. And after hurricanes, children digging holes in the beach—as they are known to do—are said to unearth a doubloon or two. There are even guidebooks telling metal-detector enthusiasts where to look when visiting the Treasure Coast. And even as late as 2015, a salvage team would rework one of the wrecks thought to be depleted, and recovered another $4 million in gold.

Of the eleven lost ships, three have never been found.

One of the people still looking for them was a crusty salvage operator named Cale Munson, but everybody knew him as

"Captain Crack Nasty." You don't want to know where the nickname came from. Cale tried to shake the moniker for years, then embraced it. He figured it was always good for a seafaring man to have a gritty air of reputation, even if it resulted from personal grooming.

On his business card, Crack wasn't a true treasure salvager, but the regular kind. He operated one of those boat-towing services for when engines blew at sea or a vessel began taking on water. His fees were steep, like all the others in his field, because it was a sellers' market. But the real money came when a boat went down, thanks to state and federal law. The government sought to provide high incentive to rescue unfortunates on the water, as well as mitigate ecological damage from a grounded ship. The statutes so heavily favored salvagers that it meant this: If a boat went down and was raised, the salvager now owned it and could sell it back to its original purchaser.

Captain Crack mulled these codicils as he became increasingly bitter about towing the ultra-wealthy back to shore. He wanted to be wealthy, too, like the owners of the mini-yachts he aided, and especially like the now-famous treasure hunters who pulled up millions in precious metals and gems. He already had scuba equipment from his current gig, which could easily reach a sunken galleon. All he needed was a break. Only one problem: He was lazy. The successful treasure finders did extensive homework, even flying to Spain and spending hours in special libraries poring over parchment ship manifests from the eighteenth century. Crack just put on his scuba suit and dove to scour a site that someone else had already put in the elbow grease to find, like being the second person to discover the *Titanic*. After years of diving, he had exactly one cannonball to show for his efforts.

On a sunny afternoon, Crack was motoring out to a fancy disabled boat that was sitting lower than usual in the waves. The emergency call over the radio said it wasn't a fast leak, but would eventually turn fatal without intervention. From a distance,

Crack could tell it was one of those boats where people didn't fish but sipped champagne. He began thinking about salvage laws again. He pulled back on his throttle. Another call over the radio. *What's the holdup?* Crack answered that everything was under control. He leisurely arrived at the boat to find a bunch of polo and tennis people standing in shin-deep water.

"No problem," said Captain Crack, climbing aboard with an assistant. "Have you out of here in no time." He explained the procedure with the water-pumping machine back on his vessel and the hoses he was sticking down in their bilge. Plus the temporary patch to help the pump outpace the leak.

A half hour later. "We have a problem." He said the patch wasn't holding and the leak was faster than his pump. He didn't tell them that he was running his pump at one-third steam. "Everyone grab your valuables and get on my boat! We don't have much time!"

The theatrics worked. They were actually grateful as they watched their pleasure craft disappear beneath the water. And after bringing the thankful party back to shore, the good captain went back out, strung inflatable bladders under the sunken hull and raised the boat. This time he used a real patch and quickly pumped her dry. Not a bad day's work for $200,000.

From there it was the rhythm of routine. Distress calls came in, and Crack waved off all the other salvagers, saying he was closest. Closest but not fastest. He built in delays and excuses and deliberately incompetent water pumping, until once again: "Everyone on my boat! Hurry!"

And so it went, scuttling vessel after vessel. Captain Crack suddenly had a lot of money. But to him, it wasn't real money. That required treasure. He sat in his dockside office one afternoon, windows open to the cross-breeze, staring at the cannonball on his desk. He got an idea. He wouldn't dive for Spanish wrecks that had already been salvaged. He would go after sites that were *still being worked*. Which was highly illegal because of the claims filed by the rightful discoverers. Which meant cover of night. Crack went down to a government auction and bought on the cheap a sleek black ultra-fast cigarette boat that had been seized from a cocaine cartel. He promptly put her back into criminal service.

The Treasure Coast officially stops at the Palm Beach County line, where the Gold Coast begins with Tequesta and the surrounding communities. But hurricanes don't take their orders from the chamber of commerce.

A highly professional salvage crew began faithfully showing up at the same spot offshore for two weeks. The descriptions in their claim were deliberately downplayed: just exploring for scant artifacts. But rumors began sweeping the treasure-hunting crowd. Could they have found one of the three missing ships from the 1715 fleet?

Captain Crack anchored a safe distance away and staked them out with a telescope. Divers were making too many trips up to the boat for simple historical excavation. Handing too many baskets of whatever up to a deckhand.

After three days of surveillance, Crack headed out at night with two trusted assistants he had handpicked because of their prison records. They anchored over the site and dove.

Jackpot.

The only pressure was time, and it wasn't how long it took to find the loot, but how fast they could fill their baskets. Gold, silver, rubies, sapphires. It all went up to the cigarette boat.

After the sixth dive, the baskets came aboard. Suddenly: "Uh-oh."

A bright search beam shone in the distance. It came at them fast from the deck of a speeding vessel. Then a megaphone. "What the fuck are you doing on our site?"

Soon they were side by side in the water. Because of the lawlessness of the seas, everyone out there has guns, and now they were all drawn in a standoff.

Captain Crack tried to chill it out with lies. "We had no idea the site was claimed."

"Bullshit! Give us everything you have on your boat!"

"We didn't find anything yet," said Crack.

"Then we're coming aboard!"

"Then we'll kill you," said Crack. "And we'll get away with it under federal piracy laws for illegal boarding at sea."

The professional crew fumed. They were hardened, but not tough enough to get in a gun battle over a fraction of their find. Their leader finally waved his rifle toward shore. "Get out of here and never come back! Or next time we *will* shoot!"

Chapter 10

CENTRAL FLORIDA

The back road ran through God's country.

Town after small town. Little Florida places with names like Weirsdale, Citra, Lochloosa, Waldo, Starke and several more that were so tiny they didn't appear on maps. Volunteer fire departments, hardware stores, barbershops, old movie theaters on Main Street playing only one film, always rated G. Signs at the city limits indicated the Kiwanis and Rotary Club were still at it. Other signs were handmade by Girl Scouts for a spaghetti dinner that Friday. There were antiques stores and ice cream stands, billboards for salvation and speed traps, water towers of all shapes, some celebrating high school championships.

And the churches.

Bright white wooden churches, red-brick churches, and churches in converted farm buildings. Some houses of worship sat crowded together in competition; others alone in cattle pastures.

There were short steeples, tall steeples, and open-sided steeples with big bells. Lutheran, Presbyterian, Pentecostal, and AME Zion. Baptist, Anabaptist, and Primitive Baptist. Some had lighted signs with attempts at humor: ETERNITY: SMOKING OR NONSMOKING? CHOOSE THE BREAD OF LIFE OR YOU ARE TOAST. Some unintentionally so: ACCEPTING APPLICATIONS FOR MISSIONARY POSITION.

The back road was actually several roads, stitched together on an old gas station map the night before by Serge. It would be a long drive to the next tour stop, and he shuddered at the thought of spending all that time on an interstate.

The '69 Plymouth entered Ocklawaha. Soon, a two-story country home with a sweeping front porch came into view. Serge's camera was out the window again. *Click, click, click.*

"It's just an old house," said Coleman.

"And one so historically important that when the land was sold from under it, they barged the whole thing across Lake Weir to this location."

"So what's its deal?"

"Back during the Depression, the infamous Ma Barker Gang terrorized the nation with a spree of bank robberies and kidnappings. In 1935, the FBI finally traced the outfit to Florida and this house, where Ma Barker—also known as Machine Gun Kate—was hiding out under an assumed name with several associates. A gun battle ensued, and the house was sprayed with more than four thousand bullets. Apparently the holes have been patched."

"That's a stone trip," said Coleman.

"It was a different era," said Serge. "They actually laid out the bullet-riddled bodies and sold the photos as postcards to mail back to loved ones: 'Having a great time in Florida, unlike these assholes.'"

Serge stowed the camera and sped north. They passed citrus stands and boiled-peanut stands and someone in overalls walking along the side of the road with a sewing machine in a wheelbarrow. They continued on over hill and dale. One of the countless churches was coming up. Threshing machines worked the field next door. It was a Sunday morning, and the last service had long since let out.

As Serge passed by, he noticed three people on the front steps. A pastor was comforting a distraught couple. The woman cried inconsolably.

"Uh-oh," said Serge. "That's my bat signal."

He made a fishtailing U-turn in the middle of the lonely road and sped back. He ran up to the steps in no time. "Pardon me, but I couldn't help but notice you're upset."

The pastor had an arm around the woman's shoulders. He looked up. "It'll be fine."

"No, it won't!" sobbed the woman.

"Why don't you tell me about it?" said Serge.

"Excuse me," said the preacher. "Who are you?"

"Who are *you*?" said Serge.

"Pastor Donovan, but I—"

"The name's Serge." He shook the preacher's hand. "I roam the countryside, enjoying fresh air, monitoring my hygiene, and helping the downtrodden. Favorite food: pizza. Turnoffs: the word *conflate* and women who think a small dog in a purse is a fashion accessory."

A voice arriving from behind. "I'm Coleman . . ." Trip, splat.

Serge looked down and shook his head, then raised his face again. "Now, how may I be of assistance?"

"I don't think you can," said Donovan.

"Then what have you got to lose?" He turned toward the couple. "And you are . . . ?"

"Buford and Agnes Whorley, of the Nantucket Whorleys," said the man. "We retired here ten years ago."

Agnes broke down again. "And now we have no place to go!"

Serge straightened up with an odd look. "Why not go to where you've been the last ten years?"

Her face was buried in her hands. "We can't! It was stolen from us!"

"This is sounding complicated." Serge turned to address Buford. "Can you back up and explain from the beginning?"

"The house was all bought and paid for, our life savings," said Buford. "But then we began running short on the monthly bills. Who knew we'd live this long, or stuff would get so expensive?"

"What did you do?" asked Serge.

"We thought it was a sign from God," said Agnes. "We began seeing all those ads on TV for reverse mortgages, and it sounded like the answer to our prayers . . ."

Buford nodded. "But then we mentioned it to Tyler from our congregation, and he told us that those reverse things were the biggest racket going. They'd gouge us on the interest rate, then compound it, not to mention hidden up-front costs."

"Let me guess," said Serge. "He offered to help you with a better deal?"

"Told us that a conventional equity loan from an upstanding local bank would accomplish the same goals but on much better terms. He even went and got the loan documents from the bank—"

Serge held up a hand. "I've seen this movie before. Then he asked you to sign some title documents that the bank needed for collateral. And the next thing you knew, the bank called to report a loan problem with the title, and the sheriff was at your door saying your home had been sold and you needed to leave."

"The deputies were so nice," said Agnes. "They told us they had investigated and knew exactly what was going on. But their hands were tied because, while it was totally immoral, it was also totally legal."

Buford nodded again. "And the people who bought the house were another retired couple who used *their* entire life savings. What can you do?"

Serge took a seat on the steps next to them. "This one really breaks my heart. The reverse mortgages on TV are generally legit—it's the lone wolves you have to watch out for. Scams in this department have gone so sky-high in Florida that it's an epidemic waiting to make the press. Worst of all, the predators come to town and weasel their way into positions of trust. The newest trend is joining churches to prey on your virtue and trust in a fellow worshiper. Let me guess: Was this Tyler character in the choir?"

"How'd you know?" asked the pastor.

"And he just joined your congregation?"

"Two months ago," said Donovan. "Seemed like the greatest guy. Explained he had just relocated for employment, and that his wife and children would join him as soon as the school year ended up north. He even showed me their photos."

"Probably came with the wallet," said Serge. "I've heard enough. I assume Tyler has made himself scarce."

"Nobody's seen him since the sheriff knocked," said Buford.

Serge shook his head again. "Anything at all I can go on to track him down?"

"Not really," said Agnes.

But Serge noticed the pastor making a furtive head tilt out of their view. "Serge, I'm sorry there's nothing you can do, but it was kind of you to stop by. Why don't I walk you back to your car?"

"How gracious." Serge looked down. Kick. "Coleman, time to get up."

They all met back at the Plymouth.

"Look, I don't know who you are," said the pastor. "Undercover law enforcement? Private investigator from Tyler's last victim? Bank auditor? But something tells me it's information you can't divulge for professional reasons."

"That would be accurate," said Serge.

"I may be a pastor, but I'm not naive about the world."

"Really?" Serge looked toward the edge of the street. "You had me fooled by your sign."

"What?" Donovan turned. "Whoa. 'Missionary Position.' Slipped right by me."

"Not everyone's an editor."

"What I'm getting at is that I did research on the Internet, and I found out about the angle you were describing," said the preacher. "How these predators are increasingly using churches as their hunting grounds. I rarely curse, but this was more than I could take."

"Understandable."

"I also read how they move on before the locals can figure out their dishonesty, but the land is too fertile in Florida, so they can only go so far."

Serge rested an elbow on the roof of the car. "What are you trying to say?"

"The pastors around these parts keep up with each other. Personally, we're not the Internet types, but our chat rooms have their purpose," said Donovan. "Usually it's positive, like how to pump up congregation attendance. But this time I put out a warning on this Tyler guy so it wouldn't happen to anyone else in the area. I also posted a photo that my secretary was able to grab from the last video of our choir performance."

"I think I see where this is going," said Serge. "Where is he?"

"Goes by 'Nicholas' now." Donovan pointed north up the empty road splitting wild meadows. "Pastor four towns up gave me the word. Joined his church two weeks ago. He's keeping an eye on him so he doesn't pull anything before we can explore our options."

"When is the next service with the choir?" asked Serge.

"Started at noon." The preacher checked his wristwatch. "That gives you forty minutes max to catch him before he leaves."

"How long a drive?"

"Hour."

FOUR YEARS EARLIER

A tiny cork ball rattled around the inside of a small metal enclosure. It had an extension that fit in a coach's mouth. A shrill whistle blew for the hundredth time that afternoon. But this time it was followed by the head coach storming onto the field.

"Dougan! Get over here!"

The player trotted up. "What?"

The coach grabbed a fistful of the wide receiver's jersey between the numbers. "You quit on that play! You were practically walking like my grandmother at the end of your route!"

"But it was a screen to the other side—"

"And now you're arguing with me?"

"No, sir."

"You never, ever quit on a play! You always run through the whistle!" The coach released his grip on the uniform. "Stadium steps! Now!"

The other players winced as Dougan removed his helmet and jogged toward the stacked rows of aluminum benches.

"Helmet on!" the coach yelled after him.

Another collective cringe.

Stadium steps were the worst. The punishment took place where the parents sat for all those Friday-night games under the lights. The punished player ran up the steps all the way to the top row of the viewing stands, then down, then up again, over and over as lactic acid built up in the legs and muscles cramped. But that was no excuse. You kept going without end in sight until the coach mercifully called you back to the field. Then, hopefully, lesson learned.

The exiled receiver's cleats began clanging off the steps. The rest of the players got the message. There would be no more letups before the whistle this day. Play resumed back on the field with noticeably renewed purpose. The blocking harder, pass routes fully run, tackles like car accidents.

It was now taking two or three whistles to stop each play.

Lamar Calhoun was on the sideline, bent forward with hands on his knees, studying the technique of his starting halfback taking a delayed handoff and waiting for the block to open daylight next to the noseguard.

Another assistant coach stepped up next to him, the same one as the day before. Receivers coach named Odom. "Lamar, isn't that you-know-who?"

"What do you mean?"

"Up there." Odom shielded his eyes against the sun. "Just below the press box."

Lamar squinted. "You've got to be kidding me."

Over in the viewing stands, there was now a second set of feet clanging up and down the aluminum steps.

"What's the deal with that kid?" said Odom. "Who the hell runs stadium steps because they *want* to?"

"Good grief," said Calhoun. "Can you take over for me again? . . ."

Lamar arrived at the bottom step just as Chris touched it— "Hey, Coach"—and pivoted to head back up."

"Stop," said Lamar. "What do you think you're doing?"

Heavy breathing. "Getting in condition, Coach."

"Didn't I tell you yesterday that only players were allowed on the field?"

"I'm not on the field, Coach. I'm in the stands."

"And stop calling me Coach."

"Sorry, Coach."

"Sit down." Lamar joined her on the bottom bench. "Maybe I wasn't perfectly clear yesterday, but when I said you couldn't be on the field, I meant the entire grounds, including the stands."

"You didn't say that."

"Now I am."

A pout. But not one of self-pity. Just a moment of frustration until Chris figured out her next move.

"And please don't pout," said Lamar. "Not that."

"Then make me a manager."

"I'll make you a *deal*," said the coach. "Just relax and stop all . . . this . . ."

"This what?"

"All of it. You're driving me nuts," said Lamar. "And when you're a freshman, I think you'd be a great manager."

Chris shook her head. "I'll lose a whole year."

"Of what?"

"Getting better. I want to learn."

She got up and began jogging away. "See you tomorrow, Coach."

"Stop calling me—"

"Sorry . . ."

H ut! Hut! *Hut!*"

The football was snapped. Players violently collided. The quarterback got leveled just after releasing a perfect fade route to the back corner of the end zone. Couldn't blame that one on the defender.

A whistle. The head coach clapped hard a single time. "Now that's what I'm talking about!"

Behind him, two assistant coaches stood next to each other, looking in a different direction.

Odom canted his head and said out the side of his mouth, "Technically she's not on the grounds."

"What do I have to do?"

They continued watching Chris run laps around the outside of the fence.

Odom shook his head, "I don't think she's going to quit."

"You don't have to smile about it."

Practice ended. Everyone headed for the locker room. Almost everyone.

Lamar strolled toward the student parking lot. Chris came dashing around the corner of the fence, head down.

"Sorry, Coach, didn't mean to run into you."

"You win," said Lamar.

"Win what?"

"You can be a manager."

Big grin. "Really?" Jumping up and down now.

"And no jumping when you're manager," said Lamar. "You need to take this seriously. You need to be a help, not a distraction. Meet me in my office before practice tomorrow. And bring your last report card."

"You got it, Coach." She began jumping again.

Lamar turned toward the locker room. "I'm already regretting this."

Chapter 11

CENTRAL FLORIDA

T he Plymouth Satellite blazed north through that rural swath
of the state where you were never more than five minutes
away from the ability to purchase marmalade.

Coleman looked down and found a Cheeto stuck to his shirt.
"Ooooh, my lucky day." He popped it in his mouth. *Crunch,*
crunch. "Serge, don't take this wrong, but a cemetery tour is kind
of dull. Nothing's moving."

"Visiting these final resting places is in large part a pretext."
The speedometer needle climbed as the muscle car raced down
the orange center line of the two-lane road like a 1970s B-movie
starring Steve McQueen. "The graves of people who lived life to
the fullest are highly inspirational. They're the perfect place to
reflect and remind yourself to never stop chasing your dreams."

"I had a cool dream last night," said Coleman.

"It's not that kind of dream."

"Wait, I want to tell you," said Coleman. "I was sleeping."

"That's usually when you dream."

"No, I mean I was sleeping *in* the dream," said Coleman. "Nothing happened."

Serge turned and stared curiously. Coleman was nodding to himself. "Much better than my nightmares. A few days ago I dreamed that I had a job and had to work all night in the dream and then I woke up tired. I hate that. What about you?"

"Okay, here's the thing I love about dreams." Serge took his hands off the wheel and rubbed them together. "You get to meet famous people throughout history. I've gotten to know Genghis Khan, General Custer, Joan of Arc, Tolstoy—who by the way was really long-winded—Galileo, Gandhi, Gershwin, the Marx Brothers, Richard the Lionhearted. But the high expectations can also lead to major disappointment. For some reason I have this recurring dream that I'm on a passenger train with Jesus, and it begins with him showing me magic tricks, like pulling quarters out of my ear, and I'm like, 'We get it. You're Jesus. Give it a rest.' And every time, before it's over, we somehow end up in a fistfight. But here's the weird part: He's the one who always starts the shit, poking me in the chest with a finger, over and over: 'What are you going to do about it? Huh? Big man? What have you got to say now?' And I tell him, 'Christ, this isn't like you.' And then he sucker-punches me! Who would ever see *that* coming?"

The Satellite sped on down the winding road. Vultures were picking apart an armadillo and took flight. Coleman cracked a can of Pabst. "You're driving pretty fast, even for you."

"Nobody could ever write a better job description for me: Florida, no appointments and a tank of gas," said Serge. "Haven't I mentioned this to you before?"

"Only about a gazillion times."

"Unfortunately, today we have an appointment." He checked his wrist. "And it's going to be close."

Serge gave it more gas, and the red needle in the dashboard climbed higher. Twenty minutes later, they skidded onto the shoulder of the road, next to a barbed-wire fence and bales of hay. Across the street, bells rang in a steeple as congregants poured out the front doors.

"How do you know what he looks like?" asked Coleman.

"I don't." Serge climbed out. "I can narrow it down with choir robes, but then it's just my gut."

They walked against the stream toward the front of the church. Most of the choir people were still up at the altar, stretching out their fellowship time.

"I think I see him," said Serge. "That young guy on the end of the second row."

"How do you know?"

"Most of the others are a bit older. And he just has that entitled shit-grin. It's got to be him."

"What's the plan?"

"Pull the car around back, then wait outside by the entrance."

Ten minutes later, the first of the choir began dribbling out and strolling down the walkway, checking with each other about their next practice time. Serge stood in the grass next to the path. Then, like someone who steps off a curb in front of a bus, he just ambled into the flow.

Crash.

A taller man grabbed Serge by the shoulders for balance. "Are you okay? Sorry, I didn't see you."

Serge had his head down. "No, it was all my fault. I apologize. I just have a lot on my mind." He raised his face and wiped Oscar-winning tears from his eyes.

"Hey, hey, hey, what's the matter?" said the man, holding a folded choir robe.

"It's nothing I need to bother you about." Then Serge covered his face and resumed sobbing. He parted two of his fingers to peek.

"Take as much time as you need." The man placed a hand on Serge's shoulder. "If your life's troubled, you're at the right place. We're all family here. I insist you allow me to help, brother."

Serge finally dropped his hands and sniffled. "It's my mother."

Alarm: "Her health? Is she okay?"

Serge nodded. "It's about money. She might lose her house."

"What? She can't afford the mortgage?"

"No, the house is completely paid for," said Serge. "It's just that between the insurance and all the rising monthly bills, her Social Security doesn't make it anymore. If she can't pay next month's property taxes, the county will seize her house, and she's been there fifty years." He kicked the ground in anger. "I feel so guilty!"

"Why? What did you do?"

"I'm not a good son." Serge wiped his nose on the back of his hand. "I'd pay the taxes myself, but I got laid off, and my own family is behind on everything."

"Then you're in luck."

"Why are you smiling?" asked Serge.

"Because this is my field of expertise. I handle real estate matters all the time." He held out a hand to shake. "My name's Nicholas. Call me Nick."

"Serge."

"Well, Serge, your problems are already behind you," said Nick, extending an arm all the way around his new buddy's shoulders. "I can easily structure something to get more than enough equity out of her house to take care of those taxes. Heck, she'll have so much left over that this time next month, she'll probably be waving bon voyage from a cruise ship."

"But how is that possible?"

"Not only is it possible, it's easy." Nick interlaced his fingers. "But it involves knowledge of how banking and real estate knit together. I'm always amazed at how much needless grief people are going through these days."

"It must have been God who made me bump into you."

"He works in mysterious ways," said Nick.

"You have no idea." Serge's head swiveled as he watched the last of the other people at the church drive away. "How do we do this?"

A hearty laugh. "See? You're already bouncing back . . . The first thing I need to do is take a look at your mother's house to gauge how it will appraise, then check some of her documents to make sure the title isn't clouded. Tell her to get ready to limbo in Cancún." Another laugh.

"I don't know how I can ever repay you," said Serge.

"No need to repay," said Nick. "At this church, it's what we do for each other in His name."

"Okay, when can we start?"

"How about right now? Let's go."

"Fantastic," said Serge.

Nick pointed at the only car in the otherwise empty parking lot. A late-model BMW sports coupe. The vanity plate read: WINNING. "That's mine." He reached in his pocket for a blue-and-white key fob.

"Mine's around back," said Serge.

"I'll follow you out to her place."

"Actually, I'd like to show you something first."

"What is it?"

"When I was going through Mom's papers on the house, I found these other files with financial accounts and securities certificates that I didn't know she had. And I also don't know what they mean. They're in my car. I was hoping maybe you could make heads or tails out of them."

Nick thinking: *Can this get any better?* He stuck the Beemer's keys back in his pocket. "I'd be more than happy to look at those files."

They walked around the rear of the church to the glowing gold Plymouth. Serge stuck a key in the back and popped the lid. Nicholas leaned toward the trunk. "Hmm, I don't see any files."

"Because there aren't any," said Serge.

"Huh? What's going on?"

"I didn't want to embarrass you in front of the others, so I waited until we could have a private little chat back here." Serge held out his hand. "A hundred and fifty thousand dollars, please."

Sincere confusion. "What are you talking about?"

"That's how much you stole from the couple up the road. I'm sure you remember the Whorleys. The Nantucket Whorleys?"

"Oh, now I get it." A smirk. "Yeah, I heard about that. Terrible tragedy. I honestly tried to help them, but they made some bad financial moves. Retirees really have to watch out these days."

Serge's hand remained extended. "I'm still waiting."

"For what?"

"The only mistake they made was trusting you," said Serge.

"Now wait a second," said Nick. "I've tried to be nice, and now you're accusing me? This is all on them. Sorry, but those are the breaks."

"I've seen a lot in my years and didn't think the bar of human behavior could drop any lower, but joining church choirs to exploit people's faith?" said Serge. "There's a little chestnut out there about a special place in hell."

"I've grown weary of you," said Nick. "Okay, say I did it. So what? In fact, now that you've pissed me off, I'm *glad* I did it."

"Then I guess there's nothing more to say."

"Yes, there is," said Nick. "Go fuck yourself!"

"In that case . . ." Serge lunged. "In you go!"

"Ahhhhhh!"

The trunk slammed shut.

FOUR YEARS EARLIER

A bottle of Johnnie Walker sat on a desk next to a cannonball. Captain Crack sat behind the desk drinking Scotch and fingering gold doubloons. He had gotten the taste, and it put the fangs in him. The nerve of those guys! How dare they point guns at *him*?

After much tortured moral gymnastics, Crack decided that it was the guys who'd found the ship who were in the wrong. He made the decision. He looked up at his two associates, sitting in wicker chairs against a wall under an antique harpoon and a stuffed wahoo.

"Suit up," said the captain. "We're going back out tonight."

"But what if they're there?"

Crack stood and grabbed the bottle by the neck. "I'm actually hoping they are . . ."

The night was moonless, and the wind howled.

A black cigarette boat with all the running lights off skipped across the waves at top speed. There was an element of stealth, but the prime strategy was a blitz attack. Come in dark and fast before they knew it.

From distance surveillance, Crack knew all the divers were in the water, leaving a single hand on deck. And from experience, Crack knew that the person would be monitoring the divers and sonar screens. The black boat circled for a downwind approach to cloak the sound of their engines until the last moment, which was now. The deckhand heard the distinct noise a hundred yards out and lunged for a shotgun.

Seconds later, another standoff.

"It's three to one," said Crack. "Give us your shit."

"Go to hell!"

"Then we're coming aboard!"

"I'll shoot!"

"No, you won't."

Bang!

Crack's eyes widened. He quickly looked down at his chest. No blood. He looked up at the salvage boat. Nobody standing.

Crack peered down into the deck at the still body of the deck-hand. Then he shot glances side to side at his henchmen. "Who fired?"

"It was an accident. My finger slipped."

"Fuck it," said Crack. "I'll deal with you later. Let's get aboard and off-load their haul before the divers surface."

The gang efficiently began passing expensive baskets over the gunwales.

Naturally, the divers surfaced. "What the hell's going on? Get off our boat!"

"You're not in a bargaining position," said Crack. "I suggest you just swim away."

"Fuck you!" The first diver started climbing up the swim ladder.

"Screw this!" A henchman dropped his basket and grabbed a rifle. "I'm not going back to prison!"

"What's that mean?" said Crack.

"One dead in a robbery gets you the same as four. No witnesses!"

Bang!

So the others got into the act.

Bang! Bang! Bang! Bang! . . .

When the proverbial smoke cleared, three lifeless wet suits floated and bumped against the hulls of both boats.

"What do we do now?" asked the second henchman.

"What the hell do you think? Finish loading!" Crack went to the inboard motor station of the divers' boat, lifted a hatch and pulled the gas line free, liberally splashing the stern and port.

When they were all back in the cigarette boat and drifting away, Captain Crack pulled out a Zippo and patiently lit an entire roll of toilet paper. It was hurled into the salvage craft. A yellowish fire flickered at first. Then blue flames violently shot out from any vulnerable aperture before a fireball billowed into the sky. Crack threw the cigarette boat in gear and took off.

After a couple hundred yards: "Stop the boat! Stop the boat!"

Crack pulled the throttle all the way back, and the boat settled. "What is it?"

A henchman stretched out an arm. "Someone's coming!"

Crack grabbed night-vision binoculars, and all three crawled out onto the bow on their stomachs.

"What's going on?"

"Shhhhh!" Captain Crack focused the binoculars on a wayward shark fisherman named Remy Skillet as he arrived at the burning boat and poked around, then inexplicably began firing a gun at the already dead. "Unbelievable."

It became even more unbelievable as Remy turned his boat and, instead of motoring off in any number of logical directions, decided to come straight at them.

"Shit!"

The black cigarette boat bolted out of its path at the last moment, and the henchmen turned around just in time to see the physics of the spinning vessel.

"He got thrown overboard . . ."

Crack decided to set a course south, parallel to land, putting distance between his boat and the natural vector out to the murder scene. A few miles later, he cut the engine again and admired the far-off ribbon of lights defining Singer Island.

"Why are we stopping?" asked a henchman.

"To celebrate," said Crack, reaching into a watertight compartment for three glasses and the bottle of Johnnie Walker he had dragged along. "I was planning to celebrate anyway, though I didn't think it would be under these exact circumstances. We had a few bumps, but all in all a successful run tonight."

He handed out the glasses and poured several fingers of the Black Label in each.

"We really appreciate the opportunity," said the first henchman.

"Definitely," said the second, sniffing his drink before sipping.

Crack clinked his glass with theirs. "Congratulations! We're all rich men now."

The first henchmen sipped. "I could seriously get used to this."

Crack turned his back. "Then be quick about it." He faced them again.

One of the henchmen's hands opened, and a glass of Scotch shattered on the deck. "W-w-what's the shotgun for?"

"Do the math," said Crack. "Six dead is the same as four. No witnesses."

"But—"

Blam! Blam!

The henchmen toppled backward into the water.

Captain Crack Nasty set the gun down and picked up a glass. He calmly finished his drink and headed back to shore.

Chapter 12

NORTHEAST FLORIDA

A Plymouth Satellite raced north along the shore of a formidable river.

"You know what really separates the United States from the rest of the world?" asked Serge.

"Cowbell?"

"Soccer."

"How so?"

"We're the only country that gives such a small shit about it that we deliberately call it by the wrong name."

"I don't know," said Coleman. "I've heard of some pretty scary soccer riots."

"How scary can it be when the rioters are called hooligans?" said Serge. "Visit Philadelphia after any championship game and watch tipped-over police cars burning. And that's when they *win*.

Soccer, on the other hand, has no upside, other than our women's team."

"What do you mean?"

"A little while ago I read where the U.S. national team narrowly defeated the island of Martinique three-to-two," said Serge. "That's like barely beating a Sandals Resort."

"It's just embarrassing." *Belch.* Coleman looked out the window as a swamp gave way to vegetation that thickened and seemed to crowd the road. Pines, oaks, palmettos. Moss hung from branches in a canopy. "Where the hell are we?"

"On the William Bartram Scenic and Historic Highway just southwest of Jacksonville," said Serge. "We're in St. Johns County, named after that big river off to our left. I'll save you the details on Bartram. Okay, I won't. Born in 1739, Bartram was a groundbreaking naturalist known for his colorful drawings of birds and plants. In 1774, he entered Florida and sailed down the river, encountering alligators and Indians and otherwise exploring in a fashion that makes people want to put your name on street signs."

"I see one of the signs now."

"But Bartram is just the aperitif. The main course is still coming up." Serge snapped photos out the window. *Click, click, click.* "Man, I love this highway. The flora is so much different from the southern part of the state, much denser." *Click, click, click.* "Do you realize what's happening again? We're in danger of too much linear thought. We must rage against the machine!"

"I thought soccer was our exit ramp."

"True, true," said Serge. "But now the whole country is into tangents, whether they realize it or not, so we amp up our game!"

"The nation is into tangents?" Coleman's construction-paper robot was starting to fall apart from saliva. He reapplied the wacky eyes and took another double-clutch hit. "How so?"

"Comment threads!" Serge handed Coleman his smartphone. "I've already dialed one up for you. Go to any news site that invites reader comments at the end of stories and start reading. Doesn't matter what the story is about: a new high-altitude diet from the Andes, debt restructuring for the mathematically deranged, royal wedding gaffes in pictures through the years, why Selena Gomez is mum about one sexy topic. The article I just gave you is about a seven-state egg recall for salmonella."

"What am I looking at?"

"Just scroll down. It's like the threads for all the other stories. This one starts with comments about food safety and the FDA and communicating with school cafeterias. But inevitably . . . wait, wait . . . Here it comes! . . . Here it comes! . . ."

Coleman squinted at the tiny screen. "'Food is regulated more than assault rifles! . . . During a robbery do you want to be holding an egg or a gun? . . . It's all the orange president's fault! . . . Lock her up! . . . Snowflakes! . . . Republic-tards!' . . ." Coleman handed the phone back. "I had no idea it was that bad. How did this happen?"

"Technology outpaced our evolution," said Serge. "All of humanity falls along a spectrum of love to hate, and the people bunched up on the shitty end are now defined by too much spare time and keyboards. It happened once before when some pricks got hold of a Gutenberg press—'Bullshit on the Renaissance'— until calmer heads prevailed."

Thud, thud, thud.

Coleman spun around in pot paranoia. "What the hell was that?"

"Relax," said Serge. "Just the guy in the trunk."

"I remember now," said Coleman. "Clyde, who's mean to birdies."

"No, you idiot. We got rid of Clyde back on the beach in Fort Lauderdale," said Serge. "This is the new guy."

"Sorry," said Coleman. "There's so much traffic through your trunk that it's hard for me to keep the players straight."

"Me too," said Serge, pointing up at names written on a row of Post-it notes stuck to the sun visor.

The Plymouth dramatically slowed down as Serge scanned the side of the road.

"What are you doing?" asked Coleman.

"We just passed Cricket Hollow, so it's coming up."

"What is?"

Serge eased off the right side of the road and pointed at an easily missed piece of crooked, weathered wood with carved lettering: BELUTHAHATCHEE.

Coleman sucked his robot. "I still don't know where we are."

"Beluthahatchee is the name of the historic four-acre compound of preeminent Florida folklorist Stetson Kennedy. It's from the Miccosukee tongue, meaning Dark Water. I love it when I find these compounds, like Graceland without amphetamines and sequins."

Serge turned down a dirt road covered with brown leaves. "Stetson is one of my all-time heroes, traveling the state writing books and recording oral histories. He studied writing under Marjorie Kinnan Rawlings, worked on the Federal Writers Project with Zora Neale Hurston, and Woody Guthrie often slept on his couch. Coincidence? You make the call!"

"I say nope."

"Our tour is like the Kevin Bacon game of Florida with lots of dot-connecting that will become more evident as our odyssey continues."

Coleman stared out his window, catching glimpses of water between the trees. "Is there a cemetery around here or something?"

"It's like Mitzi the Dolphin, just a single resting place." Serge slowed as the narrow road curved through an untamed southern jungle. "After Stetson passed away in 2011, they scattered his ashes on the pond next to us, and Woody's son Arlo gave a concert."

Serge finally parked behind the old cedar barn of a home perched on piers over the edge of the water. "I love how Stetson let most of the compound continue to grow wild. But what I love more is that back in the 1950s, he infiltrated the Ku Klux

Klan. He wasn't working with law enforcement or anything, just thought it up and did it all by himself on spec."

"What balls," said Coleman.

"Then he passed what he'd learned over to the authorities and journalists. It was a difficult time in America, and Woody Guthrie was roaming the countryside with an acoustic guitar that had a sticker on it: 'This machine kills fascists.' Woody became quite controversial, and when he needed breaks, he began spending a lot of time at Stetson's to retreat from it all. He was even staying here the night a fire started in the woods and threatened the house, but they put it out. Then they found a note on the front gate from the Klan threatening Kennedy. Mind you, this was after a previous incident when Stetson came home to discover the interior destroyed and all his writings thrown in the water. Anyway, Guthrie was crashing on the couch at Beluthahatchee so much that this is where he finished his memoir, *Seeds of Man,* and composed more than eighty songs, including 'Beluthahatchee Bill,' about Stetson. That resulted in this place being named not once, but twice, as a national literary landmark, for both Woody and Stetson. That's beyond exciting. Think of it, *two times!*"

"I remember when you got all excited after having two orgasms in a row and put that number two NASCAR racing sign on your driver's door."

"It's close, but I think this is bigger." Serge stared wistfully out across the water. "I'm on an urgent quest for the high-water marks of letters in this fine state."

"How come?"

"It's necessary," said Serge. "The state's literary laurels are a needed counterbalance to our recent cultural reputation."

"Which is?"

"Florida Man."

"Oh, yeah," said Coleman. "That maniac who's raising hell all over the place."

"Coleman, it's not just one dude. It's a whole army."

"Really? I thought he was just ambitious."

Serge shook his head. "The entire nation is into the embarrassing craze of Googling 'Florida Man' and seeing what pops up. Last year there was a spike in guys pooping in unpopular locations and contexts. This year they're getting naked."

"Naked?"

Serge pulled out his smartphone again, pressing buttons to enter search terms. "Check out these headlines: 'Naked Florida Man Eats Noodles and Plays Bongos at St. Petersburg Restaurant,' 'Naked Florida Man Rides Bicycle through Interstate 95 Traffic,' 'Naked Florida Man Chases Customers around Chick-Fil-A Parking Lot,' 'Naked Florida Man Continues Gardening Despite Pleas from Neighbors.'"

"But, Serge, how is it possible to fight that?"

"The answer is the written word," said Serge. "Let's just sit here quietly for a moment and take in the tranquillity as Stetson and Woody would have——"

Thud, thud, thud . . .

Serge closed his eyes for a long pause, then opened them. "Wait here."

Coleman turned around to see the trunk open.

Wham, wham, wham . . .

The lid closed and Serge got back in the driver's seat. "Where were we?"

"Tranquillity."

"Right," said Serge. "Here's my favorite impression of this place. When I was here for Stetson's memorial service—"

"Wait a second," said Coleman. "When you mentioned that before, I thought you read it somewhere."

"Nope, here in the flesh," said Serge. "How could anyone living in Florida at the time miss it? But I guess twenty million found some bogus excuse. Moving on: The best moment celebrating

Stetson's life came just before they went down to the pond to spread his ashes, when all those in attendance sang 'This Land Is Your Land.' Can you imagine the emotion?"

"Not me," said Coleman. "Are you about to cry?"

Serge wiped his eyes. "Just a little pollen." He pulled out a tissue and blew his nose. "Okay, I'm busted. It is getting to me a little . . . Mind if we sit until I compose myself—"

Thud, thud, thud . . .

Serge looked down to his lap, then over at Coleman without speaking.

"What?"

Thud, thud, thud . . .

Serge threw up his hands. "I can't live like this. I'm trying to have a private moment of reflection. But no . . ." He pointed back over his shoulder with his thumb. "Some people are so inconsiderate. Do *I* go around bothering people like that?"

"Not from where I'm sitting." Coleman looked down at two handfuls of soggy, falling-apart chunks of construction paper. "My robot's fucked up."

Serge twisted the key in the ignition and the Plymouth came to life.

"Where to now?" asked Coleman. He looked over his shoulder at the trunk. "I mean, I know we're going to have to stop at a motel first, but after that."

"The next visit really is a cemetery." Serge blew his nose a final time and stowed the Kleenex in an anti-litterbug bag hanging from his door. "It's the state's connective tissue I was telling you about. We just picked up the trail with Rawlings back near Cross Creek, now Stetson off Bartram Trail, and the rest of the stops will soon start falling like dominoes, as if actual planning was involved."

Thud, thud, thud . . .

"I forgot what that guy in the trunk did," said Coleman, picking paper off his tongue. "Not that I'm questioning your judgment."

"You were fading in and out back at the church," said Serge. "I'll refresh you on the way to the motel."

"Ready when you are." Coleman was about to toss damp kindergarten paper out the window.

"Stop! Hand it to me for the litter bag."

"Oops, my bad." Coleman passed the trash. "You're always thinking of others."

Thud, thud, thud . . .

"Sometimes even when I don't want to."

Chapter 13

Coaches led the team running out of the locker room for another day of torture in the Florida sun. The managers brought up the rear with sacks of balls and tees, ankle tape, first-aid kits. Everyone arrived on the field to find the newest manager already there, sitting quietly on the bench along the sideline, proudly wearing a new Pahokee Blue Devils T-shirt that Coach Calhoun had given her, now the nicest item in her wardrobe. In front of her, coolers of water and Gatorade were already in place. Paper cups arranged neatly in rows. She had kind of arrived early.

An afternoon of athletic violence and exhaustion wore on. Chris was Johnny-on-the-spot, dutifully keeping the paper cups filled, dashing on and off the field with water bottles and towels, and quickly volunteering for any errand. The reaction of the team was varied. Most didn't notice, others didn't care, the rest were amused.

Weeks went by. Chris kept her word. She didn't say a peep, didn't get in the way, just did her job. Players almost started taking it for granted that whenever they needed something from one of the managers, Chris was just right there in front of them, like a mind reader.

On a recent afternoon, the players didn't gather on the field for practice. It was a conditioning day, no pads or helmets. And it involved something else that made the kids from The Muck just that much tougher.

The Herbert Hoover Dike.

The dike was constructed in response to the hurricane of 1928, stretching 143 miles around Lake Okeechobee to contain the water in case of another deadly strike. From the outside, all that could be seen was an earthen berm rising thirty feet.

The players hated that damn dike.

At some forgotten point in the school's history, a coach was driving by the dike and got an idea. It was walking distance from Pahokee High. Make that running distance. And now, this afternoon, players grunted and cursed under their breath as they ran up it and down, fighting for footing, slipping, getting back up.

Chris kept her mouth zipped but kept glancing at Coach Calhoun. He could see her from the corner of his eye, knew what was in her head. Since it wasn't a contact practice, what the heck? He turned. "Go ahead."

"Thanks, Coach." She took off and headed up the dike.

The other players didn't have the luxury to react. They were too busy with the pain in their legs and lungs. But a few did wonder: *Who* wants *to run the dike?*

The receivers coach stepped up next to Calhoun. "She's faster than I thought. Practically keeping up with the boys."

"Told me she chases rabbits."

"Mm-hmm, one of those," said Odom.

Chris raced to the bottom of the dike, touched the ground and began sprinting back up.

The head coach blew a whistle. "Now backward!"

A chorus of quiet groans, then slow backpedaling and more suffering on the berm. A few repetitions of that and another whistle. "Now crab-walk . . ."

Chris got that burning in her calves but didn't quit.

Fifteen minutes later: "All right, bring it in!"

The players staggered down the hill like refugees, and Chris ran around with the water bottles.

The following day's practice was back in the friendly confines of the high school field.

Halfway through, one of the safeties came over to the coolers. Chris recognized him from the rabbit hunts. She held out a paper cup. He stumbled and bumped it, spilling the Gatorade on her T-shirt. *Accidentally.*

Coach Calhoun happened to notice, but it didn't register.

During the next break, the same player trotted off the field to the coolers. In a voice nobody else could hear: "Girls don't run the dike." Then he had another accident, bumping into her hard before running back onto the field. Chris crashed into the table with the paper cups.

This time Calhoun didn't dismiss it. He took a step forward. He felt a hand on his arm. It was Reggie, his first-string halfback. "I got this one, Coach." He put his helmet back on and ran out to the huddle.

Four plays later in the scrimmage, Reggie's number was called and a perfect block off-tackle broke him into the clear. Only one safety to beat. It was open field, which called for a cut, then easily outrunning him for the sideline.

Reggie cut, and the safety reacted. Then something happened that the safety never expected. Reggie cut again, this time the other way, straight *at* the safety.

Reggie caught him running sideways, trying to twist back, and plowed right through him—lifting him off the ground and dropping him on his ribs—before trotting into the end zone. On his way back to the sideline, Reggie bumped into the safety from behind. "Don't mess with Chris."

Practice eventually ended as they all did. Players wrung out beyond what they imagined they could endure. They headed for the locker room.

Chris ran after one of the boys. "Hey, Reggie, thanks!"

"For what?"

"You know, out there."

"I don't know what you're talking about."

"Can I ask you a question?"

"You just did."

"Can you teach me to cut?"

"To what?"

"Cut. You're the best! All-state first team from last year and sure to repeat!"

"Why do you want to learn to cut?"

"I'm going to be a running back."

A chuckle. "Okay, I'll play along. I'll teach you to cut."

"Great!" Chris stopped walking.

Reggie looked at her oddly. "You mean *now*?"

Eager nodding.

"Why not? . . ."

Coach Calhoun finished the day and locked up his office. He grabbed his briefcase and headed out of the locker room for the parking lot. The field was empty. Except for two people in the distance on the far sideline. He stopped and stared. Could it get any stranger?

"Okay, stand here," said Reggie. "You're a cornerback or safety."

"You got it."

"Now, here's the mistake most backs commit." He tucked a ball in the crook of an arm. "They have to make a defender miss an open-field tackle, so they juke or shake-and-bake"—Reggie shuffled his feet quickly in the same spot—"trying to fake him out. The problem is that the runner is waiting to react to how the *defender* will react. That's way too much time."

"So what do you do?"

"Totally commit. You plan your cut ahead of time and take it no matter what the defender does."

"What if he doesn't bite?" asked Chris.

"Then you're tackled."

"Doesn't seem like a good plan."

"It does if you're good at geometry."

"I like math."

"Then you'll understand this. We'll take it in slow motion." Reggie backed up twenty yards and shouted: "We're coming straight at each other." He took a single deliberate step. "So now I begin a slow turn to the right, toward the sideline. And you're going to follow." They each took two steps in unison. "The closer you get, the more I increase my angle until I'm almost running east–west."

"But that gives the defender the angle to run you out of bounds."

"And that's the whole key to selling your fake. You make it too good to be true. You run into their strength, which makes *them* commit." More slow, tandem steps. "Now you're just about on me, and I make my cut . . ." He sped back up and dashed by.

"Cool," said Chris.

"Unreal," said Coach Calhoun in the distance, and he walked to his car.

C oach Calhoun sat in his office going over the playbook for that Friday's game.

Knock knock.

He looked up. "Chris, come on in. Have a seat."

"Thanks, Coach."

"I have to admit, this is working out a lot better than I'd expected. And as for your report card..." He leaned back in a creaky chair. "I'll confess that part of the reason I did this was to hold the manager thing over your head to improve your grades, but they're already straight A's. I didn't know you were that smart."

Chris shrugged. "I like school."

"So what can I do for you today?"

"I need a favor. And I hate to ask, because of what you've already done for me..."

"Go ahead. You've earned it."

"I kind of need to borrow a football."

"Knowing you, I thought you'd have ten footballs."

"Not really."

"You can't afford a football?"

She looked at the floor. The answer was worse. Certain neighborhood boys always stole them.

The coach got up and went to a bookshelf and grabbed a ball off a stand. He returned and tossed it over his desk to Chris.

She caught it and noticed writing on the side in white letters: Lamar Calhoun, a date from the eighties and 216 Yards. Chris looked up. "I can't accept this."

Lamar just smiled and looked down at his playbook. "Anything else?"

"Uh, actually there is one other thing..."

It was a coaches-only meeting.

Calhoun and Odom arrived early.

The field was empty save for a tiny person at the far end. A ball was kicked. It landed pitifully short and left of the goalposts. The person ran after the ball, then ran back. The process was repeated with the same results.

"Where'd she get a kicking tee?" asked Odom.

"I gave her one."

"So now you're a kicking coach, too?"

"She wants to be a running back."

"How does this lead to that?"

"She said she read articles where a few girls in other parts of the country are now playing on boys' teams," said Calhoun. "I made the mistake of pointing out that those were kickers."

"So she's exploiting a loophole?"

They stared a few more minutes at sheer futile relentlessness. Then they went inside for the meeting. It was a marathon: rosters, films, discussion of college recruitment visits, and most importantly, the game plan for Friday. Their opponent was big on zone defense and double-teaming their best receivers, so they decided to rush between the tackles until it opened up the passing game. The agenda ran so long that it was night when they adjourned.

Calhoun and Odom were chatting about auto maintenance as they headed to the parking lot. They heard something near the far end zone. To them, the sound was unmistakable. A football being kicked.

"She still out there?" said Odom.

"I don't know," said Calhoun. "I can't see her."

"She's kicking in complete darkness."

"Maybe her eyes have adjusted."

They stopped and listened to a few more kicks.

"Something about kids like that," said Odom. "I've only known a few, but they're easy to spot."

"What do you mean?"

Odom faintly watched her tee up again, and miss again, and run after the stray ball again. "There's a big emptiness in there somewhere."

Chapter 14

COCOA BEACH

A gold Plymouth sat in a parking space. The sign on the motel roof was a rocket ship. A broken ice machine stood next to the dumpster.

Serge dragged a chair across the mauve carpet of room number 7.

A belch from the bathroom. Coleman emerged guzzling a bottle of Boone's Farm, then bites of jerky. "What are you doing?"

Serge was sitting with his face a few inches from the TV tube. "Ruining my eyes."

Coleman glanced at the screen. "Another protest march?"

"The new women's movement," said Serge. "I'm forcing it on myself."

"Why?"

"Because I'm embarrassed by my gender." Serge's eyes followed the sign-waving parade. "I'm in total solidarity with everything the protesters stand for. But something has become increasing clear to me: Because I'm a man, I'm not reminded fifty times a day of the shit women are expected to put up with. And I thought I was worldly-wise."

"You're not?"

"Until now, my experience has been limited to witnessing the cliché construction workers catcalling to the fairer sex. But I figured Darwin already had that one covered. I mean, when in the course of human history has that ever worked? Some woman in a business suit is hurrying down the sidewalk, and suddenly a guy in a hard hat starts whistling and making slurping sounds and yelling, 'Give me some of that *pussy*!' . . . And the woman stops in her tracks: 'Hold on a minute. I've got my priorities all screwed up. Forget that big board meeting I'm heading to. Why yes, I will give him pussy.'"

"That's pretty bad," said Coleman. "And you're saying it's even worse?"

"Way worse." Serge inched closer to the TV. "My mistake is that all these years, I've been projecting. In other words, if some notion can't remotely enter my head, I figured other guys were the same. And if it wasn't for newspapers, I never would have imagined that all across the country, men are just pulling out their dicks in unwelcome settings."

"Really?"

"And I'm not talking about Sterno bums or bowery flashers. I'm referring to wealthy, famous, powerful men who are supposedly educated. It's happening in hallways, elevators, during innocuous conversations in hospitality suites."

"It's just not right," said Coleman.

"You'd think this would go without saying, but as a general rule of thumb, if you're chatting with some woman you've just met, your best foot forward isn't to start spanking the monkey."

"That's obvious even to me," said Coleman. "I get embarrassed if there's a cat in the room."

"Speaking of cats in the room . . ."

Serge turned toward yet another motel room chair with a bound and gagged guest, wedged away in the far corner.

"He's been so quiet that I completely forgot about him," said Coleman. He covered his own face with a hand. "I'm so embarrassed."

"Why?"

"When you left me here and went to the store," said Coleman. "I think he saw me."

"Saw you? Doing what? . . . Wait, don't answer that. I think I'm getting the picture."

"I made some noises, too."

"For the love of God, please stop! It's going to be hard enough getting the image out of my head without audio as well." Serge walked over to the hostage. "I think you traumatized him. They may be naming a new syndrome after you."

He ripped duct tape off the mouth. "Sorry about my friend," said Serge. "That should be more than enough punishment for you, but I don't make the rules."

"Please let me go! I did everything you asked!" Whimpering. "I went to the bank with you and got a certified check for those people . . ."

Serge held up a driver's license. "What's wrong with Malcolm Reynolds Greely? Much better than Tyler or Nicholas."

"How many times do I have to say I'm sorry?"

"Yeah, but you don't mean it." Serge tossed the license in the trash and taped the captive's mouth shut again. He grabbed a shopping bag off the dresser.

Coleman came over. "Is that what you bought at the store while I was—"

"Shut up! The image was almost gone." Serge walked over and dumped the bag on the bed.

"What's that stuff?" asked Coleman.

"Everything I need for my next science project."

Coleman picked up each item in turn. "A barber's electric razor, cheese grater, box of small trash bags and . . . I don't recognize this thing."

"It's a time lock." Serge picked up the razor. "A lot like a regular padlock, but you can set the timer to open it at a preordained point in the future."

"This isn't much stuff," said Coleman. "Usually your projects are a lot more complicated."

"It'll be more than enough."

"So what's the timer for anyway?"

"I've fallen into a rut," said Serge. "Different day, same shit. Into the trunk, out of the trunk, into the chair, duct tape, blah, blah, blah . . . But even though this started out predictable, I'm throwing in a twist at the end so nobody can say I was snoozing at the wheel."

"You're just being responsible."

Serge walked over to Malcolm and held up the razor. "A little off the top? . . . Ha! Ha! Ha! . . . Just kidding. Actually a lot off the top."

"Mmmmmmm! Mmmmmmm!"

Serge flicked on the razor and placed it at the back of Malcolm's head just above the neck. He pushed the device upward and deep. Huge clumps of hair fell off the front of the razor as it continued over the top of the captive's scalp, right down the middle, until it reached the edge of his forehead.

Serge turned off the razor. "There you go. I hear reverse mohawks are coming into style." Next he grabbed the cheese grater. "I'd be lying if I said this won't hurt . . . Coleman, grab a towel and come here!" He placed the grater where he'd just shaved and began rubbing.

"Mmmmmm! Mmmmmm!"

"Pipe down," said Serge. "I'm only using the extra-fine side."

Coleman arrived with the towel. "Here you go . . . Jesus, he's bleeding."

"Just a few scrapes." He tossed the grater on one of the beds and applied the towel. "Coleman, hold this in place while I go out to the car."

Serge ran out the door.

Coleman bent down to the captive's face and whispered. "Malcolm, is it? Listen, what you saw earlier? I'd really appreciate it if we could keep that between you and me. If it ever got back to my mom—"

Serge returned. "What are you talking about?"

"Nothin'."

Serge placed a clear rectangle on the bed.

"Hey, I remember that," said Coleman. "It's the storage bin you were putting bacon strips in down on Big Pine Key."

"And it worked. You can let go of the towel."

Coleman joined Serge as they crouched down and peered through the side of the bin.

"It's a bunch of flies."

"*Cochliomyia hominivorax,*" said Serge. "Otherwise known as the dreaded screw worm flies that recently plagued the Florida Keys."

"Most of them are dead on the bottom."

"That was inevitable," said Serge. "But there are enough left to do the trick. They have a twenty-day life cycle under ideal conditions."

"How did you know that bacon would lure them into the bin?"

"Read it in a medical journal." Serge ripped open the box of plastic garbage bags. "As I said before, sometimes the best cure is to go low-tech. In the rare cases where screw worms attack humans, doctors use bacon, because the larvae are more attracted to that than human flesh, and the parasites unscrew themselves from their hosts. All completely true: Type 'bacon therapy' into any search engine."

Serge opened one of the trash bags, inflated it with air and fit it over the storage bin. "This is the tricky part. I'll hold the mouth of the bag in place, and you carefully pop the lid and slide it out from underneath."

It went off without a hitch, and Serge shook the bin until enough of the flies took flight into the bag. "Coleman, slide the lid back on."

Serge cinched the mouth of the sack and strolled over to Malcolm.

"Mmmmm?"

"You must be getting pretty confused about now." Serge carefully fit the bag's opening over the top of Malcolm's head. "Coleman! Duct tape!"

"Coming right up."

Several strips were wrapped around Malcolm's forehead, sealing the bag in place. "It's not your fault you don't know what's going on. You simply don't have the scientific background. So I'll tell you a little story . . ."

He did, explaining all about the gruesome infestation in the Keys, right up to: ". . . And I used a cheese grater to mimic lesions when those little deer have antler fights. That's pretty much it."

"Mmmmmmm! Mmmmmmm!"

"Why so glum?" said Serge. "I always give my contestants a bonus round and a chance to survive."

A tap on his shoulder.

"What is it, Coleman?"

"Uh, hate to mention this, but you didn't give the seagull guy a bonus round."

"Of course I did."

Coleman shook his head.

Serge pondered; then: "Damn! . . . I'll just have to make it up to Malcolm to balance my karma account . . . Malcolm, did you hear that? Another jerk's loss is your gain. I'm adjusting the time lock in your favor." He knelt behind the chair. "What you're feeling is me refitting your wrist restraints so the lock will free your hands in, say, three days?"

"Mmmmmm! Mmmmmm!"

"You're going to get pretty hungry, but the key is hydration, so I'll get you some sports bottles and stick the tubes through the tape. Just remember to conserve." Serge hopped and clapped. "And most important of all, when the time lock opens and the bonus round begins, what do you need to do?"

"Mmmmmm! Mmmmmm!"

"That's right!" Serge said with a widening grin. "Find bacon!"

Chapter 15

FOUR YEARS EARLIER

A stuffed wahoo stared down from the office wall with glassy eyes.

Captain Crack Nasty tilted his head to consider the fish. Then he considered his career position. That shootout on the high seas the previous night wasn't exactly tailored for the long game. He glanced at the bottle of Johnnie Walker on his desk and stuck it in a bottom drawer: *Last time I make business decisions on that stuff.*

Overall, though, Nasty viewed the evening a huge success, even if it was a one-timer. He'd recovered a serious amount of treasure, and he didn't have to split it with anyone. Then there was that ugly violence. Crack hadn't known this about himself before. But he liked it.

Now it was just a matter of tweaking his corporate model. Minimize risk. Captain Crack opened another drawer in his desk and pulled out an empty notebook. He turned on his computer. He had decided to do something quite unnatural to him: homework.

He found a number of wreck sites that weren't exactly inactive. The original salvagers still had valid claims. It was just that they had reached diminishing returns, and the locations were being worked more sporadically. Also, Crack began employing a spotter boat, on the off chance that the claim holders picked the wrong day to come back. He employed more care in selecting his associates, more stable, reliable, less trigger-happy. The bottom line: Take it slow and there could be a long future.

His new crew began doing quite well at five sites from Cape Canaveral to Port Salerno and Hobe Sound, never staying too long, never taking too much at once. Treasure would still be there when they came back, as they did, time after time, until there were only a few items in the bottom of a single dive basket. Then on to the next location.

But there were only so many sites off Florida—even dormant ones—that could produce any decent yield, especially if you had to dart in and out like thieves in the night. That meant even more homework for the good captain. And a funny thing happened. He began to find the research interesting, even enjoyable. The history of maritime trade routes back to the Old World, the life and times of sailors on the galleons, all the unnamed and forgotten hurricanes.

Captain Crack pored over notes he had recently scribbled. Of particular interest was a bit of treasure folklore that didn't have any foundation in the official records. Which meant virgin territory. He was intrigued at the prospect of his first legitimate find . . .

The sun had just gone down when he was interrupted by a knock on his office door. "You wanted to see me?"

"Yes, yes, come in."

It was one of his newest hires, a former marijuana bale loader released from Raiford. Went by Corky.

"What's up?"

"Follow me, Corky." He led him down the dock, making a mental note to hammer down some of the rusty nails that were popping up. They arrived at a black boat. "Climb in. We got work."

"Okay." Corky jumped aboard and looked around. "Where are the other guys?"

"Just us." Crack untied the bowline from a mooring cleat. "No diving. Only recon to GPS a potential wreck with sonar . . ."

Since there wouldn't be any violation of a claimed site, there was no need for speed. Crack motored unhurriedly out to sea, sipping coffee and Scotch. He became quite chatty. It was a new development ever since he'd gotten the research bug, and the crew was getting used to it, in a negative way. They rolled their eyes at all the boring knowledge that Crack now spouted. But only behind his back.

"Corky, you wouldn't believe what I've been researching. Potentially my first legitimate find. It's fascinating!"

"Really?" Corky concealed a sigh. "Tell me about it."

"Our work is inextricably entwined with hurricanes and their storm surges that sent doomed ships down off our coasts." The captain adjusted his course bearing. "Corky, did you know there was a hurricane in 1928 that had a storm surge unlike any other?"

"I can't say that I did."

Crack nodded earnestly. "The surge didn't come from the ocean, but from Lake Okeechobee, producing a tidal wave that wiped out entire neighborhoods of fieldworkers. Then I stumbled upon a wild coincidence. I began hearing about a folktale circulating to this day out at the lake. A treasure was lost in the hurricane! Some sugar baron supposedly squirreled away a fortune. When the storm hit, it took him, his house and whatever he was saving, and decades of farming have since covered up all traces. But to this day, it's said that children playing out in the sugarcane fields occasionally come across an old gold coin. Can you imagine it? An *inland* storm surge producing an *inland* wreck?"

"Wow," Corky said with feigned enthusiasm. "So you're going to go after it?"

Crack sagged slightly. "More homework first. I don't know anything about this sugar baron, which is the key to narrowing the search to a specific location." He cut the engine.

Corky looked over the side as the quiet boat rolled mildly in the swells. "We're here?"

"Yes, we are."

Corky climbed over gear on the deck. "I'll start checking the sonar."

"I've got something I want to show you first."

"What is it?"

"See this tube on the side of the shore radio?" asked Crack.

"Yeah, but I still don't know what I'm looking at."

"It's a pinhole video lens. Covers the whole boat from here on back, kind of like a nanny cam."

"I'm not following," said a bored Corky.

Crack reached down into bow storage and pulled something out. "Now do you follow?"

Corky was no longer bored. He'd had guns pointed at him before, but a twelve-gauge always dials it up to eleven.

"What's going on, Captain?"

"I'm sure you have a pretty damn good idea." Crack gestured with the end of the gun. "That tiny camera was filming every time you stuffed shit in your pockets when we came up from a site. Have I not treated you well? And then you steal from *me*? Don't even try to lie. I could show you the tapes, but I don't care about your opinion."

Corky silently reviewed options.

The captain racked the shotgun with the distinct sound that is a natural stool softener.

"Wait! Wait! Wait!" Corky began babbling. "I just took a little. I was going to give it back. I had car troubles. The electric bill. I was drunk. My girlfriend needed braces—"

Blam!

Corky hit the water and bobbed, well, like a cork.

"That was fun." Crack throttled back up toward land. "Now to do some homework on this sugar baron . . ."

MR. FAKAKTA

Sugarcane is actually a grass.

A grass that changed the march of history in the New World.

It can't entirely be attributed to rum, but that's a good start. During the colonial period, from the Caribbean to the South American coast surrounding French Guyana, farming took off due to the region's conducive blend of climate and rich soil. Bananas, coffee beans, nutmeg, rice, cocoa. But when they started using sugarcane to make molasses, which was shipped north to rum distilleries, sugar took the lead and never looked back.

Jamaica, Trinidad, Barbados, Belize, Cuba, Guadalupe. Plow that other stuff under, boys, and plant that cane. The cash flowed in, but at a price. Brutal conditions in a brutal business, cutthroat competition and politics.

On the island of Hispaniola, in the Dominican Republic, there was a particularly heated rivalry among the four chief growers in the early twentieth century. And it wasn't gentlemanly. Threats, vandalism, workers attacked and maimed. Alliances shifted back and forth like on one of those survival reality-TV shows, until one of the four growers was voted off the island.

Fulgencio Salvador Fakakta drew the short straw. But it was impossible to feel sorry for him. Fakakta was one of those rare comeuppance cases where the bad guy actually lost. He had bribed, cheated, stolen and even murdered his way to wealth and power. And now it had come full circle. In short, the other growers were just tired of this asshole.

Fakakta saw it coming, and it wasn't going to be a polite eviction notice. If he was lucky, they'd burn his plantation home, seize everything he had down to the last penny, and allow him to escape with the shirt on his back. If he was lucky. So Fakakta quietly and quickly liquidated everything into gold, which was all crated up one night and packed onto a chartered ship.

"What's in these crates? Rocks?"

"Shut up and keep loading!"

Fulgencio set sail. The other growers still burned his place to the ground, but at least he had enough for a new start.

Besides the Caribbean, there was one other place where sugarcane had just started to catch hold.

Florida.

It would be years before the crop asserted dominance, so for now, a fugitive sugar baron from the Dominican could affordably buy up bean fields around Lake Okeechobee to plant his stalks.

Fakakta had the experience and ruthlessness to make it work, and soon he was one of the wealthier farmers in the lake region. It wasn't enough. He began stealing from his workers. Docking pay for non-reasons, overcharging for rent on their ridiculous shanties and the food he required that they buy from him as a condition of employment. Then he realized there were far more people looking for work than there were jobs. Can't let that equation go to waste. So he took it up a notch and started not paying some workers entirely. Of course they'd yell and argue and quit. But what else were they going to do? He was white. He'd just hire more guys.

But one particular worker, named Jacob, wouldn't let it go. He kept demanding his money, day after day. Finally, Jacob went out to Fakakta's stately colonial plantation house on the edge of town and pounded on the front door. The next morning he was found hanging from a prominent cypress tree with signs of torture. It was meant to be obvious, unlike the other missing workers, who were never found. The white law didn't care, and everyone else got the message. Fakakta continued amassing his fortune, which he kept in gold. But nobody knew where.

Chapter 16

COCOA BEACH

Malcolm sat quietly in his chair.

Serge and Coleman sat quietly at a table.

Malcolm's eyes stared up at the plastic bag taped to his head.

"Mmmmmmm! Mmmmmmm!"

Serge and Coleman wore plain white T-shirts. Open bottles of various colors were scattered across the table. Stains representing the same colors covered their shirts. Coleman leaned over and rubbed feverishly. "I'd completely forgotten about finger painting."

"Finger painting is the best!" Serge made a blue circle with his thumb. "I don't know why society cuts that off after kindergarten. I had dreams of becoming a world-class finger-paint artist. Huge gallery openings in SoHo, the toast of Paris. Then I found out it was just some bullshit to keep us busy until recess. It was the beginning of the counterculture, and that's when I started seeing through all the lies. Finger painting, Vietnam."

"This is excellent when you're high."

Serge looked across the table. "Not bad. You're painting a pumpkin."

"It's a bong," said Coleman. "What are you painting?"

"An egret." Serge chugged a mug of coffee, then stood up and grabbed the page. He taped it to a wall.

"Why are you doing that?"

"Because this motel room has no artwork. We got screwed." He straightened his egret and sat back down. "All motel rooms are supposed to have artwork. But sadly, most guests never notice. You ask ten people what the painting was in the room they stayed in last night, and dollars to doughnuts none will have a clue. Not me! It's the first thing I look for when I open the door!"

"Why?"

"Reminds me of baseball cards, because you never know what you'll get." Serge grabbed a fresh page and resumed work. "I'd buy a pack of cards at the five-and-dime and then sit on the curb out front, gently and affectionately removing each card to reveal surprise after surprise: 'Cool, Carl Yastrzemski. Cookie Rojas, not bad. Do I already have Rollie Fingers? It says on the back of Félix Millán's card that he led the National League in triples. Who the fuck is Buzz Capra?' . . . Same thing with motel paintings, especially budget motels. You go to a fancy *hotel* and get high-quality art that makes sense, following the room's color scheme and local milieu. But the economy joints are the best, especially the kind with old wood paneling. They don't give a shit anymore and buy stuff from art-clearance warehouses that sell paintings by the pound. You're always in for a treat, so when I first arrive at a room, I stop outside and let the anticipation build, like holding that shiny new pack of sports cards. Then I quickly open the door and pump a fist in the air. 'Yes! Sailboats!' I can still see them to this day."

"You remember the sailboats?"

"I remember all the paintings!" said Serge. "The sailboats, a beach scene of three children playing with pails on the sand and each pail was a different primary color, a vase with sunflowers, a cherry pie on a windowsill overlooking corn, magpies on a power line, a train station when they still had baggage porters, a bowl of fruit, a cowboy leaning against a post, a lighthouse in Maine, a terrier, President Coolidge . . ."

"How do you recall all that?"

"Because I care." Serge dipped a finger in the green bottle while swigging coffee with the other hand. "If people don't watch out, there can be a lot of needless tedium in motel rooms by squandering spare time. But I rarely encounter that problem because I want to squeeze every second out of life. Even if I don't have spare time in a room, I'll *make* time, sitting in a chair staring relentlessly at the wall and metaphysically contemplating all aspects of the painting. What were the headlines of the day when it was created? How many people have straightened it on the wall? Who painted it and why? What about the backstories of the people on the sailboats? I imagine the painting hanging steadily and all-knowing in here since the mid-twentieth century, during poker games, extramarital affairs, kids jumping on beds, someone repeatedly peeking out the window, salesmen with straw hats from a plumbing supply convention, a coroner wheeling out the victim of a heart attack that everyone saw coming. Then I envision a woman at an easel in 1953 who decided to broaden her background of dependable typing skills by taking a mail-order art class, only to have her husband leave her for a Pan Am stewardess, and now she paints just to forget but has never been to the beach. And the little people on one of the sailboats are a family of six from Knoxville who take the same vacation every year to Myrtle Beach, where they always line up the children for an annual photo to document their growth, which after three decades will become the subject of a feel-good magazine article. But what are their political beliefs? How would they view the woman who painted them? Do they even know they're in a painting? These are questions for the ages." He raised his mug. "I'm out of coffee."

Malcolm heard buzzing in the bag taped to his head.

"Mmmmmm! Mmmmmm!"

Serge walked over to the captive. The trash bag had all but deflated on his head, and Serge held it upright and shook, giving the flies renewed space to work. He pointed at a page on the wall. "If you're bored, you can look at my egret and ask metaphysical questions."

He returned to his table and paint.

Coleman leaned toward his friend's new page. "What's this one?"

"Great blue heron." Serge got up and placed it on the wall.

Coleman noticed there was now a long row of overlapping finger paintings along the side of the room. "Serge, what are you doing?"

"Making a mural to compensate for this motel room's lost time without art." Serge aimed a yellow finger at Malcolm. "This science project requires an extended duration of babysitting, so a mural is the only way to go. The room's next guests will seriously get their money's worth."

"Why so long?" asked Coleman. "Can't we just leave him like the others?"

Serge shook his head and drew cattails with a finger. "I'll need to remove the bag and dispose of the remaining flies or I could be responsible for some kind of outbreak from breaching the Keys quarantine. It's the right thing to do."

"What kind of mural?"

"In full disclosure, it's not original." He sat down with another page. "I'm inspired by one of Florida's finest and most enduring works of art. While the state has a wealth of fine galleries, my favorite native painting of all time adorns the lounge of a historic erstwhile grande dame of accommodations in a small town on the southern shore of Lake Okeechobee."

"Mmmmmm! Mmmmmm!"

Coleman packed his alligator honey bottle. Puff, puff. "Even our hostage is into this now. Please tell us more."

"Unlike other swank hotels of bygone eras such as the Breakers or Biltmore, this place is now a bargain. But not because it's hit the skids. Far from it. In another freak of *Freakonomics,* the glory days faded and revenue dropped. But then an interesting thing happened. The place remained just popular enough to create a Goldilocks effect, not overheating or cooling off. Instead, it remains strangely suspended in time as a freeze-frame snapshot of the past. It's so quiet and peaceful that you're often the only person in the opulent period lobby, like staying in a museum."

"But, Serge, what is this fabulous place?"

"The Clewiston Inn, built 1938 by U.S. Sugar in Classic Revival architecture with stately white columns out front, now in the National Register of Historic Sites. It's unexpected to find one of Florida's most impressive hotels in such a modest community, almost nothing but miles of agricultural fields in all directions. The Everglades Bar and Lounge itself remains essentially closed because of lack of traffic, but the management is hospitable enough to open it up upon request for guests to bring their own beverages and food and sit just to enjoy the mural. That gets my five-star rating for dedication to heritage."

"But what about this mural?"

"Commissioned in the early 1940s and painted by J. Clinton Shepherd, director of the Norton Gallery and School of Art over on the coast. I can't tell you how many field trips my classes took to the Norton when I was a kid. And there are countless exquisite features that make the mural stand out from all the pretenders. First, it's not a traditional mural that stretches out straight, but instead wraps three hundred and sixty degrees around the whole lounge.

Also, the mural itself is a panorama of the Everglades, depicting a full menu of its wild inhabitants, from alligators, raccoons, deer and turtles to ibis, ducks and storks. Shepherd prepared for the task by making frequent excursions to the Glades to sketch his wildlife subjects. Then he began painting—and this is the funky part—not on the walls of the bar, but back in his gallery in West Palm Beach. He set up a series of separate, massive canvas panels and, along with his students, went to work with his brushes. When it was complete, they transported it all through empty acres of sugarcane fields until reaching the inn, where they permanently assembled it. But wait! There's more! In the hallway leading to the lounge hangs a row of gold-framed black-and-white photos showing the mural in progress back on the coast. That bonus material alone is so overwhelming that it's easy for visitors to get dizzy and knock over chairs. Actually, that was just me."

"Plus it's a bar," said Coleman.

"Normally I'd smack you, but in this case you're right," said Serge. "No snooty gallery patrons standing back and rubbing their chins in a passive-aggressive jab that you're a Philistine. Just a bunch of regular folk who know what they love."

Coleman crumpled a beer can. "I dig art." A fat finger made a red line on paper.

"Then your big chance is at hand, because the inn's upcoming on our tour." Serge walked over and taped another page to the wall. "Meantime, I'm going to keep working until my paintings encircle this entire room in homage to Shepherd and the hotel."

"But do we have enough time?"

Serge strolled over behind Malcolm. "The time lock says definitely." He raised the drooping bag again over his contestant's head. Buzzing increased.

He rejoined Coleman again at the table. "But I do need to pick up the pace." His index finger mixed red and white paint for a roseate spoonbill. His other hand clicked the television's remote.

"Excellent! I love it when you turn on a motel TV and *Law &
Order* is automatically rolling through a marathon! It's like a sign
from God."

"Why are you so into that show?"

"Because it's a comedy. Or at least the chase scenes are."

"How's that?"

"The writers apparently spend so much time on the genius of
the legal twists that they just backhand the action sequences into
the script."

"For instance?"

"If I've seen it once, I've seen it a hundred times: Lenny goes
to question a suspect at an automotive garage and flashes his
badge at the boss. 'Is Frenchy here?' And the boss turns to some
guy repairing a car up on a lift: 'Hey, Frenchy, the cops want to
talk to you.' So the guy now has this data: The cops know his
name, where he works, and most likely his home address. And
what's the logical thing he does every time? Throws a wrench at
them and runs out the back. Okay, first, that's a serious uphill
explanation to your boss later. Although I don't know the auto
repair culture. Maybe everyone's constantly throwing tools and
running away, and after lunch they all have a big laugh. Anyway,
they always catch Frenchy trying to climb a fence or cornering
himself on a rooftop. To mix it up, sometimes it's a loading dock
at a shipping company. 'Hey, Three-Fingers Louie, the police are
here again.' And they catch Louie every time because he runs
into a huge stack of empty cardboard boxes that are placed right
where everyone walks."

"How do you know they're empty?"

"The way they fly like they're filled with helium," said Serge.
"Let's watch."

They turned toward the TV.

"Hey, Bugsy, the police want to talk . . ."

"There goes the wrench," said Coleman. "He's running . . .
damn, cardboard boxes *and* a fence."

"I called it."

Coleman pointed with a purple finger. "Where's the science project at?"

Serge swirled his own finger on a page. "The screws have definitely begun anchoring, just a matter of reaching their depth."

"Mmmmmm! Mmmmmm!"

Serge sat back and sighed. "Am I the only one he's annoying?"

"No. He's getting under my skin, too."

They leaned over the table again and continued painting in silence . . .

The next morning, Serge shook Coleman's shoulder. Bloodshot eyes cracked open as he sat up and bonked his head. "Ow! Where am I?"

"Between the toilet and sink again." Serge checked his watch. "Look alive, we have miles ahead."

They went back into the main room.

"Damn, you really did finish your mural," said Coleman. "There's even a wild turkey. I recognize it from the bottles."

"You had any doubts?"

"Don't take this the wrong way, but sometimes you get super excited and throw yourself into a really long project, and five minutes later you say fuck that and trash everything and take off in the car with your camera."

"You're thinking of the time I wanted to build an exquisitely detailed cardboard model from my own design of the old Orange Bowl during Super Bowl Three in Miami, complete with the Jets and Colts players and each person in the stands. I misjudged the seating capacity."

"What was the seating?"

"Eighty thousand."

"How many seats did you make before you quit?"

"Five. But let's not dwell on setbacks beyond our control." Serge stood behind Malcolm, carefully peeling the tape off his forehead and gathering up the edges of the plastic garbage bag.

At the first glimpse of the captive's head, Serge sprang backward. "Jesus!"

"Mmmmmm! Mmmmmm!"

"Can I see?" asked Coleman.

"It'll give you bad dreams."

Coleman looked anyway. "God-*daaaaaamn*! . . . Man, this is you at your sickest."

"Not my intention. I underestimated the gross-out factor." Serge tied off the plastic trash bag and threw it in a motel garbage can. "Oh, well. I'll just think about that retired couple he tried to swindle and it'll balance the scales . . . Get your luggage."

Coleman grabbed a handle. "He doesn't look like he feels so hot."

Serge opened the motel room door and turned to the hostage one last time. "Remember: Bacon, it's not just for breakfast anymore."

Chapter 17

Friday. Game day.

After school, Coach Calhoun was at his desk finishing up notes on the opponent's defensive line.

A light knock at the door. "You wanted to see me, Coach?"

"Yes, yes, come in."

Chris respectfully took a seat, and Calhoun walked around his desk, leaning casually against its front edge, just as he had during so many other player discussions. Like most of the coaches in The Muck, he knew that football was often the only anchor in these kids' lives. A whistle hanging from your neck meant serving double duty as a priest.

"Chris, other than your report cards, I realize I really don't know anything about you. What's your family like?"

"You mean my grandmother?"

"I mean your whole family."

"It's my grandmother."

"What about your dad?"

"I don't know."

"Mom?"

"I don't know."

"Brothers and sisters?"

She shook her head.

"How old is your grandmother?"

"Old."

"Friends?"

"A few. Mainly boys. All the girls where I live are much older."

"Where do you live?"

She told him. He knew the place. One of those long two-story apartment buildings that looked like a converted motel, because it was. Not a blade of landscaping, just hot dirt and litter. People coming and going at odd hours for wrong reasons.

Calhoun took stock. "You said you had a few friends?"

"Mainly at school. Actually all."

"So what do you do for fun when you're at home?"

"I like to read."

"Like what?"

That got her bubbly. "Oh, wow, I found this great book at the library." She unzipped the backpack in her lap and handed a volume to the coach.

He examined the front cover. "What's this?"

"Astrophysics."

"You're reading about the big bang?"

"It's the foundation for everything. You have to learn that if you're going to study anything else." Chris grew animated with excitement. "Most people don't realize that the bang wasn't an explosion but actually an expansion of space and time, like a balloon inflating, which allowed early matter to exceed the speed of light without violating Einstein's theory."

The coach blinked hard and flipped the book over to the back cover. "You actually understand this stuff?"

"Sure, the author breaks it all down and makes it real easy."

Calhoun handed the book back. "Chris, I know this might be sensitive, but . . . are you okay?"

"What do you mean?"

"Well, I mean, for example, have you ever been bullied?"

Excitement stopped. Chris folded in . . .

I f you've ever had a full handful of sand thrown directly in your eyes at point-blank range, it's something you'll never forget. It's not like you've *got* something in your eyes that you have to get out; you're totally shut down. Disabled in every way. Nose running. The insane pain from the first time you try to raise your eyelids. The only option is to stagger and grope blindly for a place with a water source to flush it out.

It helps if there's someone to guide you. It doesn't help if there's only cruel laughter as you stumble for safety that isn't available. Especially if the nearest water source is a canal full of alligators.

It was one of her earliest recollections. Followed by the sound of a rusty old pickup truck speeding away on a dirt road from another rabbit hunt. Then quiet. Chris felt along with her feet to locate the edge of the road, then down the embankment into the reeds. Fortunately there were no gators today. Chris splashed her face until she could manage to open two red slits and find her way back to town.

The public health clinic gave her prescription ointment for scratched corneas.

"Who did this to you?" asked the nurse.

"I did it to myself."

There were the other times. *All* the other times. It never involved sand again, but you get the picture. Some of the boys actually felt sorry for her and knew it would be the right thing to step in, but they lacked that certain gravitas in the pecking order, and so life went on as it does in the jungle of childhood.

One time that was different. A new mix of boys in the pickup truck. Before long she was facedown again between cane stalks, a large boy pinning her with knees in her back, twisting her right arm almost to the point of a radial fracture. Chris prayed for him to let go, but she never screamed.

Then, suddenly, her arm was free. And the weight was off her back.

"Dammit, Reggie! Why'd you punch me in the head?"

"What's wrong with you? She's half your size."

"Fuck off!" The tormentor ran away.

Chris rolled over in the dirt, and the boy named Reggie helped her up. "Maybe you shouldn't come out here with these guys."

"I want to play football."

That was the last day Reggie was with her group, and then it was back to old routines again. At least she did catch the occasional rabbit, which meant a buck or two toward her football fund. Chris had bought a number of footballs in her short life. Sometimes she was able to play with one for two or three days before it was gone. A football was too precious for Chris to forget and leave somewhere. It was just snatched from her hands. One ball was even stolen as she stepped out of the store where she bought it. She stopped buying footballs and started sitting.

Chris would sit on a milk crate on the balcony outside her grandmother's apartment. Elbows on her knees, chin resting on her fists. She stared out into the empty street with eyes that were lasers of rage. She was one of the happiest kids you'd ever meet, which meant other kids had to make her sad. An hour could easily go by with Chris not moving, eyes locked in that fierce gaze. But it wasn't a gaze of negativity that eats you alive from the inside. It was a look of ferocious, distilled determination. She began sitting out there so often and so long that many adults in the apartment building began subconsciously associating her with that milk crate.

She usually sat on the crate after being run off from whatever the neighborhood boys were having fun doing. The few girls who were around were much older, with their own social castes and more subtle ways of hurting. Chris just kept sitting and glaring with such intensity you'd think she was going to hemorrhage. What was she thinking about all that time?

When Chris wasn't sitting on that crate or getting run off, she spent time in her room, tending curiosity. That meant books from the school library. She loved the science ones. Volcanoes, the planets, how clouds form, photosynthesis. But her all-time favorite was a book about sea creatures. The only thing she knew from Pahokee was Lake Okeechobee and all the bass fishermen, because it was fresh water. But this book brimmed with gripping pictures that filled her imagination with the faraway world of the ocean. Urchins and rays and giant squid. She was particularly fascinated by every detail in the life cycle of the hermit crab. Then there was another book she had purchased, one with holes in it. A collector's book. She would press pennies into the holes according to year, and read voraciously about the mints in Denver and San Francisco, and the wartime pennies made of zinc because artillery shells needed the copper.

But a child like Chris was meant to be outdoors, which meant she was relentless at trying to join in and being run off and sitting on a crate. Here's what she was thinking on that crate: *I'll show them. Someday they'll want to be my friend. They all will . . .* Of course she was just a little kid and only had so much life experience to work with, so she thought: *Yes, something urgent will come up with the boys. Suddenly they'll all need really important information about hermit crabs or Lincoln pennies, and then where will they have to come? That's right, me . . .* She maintained her severe glare of tunnel vision, fantasizing about all the kids in the neighborhood coming up the street in a V formation, led by the biggest and most popular. They'd climb up to her apartment balcony and beg forgiveness, and she'd tell them about crustaceans or loose change or both.

Adults weren't the only ones who observed Chris's devotion to that milk crate. Some of the boys also began to notice. They pointed up at the balcony and laughed. Then it became a running joke. Whenever she tried to hang out and participate in whatever they were doing: "Why don't you go home to your milk crate?"

It began following her around, even when she wasn't trying to join in. She'd be walking down the sidewalk and then shouts from across the street, in a shitty, singsong taunting chant: "Milk *crate* . . . Milk *crate* . . ."

Then they took it further, and it became her nickname. "Where are you going, *Milk Crate*?"

It only made Chris stomp her feet harder on the way home. Ironically, her main source of solace and strength became sitting on that crate. So sit she did. *One day!* . . . *One day!* . . .

Then one day Chris came home from school and found that someone had stolen her milk crate.

"Chris? Chris?" said Coach Calhoun. "Did you hear me? Have you ever been bullied?"

"Huh, what?" She raised her chin from her fists. "I'm sorry. I drifted there for a second."

"I was asking about bullies."

"Oh no. Not really."

"I've never seen a look like that in your eyes before," said Calhoun. "You almost scared me."

"Just tired."

"I heard they call you Milk Crate, not out of affection. And they stole yours."

"No big deal. I got another."

"Okay, if you say so . . . We need to start getting ready for the game."

"You got it, Coach." Chris went to a storage locker for the paper cups.

The game went pretty much as expected, a rout by Pahokee. Reggie was awarded the game ball.

An hour later, the last of the team dribbled out of the locker room in street clothes, laughing and recounting key plays that now loomed larger in their imaginations. Coach Calhoun emerged and headed for his car.

He stopped. The field and stands were empty now, just a single small person at the far end repeatedly trying to kick a football through the uprights.

One of the field maintenance people walked past the coach, opened the main power box and threw a large circuit breaker, turning off the stadium lights. Chris just teed up again and kicked one in the dark.

"Excuse me," Calhoun said to the maintenance guy. "Could you turn the lights back on?"

Chapter 18

THE ATLANTIC COAST

Florida has a lot of cities and towns with *fort* in the name. Given everything else, why not?

Fort Lauderdale, Fort Myers, Fort Meade, Fort Lonesome, Fort White, Fort Walton Beach. Tampa used to be Fort Brooke, and Ocala was Fort King. And there are more than a hundred other well-known actual forts, many still in existence, for which communities are not named. As late as the early twentieth century, the Sunshine State was still frontier country. While people in Manhattan attended operas and Yankee games, many Floridians were, well, Seminoles, the unconquered people, living down in the Glades.

A gold Plymouth Satellite revved south down coastal Highway A1A, through one of the last long, relatively empty and nonberserk stretches of Florida seaside where you can hear yourself think, and that voice is whispering not to take it for granted. Driving by Patrick Air Force Base, through Indialantic, Melbourne Beach, Sebastian Inlet, Wabasso Beach, past the Navy SEAL Museum before turning inland at the jetties.

Into Fort Pierce.

The city is located on the east coast of Florida about sixty miles north of West Palm Beach, named after the army fort built during the Second Seminole War in 1938, which in turn was named for Colonel Benjamin Pierce, brother of the fourteenth president of the United States, for what that's worth. Fort Pierce is the home of the A. E. Backus Gallery, in honor of the famous natural-landscape artist, and birthplace of the Florida Highwaymen painters movement. But in more recent years, as more and more people discover the past, it's developed a growing reputation for something else.

Zora Neale Hurston was a black woman traveling Florida in the 1930s. Not the best time for that combination in the Jim Crow South. Yet she carried it off with such class and dignity that you can only genuflect. She was a novelist, historian, anthropologist and a standout in the Harlem Renaissance scene. Or that's how one avid Floridian put it.

"Stetson Kennedy was often at the wheel of the car," said Serge, at the wheel of the gold Plymouth heading west on Avenue D. "The state's connective tissue I spoke of earlier. Rawlings to Stetson to Zora. She roamed the back roads with him, preserving local history and chronicling her times, kind of like us."

The Plymouth turned north as Serge chugged a travel mug of coffee. "Zora is often associated with Eatonville, one of the first self-governing African American communities, which used to be north of Orlando, and is now engulfed by it. They have a festival for her each year." The car continued a short distance until easing to a stop at 1734 Avenue I. "But Hurston spent her last years here." An arm pointed.

Coleman looked oddly out the window. "That tiny-ass house?"

"Realtors prefer to call it cozy." Serge got out of the car with his mug. "While Zora was well known and respected in literary circles, her body of work never really gained traction with the general public until well after her death in 1960. In fact, Zora lived out her last decade in destitute obscurity. She taught briefly at a local school, wrote a few articles for the local paper, even worked as a motel maid. But her undaunted pride and individual spirit never waned. Near the end she wrote: 'I have made phenomenal growth as a creative artist . . . If I die without money, somebody will bury me.'"

They walked across a tidy lawn toward a modest light blue stucco house with a flat roof. Couldn't be more than five hundred square feet.

"This was her last home." Serge stopped to absorb invisible rays coming off it. "Sometimes history puts the right person at the right place at the right time. Just after Hurston died, a sheriff's deputy named Pat Duval happened to be driving by here when he noticed someone burning trash in a big oil drum. He stopped to inquire, and the man said he was disposing of stuff from the house. Now, the deputy happened to be one of the few people at the time who had read Hurston and knew her worth. He quickly put out the fire, saving invaluable manuscripts and personal papers. Doesn't that spin your derby?"

Coleman was paying attention to something else. "What's with that big sign?"

"Official marker for the house, stop number three of eight on the Hurston Dust Tracks Heritage Trail," said Serge. "The city of Fort Pierce rightfully stepped up to honor Hurston and educate the masses, which I'm totally down with."

"Then why that look on your face?"

Serge finished his coffee in a long swig. "I like to dig up these off-the-path places on my own, and the sign makes it look like I cheated. But I knew about this place before the sign, I swear!" He grabbed Coleman by the front of his shirt. "After I'm gone, you're the only one who can set the record straight!"

"Sure thing," said Coleman. "My shirt . . ."

"Sorry." Serge released him. "Do you think I'm over-reacting?"

"Who am I to judge?"

"I've been thinking of getting a service animal," said Serge. "Or switching to decaf."

"Service animal?" said Coleman. "You're not disabled."

"Oh, how wrong you are," said Serge. "I'm crazy, whack job, nut-bar, basketcase, Looney Tunes, Froot Loops, cuckoo for Cocoa Puffs, screws loose, not playing with a full deck, batshit, bats in the belfry, off my rocker, off the deep end, out where the buses don't run. Stop me when I've made my point."

"No, I get it. I already knew but didn't want to say anything." Coleman whistled. "Wow, you're really admitting that to yourself?"

"Of course. What's the big deal?" Serge got out his camera. "Everyone's a little bit crazy, but my case is state-of-the-art. Usually it's a blessing, endowing me with supernatural powers of free-range thinking: Pavlov's dog, pinecones, softer bath tissue, covalent molecules, Pyrrhic victories, Lou Gehrig, nuance, the induction cooktop, the Yalta Conference, rationalization, pasteurization, Lou Gehrig's *disease*, Lemon Pledge, the number fifty-six, 'Jailhouse Rock,' opening products to void warranty, Hot Pockets, rainfall at the airport, Aztec beating hearts, osmosis, buy-one-get-one, frequent having to go, Netflix original series . . ."

Coleman crushed another beer can. "What about the rest of the time?"

". . . Hydraulic fluid, *Portnoy's Complaint,* the camel's nose under the tent, vote motherfucker! . . . What?"

"The rest of the time?" said Coleman. "When it's not a blessing?"

"Then there's screaming and pointing, and we have to run away again."

"I don't see how a service animal can fix that."

"When you say service animal, most people think of a guide dog leading the blind or performing other essential tasks for the handicapped." Serge handed his camera to Coleman. "But there's a whole other sub-category called 'emotional support animals,' who take the edge off mental conditions. Except that when you're dealing with crazy, you get the kind of animal selections you'd expect. And you wouldn't believe the growing list that is now confounding the transportation industry: from tiny pigs and iguanas to parrots and even boa constrictors, who are said to be able to detect certain seizures in advance and give a little warning squeeze. Other times the squeeze is a different warning—'Get this fucking snake off me!'—so there's an obvious downside. Even some *animals* have support animals. Thoroughbred horse breeders often place a donkey in a stall if one of their studs has a history of spazzing out."

"That's weird."

"I'm thinking of getting a meerkat."

"You mean those cute little guys on nature shows who stand up to look for trouble?"

Serge nodded. "A meerkat could level me out." He walked to the front of the house and smiled. "Take my picture at Zora's. Make sure not to get the sign . . ."

MEANWHILE . . .

In a Cocoa Beach motel room: a ticking sound, then a loud snap.

Malcolm frantically pulled his wrists free from the time lock. He felt the top of his head. "*Ahhhhhhhhh!*"

He ran out of the motel room and into the office.

The jaundiced manager jumped back from the counter. "Ahhhhhhh! What happened to your head? . . ."

Ten minutes later, the motel parking lot swarmed with police vehicles. In the motel office, someone pulled a sheet over a body. The officer in charge looked up. "What the hell happened?"

The motel manager shrugged. "He came in here demanding bacon and then collapsed."

An officer stuck his head in the door. "Lieutenant, I think there's something you need to see."

They rushed up the walkway and entered room number 7. The officer nodded toward a wall.

"Finger paintings?" said the lieutenant.

"I recognize it," said the officer. "The Everglades mural from the Clewiston Inn. The lounge is closed now, but they're really nice about letting guests in. You should go."

The lieutenant glared. "I thought you had some key evidence." He pointed in the general direction of the office. "What's wrong with you? There's a body getting cold back there."

The officer told the lieutenant to take a closer look at one of the paintings.

He did.

It was signed by the artist.

Chapter 19

A faithful stuffed wahoo with glazed eyes stared down from an office wall at a man cradling the receiver of a desk phone between his shoulder and neck. That left his hands free to take vigorous notes.

"Thank you very much for your time." He hung up.

After that final international call to a Dominican Republic historical society, Captain Crack Nasty had everything he could possibly find on one Fulgencio Fakakta, right up until he fled the island in 1921. After that, the years in Florida were still a mystery that phone calls couldn't solve. From here, it was in-person homework.

Time for a road trip.

Crack climbed into the cab of his Dodge Dakota pickup and headed west on Southern Boulevard. He left the outskirts of coastal development, passing the vintage Lion Country Safari roadside attraction, subconsciously thinking, *How old are those animals?* Then onward through Twentymile Bend, all the way out to where the first fumes of development picked up again as he neared the big lake. The road's name changed to Hooker Highway. The schoolkids got a kick out of that.

The captain started at the Pahokee and Belle Glade libraries, looking through special collections of old newspaper microfilms. He drove past the hurricane monument on the way over to the courthouses for records of faded deeds. He cruised the back roads around the addresses he had jotted down. Then he widened his circles of driving out into the nearest sugarcane fields. He picked up a tail. Not law enforcement, but local young men in their twenties. He thought: *What has gone insane in this world when blacks are allowed to follow whites in the Deep South?* Except his surveillance wasn't threatening; it was concerned. The three youths were watching out for their neighbors because Crack's movements around town came off like he was planning some kind of crime. Which was accurate.

The salvager was more than relieved when he reached his next stop, the local police department. Crack asked to speak with their public-affairs spokesman, and was led into an office with a football in a display case on the desk. The captain said he was writing for one of those metal-detector hobby magazines, and he wanted to ask about some rumors he'd been hearing.

"Oh, so that's why you've been driving around here all suspicious like," said the sergeant.

"You know I've been driving around?" said Crack. "Then I need to tell you there were these dangerous characters following me."

"How do you think we found out you were driving around?" said the sergeant. "The guys following you called us on their cell phones. And they're not dangerous; they used to play on the football team. They just thought you were up to something. Are you?"

"Me? What? Huh?" Crack displayed upturned palms. "Just working on my article. I heard some folklore about a sugar kingpin who supposedly went missing in the 1928 hurricane, along with some artifacts of historical significance and maybe a couple coins."

"I've heard the same." The sergeant smiled. "And that's exactly what that is. Folklore."

"But I also heard that children playing out in the sugarcane fields have found a few of these coins over the decades since the storm."

"Another bit of fanciful folklore," said the sergeant. "In all the years, we haven't known a single actual child who found anything. And do you think little kids can keep something like that a secret? They'd bring it to school and show it all around in class, and by the end of the day it would be confiscated by a teacher for depriving others of their education."

"But I've learned so much about the history of this sugar guy from the Dominican that it seems more likely—"

The sergeant held up a hand. "My advice to you? And I mean this politely: Forget about your article. We've got a nice friendly town here, and we mean to keep it that way. Visitors are always welcome, especially all those college football scouts. But what we don't need is a bunch of people running around like headless chickens with metal detectors, trespassing and digging up the whole place. Do you see how it could get messy?"

"Well, it also won't do my magazine's reputation any good if we direct people here and nobody finds anything." Captain Crack stood and stretched. "Not all of these article ideas pan out. Guess I'll just be getting back to West Palm."

"You seem like a reasonable person," said the sergeant. He shook Crack's hand. "Stop in anytime."

Crack left the office, and the sergeant picked up the phone. "I need you to follow someone . . . Yeah, Dodge Dakota with a magnetic sign on the door for a boat-towing service . . ."

Captain Crack tapped the steering wheel to a country music tune about only being able to trust his dog anymore. The pickup truck passed vacant concrete buildings of pink, green and blue. He checked his rearview. Just as he thought. A police tail. But it was a loose one, not meant for strict surveillance as much as making sure he kept his word to leave town.

A few minutes later, Highway 98 said goodbye to the last building, and Crack left the city limits. He looked up in the mirror again, and watched the police car make a lazy U-turn in the road and head the other way. The captain drove another half mile through nothing but cane fields, then made a sharp left onto a road usually used only by the sugar company. After a few zigzags, he navigated a wide route back into town. He deliberately parked out of sight behind a small business near Main Street.

Bells jingled.

A pawnshop owner named Webber looked up from a newspaper. *Finally,* he thought. Not a kid, not police, but a real customer. He folded the paper. "How can I help you?"

"Gold pieces."

"Only have a few." Webber opened the back of a glass display case. "But a real nice one came in a few years ago. Just haven't been able to sell it because, well, the economy around here. Saint-Gaudens double eagle, 1907. If you don't know, it's one of the—"

"I know the coin," said Crack. "How'd you come by it in these parts?"

"I'm sorry, but that information is confidential." Webber set the coin on the counter for Crack to examine. "We strictly protect the privacy of all our customers."

"It was a kid, wasn't it?"

The pawnshop owner's head jerked up straight on his neck. "How'd you know?"

"Been doing my research. I'll bet you've had a number of kids bring these in over the years. What can you tell me about them?"

The owner stepped back with hands on his hips. "Mister, what's really your business here? You didn't come to buy a coin."

Crack opened his wallet. "How much?"

"You're really going to buy it? You haven't even looked at—... I mean I usually have to work harder for a sale." He glanced at the gold circle still sitting on the counter. "In that condition it books for . . ."—Webber adjusted the number upward in his head mid-sentence—". . . seventeen hundred."

Crack pulled money from the billfold. "Would you settle for, say, two thousand? In cash."

Webber scratched the top of his head. "You sure have a funny way of negotiating."

"There's a catch."

"That, I assumed."

"I'll also need the name and address of the person who sold it to you."

Webber paused again. "So you really believe kids are bringing these coins in?"

"Sure, why not?"

"Because the police think I'm fencing stolen collections."

"That's because they haven't done their homework. Do you know anything about an early sugar baron around here named Fulgencio Fakakta?"

"Everyone's heard the stories," said Webber. "Especially the part about his hidden treasure lost in the Great Hurricane . . . Wait, you're not looking for . . ."

"I never said anything about treasure. You did." Crack leaned down to the counter. "Why? You don't believe that these kids found pieces of the baron's stash?"

"Not really," said Webber. "As I was telling the cops, from the dates on these coins, that's when there were all these juke joints—"

"I've read up on the local history," said Crack. "The name and the coin? Do we have a deal?"

Webber considered the stranger a moment, then began writing on a blank sheet of paper.

"On second thought," said Captain Crack, pulling out more bills. "Make it an even three thousand."

"Another catch?"

"I was never here."

Webber handed him the paper. "You're already a ghost."

"One more thing." Crack gave him a business card. "If any other kids come in here with more coins, call me and I'll buy them. Same price and terms."

"You got it."

Bells jingled.

Chapter 20

The gold Plymouth Satellite rolled up to the corner of Avenue S and Seventeenth Street. Serge got out and looked at another sign.

GARDEN OF HEAVENLY REST.

For a cemetery, it was sparsely populated. No big monuments or even large headstones. The rows of modest markers and slabs were widely separated in an otherwise sunny grass field where kids would have room to play ball. Coleman looked side to side as they walked past graves. "I'm guessing you have a cool story to drag me out here."

"One of the best stories yet!" Serge continued on until they reached the middle of the field. A single grave sat in the grass, surrounded by a small brick walkway. The whitewashed slab was raised slightly higher than the others, although the headstone was still only knee-high. It was the only one where people had been by recently to leave flowers. There was a candle. Some had left rocks on the headstone in the Jewish tradition.

Serge got down on a knee and placed his page over the letter *Z*. He began rubbing. "Hurston's undeserved obscurity had become so complete that her grave was unmarked for years and nobody could precisely pay their respects. Then the story takes a hairpin turn, extending beyond the grave to Zora's proper place in the public's awareness."

"It was only right," said Coleman.

"The year? Nineteen seventy-three. The person? Alice Walker." Serge rubbed on. "Walker was still nearly a decade away from writing her Pulitzer Prize–winning novel, *The Color Purple*. But back in the early seventies, the budding writer, still only twenty-nine years old, stumbled across Zora's works and became intrigued, even obsessed to the point of visiting Florida to get the vibes of Zora's life. She started in Eatonville, where she learned Zora was buried anonymously somewhere in Fort Pierce. So she drove out here to the coast and—this part I love—she fibbed that she was Zora's niece to get locals to open up about her 'aunt.' To her surprise, most had never heard of her, even those now living near Zora's last home. Finally, with a history-researching tenacity to which I can only aspire, she located the lost grave and bought this headstone for it." Serge began rubbing the words on the next line: A GENIUS OF THE SOUTH. "Two years later, Walker wrote a watershed article for *Ms.* magazine, 'Looking for Zora,' using her grave search as a vehicle to showcase the forgotten literary lion. That first-person piece slowly but surely rekindled interest in Hurston's work until she now stands in the pantheon. Oh, and she's from Florida!"

The gold Plymouth left the cemetery and headed south on U.S. 1, down through Jensen Beach and Stuart.

"Where to now?" asked Coleman.

"Our next stop," said Serge. "But first I need to make a *stop* before our next stop."

He pulled into a strip mall and opened the door.

"I'll wait in the car," said Coleman.

"As a general rule, that's the best plan." Serge went inside . . .

Coleman was unconscious when Serge returned, head resting against the passenger window and trademark drool stringing down from his lower lip.

Onward, south. Hobe Sound, Tequesta, Jupiter.

Coleman stirred from his liquid-induced nap. "Hmm, huh, where am I?"

"Still in the car."

Coleman reached down between his legs and popped a Schlitz to restore chemical equilibrium. "Did you get your meerkat back at that pet store?"

"No," said Serge, racing south into Juno Beach. "I didn't have any clue that they're like a thousand bucks, and they'd have to order one. Plus the pet-store guy told me that meerkats may be social creatures among themselves, but they're a little confused by the whole pet concept. Some never conform to domesticity, constantly screeching and jumping on lamps, and the ones that do work out will keep peeing on your clothes to mark you as their owner."

"That's messed up," said Coleman.

"Not exactly the definition of a support animal," said Serge. "I want a pet to wind me *down*."

"You'll figure something out." Coleman took a long swig of beer. Suddenly: "Ahh! Shit! What the hell?" The can of Schlitz went up in the air, Coleman batting and bobbling to catch it, foam everywhere.

"Are you spraying beer all over my car again?"

"Not my fault." Coleman finally got a handle on the can and pulled his neck way back in alarm, looking down in his lap in terror. "What the fuck is that thing?"

Serge glanced over. "Say hello to Mr. Zippy, my new ferret."

"Ferret?"

"When a meerkat became a non-starter, the pet-store dude suggested a ferret because they're roughly the same size and cuteness factor, easier on the wallet, and they don't pee on you. Not much."

The ferret began chattering at Coleman. "Get him off me! Get him off!" Beer flew again.

"You're frightening Zippy!" said Serge. "You need to win him over. Give him that Cheeto."

"Where?"

"Where else."

"Oh." Coleman picked it off his shoulder and tentatively extended a hand. Mr. Zippy snatched it, munching away. Then he climbed over the shoulder of a wide-eyed Coleman. "Where'd he go?"

"To explore the back seat."

"You're just going to let him run loose in the car?"

"It's what I'd want if the roles were reversed," said Serge. "Now back to live action! Our next stop is some more Florida connective tissue, this time leading from Hurston. In her now-acclaimed 1937 classic, *Their Eyes Were Watching God,* Zora depicts the hard life of African Americans along the southern shore of Lake Okeechobee early last century, culminating with the Great Hurricane of 1928—"

The ferret jumped on the dashboard and ran along the windshield, then jumped down and disappeared again.

"Jesus, Serge, how can you drive with that going on?"

"It's actually quite comforting." A calm grin crept across his face. "After the storm, Zora described the formidable task of dealing with almost three thousand bodies, so many that it took at least four burial sites . . ."

The Plymouth entered West Palm Beach and navigated south on Tamarind Avenue, into an economically scuffling section of the city, or, among the whites, the other side of the tracks. They parked on the corner of Twenty-Fifth Street.

"Hurston's novel described the mass burial activity here, but the site became so forgotten that even those who knew about it didn't have the exact location, and a warehouse was almost built on top of it. Luckily, community leaders stepped in and hired a Miami firm that used ground-penetrating radar to discover a seventy-by-thirty-foot trench." Serge placed paper against stone. "This is the granite memorial they erected in 2003."

Coleman curiously watched Serge.

"What?"

He pointed. "Where'd you get that?"

"This?" Serge looked down at something new on his chest attached to shoulder straps. "From the pet store. It's like those things that moms wear to carry infants."

Mr. Zippy poked his head out the top of the canvas pouch and looked around.

"He's growing on me," said Coleman.

Back to the car. A couple miles south on Dixie Highway, another stop.

"There's the Norton Museum of Art. Remember? From the Everglades mural?"

"We're going there?"

"No, other side of the street."

"On one condition," said Coleman.

"Now you're setting conditions, are you?"

Coleman told him what it was. "... *Pleeeeeease!*"

The pair walked through a grand stone archway into Wood-lawn Cemetery.

"Because of segregation at the time of the hurricane, the mass grave for the whites was here. Unlike the others, they got pine boxes ... How's it working out over there?"

Coleman smiled and looked down at the pouch on his chest.

"I think Mr. Zippy likes me." A burst of chattering and then a tiny head disappeared. "So you came to see another mass grave?"

"Not this time." Serge led the way through the ancient grounds until stopping at a stone with the name Charles William Pierce.

Coleman gently patted the pouch. "Who's that?"

"A bonus find unconnected to the hurricane, so how can I not stop?" Serge knelt to rub again. "In 1888, Charlie became one of the state's first legendary 'barefoot mailmen.' Because there was no land route back then between West Palm and Miami, mail carriers would make a six-day, hundred-and-thirty-mile trek, much of it traversed on foot along the beach, hence the name . . ." He turned and began running back to the car. "We're off!"

"Come on, Mr. Zippy!"

Chapter 21

FOUR YEARS EARLIER

A loud bell rang nonstop.

The local junior high was dismissed for the day. Kids poured out the doors like the Berlin Wall had fallen. Backpacks, skateboards, cell phones. Someone pushed someone else into the bushes.

A Dodge Dakota quietly eased up to the curb across the street.

A girl texted as she crossed the road.

"Excuse me?" Crack hung out the window. "Miss?"

She looked up. Uh-oh. Stranger Danger.

"Don't be scared," said Crack, checking the scrap of paper from the pawnshop. "I'm just looking for my nephew. Do you know a Ricky Aparicio?"

She pointed back at the school gates.

Captain Crack stretched his neck. "Which one?"

"I thought he was your nephew."

"Been a long time."

"Red shirt, blue shorts." She hurried along on her way.

The boy headed north on the opposite side of the street, along with a dozen other loud, laughing kids. Crack started up his truck and drove slowly. Parts of the gang peeled off as they reached the streets to their homes. It was down to just a few when Crack hung out the window again.

"Ricky! Ricky Aparicio!"

The boy looked over. "Who are you?"

Crack waved with his left hand. "Come over here. I need to ask you a question."

"Don't go," said one of the other boys.

"See what he wants," said another.

Ricky decided to split the difference and walked halfway across the empty street. "What do you want?"

"Come closer," said Crack. "I won't bite."

"I'm staying right here until you tell me what this is about."

"It concerns the gold coin you sold to the pawnshop."

"I didn't steal it!"

"Nobody says you did." The captain held out a piece of currency. "I just need some information. I'm writing an article for a hobby magazine."

"Ricky!" yelled one of the boys on the other curb. "Don't get any closer!"

"Ricky!" yelled another. "That's a hundred-dollar bill!"

Ricky got closer. "Exactly what kind of information?"

"I've been doing some research on your town, the hurricane and everything, and I think you might have stumbled onto something historic. I'll pay you a hundred dollars to show me where you found that coin."

Ricky stood like a statue. A beeping car drove around him.

Crack hung farther out the driver's window. "Listen, I know what you've been taught about strangers. But how would I know all this information about what you found? Besides, all those warnings are for little kids. You're practically a man now."

Ricky remained a stone.

"What do you say?" Crack waved the bill tauntingly. "Hundred bucks. Going once, going twice—"

"Okay, okay, but give me the money first."

"Once you're in the truck, or you'll just run away."

Ricky got in, and the Dodge drove off. The other boys dashed home to tell their parents . . .

It was ten minutes of dubious directions from the youth. "Take this left. Wait, the next left, that's it. No, that's not right. It's farther up."

"Are you sure you know where we're going?"

"Positive." Ricky clutched the hundred as if it was life itself. "Uh, could we go back to town and start again? I can figure it out better if we're coming from Main Street. From this other way, I'm not so good."

"Jesus," Crack said under his breath. But greed had gotten the better of him, and he was locked in for the ride, seeing nothing but piles of those coins.

T he Crossroads.

If the intersection had one of those signposts with wooden arrows pointing different directions with names of places and mileage, all the arrows on this post would have said Nowhere.

Three of the corners were empty except for concrete-block ruins with collapsed roofs, and weeds now grew where there had been carpeting.

On the fourth corner sat a gas station that sold as much malt liquor as unleaded.

Signs said No Loitering, at least under the spray-paint graffiti.

Three young men lounged on a stoop. All high school graduates, all football players, all with onetime dreams of making the NFL. Now they spent their days here. This was not the NFL.

Wasn't their fault. Life had dealt them truly cruel hands of cards. If you take a hundred successful Wall Street types and have them born at the very bottom with no breaks, see how far they go. This particular trio all had jobs. The operative word was *had*. When the economy coughed, The Muck got pneumonia, and layoffs were a lifestyle. The three currently had a bunch of job applications submitted all over town, but where were the jobs? So they hung out here until something turned up.

"Remember that pass I caught in the fourth quarter? Right sideline?"

"You and that one freaking pass! All we ever hear: 'Remember? Right sideline?' Shit, I had three receptions that game."

"But all short yardage over the middle."

"Moved us into scoring position, didn't it?"

"Both of you are bullshit," said the third young man. "Just remember who *threw* all those passes."

They stopped talking and watched as a lone vehicle slowly rounded the corner at the station and accelerated east. Magnetic door sign for a boat-towing company. They all sprang to their feet.

"That son of a bitch!"

"He's back!"

"And he's got Ricky!"

They piled into a low-riding Datsun and took off.

"I knew that asshole was up to something, but I didn't know what. He's a pedophile!"

"He'll kill Ricky for sure if we don't stop him!"

"Shouldn't we call the police?"

"Screw that! We can take care of our own . . ."

A mile out of town, Ricky pointed. "Turn here. This time I'm sure."

"If you say so." The Dakota made a skidding left onto a dirt road.

Moments later, a tricked-out Datsun sailed by the turnoff. "I don't see his truck anymore."

"Drive faster. We'll catch up . . ."

Back in the cane field, Ricky hopped down from the pickup's cab and climbed through a couple rows of stalks. "It was right around here somewhere."

"You don't seem that sure."

Ricky stopped and stomped a foot into the black soil. "Right here."

"Exactly?" said Crack.

Ricky nodded vigorously. "Take me back now."

"Are you joking? I gave you a hundred. Show me!"

"How?"

"Dig!"

"What?"

"If you're so fucking sure, dig!"

Panic now. Ricky got on the ground and scooped dirt with shaking hands.

"Don't keep looking up at me!" yelled Crack. "Pay attention to what you're doing! Dig! . . ."

Up the road, parked on the right shoulder, more panic. "We just got Ricky killed!" said the wide receiver.

"Don't say that!" yelled the tight end.

"I knew we should have called the police," said the quarterback.

"What's done is done. We need to chill out and figure this thing out. What would a pedophile do?"

They looked all the way around the horizon. "Bring him out in a cane field," said the wide receiver. "For privacy and body disposal."

"Don't say that!" snapped the tight end.

"He must have taken a turnoff." The quarterback swung the car around. "Keep your eyes open . . ."

Somewhere out in the stalks, small hands flung dirt. A whimper.

Captain Crack had gotten back into the Johnnie Walker, swinging the bottle by his side. "What the hell are you crying about!"

"I want to go home."

"Shut up and dig!"

"I want my mommy."

Ricky never saw the open-handed slap coming. It cupped the side of his head over his ear and sent him sprawling.

Louder crying now. "I didn't find the coin. A girl did."

"You've been lying to me all along?" Slap. "Who is this girl?"

"I don't know! I swear!"

Slap.

"Kathy? Karen? I can't remember . . ."

Back on Highway 98, a Datsun was on a slow roll.

"Wait! Stop!"

"What is it?"

"Back up! I saw his truck!"

The quarterback threw the car in reverse, then barreled down the dirt road toward the parked Dakota. It skidded to a stop just as Ricky came bursting through the cane stalks, bloody nose, crying, ripped shirt.

The quarterback got down on a knee and hugged the boy tight.

Then another voice from an unseen source a few cane rows over. "Come back here, you little fucker!" The boat captain broke through the final row and stopped.

The quarterback stood up. Without looking down at Ricky, he placed a hand on the boy's shoulder. "Go wait in my car."

Crack Nasty pointed at them with the hand not holding the bottle. "Now you listen here! I gave him a hundred dollars and we had a deal!"

It was a short chase.

They gang-tackled the captain only a few steps from where he started. The ensuing beating was not for the squeamish. Savage kicks to the ribs and head as Crack desperately tried to crawl for sanctuary that wasn't there. More kicking and stomping in rage. It wasn't thug life. It was family life. One of them found a stick and smashed it over his neck. Another hit him with a rock. A few more kicks and Crack finally rolled onto his back, an unconscious, bloody mess. But the kicking continued.

The quarterback jumped in and grabbed the others. "Guys! Guys! Stop or you'll kill him!"

"So what?" Kick.

"I feel the same way, but if you think our lives are shit now . . ." He looked back at the Datsun. "Plus we need to get Ricky home. His mother must be worried sick."

They took turns spitting on Captain Crack.

Then the Datsun drove away.

Chapter 22

PORT MAYACA

The gold Plymouth picked up two-lane State Road 710, also known as the Bee Line Highway: an odd, almost perfectly diagonal shot northwest up through the unpopulated part of Palm Beach County, along the railroad tracks, through the Loxahatchee Slough, up past the old Pratt & Whitney aircraft-engine plant that brought thousands of transplants to the county in the early sixties. They reached Indiantown, and turned decidedly west on Route 76, into more and more nothingness.

Coleman petted the pouch on his chest and looked out the window at scraggly woods. "Are we actually heading anywhere?"

"Lake Okeechobee," said Serge. "Another of our crown jewels, so huge it dominates photos taken from the Space Shuttle. And to hell with it: I'm going on the record right now, and will take on all comers. At seven hundred and thirty square miles, Okeechobee is the largest freshwater lake in the country. Oh, sure, everyone else says it's the *second* biggest, behind Lake Michigan. But that one's open at the top, mixing with Canadian water. How is *that* the record? Where were the referees on that one?"

"It's just not fair."

"Canada, Christ." Serge shook his head. "*Our* lake is a damn force of nature. I like to think of it as Florida's moon."

"How is it a moon?"

"Give me some latitude on this, Judge Coleman, and I will show the relevance," said Serge. "Earth's moon is an oddity of our solar system, far closer and proportionately larger than any of the other planets' moons. So much so that it creates our ocean tides, affects the seasons and even stabilizes Earth's rotation, doing nothing less than making life possible at all. On a smaller scale, same thing with our freakishly large lake. Most Floridians have never seen it, and even fewer realize the overwhelming effect it has on the rest of the state. First, it collects much of the watershed in Central Florida, from the Kissimmee River and other sources. Then below it, the lake feeds the Everglades. And the extensive matrix of canals that were dug to channel its runoff created entire agricultural industries and—even more mind-blowing—the very dry land that allows much of South Florida, from Miami to Fort Lauderdale, to even exist. Otherwise, all the residents would be tits-deep in lily pads and gators instead of blissfully working skimming nets to scoop leaves from their swimming pools."

"I had no idea." Coleman held his beer away from the pouch and looked down at his chest. "You're not old enough."

"But here's the kicker, and it's a beauty . . ." Serge slowed and tracked their position on a GPS. "The Okeechobee hurricane of 1928 is still whipping up changes in the way we live, even to this day!"

"How can a storm that old still be messing with us?"

"I'll tell you!" The Plymouth slowed even further. "The three thousand souls that were lost made it the second-worst natural disaster in the nation's history, behind only the Galveston storm in 1900. Nobody saw it coming. Everyone was always preparing for storm surges from the ocean, but then that monster storm made a direct hit on the lake. And if you ever doubt how big that body of water is, imagine a tidal wave covering hundreds of square miles, much higher than virtually every house. First the storm's rotation flooded all the communities along the southern shore. Then the backside of the hurricane hit, pushing water north through the city of Okeechobee. After all the burials, the federal government stepped in to prevent such a tragedy. They built the enormous Herbert Hoover Dike, a thirty-foot-high, one-hundred-and-forty-three-mile-long earthen berm surrounding the lake. That's why so many people crisscrossing the state above and below the immense body of water never see it; they just dismiss it as a long grassy hill and have such screwed-up priorities that they aren't curious to take one of the access ramps to the top and marvel. That's why I've decided to carve out time and make the lake the culmination of our tour. Zora led us here."

"So we're almost at the end?" asked Coleman.

"Actually just beginning, but time folds in on itself." The gold Satellite pulled over on the side of an empty road without a sign of life. "I intend to drop anchor, explore the lake in every detail and get a bone-deep understanding of her people. It's an amazingly disparate culture: the old-cracker cattle ranchers up north with their rodeos, western-wear shops and steak houses; the impoverished farmworkers to the south; and all around, the visiting bass fishermen hoping to land that prized lunker."

Serge got out of the car with another large sheet of paper. He approached a green metal historic marker and began rubbing.

Coleman arrived with the ferret peeking around. "Where are we?"

Rub, rub. "Can't you read?"

"My eyes are having that focus problem again."

"We're at Port Mayaca, a ghost town with ghosts." Rub, rub.

"Out in that field somewhere lie the remains of sixteen hundred victims of the storm. As usual, people finally realized they needed to erect this sign decades later."

"Sixteen hundred?" Coleman blinked a few times.

"Right under our feet." Rub, rub. "It's important to remember."

"Shit! Dammit!"

"I know the storm was a heartbreak—"

"No, not that!" Coleman pointed.

"How'd you let Mr. Zippy get away?"

"He was too fast."

They began running around the field.

"Hold on," said Coleman. "I think I have some Doritos in my pocket."

"In your pocket?"

"Just in case." Coleman tossed one forward. "I think he's going for it."

"Here, let me have one." Serge crouched down and extended a hand. "It's working." The ferret stopped to nibble, and was gently picked up. "Give me that pouch!"

"No!" Coleman turned sideways and clutched it. "I want to carry him."

"You're obviously a bad influence," said Serge.

"I can change."

"Are we going to have a custody battle? The courts won't look fondly on your substance intake."

"What about you waxing dudes?"

Serge walked the legal proceedings through his head and saw them inevitably leading to foster care. "Okay, for *now*. Just keep on top of him."

The Plymouth drove a short distance farther west, over the train tracks, reaching Highway 98 and more emptiness. "Port Mayaca is another Florida settlement abandoned by time. Besides the cemetery, about the only other thing left, like a sore thumb out here, is that big white plantation-style house coming up on our left: the historic Cypress Inn, currently a private residence and on the National Register. Hard to imagine now that there was ever enough business to support the hotel, but once upon a time the constant, northbound winter railroad traffic of fresh vegetables made this a bustling corridor."

The Plymouth turned off the highway and drove up the incline of an access road. Serge got out with his camera, hitching a camping product to his belt.

Coleman petted Mr. Zippy. "What's that thing you put on your waist?"

"Canteen for my coffee." He uncapped it for a big chug, then re-capped it. "I just completed a blue-ribbon time-motion study on myself, and someone needs to get fired. The canteen was the number one recommendation in the report, because I'm so often reaching out a hand for coffee and coming up with a fistful of empty."

Coleman pointed in another direction. "Did we drive all the way to the ocean?"

"No." *Click, click, click.* "We're on top of the dike. That's the lake."

"*That's* the lake?" said Coleman. "I can't even see the other side. And we're way up honkin' high!"

"That's how it got its name." *Click, click, click.* "The Seminole word for *big water.*"

"There's like a row of weird clouds all spaced out," said Coleman. "Wait, each of them has a little thing stretching to the ground like a tornado. But they're black like smoke. Is something on fire?"

"That would be the sugarcane fields burning over the horizon on the opposite shore. The size of those clouds should give you some idea of the scale of those blazes. They need that to get rid of the leaves and weeds before the harvesting machines come through."

Coleman looked the other way, at something much closer. "What's that?"

"The Port Mayaca Lock and Dam." *Click, click, click.* "Something else people don't realize is that you can sail clear across the state of Florida, from Fort Myers to Stuart, along the Caloosahatchee and St. Lucie rivers. But there's a series of five locks in order to raise the vessels to get to the lake, then a clear shot across a bass fishermen's paradise before the rest of the locks lower the boats back down to sea level. Like the Panama Canal except bigger. Not as wide, but much longer. So I'm going on the record right now with that as well. Fuck 'em."

Coleman looked left and right. "If this is Port Mayaca, where's the port?"

"Pretty much just that lock," said Serge.

"What's the big gate-looking thing next to it? Part of the lock?"

"No, that's the spillway," said Serge. "Remember when I told you the 1928 hurricane was still surprising people in ways they never dreamed?"

"Not really, but go on."

"So remember when we were on the coast in Stuart last year? Remember the *smell*?"

"Oh, my God! That stink is still in my head again," said Coleman. "I've never smelled anything so nasty in all my life!"

"That's what everyone said." *Click, click, click.* "And at first, because they don't know how the state's ecosystem is interconnected, they couldn't figure it out. They just saw all this thick green sludge completely blanketing the coastal inlets, up through the Intracoastal Waterway to the boating canals behind homes, like an ice floe. The stench was so bad that it emptied beaches and restaurants, and residents were held prisoner in their homes with scented candles, praying the air-conditioning didn't give out."

"What was it?"

"It all started here, forty miles away," said Serge. "The Hoover Dike is getting old, and the Army Corps of Engineers has been sounding the alarm for years that it's in desperate need of repairs or the next hurricane could breach, just like the levees failed in

New Orleans during Katrina. So when the water levels get too high, as a precautionary step they open the spillways, releasing millions of gallons of water. Same thing simultaneously happened on the Gulf coast when they opened the gates at Moore Haven."

"But how did that cause the stinky green slime?"

"The Corps of Engineers caught a lot of flak, but it wasn't their fault. Their only responsibility is protecting life and property from a dike failure. The problem is that, over the years, the lake has become chock-full of nitrogen-rich fertilizer runoff. Some is back-pumped into the lake by Big Sugar, but probably just as much or more was carried down the Kissimmee River from the pasture and cattle land south of Orlando. The resulting algae bloom could easily be seen from space—I'm kind of hung up on the reference point right now. But oddly, it didn't get much national press, and if you weren't there, you couldn't imagine the extent of the environmental disaster. Beautiful, flowing waterways just choking to death, rotting fish, no-swimming signs. For the first time, thousands of people on both coasts became acutely aware of this faraway but dominant lake. Our moon."

Coleman used a single finger to scratch a furry head. "Mr. Zippy, you don't like algae blooms, do you?" He looked up at Serge. "He says he doesn't . . . Ow, damn!" He quickly yanked his finger back. "Mr. Zippy just bit me!"

"What kind of sickness did you inflict on him?"

"Nothing, I swear."

"Did it draw blood or was it just a little nip?"

"Just a nip." Shaking a finger. "Still hurts."

Serge nodded in understanding. "The guy at the pet store explained it to me. If they're scared or pissed off, they can really bite, but if it's only a nip, it's because they're so smart."

"How is biting me smart?"

"Their intelligence requires constant mental stimulation, and they let you know it. That's what is known as their *I'm-bored-as-shit-please-entertain-me* bite."

Coleman looked down at the pouch, wiggling silly fingers next to his ears and sticking out his tongue. Mr. Zippy squeaked. Coleman petted him.

"He bit me again."

"Here," said Serge, passing his smartphone across the front seat. "Let him watch some stuff on YouTube."

"Like what?"

"Zany ferret videos. There's like a thousand for every occasion. One thing YouTube has taught me is that other people are drilling deep into ways to waste their lives."

"Okay, let me try . . ." Coleman got a video going and held the phone to the pouch. "I think it's working. He's getting into it."

Serge glanced over. "What's it playing?"

"There's a ferret in a sweater, and now two more are losing their minds in a pile of packing peanuts, another one is rolling a watermelon across the kitchen, another is riding on the back of a house cat like a jockey, one just crawled completely inside an empty tube of Pringles . . . I had no idea they were so talented."

Serge got out of the car and stood gazing across a stunning vista. "Time to take in one last sunset look from the top of the dike before we proceed." He unhitched a camping canteen from his belt and slugged cold coffee.

A minivan came up the access ramp and parked nearby. The vehicle's sliding door opened, belching out children, who promptly began screaming as they ran in pointless circles. Exhausted parents climbed down from the front seat.

"A family!" Serge quickly chugged and capped the canteen. "People still care! I must congratulate and share the good news!"

The parents leaned against the minivan's bumper, soaking up the view and eating granola bars. Serge blustered over, jumping like he had a pogo stick. "Thank God you made it! You don't see anyone else up here. That means you're special for caring!" He bobbed on the balls of his feet. "You just *have* to visit the mass grave next, I insist. Your thoughts on the algae bloom? Seen it from space? That lake is our moon." Serge tapped the side of his head. "Let it set in. Did you know that the top of this dike is part of the thirteen-hundred-mile Florida National Scenic Trail? My faithful pal here is Coleman, and that's Mr. Zippy, my service animal. Mental condition, nothing you need to worry about. Others, maybe." He pointed at the kids, still running randomly and screaming. "Children have the best sense of hearing, and yet they're always shouting at the top of their lungs at each other, especially in motel pools. Could never figure that one out. On the other hand, kindergarten is my religion. The children will lead us . . . Coleman, you ready?"

"I'm in."

The pair began running aimlessly around the top of the dike, screaming shrill gibberish to mimic the children: *"Wa-wa-wa-wa-wa! . . . Yi-yi-yi-yi-yi! . . . Blobidy-blobidy-blobidy!* . . . Coleman! Tag! You're it! Can't catch me! . . . Can't catch me! . . . Try to catch me!—"

A panel door slammed shut. Serge stopped and watched the minivan race back to the highway. "Man, they must really want to see that cemetery . . ."

Chapter 23

I fell down some stairs."

The doctor glared at Captain Crack. "Only if the stairs then got up and fell on your head. Someone clearly beat the crap out of you. Probably more than one."

"How much longer?" snapped Crack, butterfly bandages across his eyebrows and cheeks. "I have to get back to work."

"Hold on, just need to finish taping up these ribs."

Crack didn't really have to lie. It was one of those off-the-books doctors, the kind you call for a GSW—that would be gun-shot wound—when you want to avoid the mandatory reporting to police that the law requires. Every city's got a few, and all the shady types have them on speed dial.

The doctor finished treating the captain underneath a stuffed wahoo, and left Crack's office. Captain Nasty had some more people on speed dial who didn't advertise in the yellow pages. He punched buttons on his cell phone.

"Fallon, it's me, Crack," said the captain. "I know you probably don't remember, but we met a while back through a mutual friend. Vic Carver . . ."

The people the captain was contacting were consummate professionals, the kind he'd like working for him on his boats, but he couldn't afford their price tag for that sort of long-term employment. On the other hand, it might be for the better, because he wouldn't look forward to having any kind of business dispute with these cats.

" . . . The reason I'm calling is I have a job for you. . . . No, I'm calling from a burner phone. . . . Okay, check me out with Vic and then we'll meet . . ."

The next day, Captain Crack stood on the side of the Flagler Bridge over the Intracoastal Waterway to Palm Beach. It was one of those old, low concrete drawbridges that the people who couldn't afford boats fished from. The fish were apparently biting because the bridge was unusually full. Mainly blacks and Latinos. Straw hats. Someone reeled in a flopping catfish and tossed it in a pail. There was talk, time and again, over on the wealthy island about passing some kind of law to get rid of the people on the bridge, but it never really worked out.

Captain Crack cast a lure out into the water and began reeling. The midday sun was a challenge, even with his ventilated fishing shirt, and patience wasn't among his virtues. He kept checking his watch. He looked one way toward the modest skyline of downtown West Palm Beach, and then the other toward the tony waterfront mansions with Spanish barrel tiles and royal palms. He heard someone next to him and turned.

Another fisherman set a bait bucket down on the cement next to Crack's bucket. Both pails were orange and white. The new arrival then cast a line in the water without speaking. He was a head taller than the captain, thinner, more muscular in a formfitting black T-shirt that matched his black hat and jet-black wraparound sunglasses. A formation of pelicans glided along the bridge's ancient railing. A cheap radio somewhere was playing Cuban salsa music.

"It's all in the bait bucket," said Crack. "Instructions, money, just like you told me on the phone."

The taller fisherman stared down at Crack with unseen eyes behind the sunglasses. It meant: *The instructions also were not to talk to me.* What did he not understand about standing next to a stranger on a bridge and simply switching identical bait buckets?

"Sorry," said Crack.

The man brusquely picked up the captain's bucket and left the bridge.

A white blop of pelican poop hit Crack's arm.

T he sun had just gone down behind an emaciated gas station. The horizon was low and clear over the cane stalks from all four corners of the intersection. Someone walked out of the station scratching an instant lottery ticket with the edge of a dime. Someone else uncapped a bottle in a brown paper bag. The social circle on the stoop was more animated than usual.

"Jamal, if I have to hear about that stupid pass reception one more freaking time, I swear to God I'll slit my wrists."

"But it was an ESPN highlight moment!"

"In your dreams maybe."

A low-riding Datsun sat nearby with purple neon glowing underneath. All the doors were open for the listening pleasure of an over-powered stereo with the new Grenade sub-woofer. The song changed to Hendrix.

"*. . . I went down to the crossroads . . .*"

The traffic light changed, and a Dakota thumped to a stop in the intersection. Hank Williams blasted out the open windows.

"*. . . Kaw-Liga! . . .*"

The light turned green. Someone waved out the driver's window. A middle-finger salute. "Suck my dick, porch monkeys!"

One of the trio stood up from the stoop. "I don't believe my own lyin' eyes."

"What is it?"

"That son of a bitch is at it again!" said the tight end.

"You'd think he'd learned his lesson," said the wide receiver.

The quarterback angled his neck forward in the growing darkness. "And it looks like he's got another little kid with him!"

It was déjà vu all over again. The Datsun blasted out of the parking lot like before, except this time they took it careful not to overrun a detour down a cane road. For whatever reason, the driver of the Dakota made it hard to miss his vehicle. He drove the speed limit and left his high beams on, lighting everything up like a prison break. He turned into a cane field.

"There he is!"

"I ain't going to worry about killing him like last time!"

The Datsun raced down the dirt road following Crack's headlights. When they pulled up, they figured Captain Nasty would take off running and shitting his pants. Instead, they found him leaning against his driver's door, calmly smoking a cigarette. "What's up, boys?"

"You took another kid!" shouted the wide receiver.

"What kid?" Crack took a deep drag. "I don't see any children around here."

"In your pickup cab!" yelled the tight end. He ran up to the passenger window. "What the heck?"

"What is it?" asked the quarterback.

"A small mannequin."

"What?"

The young man pulled the straw-stuffed human figure from the car and walked back with it for all to see. "He tricked us!"

"But why?"

They were off-balance, staring back at the pickup truck with confused eyes.

Crack Nasty chuckled and snubbed out his cigarette. "Nice knowing you."

Suddenly a dark, windowless van crashed through the sugarcane in front of them. The side panel flew open and four men in black jumpsuits leaped out. There was no Hollywood final banter. They simply opened up with ridiculous firepower from the latest battlefield mercenary weapons.

At least death was quick.

Helicopters and TV trucks converged on the field the next day. Police found a burst-open bag of cocaine in the Datsun, and more residue on the bodies. The three victims had no criminal records. But they were known to be young, black and hanging out with no employment. Everything pointed to a drug deal gone south. Locals weren't buying it. They brought in the larger outside law enforcement agencies, and a joint task force went in front of the TV cameras, swearing they would never rest until their investigation brought the killers to justice. But given the area and the evidence, not really.

Captain Crack Nasty was getting away with it again.

Chapter 24

COW COUNTRY

A gold Plymouth Satellite headed up U.S. Highway 98. A Styrofoam takeout dinner box sat on the back seat.

"One thing that should be mandatory on every Floridian's bucket list is to drive completely around Lake Okeechobee."

A ferret ran from one of Serge's shoulders to the other.

"I think Mr. Zippy wants to know why," said Coleman.

"Because it will recalibrate your sense of place. That's what we're doing now. One hundred and twenty miles of dynamically changing culture and landscape. And this empty section between Pahokee and the city of Okeechobee is one of the coolest!"

"He nipped me again," said Coleman. "He needs more stimulation."

"It's like channel-surfing inland Florida," said Serge. "We're on the east side, where the highway hugs the rim of the lake, through flats with sabal palms and heron swooping over the road. Moss-draped oaks, bogs and marsh, grassy straightaways with just that looming dike. Plus it continues following the thread, which I will recap for Mr. Zippy: Rawlings to Stetson to Zora to the West Palm Beach cemetery in her book to the Port Mayaca mass grave, and now circumnavigating the lake with more interrelated stops. And people think I'm just winging it . . ."

A deep horn blew.

Serge quickly checked his mirrors and skidded off the road.

"What are you doing?"

"Waiting for the train to catch up," said Serge.

"Huh?"

Another horn blast.

"Along the east side of the lake, the old train tracks that carried fresh produce up north almost a century ago still have traffic, and they lie in that short strip of easement between this road and the Hoover Dike. You haven't lived until you've raced a train up Lake Okeechobee . . . Here we go!"

Tires spun, black smoke, screeching. The Plymouth hit the road as if shot by a slingshot.

A yellow-and-black locomotive gained quickly from behind, and Serge pressed his right foot down all the way. He began honking and waving. One of the engineers glanced over. Serge leaned out the window, making a pumping gesture with his fist for the engineer to blow his horn.

A long blare followed, and the train pulled away.

Serge fell back in his seat with an afterglow. "It doesn't get any better!"

"Then why that frown?"

"Incoming thought," said Serge. "What's the deal with sales receipts these days?"

"Are we playing another round of tangent?" asked Coleman.

"I'll go in a darn CVS or Walgreens drugstore to buy a single toothbrush, and I get a receipt that reaches to the floor. You can't be doing that to people. It's a drugstore, so they have to know a certain wedge of their clientele have disorders. And now the pressure is on me to read the whole fucking thing because *you never know*. But it's always a bunch of coupons for back-to-school supplies or feminine products that make me blush. On the other hand, the receipts at gas pumps are these teensy-weensy little bastards you can barely read. We regulate the size of eggs, but where's the quality control on this one?"

Coleman nodded. "Half the long receipts seem to have a pink stripe somewhere."

"This is what I'm talking about!" said Serge. "And another thing: Society now has something called 'revenge porn.'"

"Is that where someone steals all your porn?"

"So you'd think," said Serge. "But I just heard through the grapevine that in the middle of a sixty-nine, people are pulling out their cell phones."

"This is really going on?"

Serge nodded. "You'd think a quaking orgasm would get a thank-you, but no, now it has to be in high def."

"What do they do with it?"

"Save it for the breakup," said Serge. "And it's never pretty: 'You know how you said I could trust you and ask the most embarrassing thing that you'd like me to do in bed? Well, I have a request . . .' And the next thing you know, a bunch of coworkers are in their cubicles glued to a text video involving handcuffs and a zucchini."

"Ouch."

Serge shrugged. "If those people are going to judge me on that . . . I mean, it was someone else."

The Plymouth began curling around the northwest shore of the lake. A roar came up from behind and whipped past in the opposite lane.

Coleman's head spun as he grabbed the dash. "There must be twenty motorcycles!"

"It's a popular touring route for them," said Serge. "Which means we're on the right track. Bikers are a noble breed, stripping away pretense to live in the *now*. You can always count on them to bird-dog the finest scenic byways."

More wetlands and vines and scrub brush went by. Drivers in other vehicles wearing camo baseball caps and pulling airboats.

"Now we're talking!" said Serge. "Florida's bayou country, the whole area like a Credence Clearwater album!"

He fumbled to start a boom box.

"*. . . Comin' up around the bend . . .*"

The scraggly vegetation gave way to wild palms surrounding the first wisps of the mobile-home parks.

Serge nodded to himself in contentment. "Lake Okeechobee is Florida's heart, and its beat ripples a pulse far and wide."

"I thought the lake was the moon," said Coleman.

"Since when are you listening to me?"

The road wound past more evidence of population hugging the edge of the lake. RV dealerships and RV parks. Bass boats, a country store, a honky-tonk bar, a swamp buggy on tank treads. Signs for gravel and cremation. Then the trailer parks. Trailers on wheels, trailers on blocks, trailers on slabs. Trailers with screened porches, hot tubs and gazebos. There were flowerpots with no flowers, decorative stone turtles next to real ones, and a mailbox shaped like a lighthouse. Someone was casting a fishing line on his front lawn, and someone else walked by on the side of the road in shorts, sandals and a Santa Claus hat, indicating the breadth of the human condition.

Then the local economy. Big Lake Eye Care, Big Lake Bail Bonds, the Big "O" Flea Market.

American flags everywhere.

Another roar came up behind the Plymouth. Coleman turned around. "A bunch more bikers." They began streaming by the Plymouth. "Except these are all the three-wheel kind. Why are they riding separate from the others?"

"Probably unresolved tension between the groups that goes way back to an incident nobody can remember now," said Serge. "Most likely a few too many longnecks on a Sunday afternoon, and then one guy started some shit about the number of tires, threats were made, women disrespected. Best to let them sort it out among themselves."

The Plymouth reached the outskirts of the civilization. Signs for bait, fishing licenses and fried catfish.

"Where are we?" asked Coleman.

"The city of Okeechobee, also known as Cow Town." The Plymouth pulled into a parking lot. "We need to resupply before our excellent visit."

Twenty minutes later, they came out of the store. Coleman was pushing a shopping cart, and Serge was dragging a sales receipt across the pavement. He suddenly stopped and violently balled it up. Then into a garbage can—"Motherfucker!"—slamming the lid five times.

"What's the matter?"

"I don't want to talk about it."

Soon, they were checking into another economy motel. This one had a warning sign at the reception desk.

Coleman moved his lips as he read. "Serge, what are blind mosquitoes?"

"Tiny suckers that don't bite but sometimes swarm in biblical numbers off the lake after dark, and you have to keep your mouth closed unless you want extra protein. But they can still get in your eyes, ears and nose."

"Jesus."

"They're attracted to light, so that's why that sign asks guests to turn off all the lamps before leaving the room in the evening and close the door quickly. It's a whole different set of rules out here, and they're not in the humans' favor."

A young wrangler-Jane type stood behind the counter with a genuine smile. "I wouldn't worry too much. The mosquitoes are bad on the few nights they're out, but it's mostly quiet. What freaks newcomers most are the frogs."

"Frogs?" said Serge.

She nodded and held her hands apart a good half foot. "We have these giant ones that come out after a big rain, and people open their doors at night and see them all over the sidewalk and parking lot. They're harmless, but sometimes one or two will hop in a room. That's a lot of my night service calls."

"Service calls?"

Another nod. "I have to go in rooms and capture them because people say they can't sleep with those things under their bed making noise and just being creepy, and they're too squeamish to catch them on their own . . . So what are you fellas doing in town?"

"Historical research," said Serge. "Following connective tissue."

"History? Really?" She brightened further. "I love history!" She got out a paper and pen and began jotting feverishly. "Here are the area's high points . . ." She got to the bottom of the page. ". . . Finally, don't forget the Brighton Seminole reservation. There's a visitors' center with exhibits and souvenirs, plus they have a twenty-four-hour casino where you don't have to dress up. I usually go in my pajamas."

They retired to the room as the sun began to set.

Coleman stood in amazement. "This is like the best budget place we've ever stayed in. It's got a giant full kitchen and everything!"

"Scoped it out years ago, and now it's the only place I'll stay around here." Serge hung his toiletry bag on a mirror. "Where else can you rent a former condo unit at a bargain price? And there's always vacancy. That's why I'm keeping it a secret."

Rinnnng! Rinnnng!

Serge jumped. "What the fuck was that?"

"The phone," said Coleman.

"Of course it's the phone! But who could possibly know we're here?"

Rinnnng! Rinnnng!

Serge gingerly picked up the receiver. "Hello?"

"Hi! It's me, Cheyenne, from the front desk. I just thought of a couple more places that I forgot when I was making your list. Have a pen handy?"

Serge urgently lunged toward writing materials like he was taking a call for ransom demands. "Hit me!"

The call eventually ended, and the receiver went back in its cradle.

"Who was that?" asked Coleman.

"Our little history helper from the front desk. My love for country folk just keeps growing."

The pair commenced their respective chores. Coleman spread dope on the counter and swilled malt liquor. Serge unpacked notebooks, guidebooks, pamphlets, and recording devices. Coleman made a bong from a souvenir plastic cowboy-hat penny bank that he'd bought at the store.

"TV?" asked Coleman.

"Leave it off. I have other plans." Serge carefully arranged a configuration of needed materials on the nightstand: antiquarian novel, portable stereo, Styrofoam to-go dinner box. He took a deep breath in anticipation. Then he kicked off his shoes and lay on top of a bedspread in his stocking feet. "Here . . . we . . . go! . . ."

"What are you doing?"

"A lost art: constructing the perfect moment!" Serge bunched the pillow up under his head. "It requires the precisely engineered intersection of sensory, mental and emotional input: First, the motel room is in the ideal location: From the comfort of my bed, I have a fantastic view just outside the window of the Hoover Dike in the setting sun. Next"—he pressed a button on the portable stereo, and a growling voice came to life—"'Little Black Train' by Blind Joe Taggart, just the kind of blues song they would have been playing in the 1920s juke joints surrounding the lake's bustling packing houses . . ." He opened the Styrofoam box on his stomach ". . . And this is my soul-food takeout from that shack in Pahokee of smothered pork chops, pigeon peas and collards. Standard dinner fare in those old days . . ." Serge finally grabbed the book off the nightstand. "And last but not least, a collectible early copy of Zora Neale Hurston's masterpiece recounting the 1928 storm that struck right out there! . . ."

Serge became quiet. He turned up the tiny stereo, stuck a fork in a pork chop, opened the book and stared out the window. ". . . I'm starting to feel it. I'm getting tingly . . . Here it comes! . . . Here it comes! . . . It's almost here! . . . It's here!" Serge's eyelids fluttered uncontrollably as his pupils rolled up in his head like he was possessed. Then, a few seconds later, it was over. "Coleman, did you see it? The Moment! . . . It was just here . . . See? There it goes . . ." He closed the book and swallowed a bite of pork. ". . . Whew! Exhausting! . . . If everyone could experience motels like this, prostitution as we know it would end."

"They would have to get other jobs," said Coleman.

"Then one day you order a pizza and open the door: 'Hey, didn't you used to be a hooker?' 'Shut up.'"

Serge paused curiously and considered the closed book next to him. He opened it again and read down a page. "Wait . . . just . . . a minute!"

"What is it?"

He ran for the desk and opened another, thicker green book. "I need my bible."

"The *Bible* Bible?"

"No, the Florida bible. WPA Guide published in 1939, two years after Zora penned *Their Eyes Were Watching God* and around the time when she was crossing the state with Stetson Kennedy. The government commissioned the Depression-era guide series to put writers to work, and all these incredible people of letters contributed with flourishes never seen before in a travel guide. But nobody got a byline, and all the writing is uncredited . . ." Serge found the page he was looking for and thrust a fist in the air. "I knew it! I knew it!" He grabbed Coleman's arms and danced in a circle. "I rock tonight!"

"What did you find?"

Serge plopped down at the desk again, holding up one of the books. "I knew I recognized it from somewhere! Hurston's novel described the Seminoles evacuating ahead of the storm because of how the sawgrass bloomed." He set the book down and picked up another. "And in the guide, virtually the same description. I just discovered an anonymous Zora passage! Prostitution is history!"

"Woo-hoo."

Serge stopped and held the open books side by side, one in each hand. He looked out the window at the sunlit dike, then down at the books, up at the dike, books, dike, books, dike. His eyelids began fluttering again and his pupils rolled back up. Then it passed. "Whoa! . . . Two in a row!"

"Remember that time you had—"

"I know," said Serge. "But this is better than orgasms, give or take . . . There's nothing else in life to compare . . . unless I can figure a way . . ." He let his thought trail off.

"Figure a way what?"

"I don't want to jinx it." Serge reached in one of their shopping bags and pulled out a copy of the morning's *Okeechobee News*.

Coleman popped another can of malt liquor. "I think I'm going to use all the extra space in this room to run around again."

"Knock yourself out."

"Yi-yi-yi-yi-yi . . . Wa-wa-wa-wa-wa . . . Oops, that's enough."

"Why'd you stop so soon?" asked Serge.

"The key is to stop just before you spit up in your mouth."

"I think you've just nailed what to put on your tombstone."

Coleman strolled over to a spacious desk. "What's that? What are you doing now?"

"*Trying* to read the newspaper," said Serge. "I'm required to buy a local newspaper whenever I arrive somewhere, to get in rhythm with the residents. And these small-town papers are the best! No bullshit about celebrity Twitter feuds or a cabinet member spending ten grand on a wastebasket. Check out this front page . . ." He held it up to his pal. ". . . Big photo at the top, 'Veterans Honored,' and another photo of a teen holding up two fish that won a tournament. Over in a box on the side where the weather forecast would normally be: 'Lake level 15.51 feet.' And last but not least, a front-page story you would only find in a paper like this: 'Ball of Light Reported over Lake Okeechobee,' complete with a photo someone took with a cell phone."

Coleman leaned closer. "It's just a black square with a fuzzy circle in the middle. Looks like a streetlight."

"Good a guess as any." Serge grabbed something else. "I get the feeling a lot of people around the lake are often staring up at the sky: 'Sweet Jesus! The aliens are landing again!' 'You're looking at a streetlight like last time, Uncle Biff. Why don't you hand me that beer.' . . . And here's the free town flyer with announcements for lawn-mower races, taco night at the American Legion, and a dunk tank for charity." Serge flipped through the paper until he came to a full-page ad. He leaped up. "Coleman!"

"What?"

"There's a rodeo tonight!"

"What's that mean?"

Serge tossed a duffel bag on the bed. "It means we have to get our uniforms ready . . ."

Chapter 25

SEPTEMBER 17, 1928

The twangs of a guitar floated down the dirt street in pre-dawn hours. A gusting wind picked up pieces of cardboard and newspaper. Men in grimy pants and overalls sat on the porch steps of one of the many juke joints in Belle Glade and Pahokee that stayed open around the clock: small cabins with patrons stumbling in and out, some sleeping in the grass by the back door. Cats and dogs foraged for scraps.

The front of this particular saloon was a random patchwork of corrugated sheet metal. There were signs for Nehi and Royal Crown Cola and Atlantic Ale. Inside the cramped room, loud conversation and thick smoke from filterless cigarettes. A poker game became heated. Under a window stood a wooden pinball machine with a racehorse theme. At the front of the bar, a sweaty, rotund gent sat on a stool that looked like it might collapse from physics. He was the only one wearing a suit, but the jacket had long since been removed, and perspiration pasted the white dress shirt to his chest. A kerosene lantern illuminated other beads of sweat generously cascading down his cheeks. He hunched over his Gibson Archtop guitar, strumming a three-chord Chicago progression and howling the lyrics to "Rope Stretchin'" by Blind Blake. They don't call it the blues for nothing.

In the back corner, beneath other signs for Ice Cold Jax Stout and Cobbs Creek Blended Whiskey, three men huddled over brown bottles.

"I am so sick of this shit," said Johnson.

"Me too," said Cabbage.

"How does he get away with it?" asked Mozelle.

"How? What color is his skin?" said Johnson. "I lost two weeks' pay."

"Then you had it good," said Cabbage. "I was the fool who worked a third week after he kept puttin' me off."

"Somebody needs to do something about that asshole!"

"And end up like Jacob? You weren't there."

"I also heard he got run out of the Dominican for pulling a bunch of the same bullshit."

"They say he doesn't trust the banks or anyone since," said Mozelle. "Keeps everything in gold, who knows where?"

"That's just a crazy rumor," said Johnson.

"Is it? I know a guy who saw him at the bank—"

"I thought he didn't trust banks."

"Not to deposit," said Mozelle. "To change his cash into twenty-dollar gold pieces. Had a big-ass sack of 'em."

Johnson lit a Lucky Strike, and they got another round of Blatz. They sat looking at each other.

"You thinking what I'm thinking?" said Cabbage.

"I'm in," said Mozelle.

"No time like now," said Johnson.

They quickly finished their beer and headed out into the wee hours . . .

After brief trips home, they crept through the night with Colt revolvers and a crowbar, across tomato and strawberry fields. Then they entered rows of tall stalks yielding in the whipping wind.

"You heard about this storm that's supposed to come?" asked Cabbage.

"We always get storms," said Johnson.

"But what about that hurricane two years ago?"

"Lightning doesn't strike twice. Like that's going to happen again so soon."

A gust came through, knocking them off-balance.

"I don't know," said Mozelle. "I heard the Seminoles already came through before sunset for higher ground. They tend to be right."

"They tend to be Indians," said Johnson. "We going to do this or not?"

They finally crouched on the edge of the cane field. Ahead, one of the nicest homes for miles. Columns and a second-floor wraparound veranda. Johnson took off running, and the rest followed until they were crouched again by a side door. They all reached in their back pockets and pulled out canvas flour bags with holes cut in strategic spots. They pulled them over their heads.

Johnson stuck the crowbar in the frame and cracked the door open. They charged inside and up the stairs to the master bedroom. Fakakta was snoring.

"Where's his wife?"

"This other bedroom," said Johnson, quietly closing another door in the hall.

Mozelle stuck his gun to the baron's head and shook his shoulder. A whisper: "Wake up."

Fakakta finally roused, then sat up quickly. "What do you want?"

"Gold."

Then it all went south in an urgent hurry.

"I recognize your shirt from the fields," said Fakakta. "Blue stripes. What was your name? Mozelle something?"

"Fuck!" He yanked off his flower bag. "Where's the gold?"

"Mozelle, put your bag back on," said Cabbage.

"Why? If he wasn't sure about my name already, you just repeated it!" He swung his gun back to Fulgencio and pressed it between his eyes. "The gold!"

"What gold?" said the baron. "Go ahead and shoot. You're all dead men anyway."

Mozelle cocked the hammer. "You don't seem to be taking this seriously. You think you can just steal from everyone around here and get away with it? Not to mention lynching Jacob. You may not have known, but he was my cousin."

A loud crackle outside as lightning laced the sky. The wind was now up to a roar, whistling through the clapboards and eaves. The shutters began coming loose, banging with a violent rhythm against the side of the house. Other stuff in the yard became airborne and crashed into things. Then another crash, but this one was different. It was inside. The trio saw glass and water explode on the wall over the headboard. Mozelle spun with his pistol.

Bang.

A thud in the doorway.

"Jesus!" yelled Cabbage. "You just shot his wife!"

"She threw a vase at me!"

"We've got more trouble."

They heard footsteps pounding up the stairs. Fulgencio's adult son and chief enforcer, Pablo. With a rifle.

Johnson dashed to the door and fired his Colt, easily picking Pablo off before he reached the landing. The body slumped and tumbled backward down the stairs.

Cabbage grabbed his own head with both hands. "Shit! This was a bad idea! We never should have come!"

"We're way past that now." Johnson smacked the side of Fakakta's head with his pistol. Blood spattered. He smacked him again the other way, then a third time.

"Damn!" said Mozelle. "Aren't you going to ask him any questions?"

Another crack to the skull. "I don't like to repeat myself."

He raised the gun again, and Fakakta raised his hands. "Okay, enough. I'll take you to the gold."

Everyone marched out the back door and leaned forward in a driving rain. Fakakta led them out behind a falling-down old barn that came with the property. He placed his back against the wall, then counted out twenty measured paces. He stopped and pointed down.

Johnson shoved him out of the way and fell to his knees. "Keep him covered." His hands clawed at the dirt. About a foot down, his fingers found netting. He grabbed it and stood, pulling hard. Earth flew. They all froze. An open pit with crate after wooden crate stacked to an unknown depth. Johnson opened the first box. Gasps.

"Look at all that money!"

Then they were all on their knees, running their fingers through the coins. "How much do you think is here? . . ."

Fakakta knew the effect gold had on people. He'd been waiting for his chance. He slowly inched backward, then all at once took off for the house.

"He's running!"

Johnson stood and didn't hurry his shot. Careful aim.

Bang.

Fakakta fell forward into the mud.

"He's crawling," said Cabbage. "He's not dead."

Mozelle calmly crossed the thirty or so yards, until he had walked around in front of the slithering Fulgencio.

The sugar baron raised his face to see the barrel of a gun.

Mozelle cocked it again. "This is for Jacob."

Bang.

"We're definitely going to have to leave the state," said Cabbage. "I got some relatives in Natchez."

"First things first." Johnson grabbed the initial crate and heaved. "Let's get all this out of the ground."

The wind and rain became a brutal impediment, but they were motivated. Soon, crates were spread everywhere.

"He just left all this in a hole?" said Mozelle.

"It ain't going to spoil," said Johnson. "Gold doesn't even tarnish. We need to go back and get your brother's pickup truck. And it'll take more than one trip."

Cabbage wiped water from his eyes and looked up. "Shouldn't it already be getting light out?"

"We just lost track of time," said Mozelle, falling down in the wind and struggling to rise.

"I'll stay here and watch this," said Johnson. "You guys go get the truck—"

There was a sharp cracking sound. Louder than a rifle.

"What the hell was that?"

Then another loud report. More and more followed in quick succession.

"It sounds like trees snapping, but that can't be—"

"Shut up!"

They all stared silent at the woods a quarter mile north of the home. More savage cracking until it was a constant chorus. They strained with their eyes but couldn't make out anything. The noise became a roar of ground-level thunder.

Finally, the last rows of trees on the edge of the woods gave way and splintered and were gone. They looked up in the darkness.

"What the hell is that?" said Cabbage.

Whatever it was, it was traveling fast, at least sixty miles an hour.

When they finally figured out what they were looking at,

it was too much for their brains to process. A couple hundred yards away, they watched the plantation home explode and disappear.

Seconds later, it was right in front of them. Nothing to do but freeze and conjure one last thought: *That fucking lake.*

In surrender, they simply stared straight up into the black, twenty-foot-high tidal wave.

Part Two

Chapter 26

RODEO NIGHT

S erge drove north with a high-end tape recorder in his lap and a microphone in his hand.

CAPTAIN FLORIDA'S LOG, STAR DATE 376.693

The city of Okeechobee rests on the northern tip of the lake by the same name. You just have to love a town that runs off the cliff with its identity, and you never need to be reminded you're in cattle country: the Brahman Theater, Brahman Restaurant & Lounge, Okeechobee High School (Home of the Brahmans), Cowboy's Barbecue, the Cowtown Café, the Cattlemen's Association rodeo arena. The economic center of downtown is the bustling Eli's Western Wear. You can be driving down Main Street on a Tuesday morning and suddenly realize you desperately need a two-thousand-dollar saddle, lassos, spurs, rhinestone belt, and five-foot-long decorative steer horns to hang over the TV. You're in luck! Eli's has amassed a staggering supply. Then there are the cows themselves. Cattle dot the fields all over Central Florida, but nothing like here, where they vastly outnumber the humans, in herds not seen since buffalo covered the prairies in *Dances with Wolves*. Billboards everywhere along the pastures: BEEF, IT'S WHAT'S FOR DINNER, next to grazing livestock unaware of the advertisements for their impending execution.

Speaking of downtown, Main Street is actually called Park Street and there are two of them laid out parallel through the center of the city. Between the pair runs a wide, shaded green space like a series of football fields, starting with a military display of a Vietnam-era Huey helicopter, M60 Patton tank and a couple pieces of heavy ground artillery. From there, the public park has nowhere to go but mellow, with quiet benches, picnic tables, thatched-roof huts and vintage-style lampposts. But wait! There's more! Get ready to seriously crap yourselves! I've kind of been hung up on murals lately, and I'd completely forgotten my favorite part of Okeechobee! It's Mural City, USA! Remember the batshit town-identity thing? And just when you thought the insanity had reached critical mass. That's right: They found more mass! Most antique communities have lots of old brick buildings with empty brick sides, and the residents think nothing of it. Not the fine people here! Sometime back, they went on the mural version of a crack binge, and now you can't throw a cow pie in this place without it sticking to public art. There's a mural celebrating the arrival of the railroad in 1915 with scenes of ice delivery and catfish; another touts an important cattle drive with happy people waiting at the end; there's a car dealership that opened in 1933, and a pioneer hardware store. The side of the Big O drive-through liquor barn has marsh birds flying over the lake, and a country restaurant sports a mural within a mural: a painting of one of those old postcards, WELCOME TO OKEECHOBEE, with each of the giant letters in the city's name a separate homage. And you know how a lot of main streets have abandoned buildings that are simply boarded up with plywood, and jerks spray-paint gang symbols and FUCK THE SYSTEM and giant penises? I think we can all agree that's not going anywhere special. But at the historic and defunct 1923 tan-brick Okeechobee bank, instead of plywood, the town painted all the windows to look like a bunch of customers in period clothing are still inside conducting business! And finally the cherry on the sundae: There's even a mural depicting the history of local phone service ("First Operator, Byrd Sizemore"). I thought something like that would only reach an audience of one. Me. But these are my people! I must stop dictating this now and interact with them . . .

T he convenience store had cedar slats. It was sparsely stocked and otherwise empty except for a retired couple at the counter. A wagon wheel leaned against the front of the building, intended to drum up business, but now there were doubts.

Serge and Coleman walked up behind the old people.

The couple was taking an extra-long time with the clerk. An involved conversation, and it wasn't about a transaction.

"Serge, are you going to do anything crazy like the other times?"

"No."

"But when people take forever in convenience stores, you always flip out."

"This is different. I want to listen to small-town talk." Serge blew across the top of a Styrofoam cup. "I already have my coffee, so I can drink it while waiting. Legally they can't touch me as long as I pay."

The old woman clutched a purse in front of her with both hands. "When does Charlie come on?"

"He doesn't work here anymore," said the clerk. "Actually, I'm his son."

"You're Billy?" asked the old man. "You've really grown. I remember when you were this high."

"Billy's my older brother."

"Then that makes you Donny," said the woman. "You've *really* grown."

"Where does your dad work now?" asked the old man.

"Retired," said the clerk. "Just smokes cigars on the porch with the dogs."

"We've always thought the world of Charlie. Your whole family," said the woman. "Can you give him our best?"

"Absolutely."

The couple thanked him and left, and Serge stepped up.

The clerk smiled cordially. "How's your day been going?"

"Magically!" Serge set a cup on the counter. "I already love your family, and we haven't even met!"

The clerk looked down. "It's an empty cup."

"I know the rules." Serge slapped down a couple of dollars. "Technically, I'm still in my lane, so there's no need for trouble."

"No, I mean, don't you want coffee in it?"

Serge patted his stomach. "Already in here."

The clerk leaned over the cup. "Oh, yeah. I see the drops." He smiled again and rang Serge up. "Will there be anything else?"

"Yes!" Serge tossed the cup in the trash. "A side order of country-fried conversation."

"Uh, what?"

"Like you were having with those old folks. I love small-town friendliness!"

"Then you've come to the right place," said the clerk. "If we got any friendlier, people would think we were trying to sell something."

"You are," said Serge. "You're a clerk in a store. Isn't that the program here? Just because the wagon wheel out front didn't fulfill the big dreams, the answer isn't Communism."

Coleman raised his hand. "You should get a mannequin of a hot chick and stick her by the road."

"Coleman! Shhhh!" said Serge. "I'm talking to the guy here. The mannequins draw the wrong crowd, who just want to use the restrooms and aren't too precise about it."

The clerk chuckled. "You guys are funny. What brings you to town?"

"The *town*!" said Serge. "I love everything about it. Right now I'm mentally rocking out to your murals."

"Oh, the murals," said Donny. "Aren't they fantastic? My personal favorite is the telephone one."

"Me too!" said Serge. "Byrdie Sizemore! I know her name is Byrd, but I like to refer to her as Byrdie because it's a free country. I'm always thinking about her. Was she musical? Petulant? Did she find her life's work fulfilling, or just start smashing telephones near the end? And exactly what switchboard call was she connecting in that mural? A family reunion at the old Forsythe place? Gossip about the preacher and the Widow Milsap? An emergency involving moonshine and a two-person tree saw?"

The clerk chuckled again. "Never quite thought about it."

Serge pointed at the duffel bag near his feet, then at the corner of the store. "Can we use your restroom? I actually made a purchase, so we're not from the mannequin crowd. But I will need a while because we have to get dressed for work. Really important gig."

"Take as long as you want," said Donny. "If there's a problem, I'll tell everyone to use the women's room."

"You're good people . . ."

Donny sat back on a stool and resumed flipping through a

magazine with blueprints for patio decks. After a couple minutes, he thought he heard something. He leaned over the counter, looking down the hall to the restrooms. There was a muffled banging sound, then a crash and arguing in hushed tones. *"Let go of me!"* *"Don't screw this up again!"* Another bang. A clanging noise. The door opened and Serge stuck his head out with a grin. "Almost done. There's nothing unusual." The door closed. Bang, bang, bang. *"Dammit!"* *"Shit, my bad."* Then a suspiciously long pause. The door finally opened again.

Serge and Coleman stepped out, and Donny stepped back, scratching his head. "What exactly is this job you do?"

Serge told him.

"Ohhhh." Donny nodded with understanding.

"Don't fib," said Serge. "At first you thought this was weird. Anyway, pleasure to meet, thanks for use of the restroom, and any damage in there was from the other guys."

They left the store, and a gold Plymouth sped off north through the fading light on U.S. Highway 441. Pot smoke wafted out the windows.

"I'm beginning to see why you like country folk so much," said Coleman. "First your little history helper at the motel desk, and now that cool guy in the convenience store."

"Country folk are the best!" said Serge. "That is, most of the time."

Puff, puff. "What do you mean?"

"Don't get me wrong: Everything is usually finger-lickin' fantastic," said Serge. "Until you get lost driving through deep fog in the woods at night with no cell service or GPS. Then you notice a tiny light on in the distance at an isolated farmhouse. So you knock on the door for directions, and the next thing you know, you're handcuffed to a radiator while a family in bib overalls giggles and rubs mice on your face, and one of them says, 'Go get the twins.' And someone else opens a cellar door, and these two little albinos with pointy teeth show up, and you're like, 'Where in the fuck is this going?' But you know that all the signs so far are not positive, and then somehow you free yourself and run outside. Your car is just feet away and the keys are still in your pocket, but for some reason you tell yourself, 'That's a stupid idea. I'll run for a barn way out in that dark field.' You dash inside the rickety structure to find all kinds of thick chains hanging from the rafters with hooks and rusty scything blades, and a mottled hand is reaching up from a fresh grave in the dirt floor. Then a chain saw roars to life outside and you dive behind bales of hay as flashlight beams pierce through slats in the barn wall. And that's if you're lucky. Sometimes the family is into Amway: 'No, I don't want to join!' 'It'll change your life!' And then they're chasing you to the barn with pamphlets and brochures."

"Amway," said Coleman, shaking with the willies.

The Plymouth pulled off the road. "Here we are."

Other cars were already parked, many more arriving. People streamed toward what looked like an old minor-league baseball stadium in Oshkosh. Erector-Set girders and rusty metal sheeting over the stands in case of rain.

Serge and Coleman made their way to the entrance of the rodeo arena. A cashier in the ticket booth gave their outfits a double take, then asked for the admission fee.

Serge shook his head. "We're clowns. We're authorized."

"You're in the show?" asked the cashier.

Serge adjusted the red ball on his nose. "Why else would we be dressed like this? Just because we decided to pretend like we work here?"

"But the clowns have already arrived."

"They called for backup." Serge flashed a clown badge. "There could be trouble tonight. I'd count on it."

She shrugged and let them pass.

Coleman slapped floppy shoes on the walkway. "What do we do now?"

"Act like we belong."

They arrived at a fence along the side of the dusty arena. A cowgal in scarlet-fringed riding chaps went by on a horse. Sandy-blond locks flowed out from under her black Stetson hat. She proudly raised a giant American flag as they played "The Star-Spangled Banner."

Coleman nudged his buddy. "Look who it is."

"I know," said Serge. "My little history helper. Imagine that."

Coleman nudged him again. "She's wearing a plaid shirt."

"Shut up."

After a few preliminary announcements over the PA system, a galvanized metal gate burst open. A cowboy swung a free arm in the air as a bronco fiercely fought to dislodge him. After eight seconds, he hit the dirt in a nasty spill. The crowd stood in silent concern. The cowboy jumped right up and waved to them with his hat.

The PA announcer: "Let's hear it for Sundance Cassidy."

Wild cheering.

Serge wound his way through spectators along the fence— "Excuse me, excuse me, coming through . . ."—until he came to an access gate and a security guard. "Thank you for your service. Could you please open that?"

"Who are you?"

Serge looked at Coleman. "Who are we?" Then back at the guard. "Who does it look like we are? Is this your first rodeo?"

"But the clowns are already out there."

"New liability insurance rule: more clowns."

"I'm going to have to check with a supervisor."

"Go ahead," Serge said as a bronco thundered by, throwing the rider into the fence. "Meanwhile, someone gets hurt, lawsuits fly, and then you're stuttering on the witness stand about why you withheld lifesaving clown procedures."

PA: "Let's hear it for Blueridge Grymes!"

"Well, okay, you seem authorized."

Serge and Coleman waved to the crowd as they strolled across the dirt. Coleman stopped and looked at something stuck to the bottom of one of his big floppy shoes.

"Seriously?" said Serge. "Already?"

"It's everywhere."

Serge pointed. "There's our command post."

They took up positions behind a pair of oak barrels, leaning with their elbows.

"This is it? This is a job?" Coleman whistled. "Clowns have it all figured out."

"The clowning life is extreme boredom punctuated by bursts of sheer terror."

"I remember those birthday parties."

PA: "Let's hear it for Omaha Kid Sloane!"

Gate after gate flew open, and cowboy after cowboy flew through the air. More names from the PA were announced and applauded: Boone Cartwright, Doc Hickock, Austin Buck, Deadwood Dixon, Medicine Hat McCoy.

"What are those big animals over there?" asked Coleman. "They look nasty."

"They are," said Serge, resting his chin on top of a barrel. "Brahma bulls. Unlike horses, they have vicious horns. Only the bravest ride them."

"People *ride* them?" said Coleman. "And we're going to be *out* here? What if they come after me and I get scared?"

"Just get inside one of these barrels. That's what they're for."

Coleman nodded. "You know what I'm thinking about now?"

"The panel is stumped."

"My taste buds."

"Still goose eggs. Please proceed."

"You know how you loved some foods as a kid, but unless you make it a point, you don't get the chance anymore?" said Coleman. "I miss SpaghettiOs."

"This is your news flash?" said Serge.

"Just sayin'."

"But I do feel your pain," said Serge. "Our taste buds have changed, despite all my efforts. It's no coincidence that Chef Boyardee has two different gustation formulas for kids and grown-ups, developed through rigorous kindergarten focus groups. Same thing with the little McDonald's hamburgers. They needed a gateway drug to get kids hooked, but adults were unreliable test subjects, so the winning formula had to be the result of random permutations screened by the preschool set. How else would you explain the counterintuitive final strokes of adding a dollop of mustard and diced pieces of sautéed onions? I remember when I was five taking one of my hamburgers apart: 'I must learn what kind of party is going on in this thing because Mom never comes close!' And the next time she made hamburgers at home: 'Mom, I'll get the mustard and you grab the little translucent squares.'"

"I still like peanut butter and jelly," said Coleman.

"Those sandwiches are critical to keeping your childhood taste buds in shape, or you end up an asshole in a restaurant mispronouncing *foie gras*— . . . Shit, terror time!"

"What is it?"

"That cowboy's starting to slide off the horse but it looks like his left foot is stuck in the stirrup! . . . We're on!"

Serge dashed out into the arena, just as the bronco rider hit the ground and began being dragged through the dirt. Other clowns ran in from the other direction, trying to distract the horse and slow it down. The rider was taking a beating.

Then something nobody had seen before. Serge kicked off his clown shoes, running alongside the slowed horse to get his timing right. Suddenly he leaped, grabbing the saddle knob, getting a foot in the right stirrup and pulling himself aboard. He had the advantage of being able to use both hands, while the horse was hampered by the weight of what he was dragging.

Serge leaned all the way forward, wrapping his arms around the horse's neck, stroking it and whispering in a big brown ear.

The horse began to calm until it stopped. They freed the rider's foot as Serge hopped down and walked around to the front of the horse. He said a few more words in private. The horse whinnied, nickered and snorted. Serge patted him above the nose.

Nearby, the fallen cowboy leaped to his feet.

"Let's hear it for Kyle Lovitt!"

Thunderous cheers.

An older man in a white Stetson ran out onto the dirt. "What have you done?"

"Official clown business," said Serge.

"You broke my bronco!"

Serge patted the side of the horse's head. Another whinny. "He doesn't look broken."

"I mean he won't buck anymore," said the ranch owner. "He's useless at rodeos now."

Serge held out upturned palms. "No good deed goes unpunished . . ."

Meantime, the thrown rider named Kyle had walked over to one of the officials at the fence, who relayed a message up to the PA booth.

"Ladies and gentlemen, this is quite unusual, but just before our intermission Kyle is going to ride again. Of course it won't count in the official standings, but it's the least we can do for one of our brave military veterans."

More wild cheering.

Kyle climbed onto another saddle, gripped tightly with one hand and nodded that he was ready . . .

Chapter 27

Senior year.

Coach Calhoun had finally resigned himself to wearing bifocals.

He was sitting behind his desk going over the tryout sheet for the upcoming season. Seemed everyone wanted to play for Pahokee. He ran a finger down the list of names. The finger stopped. A slight smile. No surprise there.

A knock at the door.

He removed the glasses. "Chris, come in."

"Thanks, Coach." She'd gone through a growth spurt over the last three years and was nearing five ten. The chair on the other side of the coach's desk was getting small.

"As usual, you want to talk about something?"

"I'm not asking for any favors . . ."

"I already know where this is going," said Calhoun. "You signed up again for tryouts."

"Four years in a row," said Chris. "This is my last chance."

The coach took a deep breath with paternal eyes. "Chris, I want you to listen carefully to me and take it to heart. I never saw this coming when we first met, but I can't tell you what a pleasure it's been. You make all this worthwhile. You're the kind of student that inspires teachers to teach, and coaches to coach. You've got the best attitude, been the best manager, but most important, you've kept your grades way up."

She sat silent and serious.

"Look," said Calhoun. "Yes, a lot of these boys are going to get athletic scholarships, but I'd be more than shocked if you didn't land an academic one. You're going to go on and make everyone at this school proud."

"Thank you. It means a lot." She looked down.

The coach sighed in frustration. "Chris, you're asking the unrealistic." He held up the tryout sheet. "Do you know how many students we're going to have to cut as it is?"

"Coach, I don't care if I have to ride the bench. I don't care if I never play. I would just be proud to wear the uniform." She placed a hand on her chest where the numbers would go. "As I said, no favors. If I don't earn it, so be it. But I've really been working on my kicking over the summer. Can you just come out to the field and take a look?"

Calhoun slowly began to nod. "Okay, you've more than earned a look. But promise me that this won't get your hopes up . . ."

The receivers coach, the one named Odom, had been promoted to the head position a couple seasons back. He heard a knock on his office door.

"Lamar, come in. What's up?"

The coach pulled out a chair. "I want you to keep an open mind."

"Uh-oh, I've heard that one before."

Calhoun explained what he had in mind. "What do you think?"

A long pause. "Lamar, I know how fond you are of Chris. And you know I am as well. But we already have two solid place kickers coming back from last year, and an even better punter."

"A lot of teams carry three place kickers," said Calhoun.

"I know, in case of injury or ineligibility," said Odom. "But often the third-stringer plays another position. We have a corner-back who can easily fill in."

"Would you send him out for a field goal in the final seconds?"

"Are you trying to tell me Chris will be our best kicker?"

"No, third best. But a solid third," said Calhoun. "Can you do me a favor? . . ."

Minutes later, both coaches stood with folded arms on the side of an empty field. Chris was waiting at the thirty-yard line with a big sack of footballs spilled onto the ground.

"Okay, Chris!" shouted Lamar. "Show him what you showed me."

She teed up a ball between the hash marks, took the requisite steps back and stopped. She let her arms dangle in concentration. Then she loped forward and let it fly.

It was a perfect end-over-end kick—that hooked left of the up-right.

Calhoun looked sideways. "But it had plenty of distance." Odom didn't respond.

She teed up another. It split the uprights.

"See?" said Calhoun.

"That's just one-for-two," said Odom.

Chris proceeded through the rest of the balls on the grass. Except for one that bounced off the crossbar, they were all true down the middle.

"What do you think now?" asked Calhoun.

"It's different in helmet and pads," said Odom. "Even more so in game situations . . ."

The next day, all the returning players and would-bes covered the field. Whistles blew. Students were sorted according to position. And a handful collected around the coach in charge of kickers. They started at the fifteen-yard line. The coach made notes on a clipboard as each player took shots at the goalposts.

The field had been such chaos earlier, with so many more players than usual, that they didn't notice. But now they did, nudging each other and pointing downfield at a particular player with the number 00.

Chris kicked a modest-length field goal. Then the players didn't pay any more attention. They were too busy trying to make the team. They moved the kicking tees back ten yards and the hopefuls went at it again . . .

Tryouts continued pretty much as they all do. Triage. The ones who were definitely going to make the team, the ones who had no prayer, and the middle group clinging to a dream.

The day of reckoning came. Tryouts were over. Players filled a hallway, nervous silence, waiting. A door opened and they perked up. The head coach came out of the locker room and taped a sheet of paper on the wall. The final list. Students lined up single file, taking turns, one by one, looking for their name. Then either an under-the-breath "Yes!" or demure heartbreak.

Chris's nerves couldn't take it. She had deliberately placed herself at the very end of the line, because she didn't want anyone else around when she got the news. Finally there was only one boy left in front of her. He read down the list, twice, then hung his head and walked away. She watched until he was out of sight, and took a deep breath. "This is it."

She stepped up to the wall and read down the first column with no luck. Her eyes started down the second and she had to take a break from the tension. There weren't a lot of names left, and that would be it. Chris summoned courage and went back to the list. Almost exactly where she had left off, she immediately saw it. And her hand went over her mouth. "Oh, my God."

Her name.

She kept blinking and checking again because she didn't trust her eyes. But each time it was still there.

The empty hallway echoed with joy. "*Wooooo-hooooooooo!*"

She jumped up and down and spun around, crashing into Coach Calhoun. He steadied her by the arms. "Easy, you don't want to hurt yourself before the season."

"I didn't know you were there. Where'd you come from?"

"I kind of wanted to be here."

"Oh, thank you! Thank you! Thank you!"

Now Calhoun grabbed her wrists and pulled them back. "Okay, new rule. You don't hug coaches."

"Sorry, it's just . . ."

"I know." He began walking away. "Get some sleep. Practice starts tomorrow."

Chapter 28

OKEECHOBEE RODEO

The gate burst open wide with an explosion of horse.

It was the encore performance everyone had been await-
ing from the service veteran. This bronco bucked even meaner
than the first, but Kyle Lovitt was more than up to it. This time,
the ride went flawlessly through the required eight seconds, and
Kyle jumped down like a dismounting gymnast to stick the
landing.

The PA announcer needn't comment. The crowd was already
on its feet.

A smaller gate opened, and a cowgal ran into the arena. She
tearfully hugged Kyle. "You were magnificent!"

Serge strolled over. "Hope I'm not interrupting anything."

The woman turned, and suddenly Serge had tight arms around

his neck. "I saw what you did for Kyle! Thank you! Thank you! Thank you! . . ."

"Easy now." Serge grabbed her wrists to pull them down. "All in a clown's day, Cheyenne."

"Thank you . . . Wait, how do you know my name?"

The clown removed his red-ball nose and replaced it. "It's me, Serge, from the motel. You're my little history helper."

"Serge?" Cheyenne said in surprise. "I didn't know you were with the rodeo."

"Neither do they," said Serge. "So I guess Kyle's your boyfriend."

"No, silly. My brother."

Serge extended an earnest hand. "I always appreciate a chance to thank one of our heroes who protects the cornucopia of freedoms in this land."

Kyle shook the hand. "I'm not a hero."

"And that's exactly what every single hero says, or they wouldn't be heroes," added Serge. "If you walked around all day bragging about how great you are, I guess you'd be . . . I don't know, elected something?"

Cheyenne squeezed his hand. "Thanks again for helping him with that horse."

"And thanks again for his service," said Serge. "Kyle, where were you stationed?"

"Two tours Afghanistan, one Iraq."

The cowgal glanced around. "So is your friend with you?"

"Coleman?" Now it was Serge's turn to look around. "I completely forgot in all the excitement. Where is that idiot?"

They checked in every direction, until Serge's eyes stopped. Smoke was drifting out of one of the barrels. "Excuse me," he said. "This will only take a sec . . ."

The lid of a wooden barrel was raised, and Coleman looked up. "Hey, Serge."

"What the hell do you think you're doing?"

"Nuthin'."

"I never thought I would utter this sentence, but you can't smoke dope in a clown barrel."

"I got scared," said Coleman. "Just trying to take the edge off."

"Well, don't!" snapped Serge. "Now get out here. There's someone I want you to meet . . ."

Serge grinned with embarrassment as he led his pal back across the arena. "Coleman, I'd like you to meet Cheyenne's brother, Kyle, one of our nation's military heroes."

Coleman stared at an empty sleeve in Kyle's cowboy shirt. "You only have one arm."

"Coleman! For God's sake! You can't just go up to people and say they only have one arm. *Especially* when they only have one arm." Serge turned. "My deepest apologies."

"Don't worry about it," said Kyle.

"What happened to the arm?" asked Coleman.

"Jesus!" Serge smacked his forehead.

"That's all right," said Kyle. "IED went off outside Kandahar. We lost a good woman that day. She was my flank. Next to that, the arm's nothing."

Serge lowered his head. "Your breed never ceases to amaze me. Living by your own high moral code when the rest of us seem to be living by an anti-code. Just so you know, I also live by my own code, drawn from ancient Greeks, Renaissance thinkers, the Age of Reason, President Lincoln and Stones lyrics—'the better angels of our nature,' and 'you can't always get what you want'—if you catch my drift. A lot of my code still doesn't make sense, but that's the whole point, isn't it? Kant borrowed from the Roman poet Horace the Latin phrase *sapere aude,* which translates to 'dare to know,' or essentially, 'Challenge yourself to accept hard and inconvenient truths,' as opposed to the current prevailing wisdom: 'Fuck you and the facts you rode in on.' I don't know the Latin for that."

A pause. "What are you talking about?" asked Kyle.

"I'm not sure," said Serge.

"Uh, you don't know what you're talking about?"

"No, I mean that's the title of my life's philosophy. The only thing I'm absolutely certain of is that *I'm Not Sure,*" said Serge. "It's my catchphrase. Walk through the concrete human rain forest with that perspective, and ninety-nine times out of a hundred you'll be more correct than the people who *are* sure. Why? you ask. Okay, hold on to your hat, Kyle, because you've been out of the country for a while . . ." Serge leaned closer and dropped his voice ". . . believe it or not, it's now totally okay to make up every single thing that comes out of your mouth." He stopped and nodded hard. "I know, I know. It's hard to believe, but it's so widespread it's often the person standing right next to you."

"I agree," said Coleman, "because pot makes me smart."

"Excuse me." Cheyenne pointed to activity in the starting gates. "Intermission's ending. We need to be going before the Brahma bulls start."

"Good talk!" said Serge, glancing toward the far side of the arena. "Back to live action . . ."

Elbows rested atop the barrels again. A gate swung open. A bull bucked.

"Those were some good folk," said Serge. "Gives me hope."

"One arm, geez."

"Can you stop?"

"No, I'm just trying to remember what not to say. Anything else?"

"If someone has a mole on their face the size of a pepperoni," said Serge.

"How many times do I have to apologize for that?"

"But did you actually have to use the word 'pepperoni'?"

Yelling and gasps from the crowd.

"Uh-oh," said Serge. "We're needed again."

Serge took off across the dirt, and Coleman dove in a barrel.

A frenzy of clown activity swirled in the middle of the arena. The rider had been thrown clear, but the bull came back to stomp and gore, as they're prone to do. The clowns jumped and whooped to distract the ton of fury from the hapless cowhand . . . Across the arena, a curious head popped out of a barrel and peeked around, puffing a joint.

For some reason, this interested the bull. He turned and stared toward the barrel.

Coleman casually looked around the arena as he puffed. Until his eyes locked with the bull's. He shrieked in alarm. The joint went flying, and the bull came running.

"Crap!" Coleman pulled the lid back down on top of the barrel and squeezed his hands together in prayer. "Please, please, please . . ."

Thundering hooves approached. The point of a long white horn pierced the barrel, and the whole thing was suddenly on its side. Another horn attacked the wood as the container began to rotate across the dirt under the momentum of the raging steer. If it had been a car wreck, it would have been called a barrel roll. In this case, it literally was a barrel roll.

Coleman looped and spun and looped some more in an unending violent cascade down the length of the arena. He covered his mouth between bulging cheeks. "Starting to get a little sick in here . . ."

Meanwhile, everyone else was able to flee to safety either through hurriedly opened gates or by wildly scrambling over fences. After he helped vault the last person's butt up over the barrier into safety, only Serge was left.

He spun in highly emotional concern. "Coleman, my best pal! . . ."

Angry horns drove the barrel forward, rolling by in front of Serge.

"I don't like this anymore," Coleman yelled with an echo, as if he was shouting from the bottom of a well. "I'm too high."

"Hang tight! I'm so sorry for getting you into this! I'll never forgive myself!"

The rest of the clowns reemerged with the other rodeo staff, who were expert in handling this most dangerous aspect of the event. They surrounded the bull, speaking softly with calm movements. Then they lassoed its horns and brought the beast under control before guiding it into a secure chute.

The clowns righted the barrel, and Serge pulled off the lid. "Buddy! Are you okay?"

"What's happening?" Coleman had made himself into a ball. "Is it over?"

"You're safe now."

Coleman slowly stood up in the barrel. As soon as his curly red wig was visible, the crowd went wild.

One of the top rodeo officials trotted over in seriousness. "We saw everything that happened. We know what was going on."

"You do?" said Serge.

The official nodded. "And you guys aren't on our official list. What's your name?"

"Serge."

"No, him."

"Uh, Coleman."

"Coleman, come with me . . ." They pulled him out of the barrel, and the official took him by the arm. "This way."

Serge ran alongside. "I can explain."

"Save your breath." They reached the center of the arena, and someone handed the official a wireless microphone. He tapped it to make sure it was on, and the sound bounced off the metal roofs. "Ladies and gentlemen, we have just witnessed an amazing display of heroism. While Idaho Jack was in danger of serious injury, and the other clowns weren't having luck controlling the bull, Coleman here . . ." He turned. "It's Coleman, right? Coleman here took stock of the situation and swung into action without regard for his personal well-being, getting the bull's attention and bravely provoking it to attack his barrel, thus averting tragedy . . . Coleman, to what do you owe your quick thinking?"

Coleman leaned toward the microphone. "Pot makes me smart." He stood back up straight and grinned extra wide.

"Uh . . ." said the official. "Well, there you have it. Let's hear it for Coleman."

The standing ovation was deafening.

Serge stood next to Cheyenne and Kyle. "Unbelievable."

The quartet of new friends grabbed nachos and sat at a picnic table on the side of the rodeo.

Serge scooped salsa and sour cream. *Crunch, crunch.* "Normally I never eat sporting-event nachos because they're covered with the kind of kiosk-vat molten cheese that you're forced to deal with later, so I'm baking that into my schedule ahead of time. Don't let it affect your appetite . . . Kyle, what's next for you?"

Kyle looked at his sister. "I have that thing tomorrow morning, so I need to come by and get the flags."

"What thing?" said Serge. "What flags?"

"A funeral," said Cheyenne. "North of here an hour."

Kyle wasn't eating. "Someone from my unit."

"Sorry for your loss," said Serge. "So the flags? You're in the color guard or something?"

"I wish it was like that." He pushed his cardboard container of chips toward the center of the table. "No matter how hard I try, I just can't understand it."

"Understand what?" asked Serge.

"Protesters," said Cheyenne. "They picket military funerals."

"Come again?" said Serge. "You're stringing words that don't go together."

"And they shouldn't," said Cheyenne. "But here we are."

"What on earth can they be protesting?" asked Serge.

"Our nation's growing tolerance for gays in general, and those serving in uniform in particular," said Cheyenne. "The protesters claim that *all* our fallen heroes—gay, straight, whatever—are

God's punishment for our wicked ways. I can't bear to repeat what's on the signs they wave."

"Wait," said Serge. "Is this that wacko church in Kansas?"

"They may have started it and gotten the headlines," said Kyle. "But the movement's spread. They also picket recruitment centers and pride parades and even other Christian churches that they consider too inclusive. But the worst are the funerals."

"Not to make any excuses," said Serge, "but relative to the size of the country, we're talking about an extremely tiny number."

"How few is an acceptable number when you know the person being laid to rest?"

"True, true."

"But you raise a good point," said Kyle. "The idiots yelling in the streets are a small fraction. The problem is the complicit silence of a large segment of the population. They may not care for that kind of cruelty at funerals, but they're plenty cruel the rest of the time."

"Please elaborate."

"The bellwether is political campaigns," said Kyle. "One thing politicians can be counted on is to follow the polls, regardless of what they personally believe or who gets hurt. A while back it was 'don't ask, don't tell.' Then society evolved, or at least fifty-one percent did, and that cynical ploy is no longer reliable. So now when some elected cretin needs a poll bump, they've moved on to attacking one of the last acceptable targets—transgender citizens—which is code for broader hate that's not exactly cool to articulate anymore. And these leaders wouldn't be doing it if the polls didn't tell them enough of the public was behind them. That's what really hurts . . ."

Serge didn't know what to say, so he did the right thing and didn't say anything.

"Those of us out in the field know these people. We *are* these people, whether it personally applies or not, because all we have out there is each other, and when you know you can trust someone with your life, you wouldn't notice or care if they're a Martian. When all is said and done, you realize these are some of the finest people you'll ever meet in life. That's why it's so hard to fathom our political leaders today. Can you imagine what it's like to be in a gun battle, and you're fighting shoulder to shoulder with a member of your unit who just heard on the news that morning that some idiot back home is trying to score votes by saying people of his faith aren't welcome in the very country that he's risking his life to protect? And people cheer this shit in large arenas. The funeral protesters are just the spearhead."

"So this cause of yours is a liberal thing?" asked Serge.

"Not remotely," said Kyle. "It runs the whole spectrum. We got artsy-fartsy types, bikers, pointy heads, guys with shotguns in the back windows of their pickups. Most of us are vets, and the one principle that unites us all is: Don't mess with our brothers- and sisters-in-arms."

Serge nodded. "Explain the business about the flags tomorrow."

"Courts have ruled that the protesters are protected by the First Amendment, which I agree with because that's part of what I fought for—"

Serge inadvertently glanced at an empty sleeve.

"—But they also ruled that the picketers must stay at least three hundred feet away from the funeral. Me and my friends, on the other hand, aren't protesting, so the buffer zone doesn't apply to us. We arrive early and line up twenty feet in front of the pro- test with our huge, overlapping American flags that completely block the view of those at the cemetery paying their respects."

"But I'm sure the protesters are shouting," said Serge.

"That's why we play inspirational music on boom boxes," said Kyle.

"Like what?"

"Like 'This Land Is Your Land.'"

"Where do I sign up?"

"Can you carry a flag? . . ."

The night eventually wound down, and the friends bade each other good night with plans to meet in the morning.

Serge went back in the motel room, heading for the fridge. "I'm already regretting the nachos." He uncapped a bottle of water and turned around. "Coleman!"

"What?"

"You left the door open! Here come the frogs!"

Coleman looked down at something huge leaping through the wickets of his legs.

"Dammit!" Serge dropped to the floor and crawled under the bed. Coleman screamed and ran out the door.

Serge snagged the jumbo amphibian and scooted backward out from under the box spring. As he did, two more frogs hopped under the bed. "The door's still open! Where's that fool?"

He headed for the sidewalk to release his captive and almost bumped into someone.

"Cheyenne! Sorry, didn't see you." He bent down to let the creature hop off into the dark parking lot. "What are you doing back here?" He checked out the cowgal outfit she was still wearing. "I thought this was your rodeo night."

"If you work at a motel, you accept the hours." She gestured back over her shoulder at a sheepish Coleman. "He said you needed a frog rescue."

"Not me, but Coleman definitely needs a rescue, and frogs are the least of it." Serge looked up at a small swirl of insects around one of the porch lights on the motel's walkway. "Are those the blind mosquitoes?"

"That's them."

"What's the big deal everyone's talking about?" said Serge. "I've seen worse swarms of butterflies."

"Oh, that's not remotely close to a swarm. Just a few stragglers out for a stroll. But it does mean they're coming."

"How long?"

"Could be a day, could be three." Cheyenne didn't even know

she was doing it, but she leaned against the doorway with subconscious body language. "You know, you were pretty good out there tonight. Most clowns just run around randomly to create confusion in the animals."

Serge noticed she was absentmindedly rubbing the tip of a cowboy boot on the ground. He cleared his throat: "Uh, you wouldn't happen to have any more vacant rooms tonight?"

"Sure, right next to yours. Why? Expecting anyone?"

"Something's come up. We'll take it."

"I'll go get the key . . ."

She returned in a moment, opening the second room herself. "There you go."

Serge grabbed Coleman by the arm, shoving him inside. "And there *you* go."

"Hey!" yelled Coleman. "What's the deal? . . . Ah, frogs came in! Help!"

"And there are plenty more where that came from if you open this door. Now stay put!" Serge slammed it shut.

"What's going on?" asked Cheyenne.

"Coleman's a crowd. Please, come in."

The second the door closed, Cheyenne's head slowly swiveled around the room with open eyes. "If you're a motel manager, you develop instincts, but I didn't peg you for the damage type. Did you invite a rock star you didn't tell me about?"

Serge threw his arms up in exasperation. Just about everything was knocked over. Broken lightbulbs, torn curtains, pillows disemboweled. "It's Mr. Zippy."

On cue, a ferret jumped up to the TV, standing on his hind legs and chattering demonically. Then he hopped down and scattered Coleman's empty beer bottles like bowling pins. "He's wrapped way too tight, and I'm afraid we're unfit parents. But I've been putting off the inevitable because I didn't want it to reflect poorly on the adoption rights of two dudes."

"No problem," said Cheyenne. "This is a family-run place, and we have a large cage in the back room for the day manager, who has an older cat that needs care. I can put the ferret in there, and I know lots of pet people around here who would be more than happy to take him."

"Thank God," said Serge. "He was getting on my last nerve."

"Be right back." Cheyenne lovingly grabbed the ferret and disappeared.

Then she returned. As soon as Serge opened the door, she slammed into him without warning, and they fell onto the still-made bed. Violent kissing and groping. Clothes flew in all directions. "Can you leave the boots on?" asked Serge. "You can make requests, too."

"Shut up!"

"Haven't had that one before."

They were soon going at it like—well, they deserve *some* privacy.

Shrieking and banging came from both sides of the wall connecting Coleman's room to theirs.

Serge raised a hand. "Can I talk now?"

"Sure, just don't stop."

"That's not really my call," said Serge. "If you haven't noticed, you're the one on top."

"*Oh, yes, yes, yes, yes!...*"—pounding the headboard—"*... Yes! Yes! Yes! ...* Before we go any further, I need to ask a question."

"Further?" asked Serge. "I don't see any more stop signs."

"It's about commitment. You're not one of those guys, I mean . . ."

Great, Serge thought. *Here we go again.*

Cheyenne continued thrusting. "Did you just roll your eyes at me?"

"No, that was a twitch. Please, ask your question."

"Every once in a while I'll find a guy where there's the perfect combination of a meeting of the minds and broiling animal attraction. But more often than not, they turn out to be clinging vines."

"Wait," said Serge. "*That's* your commitment question? You were worried I'd be the smothering one?"

She nodded and thrust. "I hope you understand. There's too many places I've got to see. I'm sure you've heard the song."

"In my sleep," said Serge. "Believe me, you have no worries. And I completely understand about the travelin' jones."

More screaming from Coleman's room. A crash against the wall. "*Frogs!*"

Thrust. "Is your friend okay?"

"Not even close. I just tune out the meltdowns."

Thrust, thrust. "The whole history thing is what first attracted me to you."

"Really?" said Serge. "Me too! Would you like to see my tombstone rubbings?"

"Now?" Cheyenne thrust harder as she whipped her hair side to side. "Isn't that part supposed to come before, when you're trying to *get* me in bed?"

"You're right," said Serge. "Life is all about timing."

"Man, you're weird," said Cheyenne. "For some reason, that just attracts me more."

"And this concludes the slow middle movement of our song. Now it's time for the triple-guitar crescendo." Serge quickly flipped her on the bed, and moans became shrieks, louder and louder. To the point where Coleman stopped shrieking himself and became more afraid of the sounds coming from the next room . . .

The lovers finally collapsed on their backs in pools of sweat.

Serge wiped stinging perspiration from his eyes. "My compliments to the chef."

"I'm still fluttering," said Cheyenne. "And speaking of fluttering, what was that deal with your eyelids and your pupils going up in your head?"

"I had a simultaneous."

"Don't you mean *we* had a simultaneous?"

Serge shook his head. "Just me. I came *and* had A Moment. Thinking about all the murals in town and early telephone service."

"You're shitting me."

"You'd rather me think about old girlfriends, or picture you wearing a walrus mask?"

"I'm not sure." She turned her head on the pillow. "Let's find out."

"Serious?"

She nodded eagerly.

"Where's your cowboy hat?"

"In the office." Cheyenne jumped out of bed. "I'll go get it."

She wiggled into her blue jeans and opened the door. A truck with a full rack of amber lights was pulling up. "What the hell is that?"

"Ordered a rental fishing boat," said Serge. "They attach a temporary hitch on your car and everything. I always figure if you're going in, go big!"

"If you say so."

"Just realized something," said Serge. "What if other guests are trying to call you at the front desk with an emergency?"

"Screw 'em. They're just frogs."

Chapter 29

PAHOKEE

The Blue Devils were an early-season favorite, and they lived up to the hype. Pahokee tore through their district schedule, undefeated after six games. And it wasn't even close. All double-digit victories. You could always pick out the loudest voice on the bench shouting encouragement. Guess who?

A few weeks earlier, before a game, Coach Calhoun was smiling behind his desk as Chris sat on the other side. He actually looked forward to her visits now, and felt something conspicuously missing on the days she didn't show up.

She was wearing her shoulder pads and game jersey: 00. He noticed she was unusually serious.

"Is something wrong?"

"Oh, no, no, no," said Chris. "It's just that I feel awkward asking you for something."

"Never stopped you before."

"But you've done so many favors for me in the last few years."

"What's one more? Fire away."

"But I promised you."

"Promised me what?"

"That I didn't care if I never got on the field," said Chris. "I just wanted to wear the uniform."

"And?"

"I learned that to earn a varsity letter, you have to be in at least one play during a regular-season game."

"Is that so?"

"Coach, in several of these games we've had big leads late in the fourth quarter."

"Some actually huge."

"What I'm asking is, if we're leading by several touchdowns near the end and we score, uh—"

"You'd like to kick off?"

She nodded.

"All right, you've asked," said Calhoun. "We'll just see how it goes. Now, if I could have the office, there's a few things that need dealing with before tonight."

That evening's game proceeded like the previous six Fridays. The Blue Devils built up an early lead, and the defense held their opponent to only three first downs. By the beginning of the fourth quarter, it was 35–0. It was raining.

Calhoun walked over to the head coach for a private talk. By the body language, it seemed that Lamar had to be persistent. Finally, and in no small part simply in order to get Calhoun off his back, the head coach said: "We'll just have to see."

Rain poured harder and the field began turning to mud. Runners lost their footing and passes were impossible to catch. Referees had towels on the field to wipe the ball down between each snap.

It was time to call running plays from here on out. Not to move the ball, but to burn the clock. It was also one of those unwritten rules of football decorum. Don't pass and run up the score at the end. That's why the entire team on the field was second and third string. And even then, Pahokee was unstoppable. They consistently moved the ball five to ten yards a play. They entered the red zone, which means the twenty. Three minutes left.

Lamar Calhoun finished another chat with the head coach and walked back over to the players' bench. "Chris?"

She was leaning forward, wrapped up in the game and still shouting encouragement. She raised her eyes. "Yes, Coach?"

"Start warming up."

It froze her.

"Did you hear me?"

An eager nod. She sprang off the bench and began running toward the practice kicking net.

"Aren't you forgetting something?" Calhoun pointed back under the bench. "You're going to need that."

Chris raced back and snatched her helmet.

Pahokee scored again even faster than expected. Chris barely had time to stretch, no practice kicks. She ran onto the field with ten boys as the rain whipped even harder. Some of her teammates raced past her, slapping her shoulder pads. "Show 'em what you got, Chris."

As she teed up the ball, shouting came from the opposite sidelines. The other coach frantically waved his clipboard at his receiving team. They had just realized a girl was kicking. "Move up! Move up!"

The visiting team advanced ten yards.

The clipboard kept waving. "More!"

The players positioned themselves fifteen yards ahead of where they normally fielded a kick.

Chris stared down at the ball and took a few steps back. Thunder boomed from the clouds over the stadium lights. She looked left and right down the Blue Devil line. Boys nodded back, helmets dripping. The referee blew a whistle for play to resume. Chris ran forward and put her shoe into the leather.

Now here's the thing about kickoffs: they're live balls. Which means that after it travels ten yards, either team can grab it for possession.

It was an exceptionally high kick, which, along with the rain, threw off the receiving team's depth perception. They began slowly backpedaling. Meanwhile, the Pahokee line was sprinting full speed. By the time the visiting team realized the ball was seriously over their heads, all the players were at roughly the same spot on the field.

The ball bounced at the two-yard line and rolled into the end zone. Now it was a full-out race to see who could get there first. A player in a blue jersey leaped horizontally and landed on the ball just before it rolled out of bounds. The referee raised two arms straight into the air.

Touchdown.

The home crowd exploded.

All eyes were on the end zone. They didn't notice it at first. But back toward the other end of the field, whistles were blowing and numerous yellow flags had flown.

Pahokee wasn't trying to run up the score. But the other team felt they had done something far more insulting to rub their opponent's noses in it. They'd sent in a girl.

So here's what happened when the play began. The forward players of the receiving team usually begin moving back to set up their blocks. This time, however, the two players in the middle ran forward as fast as they could. The game was so unwinnable that penalties didn't matter anymore.

Chris had stood alone, watching the ball sail. Two seconds later, she was clobbered by a pair of players coming in from both sides. They sent her flying onto her back. That drew the first whistle and flag. After a few more seconds, as Chris started to push herself up, they pounced again, making sure to push her helmet hard into the grass. "Stay down, girl!"

More whistles and flags. People in the stands began to notice and point, and the celebration in the end zone ceased. The Pahokee team watched two cocky players trotting away from where their kicker was faltering as she tried to get up, a big chunk of muddy turf stuck in her face mask. "Chris!"

The offending players never made it back to their sideline. The Pahokee bench emptied and they were swarmed, then the visiting team entered the fray. It took a while to untangle, but coaches and cops were ultimately able to pull everyone apart.

For a victory, it was unusually silent in the Pahokee locker room. Normally a fight, let alone a bench-clearing brawl, would receive a tongue-lashing from the coaching staff. The players were waiting for the rebuke that never came. Everyone knew what wasn't said aloud. Chris may have been viewed in the past as just a girl, but now she was a Blue Devil, and nobody but nobody does that to one of theirs.

Chapter 30

THE NEXT MORNING

The sun had just peeked over the eastern sky of Lake Okeechobee when a Dodge Ram pickup with all the chrome and jacked-up tires and everything else it stands for rolled into the parking lot. There was the full complement of bumper stickers and decals: black POW-MIA logo, the yellow-green-red bar for Vietnam, silver parachutes for airborne, silver dolphins for submarine service, Purple Heart, Rangers, et cetera, et cetera.

Another pickup rolled in behind, a black Chevy Colorado with more decals, flying flags, American, Marine Corps. The pair of vehicles stopped outside an off-brand motel on the northern shore of Lake Okeechobee. The cabs of the trucks were already full, and more people squatted in the beds of the pickups as if there had been a pre-dawn street-corner call for migrant workers: *"We need ten for six hours . . ."*

A motel room door opened, and Serge and Cheyenne stepped out. He walked to the next door and knocked.

"Just a minute."

"Coleman! Come on! People are waiting!" said Serge.

"It's okay," said Cheyenne. "They have to stop anyway for the others to catch up."

"Others?"

The door opened and Coleman appeared. "All set to go."

Serge stared at a lumpy spot below Coleman's collarbone. "You're wearing the chest pouch?"

"That's right."

Ribbit, ribbit . . .

"A frog's in there?"

Coleman nodded and patted the pouch. "We worked things out last night. We're friends now."

"You do realize they're not like ferrets," said Serge. "I don't think he has any idea what's going on."

"You couldn't be more wrong." Coleman stroked the canvas. *Ribbit.* "And you wouldn't know it to look at him, but he's a raging maniac."

"Don't tell me."

"I found out that it's almost impossible to get a frog to smoke a joint—"

"Another sentence I never thought I'd live to hear."

"—So I grabbed one of the empty plastic bags that come with the trash cans in the room, and put the frog in it. Then I took a mondo, triple-clutch hit and blew it into the bag."

"I realize that among your people such gestures are tokens of goodwill, but we're bordering on animal unkindness here."

"He didn't mind at all." Coleman peeked down through the opening. "He liked the beer, too."

Serge covered his eyes with a hand.

Coleman reached into the pouch. "I know you and Cheyenne had your own thing going on in your room last night, but you missed the real fun."

"Did we?"

Coleman scooped out the frog, stroking its head lightly with an index finger. "Isn't that right, Jeremiah?"

"You call your frog Jeremiah?"

"Because he is a bullfrog."

"Naturally," said Serge. "But back to giving him beer."

"Three Dog Night let their frog drink wine, so I don't see the big fuss."

"Technically their frog *brought* the wine," said Serge. "Didn't that tell you there was some artistic license going on?"

"I don't know what that means, but you should have seen him last night," said Coleman. "When this little sucker gets his swerve on, look out! He was jumping straight up, sideways, even a back-flip. We had a contest."

"You jumped with him?"

"Duh!" said Coleman. "Then I used the plastic ice bucket to make him a little boat in the tub. But what he really liked was the toilet. Don't worry: I taped up the flush handle in case I forgot. I was responsible. And some of those blind mosquitoes had gotten into the room, and I was able to capture a few, but only crushed them a little, and then I sat on the edge of the tub throwing bugs to Jeremiah in the toilet. I wish someone had a camera."

"I can't picture anything more precious."

"I know," said Coleman. "He really had the munchies."

"But don't you think you should be releasing him now?" said Serge. "He probably wants to get back to his own kind."

"I think he's happy," said Coleman. "Remember how they were jumping all over the parking lot last night? Look at him now, happy to sit in my hand."

"Coleman, his eyes are closed. He's still fucked up."

"Then the nice thing to do is let him sleep it off." Coleman opened the pouch. "Back in you go."

A roar erupted from an unseen point around the bend, growing louder and louder until it was vibrating stuff. The source came into view and pulled into the parking lot.

The bikers had arrived.

Harleys, helmets and star-spangled bandannas. Most had black leather vests, festooned with medals and patches from every branch of service.

"Time to saddle up," said Cheyenne, and the three climbed in the bed of the second truck. The caravan pulled out of the parking lot and headed north.

Serge sat against the back gate next to Coleman. "I think I might have a problem."

"I'll do anything I can."

"It's not that kind of problem. It's Cheyenne." Serge searched for words. "She doesn't want a commitment."

"I don't see the problem."

"*That's* the problem," said Serge. "Almost every woman I've ever met wants a commitment. Some act like they don't at first, but it eventually comes up, and I'm a ramblin' kind of guy."

"I get it," said Coleman. "You think she's acting?"

"No, I think she's on the level."

"Then you're home free."

Serge was quiet a moment. "I can't describe it, but it's having some kind of effect on me. I'm oddly attracted to this. She's a ramblin' kind of *gal,* and that makes *me* want to commit. And then I'll be trapped following her around a Pottery Barn with an armload of guest towels and that feeling that I can't breathe."

"Jesus!" said Coleman. "Get a grip. You can't let her split us up."

"Thanks for thinking of me."

"No, seriously," said Coleman. "I don't know how to survive."

"You'll do fine."

"Serge!" He grabbed his friend tightly by the arm. "Don't mess around. You know I'd end up in the woods behind a 7-Eleven living on an old mattress."

"I see your point."

"Maybe it's all a trick," said Coleman. *Ribbit*. "If you find out that she secretly wants to commit, then you won't be attracted anymore."

"For once you speak as a sage, my finely toasted friend. And I know just how to find out . . ."

The patriotic procession of trucks and hogs cruised up through Osceola County, wind flapping hair and scarves. Serge scooted across the bed of the pickup until he settled in next to Cheyenne.

She smiled coyly. "Well, look who it is."

"Hi, Cheyenne. Uh, uh, I mean, uh, what I'm trying to say is, uh . . ."

"Wow, I've never known you to be at a loss for words."

"Cheyenne, would you like to go steady?"

"Is this a joke?" She had a good laugh. "Are you in seventh grade?"

"I've given this a lot of thought." Serge nervously picked at his fingernails. "I'd like to give you an ID bracelet with our names engraved."

"Whoa! Stop!" said Cheyenne. "You *are* serious. I thought I could trust you when we talked about this last night."

"You *can* trust me. That was just a test, to make sure what you said wasn't a trick."

"You sure?"

"When was the last time you were in a Pottery Barn?"

"Like, never."

"Case closed. You passed with flying colors."

Serge's butt scooted back across the pickup's bed until he was at the gate again.

"Well?" asked Coleman.

"It's worse than I thought. She's never even stepped foot in a Pottery Barn."

"Good God!" said Coleman. "How can you not love a woman like that?"

"I know, I know," said Serge. "I must think of something. She's just got to have some kind of a big turnoff that's a deal breaker."

"Maybe when she laughs really hard, she sounds like a donkey."

"She has a great laugh."

"You're fucked."

Nearly an hour later, the ad hoc motorcade arrived and parked along a remote country road where the only building had a steeple. Across the street, tombstones in a neatly manicured field. Nobody had arrived at the cemetery yet. Funeral workers had already set up the rows of folding chairs under a white sun canopy. A brass contraption with heavy-gauge straps sat over a freshly dug hole.

Across the street was a different story. Bullhorns, tightly screwed faces, and some of the most vile signs that have ever been painted.

Over a distant hill on the straight highway, various vehicles headed toward them. Moments later, the pickup trucks emptied and motorcyclists dismounted.

The new arrivals were heckled as they carried their flags to ward the protest line. The malcontents noticed the size and nature of the people coming toward them, particularly the bikers. The protesters took an intimidated step back. "You touch us and we'll sue! We taking video of all of this!"

Not a word was spoken among the flag people. They formed a precise line from rehearsal, turning their backs to the picketers and presenting fifteen huge renditions of Old Glory that formed an effective red, white and blue curtain.

"Hey, you can't block us like that! We have rights!"

No response.

Up the road came a solemn line of cars with headlights on at noon.

Someone reached down and pressed a button on a boom box.

"*. . . This land is your land . . .*"

The funeral procession pulled though the cemetery gates, and the hearse parked near the sun canopy.

The protesters screamed louder. The boom box was turned up.

Men with white gloves slid the casket out the back of the hearse and ceremoniously placed it on the support straps over the grave. It had its own American flag. An honor guard gave a salute with guns. A trumpet played. Two of the people with white gloves removed the flag from the casket and, with measured cadence, folded it into a triangle. One of them bent down to present it to a widow with small children.

The protesters had so much anger baggage, you wouldn't have thought there was room for more. But the flags in front of them were just too much. Not only did they block their view of the service, but more importantly, they blocked the mourners' view of their signs. On top of that, the boom box. It just wasn't fair!

"I'll fix this!"

The leader of the protest, a pastor, ran around the end of the line and stood facing them, waving his sign and screaming into a bullhorn.

Kyle Lovitt and the others looked up and down their ranks. They had been over this before in their meetings. In case the picketers ignored the court order: No violence. Don't even move lest there be inadvertent physical contact that could become courtroom fodder. Just get out cell phones and document the violation of the buffer zone.

Serge hadn't gotten the memo.

He handed Coleman his flag and ran over to the protest leader. "Excuse me, but you're out of your comfort zone. I suggest you slither back behind the buffer line."

"Go to hell! You and your queer buddies are interfering with our First Amendment rights. You're forcing us to step forward."

"There's the little matter of the court order," said Serge.

"What about it?" said the leader. "I don't see anybody here to enforce it."

"Oh, but I do." Serge swiftly nailed him in the chest with a stun gun, and just as quickly stashed it away. The leader collapsed, and his followers came running.

Kyle glanced back and forth. "Turn off your phones! Erase those files! . . ."

Serge nonchalantly sauntered over to his group as the picketers dragged their leader back behind enemy lines.

Kyle grabbed him by the arm. "Why did you go and do that?"

"What are you talking about?"

"You're just lucky that our flags blocked their video cameras."

"If you say so." Serge opened a brown billfold and removed a driver's license. "Hmm, his name's Jebediah."

"What's that?"

"A wallet I just happened to find on the ground." Serge replaced the license.

"Why'd you take it from him?"

"You don't want to know."

"And you didn't tell me that."

Chapter 31

PAHOKEE

Coach Calhoun strolled down the corridor outside the locker room. He heard slapping footsteps on the wax floor. A student ran past him practically in tears.

"Chris! Come back here!"

She stopped, embarrassed, trying to hide emotion.

"What's wrong?"

"Nothing."

"Don't 'nothing' me. In my office, now."

Chris sat quietly in a familiar wooden chair. Calhoun kept trying to get her to open up, but it was like prying answers from a hostile witness. She was staring at the floor, lips trembling, so shaken that the coach's mind ran through the menu of worst cases that can befall teenagers. The list was long and ugly in these parts.

All she kept saying was that it was "her fault." That only made the list grow in Calhoun's head. Finally, the coach was able to drag out enough details to learn that the problem was academic, and he practically collapsed with relief. But then puzzlement. What kind of problem could Chris have in class? So many straight A's now that he barely glanced at her report cards.

"Chris, I can't help you if you won't talk."

It wasn't that Chris was resisting the coach. She was one of those people who can hold in crying as long as they don't talk, or it all erupts. She couldn't have that. So she silently reached in her backpack with a quivering hand and pulled out a term paper.

Calhoun took it and looked at the top of the first page. A big red *F*. Now he was really confused. Chris never got an F in anything. Plus, this was a science paper, her best subject.

"Okay, Chris, I know you're upset, so can you come back here tomorrow, same time?"

She nodded.

"And can you leave the term paper with me?"

Another nod. She left.

Coach Calhoun leaned back in his chair with the paper and didn't know what to make of it. But the game plan for that Friday night's gridiron contest had just been put on hold. He scooted his chair up and logged on to his computer. Surfing the net, checking her footnotes. To himself: "What the heck is dark energy?" More clattering of the keyboard. "Quarks? Photons? Planck time?"

The next afternoon, the final bell of the school day rang. Minutes later, Coach Calhoun entered a classroom. The only person still there was a teacher behind his desk, starting to grade quiz papers. He had been a midterm replacement for the previous science teacher, who had left to accept a higher-paying position at a private school on the east side of the county.

"Mr. Garns?"

"Yes?"

"Coach Calhoun." They shook hands.

"How can I help you?"

"It's about one of your students, Chris Maples."

"Oh." Garns turned serious and looked down, making a mark on a test paper. "I guess she went running to you about her last grade."

Calhoun hit pause in his brain. This was not how he expected the conversation to begin. He reassessed. "She didn't come running to me. But I did see her paper. I've known her for a while, and I'm trying to understand this F."

Garns, not looking up: "She used the Internet."

"What does that mean?"

"Students aren't supposed to rely on the Internet for sourcing. It's unverified," said the teacher. "I made that extremely clear when I came on board."

"I agree," said Calhoun. "But I went through her footnotes. These weren't bulletin boards or blogs. They were scientific research journals with articles from professors at Caltech, MIT, Carnegie Mellon. I asked other teachers, and those Internet sources are allowed."

"The footnotes weren't in the proper format."

Calhoun took another deep breath. "I looked at your strike-throughs on her paper, like where she cited dark energy as the reason why gravity isn't slowing down the expansion of the big bang."

"We haven't covered that in class. And I don't believe it exists."

"She noted it as a theory. It has support in the research journals."

"You're a science teacher now?" Garns stood. "Second-guessing me?"

"Not in the least. I'm just trying to sort all this out."

"She also has a big attitude problem."

Calhoun's head practically spun on his neck. "Are we talking about the same person?"

"She undermines my authority."

"She talks back? That would surprise me."

"No, just smug like she's too smart for my class, challenging me in front of the other students."

"Challenging?"

"Interrupting to ask cynical questions, like the dark energy thing."

"I think she's just trying to learn."

"I see where this is going," said Garns. "You *coaches.*"

"What's that supposed to mean?"

"Pressuring teachers to keep players eligible."

Calhoun stopped again, this time to check his temper. He knew there was a widespread stereotype about coaches tampering with grades. But in reality, the vast majority take a holistic approach to developing a student, both as an athlete and a person, getting to know their parents, talking to their teachers.

"Can we dial this back a bit?" said Calhoun. "It's not about us. It's a student's welfare."

"So you coddle your players?"

"We don't need to continue in this direction."

"You sports guys think you have so much influence."

Calhoun took a final pause to choose words, because a bridge was about to catch fire. "I've seen you before. Not often, but enough to know."

"Seen me?"

"Some of the finest people in the world are teachers. They work tirelessly for little pay. But what really makes them so special is they're like parents to the whole community. They find no greater joy than helping students succeed to their utmost potential . . . Then there's some of the worst people in the world. Also teachers, the rare ones here and there. Bitter because their lives didn't work out the way they'd hoped. And when they see a great kid with a bright future, they don't take pride in helping them along. Instead, they're jealous and try to crush their spirit. That is unforgivable."

The coach walked around the desk and got face-to-face with

Garns. "But you're right about one thing. Coaches do have undue influence in our culture. I make it a rule not to use mine. I also make exceptions."

Calhoun stormed out of the classroom and slammed the door.

C oach Calhoun sat in the principal's office. He'd finished laying out his case, and now the ball was in the other court.

"I find all this hard to believe," said the principal. "But since it's coming from you . . ."

"So you'll look into it?"

"With due diligence. If it's true, this is very disturbing news. It has no place at my school."

The principal kept his word. He interviewed students and parents, and the feedback was uniform. Some teachers use a tough style of teaching, but only to push the students to do their best. This new science teacher just seemed to genuinely dislike the kids.

By the end of the week, Garns was packing up his belongings in a cardboard box. And swearing he'd find a way to get even.

Chapter 32

OSCEOLA COUNTY

C reeping was afoot.

Two suspicious figures on their hands and knees inched forward in the night. North of St. Cloud, Florida. North of sanity.

Coleman raised his right hand and sniffed the palm, then held it to Serge.

"Get that out of my face." Serge's back was like a leopard's. "You're just going to have to deal with it."

They crawled forward across the pasture like a sniper team. At least Serge did. Coleman's stealth was more like that of something in a playpen. Serge looked up: "Full moon. That's the worst for our mission, but we were in no position to pick our timing."

Ribbit.

"You brought Jeremiah?" asked Serge.

"He's good luck."

"He's loud," said Serge. "He'll give our position away."

"Not my Jeremiah!"

"Shhhh! Keep it down!" Serge lowered his chin in the tall weeds. "People are up . . ."

Moments earlier, the gold Satellite had left the highway for the concealment of a dirt road that ran through pine hardwoods. From there, Serge drove across the bumpy pasture as curious cattle watched the silhouette of the Plymouth in the moonlight. They continued on until reaching some new-growth woods and brush at the edge of a property. That's where they left the car and commenced their crawl. Now they were in the perfect position that Serge had scoped out in advance with Internet help. Ahead: the target.

A white farmhouse sat atop a small hill.

It was a large farmhouse, as they go, two stories with an addition on back. The owner's budget apparently favored size over condition. A tin roof sagged above the front porch. The wood siding had termite damage and missing paint from the sun. A pond sat off the driveway. And now two strangers lay in the woods just a stone's throw from the front door.

"What do we do?" asked Coleman.

"Wait and watch." Serge got out binoculars and scanned windows. "I picked the best spot to launch our operation, but that's where my plan ends. I knew this extraction would be tricky because I figured he didn't live alone. We must recon the social structure of this abode and find its soft underbelly."

"What's going on in there?"

"Remember the pastor from the funeral protest? He just went in the kitchen. I've picked up five other people inside, but they're all young women. Long dresses and bonnets. They're holding candles like it's some kind of ceremony."

"No guys?"

"Something weird's going on in there."

Coleman kissed his frog on the mouth. "Weird how?"

"Looks like one of those cults where the leader preaches strict obedience to the gospels in order for him to have sex with everyone."

"Is that what the gospels are about?"

"I hate to judge without all the facts, but I'm guessing he's taking liberties." Serge handed Coleman the binoculars. "Stay here."

"Where are you going?"

"To get more facts."

Serge darted ahead toward the farmhouse, sweeping around the west side, which was shielded from the moonlight. He plastered his back against the building, creeping sideways. Soon he was under a window. He slowly rose on tiptoes until his eyes were just above the sill.

Inside the living room, the women stood in a line with heads bowed over their candle holders. The pastor held an open Bible with one hand and gesticulated wildly with the other. Then he stepped forward. The women's chests heaved with anticipation. He looked up and down the row before blowing out one of the candles. He took that woman by the hand and led her into another room.

Serge resumed creeping along until he came to another window. This one was a bit higher. He found some loose bricks on the side of the house and fashioned a little stack. Two eyes again rose above a sill. It was a bedroom. Mirrors everywhere, including the ceiling. A video camera sat on a tripod in the corner. Serge watched the pastor taking off his shirt. The young woman took off her bonnet and reached for the top button under her neck.

"Holy mother," Serge said to himself. "There's no way she's even close to eighteen. I can't watch."

He crouched down below the sill, and when he did, a couple of the bricks at his feet toppled. "Shit." Serge hit the ground and rolled himself as tightly as possible against the lattice along the farmhouse's crawl space. He looked sharply up and saw the shadow of the pastor's face against the windowpane. Serge held his breath as the shadow moved from one side of the window to the other, clearly convinced something was out there.

After the longest of times, the shadow left the window, and voices could be heard inside.

"Whew!" Serge scurried in a big loop around the side of the house and dove back into the brush next to Coleman.

"What did you see?"

"It's worse than I thought," said Serge. "First, I don't see any way of extracting the pastor without raising general mayhem from the women. They've been brainwashed. So we must abort the mission and put him under surveillance until we can identify an interception point away from his flock. Second, I think the one he's about to have sex with is underage. I should burst in there under general principles to stop it. But what if I'm wrong or she's older than she looks, or some kind of common-law wife?"

"Maybe you could phone in an anonymous tip."

"That's a great idea." Serge pulled out a disposable burner phone with prepaid minutes. He looked up as clouds drifted across the moon, cutting the light. "And our luck might be turning. We're getting extra cover of darkness . . ." He began pressing buttons.

A tap on his shoulder.

"Not now, Coleman. I'm phoning in the important information."

Another tap. "Uh, Serge . . ."

"I told you I'm busy!"

Tap, tap, tap.

"Dammit, Coleman! What is it that can't wait?"

A crunching of leaves. "*Who's out there!*"

Serge looked up to see the pastor aiming a double-barrel twelve-gauge shotgun.

"Damn," Serge whispered. "Keep your head down and don't move."

"I said, who's out there!"

The pastor kept walking, straight toward them.

The gun cocked, now only feet away. Just a thin, single row of bushes between them and discovery. The clouds began thinning and drifting away. The moonlight grew brighter on the leaves.

"Come out with your hands up or I'll blast ya!"

Stone silence. Then:

Ribbit...

The shotgun's twin barrels bore down on an exact spot in the bushes.

Jeremiah slipped out of Coleman's pouch, and before the pair could react, the amphibian leaped from the brush. Another big jump, and it landed at the pastor's feet.

"For heaven's sake! I'm giving myself a heart attack over a stupid bullfrog!" The pastor propped the shotgun on his shoulder and turned back toward the farmhouse.

That was all the opportunity Serge needed. He sprang from the vegetation and caught the pastor in the small of his back with the stun gun. The victim fell inert.

Serge and Coleman grabbed him under the armpits and dragged the limp body from view as several curious people in bonnets appeared in the front window...

J ust after midnight, the gold Plymouth returned to the motel on the north shore of Lake Okeechobee. It backed up to their room.

Serge stood idly next to the car like he was bored.

"What are you waiting for?"

"Cheyenne."

"You're bringing her in on this?"

"Just the opposite." His eyes scanned every conceivable direction. "I have to make sure she doesn't get the slightest whiff of what we're up to. I'm taking a wild stab this is a touch worse than romantic commitment."

Serge began to whistle as he leaned against the back of the car, slowly rocking. "That's long enough. She's not around. Open the room and I'll get our guest from the trunk." He bent down and began inserting a key in the lid.

A woman's voice: "There you are!"

"Jesus Christ!" Serge leapt up and landed sitting on the lid of the trunk. "Where the hell did you come from?"

"Uh, just around the corner," said Cheyenne. "What's gotten into you? You're awfully jumpy."

"Nothing, nothing," said Serge. "Almost had an accident up the road. Heart's still pounding."

A wary eye. "Are you sure that's it?"

"Definitely!"

"If you say so." An off-hand smile. "I didn't know where you went, because I was kind of hoping . . . uh, you could show me your tombstone rubbings."

"Yes, yes, sure. How long are you on tonight? I just have a couple pressing business matters to tie up, and then it will be a freaking tombstone jamboree."

"Are you positive you're okay?"

"I'll ring you in the office when I'm free."

"I'll be waiting." She headed back to her office, glancing over her shoulder in suspicion. Serge had a toothy grin and waved to her with wiggling fingers. Then she was gone.

"Hurry, Coleman!"

The trunk popped, and soon a familiar scene.

Two people sat next to each other on the edge of a motel bed. Coleman smiled and petted a frog. Serge petted a roll of duct tape.

A brief scream as the pastor regained consciousness and looked down at all the tight rope and his uncomfortable chair.

Ribbit.

"Where are my manners?" said Serge. "Jebediah, meet Jeremiah. Sorry, but he didn't bring his wine."

"What do you want from me?"

"Damn, you're fast." Serge began cleaning under his fingernails with the tip of a large-bladed hunting knife. "My conditions are nonnegotiable. First, release all the young women at your farmhouse. We both know what's going on. Second, no more protests outside military funerals. Make that anywhere in the world while we're at it."

"You can't do this!" said the pastor. "You're abrogating my First Amendment rights!"

"Couldn't agree more," said Serge. "Few things are as important to me as our blessed Constitution."

"You agree?" said the pastor. "Then how can you do this?"

Serge shrugged. "I'm wrong. Sorry."

The pastor fumed with flared nostrils. "You're going to hell!"

"Meet you in the elevator."

The pastor threw a tantrum in his chair, making the legs tap-dance on the wooden floor. "Who do you think you are?"

"An angel," said Serge. "Avenging or merciful. You make the call!"

"You're no angel!"

"I was using poetic slack," said Serge. "'The better angels of our nature.' That was Lincoln. And I want you to embrace all your fellow citizens as children of God."

"I don't want to."

"'You can't always get what you want.' That was Jagger."

"You won't get away with this!"

"I don't have to get away with anything if you agree to my simple terms."

"Never, you pervert! Not in a million years."

"I was kind of hoping you'd say that, because I have so been wanting to try this." Duct tape quickly went over the mouth, and the chair began being dragged backward.

Minutes later, Serge sat at the steering wheel of the Plymouth. "Coast clear? No Cheyenne?"

"Right-o," said Coleman, leaning over a bong.

"You're not even looking."

"I'm high. I have extra powers."

The gold Plymouth slowly pulled around to the dark side of the motel and the special parking area for the bass boats favored by the sportsmen staying at the inn. Serge backed up to one, got out and fastened the trailer hitch.

"You're stealing a boat?" said Coleman.

"No, this is one I rented earlier and had waiting here on standby." Serge climbed back in the car to the sound of banging in the trunk. "It's actually a pretty good deal around here. I grabbed this baby on the wings of hope that I could employ it in my next science project." The Plymouth pulled out of the parking lot and turned east . . .

Lake Okeechobee has various access points for fishermen. There are a number of ramps over the Herbert Hoover Dike to public launches. If you have a really big boat already in the water, then you have to enter through one of three locks.

"It's not a very big boat," said Coleman.

"No lock, no problem."

Serge followed the road curling south toward Clewiston until he found one of the ramps, dark and deserted. The bass boat slid into the water, including the captive, tied up again to the chair. Serge got behind the wheel and pushed the throttle just above idle.

At this part of the lake, the open water is a few miles away. In between, marshland laced with canals, including a large one around the rim, logically called the Rim Canal. Serge rode it awhile before reaching an opening off the port side, and turned left into what's known as the Old Moore Haven Canal.

From there it was a straight shot through ferocious thriving nature. Birds and bugs and bogs.

"Listen to that racket," said Coleman.

"The swamp sizzles at night," said Serge. "Humans might be at the top of the food chain, but out here we're seriously outnumbered."

"What is this place?"

"They call it Dynamite Pass. But it's nothing like the cool name of the spot where we're heading. In fact, I chose it just for the name." Serge pushed the throttle forward again, and the boat began to plane. "Florida has some of the best place-names: Corkscrew, Spuds, Festus, Roach, Howey-in-the-Hills, Two Egg, but we're about to reach my favorite one of all."

Moments later, they dropped anchor at a crossroads of canals, sitting just a short distance from the lake proper.

"Okay," said Coleman. "I give. What's the name of this place?"

Serge stood with spread arms and yelled at the sky: "Monkey Box, Florida!"

"That is catchy."

"In this case, I'm also media savvy: If you're going to pull some newsworthy stunt like this, and aren't geographically constrained, always pick a place with a name that makes the TV people go belly up. They won't be able to resist!"

Coleman turned all the way around. "But there's nothing here."

"Florida doesn't care, so why should we? Now help me with our newest best friend."

They dragged the pastor, chair and all, into the shallow water and up onto spongy ground.

Coleman kept slapping his arms and swatting in front of his face.

"They're attracted to carbon dioxide," said Serge. "Remember me telling you down in Flamingo at the tip of the state?"

"No." Coleman spit something out of his mouth.

The captive struggled fiercely in the chair. "You won't get away with this! I'll yell!"

"*I'll* yell," said Serge. "Ahhhhhhhhhhhhhh! Damn, that feels good. You should try it."

"Ahhhhhhhhhhhhhh!" The hostage stopped and coughed and spit something out. "You're insane!"

"Thank you."

Coleman continued swatting and spitting. "What are these things?"

"The blind mosquitoes," said Serge. "Scientific name *Chironomidae*, also known as lake flies, and in Florida—you'll love this—chizzywinks. Guess what? The chizzywinks are back in season! I checked with the locals, and they expect them to be at maximum swarm strength tonight in the darkest hours just before sunrise. And that's just their activity level back on land away from the lake. Out here—hoo-wee! . . . Back in the 1800s, there were rampant cases of entire herds of cattle dying from insect asphyxiation in this region. Just read *A Land Remembered*."

Serge put on a surgical mask and safety goggles, and handed an identical pair to the now-coughing Coleman. He turned to the captive. "Oops, I'm short on supplies. I guess that's where the power of prayer comes in."

The pastor was blinking rapidly and trying to breathe through his nose.

"What a nature show you're about to experience," said Serge. "Kind of like something out of the Bible."

Serge sloshed back out to the boat and helped Coleman aboard. They motored away in the direction of Dynamite Pass.

A buzzer rang on the night window of a budget motel on Lake Okeechobee.

Serge swatted away bugs. He cupped hands around his eyes and pressed his nose against the window, looking at the empty front desk.

Someone emerged from a back room. "There you are! I was wondering what kind of business took so long."

"Totally tedious," said Serge. "But I do need to report a missing chair from our room. It kind of got away from me. I'm good for it."

"You know, I still have that extra room available next to yours, if, uh, your friend would like some privacy. On the house."

"You've read my mind . . ."

A half hour later, Serge lay on his back in the bed, holding up a series of large pages like flash cards. "Here's another cool tombstone rubbing, and here's another, and this one has a little cherub on top. I'm a sucker for that. And this is Mitzi the Dolphin . . ."

Cheyenne continued massaging him below the belt. "Um, Serge? Am I doing something wrong?"

"I can accurately say no. I believe most of my gender would concur."

"But you're still looking at your rubbings."

"Precisely." Serge flipped to another page. "What you're doing down there makes me appreciate them in a whole new light."

"Serge . . ."

"O-*kayyyyyyyy*." Serge set the pages on the nightstand and picked up something else. "What about View-Masters? No? My elongated penny collection? I thought women were into sex toys."

"Is that what you call those?"

"Who doesn't?" Serge set the penny album down. "Don't tell anyone I have all this stuff. I'd be mortified if the public knew about my kinky trove."

"What about simple vibrators?"

"You mean those things in the ads that people are using to rub tense facial muscles?"

"Those ads are kind of in code."

Serge crinkled his nose. "That would explain so much."

"Stop talking."

"What?"

Cheyenne got on her hands and knees and slowly crawled up the bed toward him like a jungle cat. She growled.

"Yikes."

Chapter 33

PAHOKEE

Coach Calhoun stuck his head in the principal's office. "You wanted to see me?"

"Come in. And close the door."

Uh-oh, that's never good. Hopefully one of his players hadn't made a mistake that couldn't be reversed.

"Lamar, I can't tell you how happy I was when you first showed up back at the school."

"It was a special day for me, too."

"I know, I know."

"But . . . ?"

"Lamar, we all kind of wondered a little bit about your missing years," said the principal.

"That would be natural," said Calhoun. "I'm sort of a private person."

"We weren't being nosy, mind you. It's just that you were so gifted, we all expected to see you someday in the NFL draft. But after a while, we simply assumed football didn't work out for whatever reason, and the rest was your business. Until you finally decided to come back to your roots."

"Life takes its turns," said Calhoun. "I worked in an auto plant for a while, then a drydock . . . But by that look in your eyes, you already know that."

It pained the principal, and Calhoun saw it all play out again like it was yesterday instead of more than twenty years ago . . .

T he winters in the upper Midwest were far more freezing than Calhoun had ever imagined. It was his senior year at the university, and while he hadn't torn up the Big Ten, Lamar was expected to go in the top six or seven rounds of the draft. He stared out at the snow that was crusting over the campus and piling up on the windowsill of the athletic dorm. His roommate was named Ted, but everyone called him Bruiser.

It was kind of a joke. Ted was a kicker, and they tend to be the smallest players on a team, usually by such a degree that they seem not to be football players at all. It held true in Ted's case. Hence, Bruiser. Ted was from a small farm in an equally small dot on the map in Missouri, and he was lost on the big campus. He didn't know the current music, how to talk to girls or even basic slang. "You mean when something's 'bad,' it's actually 'good'? That doesn't make sense." They went to a club one night, and Ted tried to dance. Lamar almost lost a lung from laughing. The huge player from Pahokee, Florida, appointed himself Ted's big brother, and they became the inseparable odd couple. That's how Calhoun first developed an affinity for kickers.

There are many scandals in big-time college sports that make headlines, and many more that never leave the practice field or locker room. The head coach was in the mold of Ohio State's

Woody Hayes, who punched a player on national TV. Which meant he was a dinosaur. It was a new era, and the assistant coaches struggled to keep him in check. It came to a head halfway through the season. Ted had shanked a thirty-yarder, costing them the game against Michigan. For the next few days, the coach's rage had been tightening in a vicious cycle until he was spring-loaded. On a Wednesday, the practice field was extra busy, pockets of activity where various specialty players honed their specialties. But the coach's eyes were locked in on the kickers. They call it staring daggers, and all the assistants went on high alert, like a domestic abuse victim detecting the first signs of that telltale mood swing.

Ted was back in form, nailing it down the middle. But the coach was just waiting. After, who knows, fifteen perfect kicks, Ted dinged one off the left upright, and the coach was on the field. The assistants chased. Before they could get there, the coach had his hands around Ted's neck. A similar incident had already hit the news, when an Indiana basketball coach was videotaped choking a player. But that was brief compared to this. It was a two-handed throttle that wouldn't let go. Ted vainly fought for breath. He was trying to cough and turning red. The assistants raced up and grabbed the coach's arms—too gently, under the circumstances, because they didn't want to lose their jobs. "Coach! Coach!" One of them looked up to an overhead booth and made a slashing gesture to stop filming practice.

Thumbs pressed harder into Ted's windpipe. A red face was becoming blue. "Coach!" They grabbed him around the waist and arms to no avail. Then, out of nowhere, a fist came flying in. It caught the coach in the jaw and he went down. So did Ted, finally free, gasping frantically before throwing up.

The assistants had a crisis on their hands. They looked around. All the other players had stopped practicing, standing and holding their helmets at their sides by the face masks. Even if they could destroy the video, there were too many witnesses. And if the coach went down, so did their assistant coaching positions. A new head coach would wipe the slate clean and hire all his own people. Panic turned into a plan. They would get out ahead of this and deflect. The solution was handed to them on a platter.

The punch.

They were initially thankful that Lamar had jumped in to help his friend. But thanks didn't pay power bills. In an instant, he was under the bus.

Handcuffs clapped on Calhoun's wrists, followed by expulsion from the team. But it was handled hush-hush, because any digging into the running back's arrest could lead back to the coach. They promised he'd stay on scholarship until graduation, to buy his silence. There was a quick plea bargain with no testimony, followed by a misdemeanor conviction and a suspended sentence.

Although it never made the papers, there was always the grapevine. Nobody knew the details, just that Lamar had attacked a head coach. It was a de facto blackball. Despite his credentials, the entire NFL draft took a hard pass on Calhoun.

He went to look for a job. "Sorry, we just can't do it." Like many athletes', his academic major was physical education, and schools weren't allowed to hire anyone with an assault conviction. Lamar began welding fenders . . .

T hat was then; this was now.

"I wish you would have said something." The Pahokee High School principal shook his head. "On the surface, it didn't sound at all like you. So we looked into it and learned the real circumstances, and then it all made sense. If we had known earlier, we might have figured something out, some kind of exemption, or gotten it expunged."

"But now?"

The principal held up a sheet of paper. "You didn't disclose it. You filed a false job application."

"I used bad judgment," said Calhoun. "It was just so long ago.

I wanted to put it behind me, and I wanted to get back to the kids."

"Dammit!" said the principal.

"I know this is putting you through a lot. I'm sorry."

"No, not you," said the principal. "That asshole Garns."

"Who?"

"The science teacher I got rid of."

"Oh, I remember him now," said Calhoun. "But what's he got to do with any of this?"

"He couldn't simply go quietly and get on with his life," said the principal. "I wish he was still here just so I could fire him again."

"I'm not following."

"He must have spent weeks digging, and then I still don't know how he found out," said the principal. "He's the one who reported you."

Calhoun sat a moment in helpless thought as the pieces of realization fell into place. "Someone like that has no business being around our kids. It was still worth it."

"Not from where I'm sitting," said the principal. "I wish there was something I could do."

"You've done enough." Calhoun stood. "I'll go get my stuff."

Chapter 34

OKEECHOBEE

The next morning it was breakfast in bed. Then Serge and Cheyenne took a brisk five-mile stroll along the Florida Trail on top of the Hoover Dike.

By ten o'clock, they were back in the room, making plans for her day off. By eleven, a crash against the wall from Coleman's room. "He's up."

By noon, it was on the news.

Law enforcement needed airboats to reach the scene, and they now sat clustered near the northern bank of the Old Moore Haven Canal.

TV correspondents in even more airboats began broadcasting from behind police lines.

"This is Soledad Torres reporting live from a place few have heard of. I'm standing here in Monkey Box, Florida, where a trio of bass fishermen heading out to Lake Okeechobee made a grisly early-morning discovery of a body in this remote swampland. The sheriff's office is releasing few details, but confidential sources tell me the victim may have been the leader of a controversial church infamous for picketing military funerals around the state. Sources also describe the murder victim as being bound and tortured with what are known in these parts as blind mosquitoes, also known as chizzywinks, which occasionally swarm in ferocious numbers. The most probable cause of death was asphyxiation, but prior to the victim's demise, the insects likely also filled his ears, eyes and even the sinus cavity via the nose, where he could feel them moving around behind his eyes. Sorry for ruining your lunch. This is Soledad Torres in Monkey Box, Florida. Back to you, Chet and Angela."

The broadcast switched to a pair of anchorpeople behind a desk in the home studio, sharing light banter and a chuckle. "I think she just likes saying Monkey Box . . ." "I like saying it, too. Monkey Box." "We'll be right back after these commercial messages. Monkey Box."

Cheyenne stared. "What exactly was your business last night?"

"Fake news! Fake news!" Serge clicked the set off and clapped his hands a single sharp time. "I'm famished! What do you say we grab a bite to eat?"

"Actually, I'm supposed to have lunch with my brother," said Cheyenne.

"Kyle? Fantastic! We'll make it a family affair," said Serge. "My treat. I insist!"

A knock at the door. Serge jumped and spun. "Who the hell is that?"

"Probably my brother. I told him where I was." She cast a suspicious eye over her shoulder as she went to the door and opened up. "Hey, Kyle."

"Hi, sis." He stepped into the room and glared at Serge without speaking.

Serge spread his arms. "What?"

The glare lasted a moment longer. "I just watched the news."

"That? Ha, ha, ha!" Serge waved a dismissive hand that signaled silly talk. "Where do they dream up all the crazy stuff they're putting on the air these days? I mean, death by chizzywinks? Is there even such a bug? Such a *word*?"

Cheyenne wanted the subject changed. "Serge has offered to take us to lunch."

"Damn straight!" said Serge. "It's the least I can do for your service to the nation. The only condition is I get to pick the place. I've been dying to try one of Okeechobee's famous steak houses.

A loud crash on the other side of the wall, followed by a scream and a thud.

Serge pointed. "I'll go get Coleman."

A gold Plymouth pulled into a parking lot.

Kyle looked up at the sign. "I thought you wanted to go to one of our famous steak houses."

"I do. This is it!" Serge slammed down an empty coffee mug. "No finer choice!"

"Golden Corral? But you can eat at these anywhere in the country."

"Accept no substitutes!" said Serge. "Golden Corral is the pulse of America, where the Forgotten Fly-Over-Country People dine, and I mean that as a compliment. Pundits mention the Forgotten People like they genuinely care, but there's an unmistakable subtext of condescension. This is why the elitists can never get their predictions right. Whether it's elections, consumer confidence, shifting social tectonics, just chuck your fancy algorithms and scientific polls. Golden Corral is the Rosetta stone, the Oracle of Menestheus and the Magic Eight Ball rolled into one. The reasons are myriad, but one rises above all others: They have a chocolate fountain. There can be no greater symbol of straight-shootin', salt-of-the-earth integrity. As the pinnacle of the Corral's ziggurat, the chocolate fountain cannot be surpassed or even questioned."

The Plymouth slowly crawled through the gridlocked parking lot. "Wow, is this place jammed! Their food must be extra popular in these parts."

"It's veteran appreciation day," said Kyle.

"What's that mean?" asked Serge.

"Across the country, all veterans eat free today."

"The chocolate fountain has just been eclipsed."

An old man in a USS *Iowa* baseball cap suddenly jumped in front of the Plymouth with hands urgently raised for them to stop. At several other nearby points, more vets halted other cars.

"World War Two vet pulling out!"

Others were positioned behind a Buick Regal, using hand signals to help the driver inch backward like a snail. Serge jumped from his car and joined the flag-less semaphore team directing the vehicle. "God, I love these people! . . ."

Inside the restaurant, a color guard and a small contingent from the high school band. Most of the people at the tables wore some kind of hat or vest commemorating their service.

Serge grabbed a plate. "I've inadvertently entered an overkill of positive vibes." He led his group along the salad bar. "Let me show you how to make a salad. Most people simply throw a salad together because it's just a salad. But it's actually a statement. Please stand back . . ." They gave him space as he became a windmill of motion. Ingredients filled his plate, first in meticulous layers, then quadrants. ". . . A true salad is about architecture and engineering. I'm borrowing from the Romans for my potato salad basilica, and now for the victory arch . . ."

The packed dining room was a southern aroma symphony. Catfish, barbecued chicken, roast beef, okra, hush puppies, popcorn shrimp, three kinds of gravy.

Kyle pointed with a fork. "Serge, aren't you hungry?"

Serge sat back in his chair with his head tilted sideways. "This salad is way too damn big." His fork hovered over the single cherry tomato on top. "How does one even approach eating this without an avalanche?"

Cheyenne took a bite of beef. "So, Serge, what are you up to next?"

"Communing with these fine folks and learning their ways." He leaned toward the next table, where four old guys in suspenders and U.S. Navy caps were cutting steak. "Excuse me! Yoo-hoo! You know my new motto? Remember the Forgotten People! I think it's got legs. Don't pay no mind to the New York–L.A. cultural axis. There's an untapped reservoir of values and enlightenment in this room."

"Are you okay?" asked one of the guys.

"Fantastic, except for this ridiculous salad. But I've learned to accept what I can't change." A grin. "So tell me, what does Golden Corral have that those pointy-headed ivory tower types don't understand?"

One of the old guys continued chewing. "A chocolate fountain."

"Bingo!" said Serge. "It *looks* like an ordinary chocolate fountain, but you and I know what it really means." Wink. "All across the country there's an economic Mendoza Line, below which the middle and lower classes are secretly viewed by our oligarchs as the *livestock* class. How else can it be explained? Our paycheck-to-paycheck toil created their staggering fortunes. In return, all our safety nets are under siege in the name of corporate greed that won't be quenched until our lives are reduced to perpetual white-knuckled freak-outs hurtling toward premature, pre-existing-condition death. Who could do that in good conscience to another human being? On the other hand, if they see us as livestock instead of people, then it all makes sense: A political consultant stands at the front of a conference room with a projector. 'Our research shows we can easily convince the beef cattle to vote for the owners of the slaughterhouse. First we get them pissed off at the *dairy* cows—'"

"Quick," Kyle told his sister. "Grab his coffee."

"Just talkin' 'bout the chocolate fountain," said Serge. "It's the secret symbol of recognition among our people, like that creepy eyeball atop the pyramid on the back of a one-dollar bill."

Cheyenne smiled. "When I asked what you were up to next, I meant where are you going?"

"Oh, that's different." Serge stuck his fork in the salad, triggering a rockslide of croutons. "You're all witnesses. Not my fault . . . Anyway, I'm continuing my Florida odyssey of sweeping ramifications, but aren't they all? This one involves connective tissue that is pulling us in a tractor beam toward the lost town of Ortona, then Clewiston, before whipping under the bottom of Lake Okeechobee and visiting Belle Glade and Pahokee, collectively known as The Muck, for its rich earth. The welcome sign to Belle Glade says 'Her Soil Is Her Fortune.' The sign to Pahokee just says 'Pahokee.' It's hard to figure people out."

"I know all those places," said Kyle.

"Me too," said Cheyenne.

"How so?" asked Serge. "You're from the north side of the lake."

"But I played football," said Kyle. "We had away games. My father was one of the coaches in Okeechobee, and around the lake, all the coaches pretty much knew each other. From the time I was a little kid, we were always having dinner at someone's house in another small town."

"I was a cheerleader," said Cheyenne. "It's hard to believe now with the way many of those towns are boarded up, but I heard that back in the 1930s the whole area was called the 'winter vegetable capital of America.' It was a twenty-four-hour operation with refrigerated warehouses and trains constantly coming and going to rush the produce north while still fresh, not to mention thousands of workers filling the juke joints and gambling houses at all hours near the shantytowns that sprang up."

"Look at the Florida knowledge on you," said Serge.

"I'm your little history helper, remember? I've heard lots of stories about the whole lake region, some not on the books."

"Such as?"

"Lost treasure," said Cheyenne. "That was a favorite on the school yard. Trunks of precious metals supposedly went missing during the hurricane of '28."

"I'm sure a lot of everything went missing in that one."

"Yeah, but this tale had other scary and mysterious details," said Cheyenne. "Like a vicious sugar baron whose body was discovered with bullet holes and buried before the authorities found out."

"Then how did you and your schoolmates hear about it?" asked Serge.

"The guys who did the burying allegedly told their families, and the story was passed down generation to generation by word of mouth. But it's probably just that, a story." Cheyenne's fork toyed with the food on her plate. "It must be fun to take road trips like you do."

"I'm sure you've taken a million."

"Not really."

"But what about you saying there's too many places you've got to see?"

"That's why."

"Okay, then come with us." Serge collapsed the other side of his salad. "Shit."

"Really?"

Kyle touched her wrist. "What about the motel?"

"I've piled up a ton of vacation."

The brother grabbed his cowboy hat from under the chair. "Then I guess I'll need to make it a foursome. When do we leave? . . ."

Chapter 35

PAHOKEE

Senior year of high school arrived with all the fanfare of raging hormones.

Social calendars filled up. A few students now had cars. Others got new clothes for the merciless battlefield that is popularity. And of course there was football season, with the mandatory post-game gatherings at burger joints. Yes, they still do that.

Chris was blossoming with her own crowd. The varsity team, the cheerleading squad, the marching band and various hangers-on. She was welcome at their restaurant tables, where they laughed and relived big plays and threw french fries at each other.

But Chris was still different. She didn't have any money. Others always chipped in for her food and told her not to worry, but good luck with that.

She never stopped smiling, but it began eating at her stomach, figuratively and literally.

One Thursday afternoon that fall, Chris thought hard about a dilemma that she'd been twisting in her mind and rotating to inspect from all angles. She made her choice. After all, how much difference can *one* make?"

That night, she left her grandmother's apartment and quietly headed down the stairs. Chris glanced around one last time before running off into the darkness behind the building and disappearing like a ninja . . .

The next afternoon, community fever grew as hours counted down to another huge gridiron contest in The Muck. The Blue Devils were still undefeated, and it was the second-to-last game of the season; the last before the Big Game. Signs that normally advertised breakfast specials and free tire rotation now had their letters rearranged into some variation of BEAT CARDINAL NEWMAN! The barbershop was full of experts and bullshit.

At a storefront on a downtown street, bells jingled.

The pawnshop owner's hand was shaking a Rolex that had stopped working. He looked up. He saw her letterman jacket. "We going to win tonight?"

"Bank on it," said Chris.

"Are you one of the cheerleaders?"

"No, a kicker."

"You're on the team?" He paused with a finger to his mouth. "Wait, I heard something about you . . . Well, that's great. So how can I help?"

"I need to sell something."

"Let's see what you've got."

Chris pulled a shiny coin from her pocket and placed it on the glass counter.

"Wow, that sure is pretty." He turned it over. "Says twenty dollars. But of course you realize that they don't use these anymore."

"I know. We effectively went off the gold standard under Roosevelt," said Chris. "Some technically argue Nixon. Now it's full faith and credit."

"What do you say I give you—"

Chris removed a book from her backpack and placed it on the counter. *The Red Book,* the bible of coin-collecting price guides. "With all due respect, I know exactly what it's worth."

It was the last thing the pawn man expected. "Okay, I'm sorry. I'm not exactly killing it here in this town business-wise. Straight up, I need to make a profit, and who knows how long till I sell it. How about half of what it books for?"

"How about the melt value of the gold?" asked Chris. "That way you can't lose, and you get the whole numismatic collecting up-charge."

The pawn man thought: *Where did this kid come from? Most adults don't negotiate this well.* He slowly began to nod. "I can live with that. You just need to fill out this form. I'll get money from the register." He began counting out hundreds . . .

The football game went pretty much as expected. The home crowd had everything to cheer about all night as Pahokee took an early lead and never looked back for the trounce. There was even a late kickoff return that went all the way for a touchdown, crowning the night.

Revving convertibles and trucks, stereos blaring, converged again on Max's Shake Spot. It was a nicely converted old gas station from the thirties in the period's art deco design. Max had used old photos to replicate the original green-and-orange neon that trimmed the building all the way around to the outside restroom doors. Team pennants and banners filled the walls, along with a couple of framed jerseys and photos of former players who had gone on to the pros. The school's fall schedule and results had been dutifully tallied on a chalkboard. All the chairs were filled in the dining room, and the crowd spilled outside to the picnic tables on the porch.

"I can't believe about Coach Calhoun!"

"What have you heard?"

"Just rumors, but they can't be true."

"We have to do something!"

"Chris, you were pretty close to him. What do you think?"

"I feel the same as you," said the kicker. "But I know what he told me: Don't worry about him. And don't let anything distract us. We have to win the Muck Bowl."

The Muck Bowl.

More than historic.

Pahokee versus Glades Central. David and Goliath. Except David always had his slingshot. Either team could go undefeated the rest of the year, even win state championships in their separate divisions, but it wouldn't mean anything if they didn't prevail in the end-of-the-regular-season rivalry.

"The Muck Bowl." Nodding around the table. "Coach Calhoun is right. We'll deal with it later . . ."

The waitress came over and they ordered. It was pay in advance, and Chris stood up with her wallet. "I've got this."

"Chris, since when do you have money?"

"Since I started doing some odd jobs."

"Put your money away," said a starting lineman. "We always got you."

Then they saw the hundred-dollar bill . . . "Please, pay away."

The jumbo basket of buffalo wings arrived first and they dove in. Some of the loyal crowd were ex-students who had graduated in the last couple of years and were still trying to get in gear. They had minimum-wage jobs, unable to figure a way out. But they all looked forward to Friday nights in the fall, the connection to their true family. They wore their old team jackets.

The kicker felt a slap on her back.

"Chris, how's it going?"

She turned around. A young man named Ricky, who used to push her down in the dirt.

"Don't you mean 'Milk Crate'?"

"Sorry about all that," said Ricky. "And I think I owe you a football or two. Anyway, great game."

"I didn't even play."

"Still, you made the team. That's something."

"Thanks." She scooted over to make room. "Have some wings."

ORTONA

Kyle Lovitt looked out the rear window of a gold Plymouth speeding down the western shore of Lake Okeechobee. "Nobody can accuse you of letting moss grow."

"Why noodle around? When it's time to ramble, it should just be a matter of packing your bags and throwing them in the trunk," said Serge. "Of course in my case, my bags are usually already packed in the trunk, unless there's no room because . . . Let's leave it at that."

Ribbit. Coleman petted his chest. "Easy, Jeremiah."

Serge looked across the front seat. "Been meaning to ask. Cheyenne is such a fetching name, yet all the parents today go for Brittany or Kirsten. How come?"

"Because I'm Native American."

He pushed her shoulder playfully. "Get out of town!"

"Supposedly full-blooded, but I think someone in my family was fucking around and lying about it."

Coleman reached over from the back seat and tapped his shoulder. "Serge, a chick who says 'fuck.' That is so hot."

Serge smacked his hand away. "Shut up, you . . ." He turned. "Sorry about that on multiple male levels. But full disclosure: It *is* hot. Don't let that affect your level of lurid lexicon, for more or less . . . Please continue."

"So that's why I'm Cheyenne." The Plymouth's A/C was broken, and the wind from the open windows made her grab a rubber band and fashion a ponytail. "Imagine me. A Native American raised in Okeechobee. Half Indian, half cowboy."

Kyle stared at Coleman a moment, sitting next to him in the back seat, trying to give beer to a frog with an eyedropper. "So what's this next stop of yours? Ortona? I've never heard of it, and I've lived my whole life around here."

"It's the best!" Serge chugged coffee with a single brown rivulet running from the corner of his mouth. "A tiny hamlet down a long, inspiring country drive through our unspoiled nature. I would say it's a forgotten place, if it was ever known in the first place. There's a modest collection of canal-front homes down by the Caloosahatchee River, and that's about it for population. Otherwise, just a wild stretch of Route Seventy-Eight between LaBelle and Moore Haven. With one major exception: an incredibly important historic site that is right-on-point relevant! Which can mean only one thing."

"What's that?" asked Kyle.

"We must balance out relevance with non sequitur or The Man imprisons us in his plastic cage of linear thought. And we all know where that leads. Except I don't know where it leads because I've escaped the cage. See how it works? . . . Coleman, ready for another round of tangent? Get the list."

"Cool." Coleman reached in the glove compartment. "Next topic: best cowbell songs."

"Right!" said Serge, reaching under his seat.

"You brought a cowbell?" asked Kyle.

"I always have a cowbell nearby for any circumstance. Why? Without warning in polite cocktail-party society, you might need to urgently change the subject: 'Serge, did your friend Coleman just scratch his butt and sniff his finger?' You can interrupt and yell 'Gas leak!' or, if a stampede isn't needed..." He began hitting the bell with a drumstick. "... Get where I'm going with this?... *'Honky-tonk womannnnnnnnn!'...*"

"Shouldn't you be paying more attention to the road?" asked Kyle.

"The other hemisphere of my brain is at the wheel." *Clang, clang, clang.* "*Mississippi queen!*" ..." *Clang, clang.* "*Fool for the city!*' ... Remember the Chambers Brothers? '*Time has come to-day!*'..." *Clang, clang.* He threw the cowbell back under the seat. "Enough of that shit. Coleman?"

Coleman checked the list. "Homeland security."

"This is an important one," said Serge. "They say that our main strategic weakness against the terrorists is failure of imagination. But I'm just the guy to fix that! Two words: toupee bomber. Are we on that one?"

"Serge—"

"Hold that thought," said Serge. "We're here."

The Plymouth pulled up to the edge of the Caloosahatchee, and everyone got out.

"Is this the historic place?" asked Cheyenne.

"Not the main one," said Serge. "We need to build up to that or we could lapse into history shock. This is the Ortona Lock and Dam, part of a system of such structures that raise and lower boats traveling across the state on the one-hundred-and-fifty-four-mile-long Okeechobee Waterway. As opposed to, say, only forty-eight miles. I'm looking in your direction, Panama Canal."

"We've got a lock like this back near the motel," said Cheyenne.

Serge walked closer to the edge, carrying a paper sack.

"What's in the bag?" asked Kyle.

"You'll find out." Serge drank in the vista. "I love locks for their engineering feats. And especially the whirlpools."

"Whirlpools?" asked Coleman.

Serge nodded and aimed an arm. "When a boat's coming over from the coast and enters the lock, valves are opened, and water from the high side flows into it, raising the vessel like a rubber duck in a bathtub. But so much fluid rushes inside that it creates a vast vortex just outside the lock's upstream doors. In fact, this lock was recently closed two weeks for repairs because, among other things, serious whirlpools were forming *inside* the lock when lowering boats. Not good for the canoe people."

"Here comes a boat now," said Cheyenne.

"Let's watch the whirlpool." Serge led them up a path to the lock's eastern doors. "I love watching whirlpools the way cats watch a toilet flush."

"The whirlpool's starting," said Coleman. "Wow, it's getting big."

"I had no idea," said Kyle. "Forget canoes. It's a monster."

"Videos of these physics spectacles are all over YouTube, and someone just posted incredible footage from the Demopolis Lock in Alabama." Serge pulled something from his paper bag. "Watch this!"

"You carry a rubber duck around?" asked Cheyenne.

"A close second behind the cowbell." He heaved the yellow toy far out into the water.

They all watched it splash, then rotate in a wide but tightening circle until it was violently sucked under.

"Ta-da!" said Serge.

"Uh, you do realize you just littered," said Cheyenne.

"What? Oh, shit! I usually play with it in the tub, so there's rarely difficulty retrieving it. I wasn't thinking." Serge covered his face with his hands. "This negates my whole moment. I must atone." He ran back along the bank and stared at the water and waited. Finally, a rubber duck popped to the surface inside the lock. He cupped hands around his mouth. "Hey, you in the boat! I need a big favor! I just accidentally littered because I was watching water like a house cat. See that rubber duck about to float by? If you could just snag the sucker, it would center my karma . . . Thanks." Serge wiped his forehead. "Whew! Another close one! . . . Back to the car!"

They drove a short distance until three people were standing beside a Plymouth, watching Serge standing proudly atop a small hill.

"And this is one of the fabulous Ortona mounds, believed to have been created seventeen hundred years ago by the Calusa, who were the busy bees of early Florida, also digging a network of navigable canals . . . Back to the car!"

Another short drive. Serge leaped from the Plymouth. "You've been properly warmed up, so here it is! But first look around and let the context sink in: nothing, deserted, not even cars on the road. The closest thing to *anything* is that remote and idle quarry we passed on the way in. And I can't get enough of it! Dig!" Serge walked fifty yards out into a roadside field that was blanketed in yellow. He called back to the gang: "Florida, literally the Land of Flowers, and all these beautiful babies around me are the state's official wildflower, coreopsis." He stretched out his arms and began spinning joyously amid the blooms. "'*The hills are alive with the sound of*—' . . . whoa, getting a little dizzy again." He staggered back to the road. "And now for our feature presentation."

Serge opened the Plymouth's trunk for his gravestone-rubbing supplies. A brief hike followed. "This is the Ortona Cemetery. It's hard to imagine now with all the surrounding emptiness, but for a few days in 1928, this was one of the busiest spots in the state. That year's hurricane was so devastating that it required three mass graves, including this last one." He placed his oversize sheet of paper against a historical marker and began rubbing. "We're back in Zora country! Can you dig it?"

"Uh . . ." said Kyle. "This has been an . . . interesting day."

"This is nothing," said Serge. "I'm getting a familiar tingle in my bones. That means the biggest day of this entire tour is about to dawn and blow your hat off! Come on! . . ."

Chapter 36

Captain Crack Nasty grabbed a stuffed wahoo by the tail and ripped it off the wall. He smashed it over and over against the edge of his desk until it was almost dust.

His treasure business was turning to shit. The losing streak had reached six wreck sites that he had been sure would pay off like slot machines. All he had to show for it was another cannonball. Some of his workers left in frustration, and the rest found a way back to prison.

He fell in his chair and grabbed a bottle and fumed. He began thinking of an older "can't miss" treasure site. The one that had slipped through his fingers.

Crack Nasty had indeed gotten away with that ugly business out at the lake with those three young men. Four years had quickly passed without a knock on his door from the cops.

But he had also screwed himself.

Pahokee was too small a town, and he had been too visible. If he wanted to keep getting away with the killings, he had to stay extremely clear of the area. Dammit! Why did he let emotions make business decisions? And after the homework he'd put in. He had been so close he could taste it. He grabbed a nautical map, out of habit, to look for another offshore site. "What's the point!" He threw it and grabbed the bottle instead.

The phone rang.

"Hello? . . . No, I don't know who this is. . . . Been a long time? You said to call and you'd pay? If you say so. . . . What do you mean, 'prepare for happiness'? . . . What! Seriously? I'll be there this afternoon . . ."

Captain Crack pulled the magnetic door sign off his pickup truck, kicked caution to the curb, and headed west into sugar country.

Bells jingled extra hard as Crack burst into the pawnshop. "When did it come in?"

The owner stuck a clarinet on a shelf. "A few weeks ago, but I couldn't find your business card until this morning." He reached into the display case for a coin dated 1911.

Crack held it to his face as waves of dormant greed resurfaced. "Who sold it?"

"Young girl from the local high school." The owner pulled out a ledger book. "Her name was Chris something . . . Yeah, here it is. For whatever reason I didn't get her address, but she plays for the football team." He scribbled on a sheet of paper.

Crack laid a stack of hundreds on the counter and snatched the coin. "Remember . . ."

"I know. You were never here."

Bells jingled.

The owner shook his head. "I will never understand white people."

The gold Plymouth swung down under the lake and passed a welcome sign: AMERICA'S SWEETEST TOWN.

"This is it," said Serge. "Clewiston. Epicenter of Florida's sugar industry. Here we begin our exploration of the southern lake culture, moving on to South Bay, then swinging northeast along the shore. See the plumes of smoke dotting the horizon, as well as these recently burned black fields we're passing?"

"We're familiar with the harvesting process," said Kyle. Still, it was always a sight, and he and Cheyenne leaned toward the window.

"Then I'll tell Coleman," said Serge. An elbow. "Coleman, you awake?"

"Just resting my eyelids. They've been going all day."

"Look alive. We're in a hallowed place." He startled everyone by swinging into a convenience store at the last second, and running for the far wall.

Coleman caught up. "Coffee. What a surprise."

Serge shook a small packet and ripped it open. "Know what I'm pouring in my coffee?"

"Sugar?"

"History!" He tore open a second packet. "And since I'm in Clewiston, I need a second helping of heritage. From the molasses and rum trade routes to modern-day Florida, the sugar industry has sparked economy and controversy. Back to the car!"

Moments later, the quartet stood quietly in the middle of a large, gleaming space.

"Have to hand it to you," said Cheyenne. "You sure can pick 'em. This is incredible."

"The Clewiston Inn? Easy call." Serge swept an arm through the air. "Now *this* is a lobby! Other lobbies today are sterile nightmares that disagree with my colon: a few chairs, artificial flowers, rack of tourist pamphlets, and the counter where they lay out the free breakfast, which has been reduced to a plastic bin of Froot Loops where you have to turn a crank like a gumball machine. And then strictly at ten A.M., they actually *lock up* the Froot Loops! Will the madness never end? But not here! I can't get enough of a lobby that is a virtual church of varnished dark-wood walls, with the original mail slots behind the vintage counter, antique sofas and bookshelves with more old stuff that makes you want to leave your room just to sit in the middle of bygone days. Check out the hotel's preserved switchboard next to the fireplace, with the old cables and everything. And this coffee table over here is a glass display case. See those shiny metal things in there that look like a baseball catcher's shin guards, except if they'd come off a medieval suit of armor? Those are the old sugar cutters' leg protectors, because back before mechanized harvesting they were working so fast and swinging such sharp machetes to slice down the stalks that they kept hitting their legs, which was no good for anybody. And next to the protector things is one of the ancient cane blades. Notice the size and width of that bastard. If I ever have to attend a machete fight, that's what I'm bringing." He marched back to the receptionist's desk, where they'd just checked in.

"Sorry to bother you," said Serge, "but could I trouble you to open up the lounge for me and my friends to see art?"

"Wait, I remember you." A smile from behind the counter. "You're the mural guy."

"In some circles."

"No problem." She grabbed keys. "Follow me."

The quartet soon stood in another fabulous space, turning slowly to take it in.

"What do you think?" asked Serge. "Snazzy, eh?"

"I had no idea," said Cheyenne, stepping toward a wall to inspect a spoonbill. "I've driven by this place a million times but never stopped in because who needs a hotel when you live so close?"

"The history we most often overlook is in our own backyard." Serge parted blinds to look out one of the lounge's windows. "It's the little things about a small town, and in Clewiston it's stuff like that bank-style sign by the road, where in any other place the lightbulbs would display time and temperature, but here it's the lake level, just over fifteen feet. Wow, that's getting pretty high."

Serge pulled out a chair for Cheyenne, and they all sat at a table in the middle of the bar.

"Ladies and gentlemen!" Serge zestfully rubbed his hands together. "Our timing here is no accident! I have a surprise! But first an essential background briefing, which is mainly for Coleman . . . *Coleman!*"

"Huh? What? Right here."

"Can you at least raise your forehead off the table when I'm talking to you?"

"Crap. Always more work. Just give me a minute . . . Okay, I'm looking at you."

"As our journey continues, we're about to enter a most amazing place." Serge raised his arms to the heavens. "Some of the hardest-working folk you'll ever meet, with an astounding sense of family and community. It's actually two separate small towns ten miles apart on the southeastern shore of Lake Okeechobee—Belle Glade and Pahokee—but they're collectively referred to as The Muck, from the rich, dark soil—"

"Wait, what's the date?" asked Kyle. He checked his cell phone and smiled. "Now I know why your bones were tingling for the biggest day of your tour. The Muck Bowl."

"Ding, ding, ding!" said Serge. "We have a winner!"

"The Muck Bowl?" said Cheyenne. "That's so cool! I've never seen one."

Coleman looked left and right at the table. "What's the Muck Bowl?"

"Just the biggest high school football game in all of Florida," said Kyle. "Forget state championships. The rivalry between those two towns is more electric than anything. I played against both teams when I was in school, and they're unbelievable."

Serge nodded. "Go to any Muck Bowl, and a few years later you're liable to see several players on TV in the NFL."

"So you have tickets?" asked Kyle.

"I was going to pick some up when we got into town."

"You can't just *pick up* tickets to the Muck Bowl, unless you want to wait in line forever."

"What do you suggest?" asked Serge.

"I know one of the coaches in Pahokee, Lamar Calhoun." Kyle got out his phone again. "He might be able to hook us up."

"Lamar Calhoun?" said Serge. "Why do I know his name?"

"Because he used to be one of the best blue-chip running backs in all the state."

Serge snapped his fingers. "That's right. He was incredible, one that I would have bet for sure would make the pros. But then nothing. What happened?"

"I don't know," said Kyle. "I wasn't even born when he graduated, but our fathers were both coaches at opposite ends of the lake, and they became great friends over the years from crossing paths on the circuit. I even met Lamar at his dad's house a few times when he visited for the holidays. I heard he moved back to coach himself a couple years ago, and I've been meaning to call, but you know how that goes."

"I remember us having dinner at their house several times when I was a little kid," said Cheyenne. "Wonderful family." She turned to her brother. "Did you read where Pahokee has a girl on the team this year?"

Kyle shook his head, listening to his cell phone before hanging up. "No answer. They must have all left school for the day."

"She's a kicker," said Cheyenne.

"Who?" asked Kyle.

"The girl on the Pahokee squad," said his sister. "I saw a small thing about it in the paper, so I started following the team this year. I always get a good feeling when I see a girl making those kinds of strides against the odds."

Serge nodded. "And I always get a bad feeling when I see Internet trolls babbling that some successful girl is just a token who only made it through favoritism. Give me a break! I've been witnessing the behavior of my gender for years. Do you have any idea what it's like to be a woman in a man's world?"

"Yes."

"Okay, well, I don't," said Serge. "But I know the burden of the kind of brains we guys have to work with . . ." He grabbed Coleman by the hair and lifted his head up off the table again. "Exhibit A." He lowered the head. "And I can't believe the crassness I observed directed at women on the street."

"And that's only the stuff that guys like you overhear," said Cheyenne. "For us, it's such a perpetual, day-in-day-out gauntlet of leering and vulgar remarks that you eventually become numb."

"Coleman and I were discussing the phenomenon the other day," said Serge. "And I want to offer my deepest proxy apology for the dudes making slurping sounds and calling out anatomy by non-medical names. Personally, it confounds me. Putting the rudeness factor aside for a moment, on the mating level this is also their intelligence audition. It's like if a guy goes to a supermarket cashier a hundred days in a row and says, 'I don't have any money,' and she says, 'Then you can't have any food,' and he says, 'Okay, same time tomorrow?'"

"Did I just start a tangent with you?" asked Cheyenne.

"Well played," said Serge.

"So we're going to the Muck Bowl," said Kyle. "I'll just need to keep trying to reach Coach Calhoun. What in the meantime?"

Serge flipped open a notepad. "There's something huge that's been looming on my Florida bucket list. And now is the perfect opportunity to strike it off."

"What is it?" asked Kyle.

"This one is best left to be revealed in real time . . ."

An hour later, two flatbed pickup trucks sat on the side of a road with nothing around but a setting sun over vast acreage. Behind the trucks was a gold Plymouth and two people leaning against the fender with folded arms.

"What do you think they're doing in there?" asked Cheyenne.

Kyle covered his mouth as he began to cough from the smoke. "I have a good idea."

Serge dashed as fast as he could down the black-dirt rows. He crashed through stalks and dove on the ground over and over. Then running full speed again, smashing through more cane and another dive.

Exhausted, he rolled over onto his back and lay in the dirt, looked up into a circle of a half-dozen children's faces. Some of the kids were grasping cottontails. They giggled at Serge and ran off.

A few rows over, Coleman also lay on his back. Eyes shut tight.

Ribbit. A bullfrog crawled out of a chest pouch and hopped away.

Serge got up and raced about, obsessively not giving up. But then it became just too dark. "Coleman! We have to head back to the car! . . . Coleman! . . ."

Coleman roused from an anesthesia fog. "Wha—? What is it?" He raised his head. "Oh, hello. It's another of my little nature friends." While Coleman had been unconscious, something had crawled onto his chest and found his girth, warmth and breathing to be a soothing elixir. He began stroking its back. He sat up and snuggled it under his chin, gently slipping it down into his chest pouch. "I'm coming, Serge!"

Over at the road, kids began jumping back into the pickups that had brought them. Most had sacks and makeshift chicken-wire cages with rabbits. Serge collapsed empty-handed over the hood of the Satellite.

"Jesus!" said Cheyenne. "You look like you're about to have a heart attack!"

"There's no other way to do a job than to end up looking like you're nearly in cardiac arrest. But you're a witness: I gave it my all."

"And then some," said Cheyenne.

The truck beds were noisy with animated tall tales from the cane fields. Then they went silent, all looking in the same direction.

Coleman strolled ho-hum out of the cane field, petting his newest furry friend. He looked up to see all eyes upon him. "What?"

Kids jumped down from the trucks and gathered around the plump, stumbling stranger. *"What's your secret?" "How'd you catch a jackrabbit?" "You must be super fast!"*

There was a banging sound. Serge's forehead against the hood of his Plymouth. Accompanied by fists.

"Easy," said Cheyenne. "You'll catch one someday."

"You're right." Serge stood and collected himself. "Besides, the big game is tomorrow. We need to be heading for the hotel to get our rest."

The gang piled back into the Plymouth and turned south on Main Street.

"Serge, why are you pulling over?"

"Just one last stop of the day on the way to the inn."

The Plymouth pulled around behind a government building.

"What is this place?" asked Cheyenne.

"Used to be the library," said Serge. "Now a museum."

Three people headed for the doors. One went another direction.

"Serge," yelled Kyle. "The entrance is this way."

"We're not going in the museum," said Serge. "Follow me . . ."

The foursome soon stood on the lawn on the north side of the building. All staring up at the same thing.

"This is just like our hotel," said Cheyenne. "I've driven by a thousand times but never stopped to really take a look."

"One of the most emotional historic monuments in all the state," said Serge. "Statues of a family of four: father, young son, and mother cradling an infant, all running for their lives and looking back up at the sky in terror, the parents raising futile arms to shield their heads. And on the monument's base, a stone-relief sculpture of giant waves washing away homes and snapping palm trees. And if you look real close in the water, there's a bunch of tiny people drowning beneath a simple inscription: 'Belle Glade 1928.'"

"Whew," said Cheyenne. "What can you say?"

"You can't," said Serge.

The monument was too much to take in at once, so they didn't.

"Every now and then, being at a place pulls at me in a way I don't understand," said Serge. "I get an odd feeling."

"Who wouldn't at a monument like this?" said Cheyenne.

"It's not the monument," said Serge. "Another kind of feeling. My bones again, but different this time. Like something big is looming just around the corner."

They all became quiet again, respectfully taking in the sight as the sun departed.

Chapter 37

GAME DAY

There had been talk of rain, but it never came. Instead, the departing clouds over Lake Okeechobee left the night air cool and crisp under the stadium lights. The faint smell of smoke from the surrounding cane fields competed with sausage grills in the concession stands.

Spectators had started arriving at the gates when the sun was still high. You had to for this one if you wanted any kind of decent seat. Those who arrived late were still more than happy to stand or watch from outside the fence, fingers clinging to chain link.

Twenty-five thousand were expected tonight. Insane for a high school. But the Muck Bowl was no ordinary game. The number of college scouts in the stands confirmed that. They always came out for the annual battle of the rabbit chasers.

The hype had been building for weeks among the nearby

communities. Signs outside restaurants and dry cleaners and lube shops cheered on the Blue Devils and the Raiders. They talked about it in the post office and the supermarket lines. Tailgate parties were planned with the logistics of military campaigns. And now it was time.

School buses arrived after the ten-mile drive up the rim of the lake from Belle Glade, and the players streamed out. Bands played, police directed traffic. The Blue Devils were already on their home-field sideline. Their uniforms were slightly different from the usual. It was the players' idea. On the front of each of their jerseys, just above the numbers, a strip of tape with lettering in Magic Marker: CALHOUN. It was unauthorized, but all the coaches looked the other way.

The cheering from the stands was like a jet taking off. And this was only the warm-ups . . .

. . . A gold Plymouth Satellite rounded the bottom of the lake.

"You sure we got tickets?" asked Serge.

Kyle nodded. "Coach Calhoun said they'd be waiting for us at the booth, but it might be standing room."

The Plymouth continued north. Even if they hadn't known there was a big game, they would've been able to tell something was definitely up. Everyone in motion, piling in cars, honking, good-natured yelling in traffic, making last-moment dashes into stores, well-wishes painted on the windows of homes and offices.

"This is what I'm talking about," said Serge, gripping his fingers against the steering wheel. "Small-town pride. The fabric of the community coming together like a Kevlar vest."

They left Belle Glade behind and then it was just an empty stretch of cane fields that connected destinies. The sun finally set over Pahokee, draping the town in darkness, except for the strings of headlights pouring in from all directions.

"There it is," said Serge.

The brilliantly glowing football field stood out in the surroundings like Yankee Stadium.

"Looks like we have a bit of a walk," said Cheyenne.

They parked down the street from the overflow lots and hiked to the entrance booth.

"Coleman, you let the jackrabbit free," said Serge. "Why are you still wearing the chest pouch?"

Coleman reached inside and pulled something out to show his buddy. Then put it back inside.

"Why are you carrying a doughnut in your pouch?"

"Emergencies."

Tickets were waiting as promised. This time Kyle took charge, leading them along the fence in front of the home section until they reached the area behind the Pahokee bench.

"Coach Calhoun!"

Lamar turned. At first there was a lack of recognition.

"It's me, Kyle."

Then Calhoun brightened, and a reunion hug. "I heard about your dad. Sorry."

"Heard about yours, too," said Kyle. "They were good men."

"Coach!" A hand extended to shake.

"And you must be Cheyenne." Lamar lowered his right palm to the height of his waist. "Last time I saw you, you were this tall."

"The years fly by," she said. "So you're back home coaching now?"

Calhoun rested a forearm on the top of the fence. "That's a complicated story."

"Where's this kicker I've been reading about?"

"Chris? Right over there. She's quite something."

They all looked down the bench at a slender girl with a pony-tail, leaning forward with spring-wound intensity.

Then more coiled intensity from another direction. "Coach! I'm Serge! Huge fan!"—shaking hands vigorously—"Can't tell you how much all of this means to our nation! Connective tissue from Stetson to Zora! This is Coleman . . ."

Coleman waved. "I caught a bunny."

"Don't listen to him," said Serge. "So what's the big plan for tonight? Razzle-dazzle, Statue of Liberty, flea flicker, fumble-rooski, triple-reverse sting operation, bark at the moon to confuse the blitz?"

Calhoun glanced over at Kyle. "You know these people?"

"Actually, yes," said the young man. "But they're harmless. Maybe not to themselves . . ."

Cheyenne pointed at the color guard marching out onto the field. "Looks like we're starting."

After the national anthem, thunder from the stands as the Devils took the field to kick off. They formed a rigid line. A referee blew a whistle. A ball sailed high under the lights.

The Belle Glade receiver took it on the fifteen and charged straight up the field, waiting for his wall of blockers to form. Then he abruptly swung left, and used ridiculous speed to curl around the end and race up the sideline. The blocking wall held. One by one, the defenders were picked off. The path to the end zone now clear.

Well, almost clear. The kicker was left, outmatched by at least eighty pounds and staring in headlights. Normally a tackle would have been impossible. But the receiver was running down the sideline. It wasn't necessary to *tackle,* just knock him out of bounds. So the kicker, as they say, took one for the team. He ran as best he could toward the edge of the field, left his feet and laid out. Which meant just diving and sacrificing his body horizontally in front of the runner.

It was a wincing collision, but it did the trick. Out of bounds at the thirty. The kicker didn't get up. Coaches ran over. They held fingers in front of his face. They gave him a pop quiz.

The referee leaned in. "What's the story?"

They shook their heads. "Concussion. He's out."

A rare moment of silence in the stands as medics wheeled the stretcher toward the waiting ambulance that had backed up through the gates. Then an eruption of applause from both stands as the player, still prone on the stretcher, raised a fist with a thumbs-up.

That bit of drama was the first of many. Key fumbles and interceptions. Lead swings. Fourth-down pass completions. Safety blitzes and trick plays. Spectators held their stomachs and hearts, not sure how much more they could take . . .

. . . Police officers kept an eye on the darkened parking lots. Every space was taken. Even spaces that weren't spaces. Vehicles up on curbs, in no-parking zones, blocking fire hydrants. It was the unwritten fine print of a small town: no parking tickets during high school games.

Just after halftime, a pickup truck arrived and drove up and down packed rows until parking on the grass behind a dumpster. The driver bought a standing-room ticket and stood as Pahokee kicked off. But the new spectator wasn't watching the field. He was looking at the bench.

Chris wasn't hard to spot. The players on the bench had their helmets off. Just look for the only girl.

Captain Crack Nasty reached into his pocket and rubbed the gold coin he had just purchased at the pawnshop. He smiled to himself and decided to enjoy the rest of the game . . .

With five minutes to go, the Blue Devils were down 27–21 and driving inside the five. But play stalled on a third-down shot out the back of the end zone. They were too close to risk another touchdown attempt and give up the sure three points. They sent out the kicker, who made good: 27–24.

The kicker trotted off the field as teammates slapped his pads in congratulation. Then he suddenly began hopping on his left foot and dropped down on the bench. His helmet came off with a grimace. The trainer arrived, then other staff.

"What is it?" asked the head coach.

The trainer rotated the leg slightly, and the player almost screamed. "Looks like a pulled groin."

"So how's he going to be?"

"He's in no condition for even an onside kick."

"Are you kidding me?" said the coach. "Can't you do anything? Tape it up?"

A headshake. "He might even need surgery."

Teeth gritted; then: "I know, I know. Shouldn't have even asked. Their welfare comes first." A frustrated kick in the dirt. "But why in a three-point game? One field goal to tie and send it to overtime? What am I supposed to do?"

"I guess you're just going to have to try for the touchdown and the win."

They carefully took off the kicker's jersey.

Chris was leaning way forward, trying to make out the commotion at the other end of the bench. She saw them removing the shoulder pads of the second-string kicker, who was in obvious agony. She leaned back. "Shit."

The Devils defense made a clutch stop on third down in enemy territory, and the Raiders had no choice but to punt. The Pahokee offense took the field. Time was running short, so they had to manage the clock. Which meant passing. And Belle Glade knew it. They loaded up deep and played soft for the short, underneath stuff. Pahokee started with a sideline route that went out of bounds for a four-yard gain. Then another for five yards. Then a short pass over the middle for a first down that stopped the clock at just over a minute. It was working, but it was taking far too long.

Chris would have been biting her nails if she did that sort of thing. Instead, her right knee nervously bounced up and down. She glanced over her shoulder at the roaring overflow crowd. She did a double take. She jumped off the bench and ran to the fence. "Coach Calhoun!" She hugged him over the top of the chain link.

"Easy now."

Chris let him go. "What are you doing here?"

"You kidding? I wouldn't miss this for anything."

She hadn't noticed because of the excitement at seeing the

coach, but someone was standing with him. He was home for a break from college.

"Reggie!" Another hug.

"Chris," said Calhoun. "There's time for this later. You need to get your head back in the game."

"Did you see what happened to our kickers?"

Calhoun nodded.

"What should I do?"

"I suggest you start warming up."

Chris nodded and dashed off. She found a spot behind the bench away from the others and began stretching.

The Blue Devils continued a consistent march down the field. But it was all still more short stuff, eating up way too much time. Both sides knew what was coming. The quarterback took the next snap and dropped back farther than before to give the receivers time to extend their routes. He looked right and saw tight coverage. He ducked and stepped up in the pocket as a defender leaped and flew by. He reached back with everything he had and launched a perfect spiral with plenty of air. It couldn't have been more on target, arcing down toward the back corner of the end zone. But Glades Central had time to shift an extra defender, and now the Pahokee receiver was double-teamed. The ball was swatted away.

Fourth and long. At the outer edge of field-goal range. The clock stopped at ten seconds. The head coach glanced at Chris, warming up at the practice net. "Time out!"

The roar of the crowd was a rattling blare of sheer white noise. Nobody had taken a seat for the last fifteen minutes. Even the cops were cheering.

The teams went to their sidelines, panting, gargling water and spitting it out. Nobody could say they weren't leaving it all on the field. Both sides had nothing left, and that's when the boys at the lake always found more. The head coach called the play. The players ran back onto the field.

Chris stayed behind the bench at the practice net.

Pahokee lined up identical to the last play. Spectators grabbed their heads and pulled their hair. The ball was snapped. The fastest receivers streaked down both sidelines. The quarterback dropped back deep. He cocked his arm to launch another long one. Then he pulled the ball in. It was a delay play. The tight end threw a block on the right tackle, then slipped over the line five yards. The quarterback stepped forward and hit him running full speed. The defense was covering all the long routes and had left the middle open. Bedlam in the stands. The end raced up the clear middle of the field. Ten yards, fifteen, twenty. The defenders converged. The end tried to get around the left side, but one of the Raiders dove for a perfect ankle tackle. The runner went down right on the hash mark at the fifteen-yard line. A second later, a horn on top of the scoreboard blared. No time on the clock. Final score: Glades Central 27, Pahokee 24.

One side of the field jumped in ecstasy, the other in furious protest. The referees were already huddling. They already knew they had a serious mess on their hands. They realized the implications of what they had to do, and in the back of their minds were thinking how to get out of the parking lot as fast as possible when it was all over. The runner was down, but the scorekeeper up in the booth hadn't stopped the clock in time. The refs all nodded in agreement, and the head official broke their huddle and signaled to the booth to put a single second back on the clock.

Now emotions reversed in the opposing stands.

The Pahokee coach yelled at a ref and made a T with his hands. "Time out!"

Then he turned. "Chris!"

There wasn't need for any strategy discussion. It was a straight field goal. If she made it, then overtime. If not . . .

"You got this one, Chris," said a teammate, slapping her on the butt. "Oops, sorry."

"Don't worry about it."

The crowd was apoplectic. Spectators dug fingernails into each other's arms. Some gasped for air. Others grabbed their hearts. Coleman reached in his pouch for the doughnut.

The intermission ended, and the players trotted back out under the bright lights.

To this day, almost everyone involved remembers what happened next like the climax of a sports movie, drawn way out in extra-excruciating drama. Not that it needed any more.

Chris stepped up to the holder and addressed where the ball would be placed. Then she took measured steps backward and two more to the left. She shook her dangling arms at her sides to loosen nerves. She looked up at the home stands. Berserk people jumping and clapping. She saw their mouths shouting but she couldn't hear them. She couldn't hear any sound. Then a shrill ringing grew louder in her ears, and a pounding heartbeat. She looked toward the holder and nodded. The holder turned toward the blocking line and nodded at the center. People held breaths, prayed.

The ball was snapped.

It was ultra-slow motion. A tenth of a second ticked off the clock. Shoulder pads violently collided. Chris had done this a million times. She began running toward the holder, synchronizing her approach with the arrival of the ball. *Click.* Another tenth of a second. The ball seemed to hang in the air forever on the way to the holder. More shoulder pads crashed. She saw the linebackers take their first step forward for their leaps to attempt the block.

The ball reached the holder's hands. *Click.* She could see individual laces. The ball went toward the ground. Chris took another step and got ready to plant her left foot. There would be another step after that. Her kicking leg would swing.

The holder got the ball to the ground. *Click.* He spun the laces away.

Chris was suddenly hit in the chest with utter terror.

While spinning the ball, the holder had muffed it. The ball slipped out of his hands and it now lay sideways on the ground.

He tried to right it, but too late. Chris was already there. She had to pull up and abort the kick.

The team had a plan for such a misplay. They'd drilled it and drilled it in practice. But it was never conceivably meant with Chris in mind. Nonetheless, she had dutifully gone through all the practices with the other kickers, and now it was the mindless instinct of repetition.

Click. The horn sounded. The clock read zero.

Chris swung out of her kicking approach, running wide right. The holder pitched her the ball. She caught it in stride. The Belle Glade defense had loaded up for the block, and now most of their players were entangled in that snarl of limbs at scrimmage, allowing Chris to round the end. And damn if she wasn't faster than anyone would have guessed. Rabbits.

But all appeared to be for naught. The Raiders were anything but slow, and a pair of them bounced outside and swept toward her path. The farther one was toward the middle and had a ways to go, but the closer was almost straight ahead and in perfect position.

He'd placed himself to be able to beat her to the sideline. Unless she wanted to run out of bounds and end the game, her only option was to do what he wanted: to veer inside toward the middle of the field, where he'd have help from the other player, and maybe more. She'd easily be tackled.

Either way, checkmate.

She kept running full sprint. Then she did something the defenders didn't expect. She began curling *toward* the sideline. Those in the home stands who had been holding their own heads began slapping them. *"What's she doing?" "He'll run her out of bounds!"*

The closest player couldn't believe his luck. *Must be her lack of experience, probably thinks she can beat me to the corner and tightrope it into the end zone.* He adjusted his course along with hers. Then Chris surprised him even more. She increased her angle toward the sideline. He thought: *Has Christmas come early?*

They were only yards away, a split second left. He leaned forward to shove her out of bounds.

Chris took a last stride with her right leg toward the sideline. But instead of continuing, she dug her foot into the turf, hitting the brakes. The player flew by in front of her. His feet went out from under him as he tried to reach back, but Chris had already hit the gas again.

She still couldn't hear the crowd, but now it was because they were almost silent, mouths open.

The last defender had expected to merge with his teammate and sandwich her just inside the five. That was off the table now, and the footrace was on. He had the edge in distance and speed, but nothing was settled yet.

Chris had no more "Reggie" cuts in her bag of tricks. No argument that she'd be tackled inside the two. It was just a question of geometry.

She reached full sprint speed and left her feet like a track star in the long jump. Except this time it was headfirst. The Raiders player had been expecting that, and dove to hit her at the waist, hoping to drive airborne Chris off the field.

As she was coming down, Chris stretched out an arm and reached as far left as she could, swiping the tip of the ball against the orange pylon in the front corner of the end zone.

The referee's arms went up. Touchdown. No need for that overtime.

Players and fans swarmed the field. The insane jumping in the home team's stands would have registered on seismic instruments.

Calhoun and Reggie stood on their toes at the fence. They couldn't have been happier as they watched the team carry Chris off the field on their shoulders.

Chapter 38

CELEBRATION

Car horns honked nonstop all over town. Screaming on Main Street. People whipped team towels in circles over their heads. The epicenter of the bedlam, of course, was Max's Shake Spot.

Chris was the talk and the toast. She was still carrying the game ball that the head coach had presented to her. No way she would be allowed to pay for anything tonight. And not just Chris. Max himself came out and made the announcement personally: All players eat free tonight.

"Hooray!"

The revelry continued into the night, players becoming bloated on free burgers, chocolate shakes and root beer floats.

"Pahokee! . . . Pahokee! . . . Pahokee! . . ."

Players took selfies and group photos with cell phones. The

students, especially the seniors, knew this was a night they would well remember into the decades to come.

And for the first night all season, there were an unusually large number of white people. It wasn't suspicious. It was the usual suspects from the scouting ranks across the southeast and all the way up to Ohio and Michigan. They knew the delicate line of what they could and couldn't say to avoid violating eligibility. All night long: *"Great game! Here's my card. Florida State . . ." ". . . Here's my card. Georgia Tech . . ." ". . . Auburn . . ." ". . . Ole Miss . . ."*

Former coach Calhoun arrived and headed toward a picnic table, smiling bigger than he had in years. Chris suddenly noticed him in the crowd. She jumped up and gave him a strangling hug. "Thank you! Thank you! Thank you!"

"Easy, you'll break my neck," said Calhoun. "And I should be the one thanking you. At my age, you don't think there's much more to learn in life, but you've taught me so much."

A Plymouth pulled up and emptied. Serge led the gang through the crowd.

"Uh-oh," said Calhoun. "I think you have some more fans."

"Chris!" said Serge, shaking her hand. "I've heard so much about you! Such an inspiration in our times of crisis!"

"Uh, do I know you?"

"No, but I'm a friend of a friend of Coach Calhoun."

"Then you're my friend."

More students arrived and crowded round the table. *"That was fantastic!" "You were great!"*

Cheyenne tugged Serge by the sleeve. "We should let her be with her friends. It's her big night."

"I was going to start a wave in her honor, but I'll defer to your female judgment," said Serge. "That's my new life motto: When in doubt, ask a woman. Because us guys are doing such a bang-up job, right?"

She tugged his sleeve harder. "There are some seats in back . . ."

Chris said she had to go to the bathroom.

"Too much information."

"Just hold my seat."

She walked around the dark side of the building for the restrooms.

"Chris!" someone yelled. "Great game!"

She turned around. "Thanks . . . Do I know you?"

"Doubt it," said the man in the cab of the pickup. "I'm a college scout. If only you were a boy . . . I didn't mean that like it sounded."

"I know what you meant." She grabbed the handle of the door to the women's room.

When she walked out moments later: "Could you come here a second?"

"Why?"

"We don't recruit girls for football in Division One, but you're a natural," said Crack. "There are a number of sports you could easily adapt to."

Chris walked halfway to the truck. "Like what?"

"Tell me what else you play," said the captain. "You're probably thinking we're just trying to comply with Title Nine, which we are. But this is no charity: You can definitely play. Full scholarships rarely come along for girls. Ever try volleyball? Lacrosse?"

A couple more steps. "I really haven't tried any other sports."

Captain Crack opened his door and stepped out. "Let me show you these brochures from the school I represent."

"What school did you say that was?"

"I didn't."

And before Chris knew it, Crack had her by the arm, twisting hard. She yelped as he tried pushing her into the pickup. She was putting up a lot more fight than he had expected from a girl, but a sock in the jaw ended that nonsense.

Two boys came around the side of the building, yucking it up. Chris screamed from the open window as the pickup patched out.

The boys raced back to the picnic table. "Some guy just snatched Chris!"

"What? Who?"

"I got a picture on my cell phone." He held it up.

Someone leaned over his shoulder. "I know that truck!" yelled Ricky. "I know that *guy*. I'll never forget him as long as I live!"

It took mere seconds for alarm to sweep the crowd. Serge burst through and saw the phone. "I overheard you say that you know where he took her?"

The boy nodded.

"What's your name?"

"Ricky."

Calhoun frantically pushed his way in. "What's going on? Where's Chris?"

"No time," said Serge. "Seconds are precious . . . Ricky! Coleman! Come with me! . . . Coach, take the others in your car and follow us!"

Soon the Plymouth was barreling out of town, out into the darkness of flowing cane stalks. The needle spiked at over a hundred, leaving Calhoun and the others in the dust. Ricky filled Serge in along the way: His own beating in the cane fields years earlier, sure he was going to die until his rescue. Then the murder of his rescuers in the exact same spot, which the authorities ruled to be a drug deal gone sour, but Ricky knew better.

"Slow down," said the boy. "The turnoff's coming up."

The Plymouth rolled to a crawl.

"There it is," said Ricky.

Serge couldn't see anything down the dirt road, but he did make out fresh tire tracks leading into the field. "Ricky, you need to trust me. Get out and wait here by the road for the others for your own good. This is my specialty and I work alone." He pulled something from under the seat and Ricky opened the door. "And you didn't see this."

"What gun?" Ricky closed the door.

Serge hit his high beams and sped off into the black desolation of the cane field . . .

Soon, other headlights came up the highway. They caught Ricky waving madly on the side of the road. Calhoun pulled alongside. "What's happening?"

Ricky stuck his head in the window. "He went in after him. And I'm not supposed to tell you, but he has a gun."

"Shit!" Lamar cut the wheel and raced his car down the dirt road . . .

Serge's lights eventually hit the back of Captain Crack's pickup. Dark and empty. Bad sign. "Coleman, wait in the car. I may need you to drive this out of here in a hurry."

Serge planted his feet in the soil and crouched to listen. A brief gust of wind carried a snippet of noise. He crept like a ghost in its direction, quietly parting cane stalks. The sound grew louder. Voices. Soon they weren't hard to follow. The captain had chucked all his business rules. He chugged Johnnie Walker straight from the bottle as Chris lay crying in the dirt at his feet. "Please don't hurt me."

"Shut up!" A swift kick to her ribs. "Just dig!"

"I'm trying!"

More weeping, more kicks, more Scotch. Chris trembling too much to make progress in the soil. It wasn't going anyplace good.

"What the fuck is wrong with you?"

She heard a click and looked up and saw the cocked pistol. "No!"

Then another sound, unexpected. The clack of metal on skull.

Captain Crack thudded to the dirt like an unhooked punching bag. In the space where he had been standing, another person now stood. Chris recognized him as someone she had just met back at the burger joint.

She ran crying into his arms.

He quickly held Chris out by the shoulders. "You have to pull yourself together. I know you can do it! Others are counting on you, okay?"

She nodded and stifled her sobs down to sniffles.

"Good," said Serge. "If I'm correct, Coach Calhoun should be arriving just about now. I need you to walk straight down this one row of cane and start calling out for him."

"What are you going to do?" asked Chris.

"You and Ricky and the other kids deserve to be happy. And safe. And that will never happen under the status quo." Serge nodded in the direction of the cane. "Now get going. And don't look back . . ."

C oach Calhoun! Coach Calhoun! . . ."
Lamar's headlights had just hit Serge's Plymouth parked behind a pickup truck. He slammed the brakes and got out.

"Coach Calhoun! Coach Calhoun! . . ."

Lamar looked at Kyle and Cheyenne. "Did you hear that?"

"It's coming from over there!"

They crashed through stalks. "Chris! We're over here! We're on the way!"

Moments later, they all burst through the last rows of cane, and everyone embraced in terrified relief.

"What happened?" asked Calhoun.

"I don't know," said Chris. "The guy was going to kill me for sure. I just know it. But then that friend of yours came out of nowhere."

"And where are they now?"

She shrugged. "He just told me to leave and not look back."

Kyle and Cheyenne glanced at each other. They heard sirens in the distance. A lot of them.

Calhoun took off his Pahokee football jacket and wrapped it around Chris's shoulders. "We need to get you to my car."

Back at the highway, Ricky was waving a long line of police cars down the dirt road. Blue and red lights flashed through the crops as the speeding vehicles kicked up a long plume of black dust.

The officers arrived at Calhoun's car just as the former coach and the others emerged safely with Chris.

But the '69 Plymouth and pickup truck were gone.

HIGHWAY 78 REVISITED

High beams pierced the black countryside.

Nothingness for miles. The pickup's windows were down, allowing a cool night breeze to accompany the peaceful, silent, green glow from the instrument panel.

It hadn't started that way. In the passenger seat, the captain had been quite chatty. *What do you want? I have money. I'll give you anything. Blah, blah, blah.*

Serge put a stop to the annoyance with another bloody skull crack from his Colt .45. Calmly as a librarian: "Shhhh . . . I'm enjoying the tranquil drive." He kept the pistol in his left hand, aiming across the pickup's cab as he steered with his right.

It was indeed a mellow ride. Dim fields of wildflowers under the economic light of a crescent moon. More miles of blood-pressure-reducing serenity through the wilderness.

Finally, Serge let off the gas, and the pickup truck from a marine-towing company uneventfully rolled to a stop with the sound of small crushed white rocks under the tires. He ordered the good captain out of the car at gunpoint.

A gold Plymouth arrived and parked behind. "Coleman, wait here until I get back."

A hike began. Crack Nasty looked around in the night landscape. Emptiness only led to even more emptiness. His thoughts pinballed as they can at a moment like this. Heaven, hell, God, the devil. *Anything you want! I'm begging!* Crack!

Another half hour.

Serge poked a gun barrel in ribs. "Walk down the bank and watch your step."

It was precarious, with loose soil and gravel collapsing and rolling down the incline under their feet, but they made it with only a couple of stumbles. They arrived at a modest shoreline.

"We're here," said Serge. "Sit down."

"What are you going to do?"

"Wait for someone."

"Who?"

"I don't know."

"I don't understand."

"That's your problem," said Serge. "Your least."

They sat, as they say in kindergarten, crisscross applesauce, amid sounds of insects and bullfrogs and rustling leaves.

Serge's ears perked, and he stood. "Here they come."

"Who?"

"Like I said, I don't know."

"You're insane, aren't you?"

"My gain is your loss."

Crack Nasty opened his mouth to scream, but Serge bashed him once more before he could get it out. "Try to yell again, and it's game over. Two taps to the head. But play nice and you might get away. Here's my offer: If you behave and wait until I release you, you're free to swim for it. But utter a peep, even in the water, and I can plug you way over here. Deal? Just nod."

He nodded.

"Great! A cooperator! Sit still . . ." Serge listened intently as the distant motorized sound grew louder. "That's the person I've been waiting for. Okay, Florida Man, take off all your clothes."

"You want me to get naked?"

"I'm doing you a favor." Serge stretched out his shooting arm. "Play your cards right, and you could become an Internet heart-throb."

"But—"

"You'd rather stay here with me? How sweet."

"No, no!" Crack quickly ripped off his shirt and pulled down his pants. "I'll skinny-dip . . ." He looked around. "But where is this person you were waiting for?"

"They're arriving by boat." Serge aimed his pistol. "You're free to go. Swim . . ."

Crack didn't need to be told twice. He dove in the water and swam like it was the Olympics. He neared the halfway mark across the river and found he was veering in the wrong direction. He lifted his head and corrected course. It happened two more times, but no matter how hard he tried, the captain always found himself swinging back to face Serge. What was going on?

Then it became clear. He didn't know the name of the place he was at, but he understood the concept. Captain Crack began spinning wildly, screaming with abandon as he stared up at the large metal wall at the Ortona Lock and Dam towering over him.

And the violent, twenty-foot-wide whirlpool flushed him down like a turd.

Epilogue

As football signing day approached, college scouts again descended on The Muck like a migration of birds. Or locusts.

One particular scout from a perennial midwestern contender was interested in the star running back. The principal pulled him aside and reminded the scout that, years earlier, his university had recruited another of their running backs.

"That's right," said the smiling scout. "I remember him."

Then the principal adopted a grave tone and explained how it would be.

Now, mere mortals cannot comprehend what the power and money of big-college football are able to accomplish, just short of interstellar travel. And even that's arguable. It's only a matter of motivation, and the college boosters really wanted this tailback. The principal's conversation was highly inappropriate and totally the right thing to do.

A few weeks later, a knock at the front door of a modest concrete-block ranch house on Pahokee's south side.

"Principal Jennings, what brings you around?"

"May I come in?"

"Be my guest," said a former running back named Calhoun.

"Lamar, funny thing. We took another look at your situation, and it turns out there are no records whatsoever of any incident between you and a coach." He opened a file with stamped pages. "We've received notarized statements from both the university and local police department that your name is squeaky-clean up there."

"What? But how—?"

"Lamar, listen to me . . ."—telegraphing the unspoken with his eyes—". . . there are no records."

"Uh, okay."

The principal headed for the door and turned around just before he left. "Why don't you swing by my office Monday morning. I'd like to hear your plans for the team this year."

T he body of Captain Crack Nasty was discovered sticking halfway out of an underwater valve at the Ortona Lock and Dam. Due to his blood-alcohol content, nudity and other factors, it was officially ruled death by misadventure, as if someone had planned it that way. Some of the locals had other theories about an unusual stranger who'd breezed through town, but none felt the slightest inclination to come forward.

C heyenne Lovitt actually cried after opening the letter that had been slipped under the motel office door in the middle of the night: "For reasons that are now all too obvious, I must go away for a while and not have any contact with you or your brother, for your own protection. I guess there are too many places we've *both* got to see. I can't say when, but I promise after things blow over, I'll find a way to get back in touch with my little history helper. Serge."

Kyle Lovitt's passion for the rodeo only grew, and he became a crowd favorite on the southern circuit. He was back home again a year later for the annual Okeechobee Rodeo. It immediately got dicey in the starting chute. An extra-ornery bronco named Diablo crashed and bucked against the railings. Until now, nobody had been able to complete a ride, and most no longer dared try. "Hold on!" yelled one of the rodeo hands trying to steady the horse. "No, I've got it," said Kyle. "Just get that gate open fast." He practically had to jump into the saddle, and the horse blasted off. It was a magnificent ride, and after the full eight seconds, Kyle jumped down to a standing ovation from the crowd.

Cheyenne had begun nursing school, but still always found the time to slip into her cowgal duds and proudly carry the American flag to open each rodeo. After Kyle dismounted Diablo, she ran out across the dirt to congratulate him with a hug. "You were fantastic! Listen to that applause!" As their eyes moved around the arena, taking in all the standing, cheering people, they happened to look at the far end of the dirt and a pair of barrels. Suddenly, two clowns popped up and waved. Then ran off into the night.

"Did I just really see that?" asked Cheyenne.

Kyle turned to his sister. "Is this good or bad?"

C hris never played organized sports again.

Instead, she received a full academic scholarship to Johns Hopkins University. She had the grades and aptitude to become a highly paid, top-notch specialist in any number of disciplines, but her personal calling required her to become a general practitioner.

After graduation, she hired a lawyer. He had never heard such a story, about a little kid who discovered treasure in a cane field and patiently carried a little bit home every day until, over the course of years, she had buried, well, a lot of it in the woods behind her grandmother's apartment. He researched applicable law, and sure enough, the hurricane had given her the same salvage rights as if it had been a Spanish galleon. The question of a proper lease and trespassing were another matter, but the land had since changed hands, wiping the slate clean. She was free and clear. He set up a trust and took care of taxes.

Chris used the trust and her degree to return to The Muck, where she opened a much-needed pediatric health clinic. She accepted all kinds of insurance and Medicaid. If you didn't have any of that, it was free. She couldn't have been happier, and neither could the town.

This is how much the community loved Chris for all she had given to them: Four decades later, in the wrinkled winter of her career, they unveiled a bronze statue of a young girl running with a football.

A few days after that, Chris and her staff finished a Friday afternoon of treating the latest crop of local kids who came through her door. The staff and patients had all gone home, and Chris stayed behind to deal with some government forms.

A number of professionals in various walks of life like to decorate their offices with mementos of success: diplomas, plaques, trophies, medals and ribbons. Chris had her own idea of decorating.

She finished the paperwork and grabbed her briefcase. Just before turning out the lights, Chris did what she always did at the end of each day. She looked around at the various walls, completely covered with overlapping photos of children and thank-you cards.

Finally, Chris's eyes went over to her favorite trophy, displayed on a bookshelf. And she smiled.

She was looking at a milk crate.

ABOUT THE AUTHOR

Tim Dorsey was a reporter and editor for the *Tampa Tribune* from 1987 to 1999, and is the author of twenty-two other novels: *Florida Roadkill, Hammerhead Ranch Motel, Orange Crush, Triggerfish Twist, The Stingray Shuffle, Cadillac Beach, Torpedo Juice, The Big Bamboo, Hurricane Punch, Atomic Lobster, Nuclear Jellyfish, Gator A-Go-Go, Electric Barracuda, When Elves Attack, Pineapple Grenade, The Riptide Ultra-Glide, Tiger Shrimp Tango, Shark Skin Suite, Coconut Cowboy, Clownfish Blues, The Pope of Palm Beach* and *No Sunscreen for the Dead*. He lives in Tampa, Florida.